T. Vincent Beck

# Wading On

Wading On by Thomas V. Beck

Copyright © 2017 by Thomas V. Beck

Cover by Alexandra King

188p. ill. cm.

ISBN 978-1-935795-50-6

LCCN 2017963591

___________________________



Michael Ray King Publishing

PO Box 353431

Palm Coast, FL 32135-3431


Printed in the United States of America

A special Thank You to

Barbara Rose Hege
Linda Beck
And a bunch of friends who believe
in me.
Love you guys.

# Table of Contents

# Table of Contents

# Table of Contents

## *Wade Ivan Nash*

THE DOG DAYS OF SUMMER are thought to be the sultriest days of summer, from mid-July to mid-August. The heat and humidity combine to form the greatest discomfort on the human body. The term "Dog Days" began in countries surrounding the Mediterranean Sea and then migrated to other countries over time. It had something to do with Sirius, the Dog Star, and the sun. All I knew was it was hot as hell. The heat and humidity had all of us sweating intensely in minutes.

I'm Wade Ivan Nash. I'm 63 years old, stand six feet one inch tall and weigh one hundred and eighty-two pounds of mostly solid flesh and bone. My chiseled stature is thanks in large part to a decision I made forty-four years ago to join the U.S. Marine Corps. Once a Marine, always a Marine.

Over time, I've worked for many branches of the government. In the process, I received a great deal of clandestine training. The last seven years found me semi-retired which is kind of like saying I've taken a paycheck and did little but put my two cents in on meetings with some very influential people in our government that are dedicated to keeping our country safe.

A few months ago, I got involved in a with murder case right here in my back yard. All those years of training came back to the forefront of my life until the case was solved.

I stood in the back yard on the Intra-Coastal waterway, half way between the two inlets serving this area. Matanzas Inlet to the north and Ponce Inlet to the south. It is a fifty-four mile stretch between the two inlets with hundreds of miles of channels to fish, connecting to the Intra-Coastal. My home is about fifteen miles north of Daytona Beach and thirty miles south of St. Augustine, our nation's oldest city.

Seven years ago, after a tough career, my wife Catherine and I discovered this area pretty much by accident and fell in love with it. It's quiet and not too fancy. Best of all, it's on the water.

I rediscovered that I loved fishing. My grandpa, Ivan, often took me fishing for perch on Lake Michigan in Chicago, where we lived just three blocks from Midway Airport.

The Intra-Coastal has many names as it runs from Maine to the Florida Keys. Here it's called the Halifax River and yet it's all just a part of that big body of water between the mainland and the barrier islands along the way, with the Atlantic Ocean feeding it.

I've always loved fishing and didn't know a lot but with the help of a good neighbor John, and a few others, I quickly learned many skills. Soon I could read the water and tell what the tides meant, identifying the moon phases, and know where to look for the often elusive fish that were residents here. When I wasn't fishing, I read about it and soon got the reputation for being a good hand on the water.

All was as good as it can get for Catherine and me as we took two nice "vacations" a year. We had lots of friends and even joined the Yacht Club, mostly for a place to dance and to be with people who liked the water. Hell, I live in a resort as far as I am concerned. Until the day Catherine went shopping and didn't come home. She was killed by a truck crossing the median on Interstate 95, just ten miles from our home.

The no-fault accident was the result of a mechanical error on the truck. That knowledge was little consolation, though. It didn't bring my Catherine back and I felt as low as a man could get. I knew I wasn't alone. Many people lose loved ones and are in the same boat, so to speak. I felt alone for a long time. With too much time on my hands, I started a fish charter then expanded to ecological tours for tourists. Soon, I hired a partner, one Bobby Joe Green, fresh from the Okefenokee swamps of Georgia. That was almost two years ago.

As I stood at the helm of my deck boat, I felt very comfortable. The breeze wafted through my salt and pepper hair, ruffling my short sleeve business fishing shirt with some SPF rating to ward off the sun's rays. I wore khaki shorts and my brown deck shoes I worn without socks which had me looking professional.

This boat, I have two, is my 23-foot deck boat with a powerful 250 horsepower Yamaha outboard motor. The Ericson family beamed happily in the boat with me as we motored down south to Ponce Inlet and the restaurant there.

We were only four or five miles from home and already the family was totally caught up in the trip despite the heat. Don and Julie were as engrossed as their two kids, twelve-year-old Eric and fourteen-year-old Jasmine, all lathered up in SPF 40 sunscreen.

Dozens of pictures were taken as they encountered several bottled nosed porpoise. Two of the creatures entertained the family as they jumped out of the water, passing a mullet fish between them, as though trained at Sea World in Orlando, an hour's drive by car from here.

As we neared the mouth of the Tomoka Basin, a huge body of water that resembled a big lake, I spotted something that was sure to entertain the Ericson family.

"Look ahead to the left a little. See those two rings on the water? Under those rings are two manatees. When we get next to them, they may come to the surface and you'll get a good look at them."

I cut the power to barely an idle and eased my way slowly past the two circles. As I hoped, the two giant sea cows, so ugly that they are beautiful, rose to the surface. Each sea cow was probably a thousand pounds of friendship that lived in the intra-coastal. When cold weather set in, they would be forced to find warm water for the winter.

After taking several pictures, Don passed the camera to Julie and then reached over to touch one of the manatees. Jasmine squealed in delight. Eric wasn't sure whether or not he wanted to touch one but put his hand near the lead one and said, "Mom, take my picture. This is so cool. I want to send this to my friends. They won't believe it."

Because of the manatee, I let my boat get close to the west bank of the channel. We were barely floating as I felt the skeg, the rudder on the outboard, just below the propeller, scrape the sandy, muddy bottom.

I started to ease my way back toward the channel, captivated by the sea cows. When I looked up I was shocked to see a sailboat coming at us, heading north in the middle of the channel.

It was an Island Packet and it looked like a brand new boat. As I looked again, I could see something missing. Nobody was steering the boat. The helm was empty.

The channel was narrow, and yet, we had a hundred feet or so between us. To see no one at the helm had me very concerned. I hit the horn on my boat once to let the other boat know they had company. I felt one of the manatee bump into the side of my boat, pushing me even closer to the muddy bank.

Ten seconds later, the gleaming white sailboat with the blue stripe along the hull showed no signs of life, so I hit my horn two more times.  From the deck below, a hand reached up and grabbed the steering wheel and gave it a single tug downward, sending the sailboat on a collision course with us. The hand was huge and black and covered with red. Paint? Blood?

The Ericson family suddenly forgot about the sea cows and looked at the fast approaching sailboat in fear as I hit the throttle on my boat to take us past the impact of the sailboat. In my excitement and haste, I pushed the throttle a bit too hard, which caused my boat to dig down into the mud, anchoring it in place for a few seconds. I backed off the throttle and the boat floated again, giving me one more chance to get out of the way.

My next attempt was too little, too late. I jerked around and yelled for Don and Eric to get to the front of my boat. Neither moved, but like the girls, they too raised their hands and arm as if to ward off a fifty thousand pound boat traveling at six miles per hour. It was an instinctive reaction.

The sailboat struck us just behind amidships. Don went flying toward the bow, hitting his head, knocking him to the deck with a nasty cut on his forehead. Eric was fast enough to move toward the back of my boat and avoided a direct hit. Julie screamed a blood-curdling note as Jasmine was knocked into the water by the force of the collision into less than two feet of water. Her life vest flipped her on her back, face up. Just as it was designed to do.

The speed and the weight of the sailboat forced it to climb over my boat, pushing mine deep into the bank. I pulled the kill switch on my motor and with an exuberance that I somehow found at the moment, I reached up to the bow cleat on the sailboat and vaulted up on the deck, already on a steep angle over my boat.

Half running, half sliding on the deck, I arrived at the helm in seconds. I shoved the throttle to neutral, then found the key and switched off the engine. The sailboat was now completely over my boat.

Adrenaline surged through me as I looked around and saw Jasmine, now on her feet in front of my deck boat as Julie and Eric lowered the front boarding ladder help her back on the boat. Don was hunched over the front seat, clutching a handkerchief over his cut forehead. Streaks of blood trickled down his left cheek and dripped on his Hawaiian shirt.

My mind raced as I attempted to put together what just happened. A hand grabbed my ankle and yanked hard, nearly pulling me off my feet. Holding the steering wheel, I barely managed to avoid falling. With a spine-tingling roar, a huge man appeared from below. A monstrosity of a black man covered in sweat sheen from his bald head down. Ivory teeth grimaced as he stood a head taller than me. He screamed and I could see the red color was not paint but blood. He trapped me between the helm and the side of the boat. The only way out was to get past this monster who held a barbecue fork in his right hand.

I later learned the monster's name. Moses Mendoza. He was charged with the boat and its contents. All I knew at that moment was that this giant was trying to kill me. I easily ducked a slow left he threw at me. His right hand, holding the barbecue fork, lunged at my midsection. Turning just enough, I felt the tines pierce my shirt and the cold steel grazed my left side. Had I moved a fraction of a second later, I would have been the barbecue of the day.

I could see he was obviously weak as my right punch to his chest sent him back on his heels. His balance was fading fast. His next left to my head was right of my right ear, giving me the chance to hit him with all the power I could muster. My fist broke his nose, staggering the giant back another step. I moved closer and hit his Adam's apple with a left cross thrown from my shoes upward.

It's all the power I had.  It was enough to send the monster to the deck, grasping his broken throat, struggling for elusive air. Suddenly, he was quiet.

I guess I looked a sight to the Ericson's as they had a look of horror on their faces. I had blood on both my fists and knew I had blood on me as I looked at my shirt front and saw splotches of red all over.

My world became quiet. I guess the adrenalin ran its course. My knees felt weak and I wanted to sit down. Old guys shouldn't be fighting monsters other than maybe in a movie.

I grabbed a line from the sailboat and secured the two boats together as the stern of the sailboat started moving down the river with the tide. That done, I had more work to do and it could not be avoided as I heard cries from below, from the cabin.

The cries were children's cries. Certainly more than one child. Perhaps several. In another life and another place, I was in a somewhat similar situation so I was afraid of what I might find below. From experience, I understood just one man would not take a trip like this. There had to be another adult aboard. I imagined myself climbing down the ladder below and getting shot on the way down. Still, there was only one way below. There was no choice. I had to go.

I reached behind my back, under my shirt and slid out my Glock 40 caliber handgun, making sure it was ready to fire. I held my breath as I took the first of five steps to the deck below. Two more cautious steps and I was exposed from the neck down. This would have been a good time for someone to shoot me since I was open and vulnerable. On the contrary, I was met with silence, so I took the final two steps into a dark tomb. It was so bright outside that the teak interior seemed like midnight on a moonless night.

My eyesight adjusted in less than a minute. I could see the head, a nautical term for the bathroom, directly in front of me. The door was wide open. The bathroom was empty. I looked left to the berth. It too was empty, except for a pile of dirty clothing strewn across the mattress.

Cries erupted, coming from the front of the cabin, in the V berth. I worked my way forward, my gun at the ready, silently praying I did not have to shoot or get shot myself. Every instinct I've learned in the past was on full alert for a wrong movement.

When I reached the V berth, I could see a mass of children huddled together on the mattress. I scanned the berth to verify that no one else was present before I reached above and pushed open the escape hatch. A flood of beautiful, welcoming sunlight entered the room. Then I counted.

I counted five girls, probably between ten and fourteen years old. They were dirty and poorly dressed. The group reminded me of a litter of kittens waiting for their mother to return and rescue them. Streaks of tears flowed, leaving wet trails through the dirt on their faces.

I slipped my gun back into its holster behind my back and indicated to the girls to stand up and get out through the hatch above them. I had to help the first girl but the rest of them got the idea and started to follow her lead. By the time the third girl climbed on deck, I noticed the final girl wasn't moving. I rolled her to her side and could see a crimson blood stain from what appeared to be a knife wound.

Scantily dressed and obviously terribly mistreated from the appearance of bruises on her body, I felt sorry for the poor girl. Then I thought of the other four. Were they the lucky ones? Or would they find themselves in the same predicament once they found their way back home to parents who most likely sold them into the sex trade in the first place? Perhaps the dead one was the lucky one after all.

Searching a sailboat was an easy task. There just aren't that many places to hide on a sailboat. I looked around on my way to the ladder and climbed on the deck above. I was happy to find the radio in perfect working order as I notified law enforcement of the situation. I used code terms, which was a joke as all the news media knew the codes and what they meant. Soon, the area would be teeming with boats and probably a helicopter or two with reporters wanting the first break in the story.

I looked at the Ericson family and noticed that their anxiety and fear was now replaced with curiosity and confusion as I told them a limited story of what I knew. I then looked down at the giant on the deck, lying in an ever-expanding pool of blood.

I wondered if I should just put him out of his misery. If I did, I would most likely be in a world of trouble with witnesses and all. Perhaps I should try and help him I thought. Just as that thought crossed my mind, the monster gave one final groan and his eyes glassed over in a fog. He was in another world now. I didn't want to be in his shoes.

The girls looked like lost kittens as we passed out bottles of water and snack bars retrieved from my boat. I tried to question them and found two of them spoke passable English. We found out they were from Guyana, sold by their parents to a man they called the "Money Man." He lied to their parents and promised that the girls would experience a better life in another country. The girl that did most of the talking on behalf of the others said her name was Ashana. Ashana continued to tell a horrific story, a story she would have to repeat over and over before the day was done.

The Money Man transferred the girls to this boat. Soon after they sailed for a better world, they discovered they were now caught up in the sex business with Moses and the second man Felipe breaking them in along the way.

I knew there had to be another guy with them. I asked, "What happened to Felipe?"

Ashana continued with her story. She said the dead girl's name was Sheliza. Felipe had sex with the girls. It was bad but better than sex with Moses who was huge and rough.

About an hour before the collision, Felipe entered the birth and pulled Sheliza toward him. As he started to mount her, Sheliza was able to get his long knife from his scabbard and stab Felipe in his heart. She killed him almost instantly, but not before a scream escaped him.

Moses ran below and grabbed Felipe and pulled him off Sheliza.  As he did, Sheliza swung wildly and stabbed Moses in his left side.

Before she could stab him again, Moses overpowered her and plunged the knife into her in the side, twisting the knife as she screamed from the pain. A moment later, she was dead.

Ashana continued: "Moses got up and walked to the table.  He sat there for a few minutes and checked his wound.  Then got up and picked up Felipe like a sack of potatoes, threw him over his shoulder and climbed to up to the deck above. A few minutes later, we heard a splash.  We think Moses threw Felipe over the side."

I looked north and could see a boat coming at a fast pace. It would be here in a few minutes. From this distance, I couldn't see if it was the police or the news. I would know soon enough.

"Folks, I'm sorry about all of this. You will get a full refund of course, but I'm afraid this trip is over. It sure wasn't our doing. I hope you like the news because you'll be on television for the next couple of days."

The Ericson family looked on in shock. Not in their wildest dreams could they have imagined that before the end of the day, they would be involved in a collision and watch their guide beat down and kill a giant of a man. To top it all off, see young girls that had been held captive as sex slaves. Yet, in a reality TV age, as horrible as this day was, it was also the story of a lifetime – in a perverse sort of way.

Don, holding the blood-soaked handkerchief on his forehead said "Wade, this was none of your doing in any way. We are all here to vouch for it. In fact, you could have saved our lives. Thank you."

I looked at the two women. I was half bewildered and half amused at the sight of them combing their hair. Maybe they were still in shock, I thought…. Ah, television, I  thought. I guess they will find out if a camera really does add ten pounds to a person on TV.

As for me, I knew this was just the beginning. My heart was already ten pounds heavier just thinking of these poor children and what they already went through and would go through before this was all over. If it ever was. I thought of Human Trafficking in my back yard. I just never considered that it would be here. Now, I'll never forget it.

## *Cleaning Up a Mess*

When the approaching boat was about a quarter of a mile away, I could see it was the Coast Guard. I knew they were stationed in New Smyrna Beach, not a mile from where we were traveling to today. Well, we wouldn't see New Smyrna Beach today for sure.

As the boat got close, I could see it was their 29-foot Defender-class inflatable used in the shallow waters of the Intra-Coastal. I knew this from a class I gave the Coast Guard a year or so ago concerning Homeland Security. Part of the class was the boats and weapons carried by the Coast Guard. Others gave presentations too in the full eight-hour class. It was interesting, to say the least.

The pilot of their craft was very experienced as when their boat touched the sailboat, barely a nudge was felt as I watched an able seaman hop from their craft to the sailboat and secure the boats together in short order.

It looked like the Coast Guard had practice drills on how to board another vessel as no sooner were the two boats secured when a spit and polish young officer stepped lively on to the deck of the sailboat. He took a few steps to me, stood at attention and saluted.

*Why is the hell he saluting me?* He was all spit and polish from hours spent with Brasso on his belt buckles and other shiny objects to the spit shine on his mirror shoes. I remembered my year at the Pentagon when I had to do this too and blessed the day I could get back to my kind of military.

"Good morning sir. I'm Second Lieutenant Robert Hooper of the United States Coast Guard," said the young officer standing at attention before me.

I stuck out my hand and grasped his giving it a good solid shake with plenty of muscle in my squeeze, just to show him I might have age on me, but I could still function. It's a man thing I guess.

"I'm Wade Nash and we have a problem," I said.

"Yes, sir. I got the gist of it over the radio. At this time, I have no idea what to do but I'm sure headquarters will get back to me in short order," said Lieutenant Hooper as he looked unwavering at Wade.

"Relax Lieutenant. There's nobody here to grade us. Let me tell you the story the way it happened. This way there is no confusion or a mixed story. Do you happen to have a recorder on board?"

"Yes sir, we do. Seaman Dawes! Front and center and bring a tape recorder."

As I looked at the Coast Guard boat, I noticed Lieutenant Hooper stood at Parade Rest, feet shoulder width apart and his hands clasped behind his back, staring straight ahead. *What the hell are they teaching these guys?*

In less than a minute, a very attractive, perky young lady dressed in jungle camouflage clothing stepped aboard and walked quickly next to Lieutenant Hooper. I knew females were in uniform for a long time. Almost forever but I never saw one so pretty in a man's world. *Oops, better keep that thought to yourself Nash or one of these beauties will shoot your ass off.*

After introductions, I told my story to the two of them and the recorder in much less time than the incident took. I then took the two of them to the little girls, sitting in the sun, some still nursing their bottle of water, now as warm as the air. I told the girls what was needed and the two that spoke some English started talking over each other.

"Whoa whoa whoa girls. One at a time." The two looked at me and nodded somberly. I pointed to one and said, "You first."

I walked away from them and looked both up the river and down. Sure enough, there were several boats coming from both directions. I didn't have to look up to see the helicopter above with a big "13" painted on the side. The news was here.

In no time we were with several official boats tied together and on us. The county sent two boats as did Homeland Security as well as the state along with fish and game and one tow boat from Tow USA painted in white on the bright red of the boat hull.

The news was more than adequately covered but kept at bay fifty yards from us. That didn't stop them from shouting questions to the Ericson's who sometimes shouted answers back. So far, nothing crazy was said that I heard. But it was just a matter of time.

Early on, I talked to the Volusia sheriff and told him of Felipe and where I thought he might be. He sent boats to the area to start looking. It could be an easy find if Felipe were just dumped overboard. Or not if weights were tied to him.

It was near noon and the heat was sweltering. The sheriff got a call and was told to bring the Ericson family back to my dock. They would be escorted to the Volusia police station for official statements. When the news got wind of this, several boats fired up and rooster tails flew from the back of each boat toward my house to get a lead on a story. Even the helicopter vanished.

As Lieutenant Hooper thought, the Coast Guard wanted the sailboat delivered to their station in New Smyrna Beach as well as the girls, accompanied by Homeland Security.
The five girls were passed over to the coast guard boat and the dead girl, Sheliza was strapped to a portable stretcher and covered with a blanket and carried aboard with them. They were about to cast off

when I noticed two of the girls pointing upstream. I looked and heard one of the English speaking girls say "alligator" while another said no, no, no.

It floated directly toward us and it was not an alligator at all but something once far more dangerous to the girls. It was Felipe, face down, arms out wide, appearing to be flying on the surface of the water.

A sheriff's deputy made a loop from the line and passed it in front of the body which floated into the loop and was secured. He pulled the body toward the sheriff's boat. The air became palpable with hate. I could feel it. I've been around a lot of hate and ill feelings but nothing like this.

Each girl vibrated with the loathing they felt. It was like a dark cloud invaded the area. The evil tortured look on the faces of those poor children will be with me forever.

They cast off, but the hatred hung in the air for a while, then became just another dog day afternoon.

Sometime during the morning, the wind switched and started blowing from the east, pushing more water to the Intra-Coastal, raising the tide a bit more than usual. The tow boat called a partner, and together, with the help of the rising tide, the sailboat easily slid off my boat which was well buried in the muck. A quick check and it was ready to be sailed to the Coast Guard Depot.

My boat came out easier than expected too. The soft muck cushioned the hull perfectly with the only damage I could see being a cracked windshield and a nasty gouge on the top rail.

I got in and opened all of the inspection plugs and found everything dry and in good condition. The big Yamaha started instantly. I was all set to go after I signed the papers for the tow out of the muck.

Lieutenant Hooper assured me I would get a copy of the tape he and Dawes made on board. I was hot, tired and totally pissed off. Pissed off that human trafficking was happening right under my nose.

Once out of sight of the others, I felt the boat was OK but needed to see if that was true. I pushed the throttle handle to the full stop position as my deck boat did its best to hit its top speed of fifty-two miles per hour. In minutes, my dock was in sight, and it was empty. Thank god for small favors.

Once the boat was on the lift, my parched throat and lips forced me to the cool confines of my house where I drained a bottle of cold water in seconds. I hit the shower and let cool water pour over me for several minutes before I grabbed a bar of soap. I was feeling a lot better now.

Ten minutes later, I was sitting in my office making phone calls. The first to my boss Floyd Johnson.

Then a call to the town where I have my boat serviced and told Mike what I needed. I helped Mike a couple of times and it was payback time. He told me he was sending a man over within the hour to pick up the boat and drive it up to him. He would have answers for me tomorrow on the damages if any.

A call to the sheriff's office and the Coast Guard rounded off my calling. I was tired. Both my hands were swollen from my fight with that monster. I didn't notice it until I took my shower and saw where the barbecue fork grazed my side. I was lucky.

I pushed the button on my computer and got on the net. I then goggled "Human Trafficking." As I read the Wikipedia site, I was shocked. The more I read, the worse the story got. Sexual slavery, forced labor, and commercial sexual exploitation were only a part of the problem. The extraction of human body organs and tissues were another part of a giant business.

Human trafficking generated an estimated $7 billion to $9.5 billion in annual revenue. That estimate came from a study dating 2004.

What was it now? Half as much again? Double? In 2008, the United Nations estimated nearly 2.5 million people from 127 different countries were being trafficked into 137 countries around the world.

All free countries were against this of course as was the United Nations and yet, the problem was growing annually. And to think that most Americans thought slavery ended a hundred fifty years ago.

I read more than I wanted to know today then thought of the beer I bought yesterday. It came recommended by a good friend who knew his beer, so I picked up a twelve pack of Modelo. This was a Mexican beer that he bragged about. I was thirsty and a little alcohol kick might just improve my sour attitude from what I just read.

I popped the top and just sat down on my office chair. I had just kicked my feet up on the corner of my desk when my private phone rang. I looked at the caller ID which had printed Mary Connors on the screen. Mary was my main squeeze now. Hell, she was my only squeeze since Catherine died. A call from Mary was always an upbeat call and conversation. I just knew it wouldn't be that way today.

This would not be a happy call. I just felt it. I picked up the phone and mumbled, "Hello."

# *Woman Trouble*

I can get pretty cranky at times.  In my youth, I was sometimes called a hothead. As age caught up with me, as it does to all of us, I've mellowed. After I retired, mellow might be the perfect definition of my personality. Until the last few months, that is, when a homicide forced me to revert back to my old ways.

Do you ever get the feeling that you just know something before it happens? You can feel it. That's how I felt when I answered the phone with Mary on the other end. Mary works as a secretary/legal assistant/ jack-of-all-trades at our office in the county office building in Bunnell. Two years younger than me, she is a cute redhead with bright green eyes.

Mary lost her husband to cancer two years ago. We both felt the same loneliness. Sometimes I still struggle with it and I guess that's what drew us together. We started dating a few months ago, and yes, we eventually ended up in the sack. We thought we had something going together but this last month, something changed between us.

Just like that, the passion fizzled. For some reason, there was no longer fireworks between us.  I never felt that way with Catherine. That was one of the reasons I answered the way I did when I picked up the phone. Intuition told me it was going to be bad news. The clock was ticking on our relationship.  I just didn't know quite when it would end.

"Wade, I'm sorry for all the troubles you've had today. Our phones are ringing off the hook with the news. I hope you're OK. I'm afraid I have more bad news too. It concerns me. Well, both of us I guess."

I didn't answer. I just looked at the frosty beer bottle in my hand and felt the cold air from the ceiling register blow on me.  I wasn't sure if I didn't want to know what Mary was about to tell me, or didn't care.  Maybe I was just so torn up about human trafficking behind my house, I couldn't think straight.

"Wade? Are you there?" Mary asked

"Uh, yeah."

*I know it's bad news. I can just feel it in the pit of my stomach.  It's kind of like when my left shoulder hurts before a storm. What is it?*

"I just got word from Mother of Mercy Hospital in Paducah, Kentucky. My sister Patty, you know, I told you about her living on a mini farm. She ended up staying after her husband, Stan, died three years ago. Well, she was in a bad accident this morning and is going to be in bed for quite a while."

"She was broadsided by a cement truck they said lost its brakes. Her Chevy pickup is totaled.  They told me her left leg is broken in two places and her left arm is broken too. So is her right wrist. A side window shattered and cut her up pretty badly.  I spoke to her doctor who said that would heal in time, but she is going to be laid up for a month or longer."

"I take it you're going to go see her?" I asked, knowing she would.

"Well the thing is Wade, Patty has a mini farm. Just ten acres, but two riding horses and some chickens she's fond of for the fresh eggs. And her beloved dog, a German Shepherd the calls Stan. Her husband picked him out of a litter and called him his Man. When Stan died, Patty just started calling him Stan. Silly huh? Naming a dog after your husband. I guess there is more than one way to take that. Her husband was no dog for sure."
I listened and just let her talk.

"Anyway, I'm asking Director Johnson for a leave of absence for ninety days. I hope he gives it to me because I have to take care of my sister and I don't want to quit. The animals need care, and of course, Patty does too."

I was probably reading too much into what she was saying but it sounded like she was anxious just to get away. Maybe she was having second thoughts about the two of us too.

"Don't worry about that Mary. I'll call Floyd and you'll get your leave of absence. That won't be a problem," I said. "I'm tied up in this new problem and I have no idea when I can run over to see you, but I'll try. When are you leaving?"

"I'm going home now to pack. I hope to be gone before three this afternoon. I think I can make Atlanta by nightfall and be in Paducah tomorrow evening."

"I'll be over in an hour," I said. "The least I can do is get your bags in the car and give you a proper kiss goodbye."

"That's great Wade. See you soon."

No 'Love you' said this time. Well, Mary was under a lot of stress herself.

I finished my Modelo beer which was very good, got up and walked into the garage to throw the "dead soldier" into the recycle bin. Dead Soldier is what we called empty beer cans or bottles back in the day. Bobby Joe Green was just getting out of our small shallow water fishing boat with his client he took fishing.

Bobby Joe Green was born and raised in the Okefenokee swamps of Georgia. When his parents died and his sister and brother moved on, so did Bobby Joe. His story should be a book someday as the boy who knew very little about the world we live in who was fast becoming one of the smarter members of our society.

I took Bobby Joe on as an employee a year or so ago. Not long after that, he soon became my partner and more. He became my friend and well He was like a son I never had. He lived above a restaurant in town called Peppers. He worked part time for the owner, Niko Georgopoulos, who like me, saw a lot more in Bobby Joe than most. Niko was grooming him to take over the restaurant one day.

Standing six-foot tall weighing about 160, Bobby Joe could be called raw-boned I guess. At least that's how I saw him. On the thin side but tough as shoe leather and quick as a fox in a hen house. Mild mannered too. Almost too polite. To say I was surprised when I heard him arguing with the client, well, I was surprised.

"You see Bobby Joe," argued the client. He appeared to be a man about my age except he didn't take care of himself, showing a big belly and the start of a double chin.

"I taught this stuff for almost forty years and I know what I'm talking about. Andersonville prison, well, the warden there, killed over thirteen thousand prisoners just to get rid of them. And that's one of the reasons nobody likes the Confederate flag now." Harold Snedeker had his teaching face on.

"Den why is it dat so many guards died from the same ting? Dey were starving too. I gest learnet dat they died cause of a lack of some vitamin. C I tink dey said. And as far as da Confederate flag, hey, it's part of our country's history. I don't tink we should change history Harold," Bobby Joe drawled.

The client, Harold Snedeker, taught American History in a high school in Albany, New York. He felt strong on his opinion. He didn't want to listen to Bobby Joe. I wondered how the hell Bobby Joe knew this information.

Ah, his girlfriend, Sharon Stone. That's where he got this. Sharon was a senior in high school and surprised most everybody when she held classes at the restaurant named Peppers, where Bobby Joe lived, during the summer. Even now when school was in session, Sharon had classes on most Saturday's.
What started out as just a whim and a few students turned out to be as many as fifty or sixty kids showing up and almost a party. Niko, the restaurant owner, gave each kid a free soda. Many of the kids

bought other items, so he made money. It got so the kids loved Sharon's lessons, which she chose randomly.

The district superintendent came to a class two weeks ago to see what Sharon was doing that worked so well. She made learning fun. The word was Sharon would get a scholarship to either be a Gator or a Seminole to get a real teaching degree.  It would be her choice.

When Harold booked this fishing trip, he said it would be a 'one time trip' to learn a little more about fishing. Harold and his wife lived in Palm Coast, just twenty minutes north of here.  He had his boat and regularly fished with little or sporadic results. He taught all his life and was now ready to learn. He could not have picked a better teacher in my opinion.

Bobby Joe and Harold weren't on the water twenty minutes and for some reason, the two of them just hit it off as though both were friends all their lives. Between fishing hints and lessons, they talked agreeably about many things. Until Andersonville Prison came up.

During the Civil War, Andersonville prison housed as many as 45,000 prisoners. Located in central Georgia, the prison was originally called Camp Sumter, located next to the town of Andersonville. The records show that 13,000 Union prisoners died of starvation while interned. The Confederates, on a few occasions, tried to offer an exchange of prisoners with the Union but the offers were always rejected.

The camp commander was Captain Henry Wirz who was tried and convicted of war crimes after the war and was hanged for his sins. It made no difference he tried to exchange prisoners. Many Confederate soldiers died there too from the same problem. Malnutrition.

I could tell it was a friendly argument and watched Bobby Joe remove two nice trout and one decent redfish from the live well on the boat. With speed only youth can possess, he cut two filets from each fish, washed them off and put them into a zip lock gallon bag, filling the bag to capacity. As he was washing the table he asked:

"Well Harold, do you tink you got yer money's worth today?"

"Oh, I sure did Bobby Joe. I learned a lot."

"Well, tell me what stuck out in yer mind?" Bobby Joe ask as he washed off the fish cleaning station with a soft brush. and The hose sprayed a mist, reflecting a rainbow in the sunlight from where I stood.

Harold went through a litany of what he learned, from bating a live shrimp to fishing line size to how to cast to reading the water and even more.  He ended by saying,

"You know Bobby Joe, I booked this trip telling you this would be a one-time trip. I think I'm gonna call you in a couple of months and do another. Oh, I'll learn more for sure but I want you to see how much I learned from this trip, thanks to you. Maybe we can talk some more about Andersonville," Harold said with a big grin and a slap on the back of his new buddy, Bobby Joe.

As Harold walked past me on the dock, I nodded a hello and walked out to Bobby Joe who had the hose spraying down the fishing boat. The overspray I felt was welcome in the heat of the day.

"Hey, boss," teased Bobby Joe, knowing I hated being called boss, "Watcha doin here? Did sometin happen wid da boat? Did somebody get sick?"

For the next ten or fifteen minutes, I told Bobby Joe about my morning with the Ericson's and the accident and human trafficking incident. Of course, Bobby Joe was stunned.

He just could not comprehend how one person could be so cruel to another. To him, even animals should have respect. He killed many animals but always just for food to survive. Never for sport. People doing such things to others was totally foreign to him.

After I wearily finished my tale of woe, I dug out my phone and hit the number 3 on my speed dial. I listened to it ring twice and answered by Floyd Johnson, my director and boss.

"I know, I know. I don't need any grief from you today. Save it. She's got her ninety-day leave," Floyd said. "I knew you'd call. What the hell do you think I am anyhow? Some heartless bastard? Wait. Don't tell me. I'd like to think we have a good relationship and I don't want an honest answer. Not today anyhow."

"But tell me, Wade, how the hell do you get yourself into shit like this? Are you a shit magnet? Now that I think about it, you've always been involved in something, haven't you."

I was glad this call didn't happen an hour ago when I was hot and miserable. I was feeling a lot better now and answered. I walked back toward the shade of the garage, looking at my Mexican Petunia plant, already shedding a few flowers.

"Give me a break Floyd. Vickie was a fluke and yet it turned out pretty damned good didn't it. You got two for the price of one. Both big Tony and his son, little Tony are gone forever." I referred to the incident we had here a short time ago.

"Now this one. Who would ever figure something like this could happen on a sightseeing cruise? It happened to me, Floyd. I sure as hell wasn't looking for this. I never gave a thought to human trafficking and never thought it could be taking place right in my back yard and it sure as hell is. I read up on it a bit, and it's beyond disgusting. And it's growing and growing fast. I don't see how anybody can stop it. Now, every boat that passes is suspect when in truth, 99.9% of the boats are totally legal."

"Well Wade, that's the problem. It's that one tenth of one percent," Floyd said back to me. "This story is going national and the news media are making it sound like we, the United States, are not doing our part to stop it. I know, it's all bullshit, but it's what we have."

"I just got off the phone with Homeland Security who got an ass chewing from the White House. We have to make a good showing and try and at least slow down the human trafficking in this area. What I am now going to tell you is from them. Not me. So don't kill the messenger, huh?"

"There's a woman who has spent the last few years working in England and Spain who apparently has done some good things to curb this problem. She's American and supposed to be really good at what she does. Homeland has now requested she come here and work with us. Homeland has also assigned you to be a co-leader on this project with her. She will be here in three days. Treat her right, Wade. I hear she's hell on wheels. I'll send over her bio and other records later today, so you'll have a heads up. Good luck."

And that is how I first heard the name, Ms. Diane Rose Mason.

# *Diane Rose Mason*

The beautiful city of Orlando, Florida is called home to a vast assortment of amusement and theme parks. Millions of children and adults visit the city annually, so it was not unusual to see a sleek, brilliant red Ford Mustang convertible, top down, luggage crammed into the back seat, make its way out of the airport.

Most would think it was a bit too hot for the top to be down this late morning as the temperature gage on the dash registered 93 degrees. For Diane Mason, coming from a cool, damp London, the warmth was welcome. Born and raised just outside Charlotte, North Carolina, this felt more like home to her.

Diane Rose Mason stood five foot six inches tall and weighed 10.2 stone which converted to 142 pounds. Somehow, her weight in stone sounded better to her. Short salt and pepper hair framed her pretty face. She sported dark red lipstick and matching nail polish. Turning the steering wheel with one hand, she followed the exit sign directing the way to Daytona Beach.

The exit speed was marked 50, so Diane nudged the Mustang to 60. This also happened to be her age, although some men believed her to be ten years younger. Over the years, she took some of these suitors home with her, but nobody ever stayed very long.

By the time she turned 30, she was far too busy to connect with a serious relationship. At 40, she began to worry about her biological clock ticking inside her, running faster every day. At 50, biology stopped that clock. Now at 60, she was what she always was. Alone and self-sufficient. Did she regret it? Sometimes.

Diane had already programmed her GPS to the address she was seeking, the home of her new short time partner, Wade Ivan Nash. She picked up on his initials quick. W.I.N. Somebody had some sense of humor about them. It couldn't be him picking his name. His bio said he was born in a small hospital in Chicago, Illinois in December of 1952 making him three years older than she was. Well, three and a half years really, not that it mattered.

She had his records for two days now and studied them quite well on her flight over this morning. A large part of his files were redacted. Blacked out. Many sections were missing entirely. Reading between the lines, he was one tough son of a bitch to do so much and yet he had to be clean to continue working for the government.

Interstate 4 ended with a choice between north and south. The GPS chose north toward Jacksonville. Long before she saw that city, she was prompted to turn off on Old Dixie Highway. Soon, she was on a beautiful tree lined curvy road with majestic Live Oak trees draped in Spanish moss. Palm trees dotted the water on both sides of the road. She crossed a draw bridge and a quarter mile on, the road ended at the shores of the Atlantic Ocean.

In five minutes, she pulled into the driveway of a Spanish style single story house on a lot bigger than most on the block. She noticed the unusual feature that the garage had an overhead garage door on not only the frontbut also the back where the Intra-Coastal water was just fifty feet away. She saw one boat on a lift and the other boat lift empty.

A man exited from a side door.  From the looks of him, Diane guessed that it could only be Wade Nash. He looked a lot better than the picture in his bio, truth be told. He was tall and obviously very fit. Broad shoulders, a narrow waist and a flat stomach. Not bad at all for a man his age. *His age. Practically my age come to think of it,* thought Diane.

Diane turned off the car's ignition and turned on her thousand-watt disarming smile.

***

I walked to the driver's side of the car and opened the door for her, offering my hand to help her out. If anything, her smile grew more intense as she offered me her left hand. She stepped out of the car.

Through that ever widening smile she said, "Wade Ivan Nash I presume. You don't look like the bad ass I read about in your file. It looks like you found a retirement job here. You must sit around all day and collect Uncle Sam's money huh," said Diane half-jokingly as she surveyed the scene and settled her eyes on the waterway.

"Nah, I don't sit around all day. I like to fish, so I do a lot of that until Uncle Sam decides to send me some woman to come here and bust my chops. You must be Ms. Diane Rose Mason?" I said with a big smile of my own.

I went on. "I got your bio like you got mine. Yours is impressive too and squeaky clean, with no redactions. Come on, let me show you around."

We both walked out on the dock, the sun at its zenith beating down on us.
I walked behind intentionally, liking what I saw. Diane had a nice ass for sure, although I was a little put off by her dark, almost gothic lipstick and nail polish. *Is she into some weird stuff?*

At the end of the dock, she turned and said, "Do you like what you see big guy? Listen, I'm here to work with you. That's it. Got that?

Thinking fast, I said, "Look here sweetie. I don't date the hired help and you work for me now. You aren't bad looking but you sure are no Ann Margret."

"Oh, you like older women huh. Those that can't run from you? Those that you can overpower huh? Well, buddy, you are not

28

George Clooney either. I'm just setting the ground rules," Diane shot back, her eyes blazing.

I was distracted by the unmistakable sound of a cigarette boat. A sleek offshore boat, often sixty feet or longer capable of triple digit sped coming from north to south and took a quick look. I couldn't help it. I loved the speed.

"Damn it, lady, you aren't here five minutes and already you're busting my ass over nothing I said or did. What's with you?"

Diane laughed deep and stuck out her right hand and said, "Hi Wade. I'm Diane, and I'm pleased to meet you. I was just having some fun. We've got some heavy lifting to do here but I want to say something and I only want to say it once. We are partners. Equal partners. If you don't agree, say so now, and that red pony car will be out of here so fast your head will spin and you can deal with the assholes in Washington."

"The way I see it, we are partners but this is my turf. How about you let me take the lead for now. At least until you're up to speed about the area here and all. We can make decisions together and if we don't agree, we can flip a coin or arm-wrestle or whatever the hell you want. I've been in this game a long time too but I'll admit, not in human trafficking as you've been," I said.

The sound of jet skis, two of them, filled the air with their high pitched whine as they flew by at least twice the speed of the posted 30 miles per hour.

"Agreed. So that you know, I'm pretty good at arm wrestling."

I asked, "Did you get the memo your house won't be available for another week? The house they rented for you?"

"No."

"Yeah, the memo came in a couple of hours ago. I can get you a room at the Holiday Inn Express, or if you want, you can stay here. I have two extra bedrooms, and you can have the whole side of the house. It's for a week but hey, it's your call."

"Really? I think I'd love to stay here for a week. I cook a great breakfast if you like breakfasts."

"Good deal Diane. Let's get your luggage in," I said just as a familiar sound entered my world. A quick glance over my shoulder and sure enough, it was our shallow water boat. Bobby Joe with a customer out fishing today.

"Hold on a minute Diane and meet my partner Bobby Joe Green.

I reached over and opened the lift control box and tripped the toggle switch lowering the boat lift. The boat was a custom made Morgan Skimmer, made locally just for shallow water fishing. The boat slid on as Bobby Joe killed the motor before the front of the boat found the lift. It glided on silently. The customer, on the other hand, was far from silent as his salty speech erupted with words one would never hear in church or good company.

*Now what*, I thought. The customer was a big man. He would bottom out a scale that went to 250 pounds for sure and he didn't look fat to me. Bobby Joe took two beautiful trout out of the live well and asked the customer if he wanted them cleaned or would he prefer filets. The grumble sounded like filets to me.

I walked up to Bobby Joe and said I'd like to introduce Diane to him but it could wait until he was finished. Bobby Joe just looked at me and didn't say a word. That wasn't like him at all. I turned to walk Diane back to the house and got three steps when all hell broke loose behind me.

The customer roared at Bobby Joe and said he was going to cut his balls off. I turned and looked at the big guy who was poised to fight, his hands up, balled into fists. He was nearly foaming at the mouth, his eyes looked red and beady.

"OK, what's going on here?" I demanded. The guy had close to a hundred pounds on Bobby Joe who could maybe handle him but why take a chance. I knew I could.

The customer, Brian Dunn, turned his anger on me.

"I'll tell you what's going on," He screamed, pointing to Bobby Joe. "That fucking hillbilly turned loose the biggest fish I ever caught in my life is what's going on. And you expect me to pay for this kind of shit? Well, fuck you too.

Bobby Joe was shaking his head back and forth in disagreement and said, "He caught a nice snook. It gave him one helluva fight, and he did real good catchin it and I got it in the boat. I measured it and it was twenty-six and a half inches long. I showed him da rule book that it hadda be twenty-eight inches long to keep it. He took some pictures wid his phone and I turned it loose. And he got all pissed off and it's been bad since den.

"Bullshit," said Brian. "It's my fish. There ain't a game warden near here. I wanted to take the chance. It's my damned fish."

"No, that's not how it works," I told him. "If we get caught with an illegal fish, we lose our license. No license, no business. We can't do that. If you think about it, I think you'll agree. Seven or eight years ago, we had a bad cold snap, and we lost all our snook. They're finally coming back. You know how much fun they are to catch. We want them back and we want to follow the rules.

The guy just glared at me. For a second, I thought he was going to make a move. Both my hands were still sore from the other day, so I figured I'd bust his knee if it came to that. Then I said, "You don't want to pay, OK. Leave the trout and get your crap and get out of here. I guarantee you'll never fish with a guide here again. It's your call."

He glared at me then picked up his cooler and started walking off the dock. He was almost off the dock then stopped. Shit. He turned and walked back, dropped the little fabric cooler and stuck out his big right hand and said, "I'm Sorry Dude."

I looked at him, prepared for the sucker punch that never came.

"I just never caught a fish like that and well, I messed up. I'm sorry Bobby," He said past me to Bobby Joe. I couldn't see Bobby Joe but bet he was glad the guy was leaving.

Brian reached into his back pocket for his wallet and handed Bobby Joe the price of the trip plus an extra fifty bucks for a tip with another apology. He took his two trout and dropped them into the cooler on the way off the dock and soon was out of sight.

"Ya know Wade. I tink it's better to have a friendly guy wid a little tip den one like him wid a big tip."

"You want a good tip Bobby Joe? This lady is Diane Mason and the tip is don't mess with her. She's one tough lady," I said with a smile

"Well that's an interesting introduction Wade. Don't believe him Bobby Joe. I'm just a big pussycat," said Diane as she walked up and delivered a big kiss on the cheek of one very embarrassed Bobby                                                                    Joe.

It was just past one and already one helluva day.

## *Lester Frabill*

"Ouch."

The little son of a bitch bit him. This little piss ant of a dog, a Yorkie, grabbed Lester on his left thumb and bit down with enough force to draw blood and hold on. Swinging his left hand with the damned dog clamped on tight did nothing to ease the pain or get the little bastard to let go.

Using his right hand, he grabbed the Yorkie by the neck and squeezed hard. Enough force and the Yorkshire terrier cried out and let go of Lester's hand. Lester's reaction was to throw the little guy across the pen into the back wall where he bounced off the wire, falling to the ground.

Max let out a pitiful cry. He was hurt. He didn't mean to cry out but it just happened. Max was never treated like this before.

It was late afternoon when the little dog bit Lester. Not that he liked the damned thing anyhow but it meant money in his pocket. He had to keep the dog healthy for the next couple of days until he could sell him.

Lester Frabill stuck his thumb in his mouth and sucked the puncture wound, hoping to suck out any germs. He reached into his right hip pocket and took out a rag of a handkerchief and wrapped it around his thumb. He wondered if he would need a rabies shot as he looked around him.

Under an ancient Live Oak tree with Spanish Moss waving in the soft breeze sat an old, falling down trailer home on a little knoll. The trailer is the only home he knew. It was on forty acres of pretty good farm land that bordered on the St. John's River to the west.

The problem always was it was forty acres, not four hundred. The land grew watermelon and cabbage very well but there simply was not enough land to make a living.

Lester's daddy owned the land, and his daddy before him did too. Passed down from son to grandson. But times changed and making a living on a small parcel was times long gone.

Lester was twenty-seven years old. He stood five foot ten, one hundred and sixty pounds. His hair, several months past a haircut, hung down to his shoulders. His face stubble now almost a full beard.  He wore cotton jean shorts, worn low and baggy. His butt crack would show if he bent over. The well-worn front button shirt showed stains from much use and little cleaning by the old fashioned washing machine in the lean-to against the trailer. He got his clothes from the church resale shop and often wore them until he just threw them out.

Lester was well into his new enterprise. A business that would keep him from tilling and toiling the rich bottomland soil on which he stood. He hated farming.

The dog was stunned.  The tag on his collar said his name was Max and he belonged to the Masters family with an address and phone number inscribed on the tag. Falling where he did, Max struggled to get up and did his best to shake off the dirt and feces from his coat.

Lester's actions caused his right leg and shoulder to dislocate. The pain made Max whine as he limped to the corner of the pen. Lester came toward him again. Max showed Lester his teeth. If only his big brother Rambo, the red Doberman he lived with along with Myra and Bob Masters were here. Rambo would protect him, but Rambo wasn't here.

Max and Rambo had been investigating today. Just having fun and seeing what they could find that was interesting. Myra was in the back of the house tending the garden and knew neither Rambo nor Max would leave the property. They were well trained to stay by the house.

It was that frog that did it.  A bright green tree frog that was in the way of his travels. The frog jumped almost straight up in front of Max, scaring him half to death. Seeing what it was, Max decided it was time to play with the Frog which kept jumping just out of range of Max and his little paws.

Soon, the Frog was by the culvert where the gravel driveway went over it.  One more hop and the frog would find sanctuary in that culvert which had a few inches of water covering the mud bottom. Water, other than the drinking kind, was something Max hated. Almost as much as he hated getting his nails cut.

Max was so intent on catching that green frog he never heard the van pull up by the ditch, next to him. Nor did he see the guy with the net reach out through the window and drop the net over him, tangling little Max in the net.  Then he pulled the net back into the van. Sitting on the front porch, Rambo spotted what was happening and came charging.  Rambo barked and chased after the van as it drove away with his buddy Max captured inside.

Rambo chased the van for a good distance, barking all the way, but the van was just too fast. Rambo's bark faded, leaving Max alone, still tangled in the net. Now, Max was facing the guy who took him from his happy home and was treating him badly.

Lester looked at the Yorkie with trepidation. He hated the little bastard because he bit him for no reason as far as he was concerned. Lester saw the dog as two hundred dollars in his pocket. Now, he was limping and if he didn't stop the limp, Lester could kiss the money goodbye.

Lester was born and raised here. Just a few miles from the town of Palatka, Florida.  Lester was the only child of Bessy and Harold

Frabill. It was a long time ago but Lester remembered his mama, Bessy, and the day she left him and his daddy. Lester was four or five when she disappeared.

Daddy told Lester to sit in the old Chevy pick up truck parked under the lean-to. He got into the truck and rolled the windows down. Then he heard the terrible argument mommy and daddy were having. Daddy yelling mommy was cheating on him but daddy had to be wrong. Mama always gave daddy the biggest fish or chunk of meat. She never cheated him he was sure.

Lester heard a hard slap and mama scream followed by more slaps from daddy. Lester was familiar with daddy's slaps. Most for no reason he could figure out. Furniture tossed and glass breaking and soon, mama came out of the trailer with her hair a mess and her lip bleeding. She sat in one of the two plastic chairs under the live oak tree in front of the trailer, holding her head in both hands and rocking back and forth for a very long time.

Lester remembered sleeping real late the next morning. Daddy gave him a vitamin the night before and that must have made him extra sleepy as he was always up before the sun. Even the old rooster crowing didn't wake him. When he woke, he could hear the old Case tractor, daddy's pride and joy, coming from the back of the property. When daddy stopped, he told Lester he was working on removing a stump back there. Then as calm as could be, he told Lester his mama wasn't coming back home again. She ran away and left them. It would just be the two of them from now on.

Life wasn't much fun anymore. Mama would read to Lester as he sat on her lap in the evening. Books she got from town and read them and brought them back. Mama also read from the Bible every day. Just a few pages each time, explaining to Lester the meaning of what she read. She told Lester over and over how God started the world and would come back one day and punish those who did bad things.

Mama would wash him with real nice smelling soap. She cut his hair and trimmed his finger and toe nails, singing a song while she did this. She gave him a hundred kisses every day it seemed and told him over and over how much she loved him. Lester would start school soon, so mama taught him his ABC's and to count to one hundred. Mama kept telling him he was a smart boy and he would do well. Now she ran away and left him with just his daddy.

At first, Lester would go to bed and cry quietly, lest his daddy would yell at him. He would pray to the God mama prayed to that she would come back but she never did. Over time, Lester didn't pray anymore. It did no good for him, he thought.

***

By the time Lester was eight years old and in third grade, he was working the land almost as hard as his daddy. They raised melons on half the land and cabbages on the other half. It wasn't much but they got by, paying the bills and keeping food, such as it was, on the table. Daddy taught him to shoot and trap and with plenty of catfish, they ate just fine. Usually.

Lester didn't have friends at school because he didn't have time for them. When the bell rang dismissal, Lester had to head straight home. Some of the boys would stay and shoot a basketball through the hoop in the back of the school.

One day, Mr. Douglas, the history teacher, got all the boys together. He wanted them to start playing a game of touch football after school, two days a week. He would coach them and teach them the rules. Lester could run real fast and he would have loved to play but his daddy said NO. He had chores on the farm.

It was about this time daddy got home just as Lester did from school. Daddy had a dead calf in the back of his truck, covered with a tarpaulin. Its throat slit. Fresh blood-soaked straw covered the bed of the truck. Daddy said he bought it cheap.

The two of them hoisted it up in the lean-to. Daddy showed Lester how to butcher a calf. They had a feast of a meal that night and several nights in a row. The first night, fresh calf's liver with fried onions and sweet potatoes from their patch garden.

The next day at school, a story was told about a missing calf from the Oakford Farm. It appeared somebody cut the wire fence and stole the critter. Nobody saw anything but truck tire marks were next to the fence. Because Lester never talked much, it was easy to just keep quiet about the calf daddy bought at a real good price. In the back of Lester's mind, he knew how daddy got that calf.

*** 

Lester began to notice how daddy would come up with something special now and again. An almost brand new shovel. A used but good running chain saw. Once, a nice fishing rod and reel, telling Lester never to take it fishing when other people were around.

He was old enough to know.  Daddy was stealing things. He remembered Mama reading the Bible to him and a part that said, "Thou shalt not steal." It was a sin. His daddy was all he had, though, and by now, daddy wasn't yelling at him so much anymore. He got to thinking he would try his hand at stealing. Maybe that would make daddy happy.

One of Lester's classmates was a big guy named Wilford Gibbons. Wilford was a thief and everybody knew it, yet he always seemed to get away with his thievery. Wil was big for his grade because he was set back two times already. It was not unusual he would steal a classmates pencil or even his lunch.

At recess, Wil would sneak out to the parking lot and steal a gallon or two of gasoline from a car, hide it in the woods then go back that evening and pick it up. It took Lester a while but he managed to make Wil a friend who taught Lester a few tricks on how to steal. "Gotta steal it like you own it, Les." He would say.

Stealing became easy for Lester. The challenge and excitement were fun too. By the age of nine, he could walk into the IGA store in town and swipe any number of items, then sell them to somebody at a discount. He would take the money and put it in a coffee can he buried under a rock in the field by his house. He didn't share the money with daddy.

At the age of twelve, he got caught stealing a car. It was his first arrest and he was proud of the attention he got.  Mrs. McClintock left her keys in the ignition of her car as she went into the Rexall drug store.  Many people left their keys back then as stealing a car was a big deal and people never stole from neighbors.

Lester had no intention of keeping the Dodge Caravan van. Just take it for a joy ride. Maybe pick up a classmate and drive around. Slipping behind the wheel, Lester had a time figuring out how to move the seat back as Mrs. McClintock was barely five feet tall.

He fired the van up, slipped the lever into D and stepped on the gas and knew he was in trouble. The van was a whole lot faster than the old Case tractor at home.  He slid out of the parking lot and almost hit the car of Deputy Duane Rawlings in his black and white Ford LTD cruiser.

The chase was fast but short. Lester lost control. He put the van in the ditch a half a mile out of town. By then, two cop cars were on his tail. Lester got probation and a scolding. Not bad he thought.

Lester's daddy Harold found out that a kid of sixteen could quit school. By now, Lester was missing more days than attending and saw no reason to go to school. His thievery was growing and improving every day.

Lester would take daddy's truck a couple of times a week and case out homes in good neighborhoods, miles away.  He had a story if he got stopped. He was a handyman looking for work. He kept a wooden box with assorted tools in the bed of the truck and a few times, the story and tools came in handy.

When he knew a house was empty, newspapers in the drive was a giveaway for him, he would break in and steal small appliances and tools until his "fence" taught him to steal good jewelry and how to tell the costume stuff from the real thing.

***

Daddy got killed by his pride and joy, his beloved Case tractor. Well, not killed by the thing but it led up to his death. The tractor got bogged down near the river one afternoon. Instead of using the bucket to push his way to solid ground, daddy hit the gas in low gear and the tractor flipped over on top of him, breaking his back and pinning him under the tractor. The steering wheel crashed into his chest, pinning him tightly to the ground.

Lester found him two hours later, barely alive.  Before he could call for help, he had to purge the trailer of items that they had been using and not purchased with a store receipt. It was a half hour later before Lester could finally call for help. His 911 call directed to the Palatka fire department got them on the scene in ten minutes. With the fire truck, they were able to lift the old tractor off daddy and rush him to the hospital.

Harold was in the hospital for three weeks.  He suffered a broken back, leaving him paralyzed from the waist down.  He had limited use of both arms which the doctors hoped would improve with surgery. The medical team told Harold he would be in a wheelchair until the day he died.  But they were wrong.

Three days after Harold came home, Lester knew he had to feed his daddy and clean the bed two or more times a day as Harold had no control over his bowels or bladder.  It was clear to Lester he was in for a very rough time ahead. Diapers helped a lot but there was still the mess.

A few days after being home, Harold asked Lester to go to town and get him a six pack of beer. He hadn't had a beer in a long time and wanted one he said. Glad to get away for a while, Lester fired up the old Chevy pickup and headed to town. His life was in one big mess now.

40

Before the noise of the pickup truck disappeared from the inside of the trailer, Harold, using all the strength he could find, managed to slide off the bed and fall to the floor. The impact of the fall stunned him to near unconsciousness. Brutal determination allowed him to carry on. With limited use of his left arm, he was able to reach between the mattress and the springs and wrap his left hand around a bundle between the springs and the bed frame.

Wrapped in an oily hunk of an old flannel shirt, Harold worked the cloth off and gripped the wooden handle of the Smith and Wesson Police Special handgun, a 38 caliber. Harold got the gun from his uncle a lifetime ago. It looked familiar and it should. It was the same gun that ended the life of his cheating wife Bessy oh so long ago.

Harold didn't have the strength to pull the trigger in double action mode. He could not cock the hammer back making the trigger pull in single action an easy task.  As he always did, he improvised. He took the hammer and slid it against the metal bed frame.  Using both hands, he pushed the gun as hard as he could, until he heard the familiar "click" of the hammer fully cocked. He rested a moment, reflecting on his past.  He looked at the gun, remembering how easy it was to cock so very long ago.

 A long time ago, out in the back field, he remembered Bessy crying and begging, pleaded her innocence. Her cries fell on his deaf ears as he stuck the barrel in a small watermelon and shot Bessy. The melon acted as a silencer, only a small "puff" heard as the bullet tore through the melon and into Bessy's left eye, removing the back of her head along its path. Bessy would cheat no more.

There was no need for a silencer today. Harold put the four-inch steel barrel deep in his mouth, his thumb on the trigger. He didn't pray. He never prayed and he didn't believe in God. He hated when Bessy would read the words from the Bible to Lester.

He needed Lester tough, not a sissy like most of those church folks. With nothing to live for, his thumb moved the trigger incrementally back until at last, the hammer tripped, falling forward, meeting the bullet primer, setting off an explosive reaction in the gun cylinder.

He never knew that the 158 grain Winchester Silver Tip bullet took off the back of his head. The exit hole the size of a baseball, sending bone fragments into the wall behind him and all around his lifeless body. The mess included brain matter on the ceiling above.

A half hour later, Lester returned to see what his daddy did to himself. The feeling he had was relief, not sadness. He knew he couldn't deal with the man who took the strap to him for many years and treated him like a farm animal. He never had it in him to not care for the man who hated him more than loved him. Lester knew what he had to do as he set out to once more remove items from the trailer, just like before when his daddy got hurt.

Two hours later, he called the Palatka police and reported what he found. Lester was pretty sure the police would investigate him and find out it was some time ago Lester bought the six pack of beer. He had two hours to account for. He would say he stopped at a Crooked Creek and fished a little. The cane pole sat next to the truck under the lean-to. He would say when he got home, he was distraught and didn't call for a while. As it turned out, nobody checked up on him that he ever knew.

That was seven years ago. Four and a half years ago, Lester got caught breaking and entering a home in Palm Coast and spent four years in jail. When he was released, he went back to the only home he knew, an overgrown jungle, hiding an old house trailer near the St. John's River. The old Case tractor sat near the house, weeds growing around and through the frame of the old workhorse. Later, Lester found out the tractor was too far gone to make serviceable again.

It took some searching but he found his hideout rock and under it, the rusting Maxwell House coffee can with his hidden money. The trailer door wasn't locked.  He walked in and sat at the table amongst the roaches and ants, dumping the contents of the coffee can on the dirty table and counted out the money. Seventeen thousand and two hundred and forty dollars had been saved. Lester was in business again.

It took $2,200.00 to buy the nine-year-old dark blue Dodge Caravan with 82,340 miles on the odometer from old man Douglas. The same man that taught history and wanted him to play touch football. Mr. Douglas was retired now for a couple of years but he kept that old van in very good mechanical shape.

The Dodge Company must have bought a bunch of discount paint as the paint on the van was more missing than on it, making the van appear older than it was. The poor paint cost Mr. Douglas eight hundred dollars off his asking price.

Lester learned a few things in prison. How to be a better B&E burglar was one. He vowed he would not get caught again

 Six months later, his B&E trade active but never close to home, was nearing its end if he wanted to stay out of jail. He was getting tired of doing this, almost getting caught twice. Modern security systems were hard to beat now.

One evening, in John's Joint, a biker's bar just out of town, he struck up a conversation with a guy he often saw in the place. John's Joint was not known for much conversation between strangers. A week or so later, Lester and this guy find out both are in the same business. Repossessing property from others. The guy told Lester he had the opportunity for a good business and an outlet for what he could steal.

The venture was stealing pedigree dogs and selling them. Some breeds are bringing four hundred dollars or more, the guy said. The problem is the guy lived in town in an apartment and no way could he keep a dog. And he was afraid of dogs too. Not a good combination or reason to start a program like this. Lester had the room and he wasn't afraid of any animal.

Stealing dogs turned out to be easy and netted him twenty-two hundred dollars in the five weeks he was at it. He had two buyers for the dogs he stole. The money was easy and should he get caught, dog theft was not a hard jail time offense. Maybe this wasn't a lifetime gig but it was good for now.

Slipping on thick leather gloves, Lester moved to the corner to trap Max once more. Max, putting on his best and fiercest look, snarled at Lester, showing his bright white teeth hoping to fend off the monster coming for him. It didn't work.

"Come here you little shit."

# Dirty Business

Clang, clang, clang, clang, clang. The rhythmic bell sound made by the ropes that raise and lower the mainsail, slapped the mast of the 42 foot Beneteau sailboat. The constant clang rang with every pitch the boat made. The boat sailed just north of the north causeway bridge in New Smyrna Beach, Florida.

The bridge alarm bell sounded its warning. The bridge was closing again as the tall mast slid through the opening the raised bridge created. The sails were furled and stowed. The boat under diesel power headed north to the channel taking them to the inlet and the ocean nine miles away.

The water was glass smooth as the Beneteau glided almost silently through the channel, the only sound, the mast clanging which all sailboats experienced when sails are furled. Below deck, Doctor Cosmin Phelan, a disbarred surgeon from Romania finished washing his hands and drying them on three squares of paper towels. He balled them up and shot at a make believe basketball hoop. A trash container.

"Three Points," said the doctor as the towels found the container. Cosmin had practiced unethical and illegal surgery for several years in Romania. The law finally caught up with him and banned him from performing any surgical procedure in his home country. In Romania, doctors were allocated a certain salary for a medical procedure. It wasn't much more than a plumber. In fact, sometimes plumbers made more than he did.

Always an entrepreneur, he started his clinic in the basement of his home and charged whatever the traffic would bear. In Romania, people often waited weeks if not months for some surgical procedures. Call Dr. Phelin and you might have your surgery the same day. He did a lot of abortions and his share of appendectomies and even hysterectomies that saved lives.

One well-to-do businessman brought his wife to him thinking her abdominal pain was due to an inflamed appendix. Dr. Phelin didn't think that to be the problem but performed exploratory surgery, only to find the poor woman would die soon from cancer spreading rapidly.

Dr. Phelan closed her up and gave the husband the bad news. "Go home and make plans. Your missus will not be here much longer."

In a few weeks, the missus died and the businessman, in his grief turned the good doctor in to the authorities. They had him dead to right as he was performing a D & C on a woman when the authorities broke down the door to his basement clinic.

Dr. Cosmin Phelan was out of business. For a while anyhow, until he discovered there was a lot of money to be made in surgical procedures, somewhat modified from what he did. The operations would be the removal of organs taken from organ donors including but not exclusive to hearts, livers, and kidneys.

The payday was great. The surgery performed on a variety of boats, mostly sailboats as they were more stable than a power boat and less likely to cause suspicion. The donors, well, mother or father or both sold their child to a man who paid up to two hundred dollars for each child. It was not for Cosmin to judge the parents. He only judged his bank account.

Many donors were available. The story was, the parents were told their child would be taken to another free country and be adopted. The parents were never to be in touch with them again.

"Your child will have a chance at a good life. One day, they may return here with gifts for you and gratitude for giving them a better life."

Cosmin boarded the boat yesterday evening at Haulover Canal at the cape. Today's schedule was typical. There were just two donors who made Cosmin's routine easy. One boy and one girl, both about ten and eleven years old. Cosmin gave each a powerful sedative just over an hour ago. Both now slept in the forward V berth. Neither would ever wake up again.

Hector Alvarado steered a course in the secure, quiet channel out to sea. Pepe, the assistant, took the head of the girl whose name tag was secured to her blouse and printed in black magic marker, indicated she was called Lorita.

Cosmin took her legs as the two of them moved her delicate body to the operating table, a makeshift slab of stainless steel, with channels pressed into the surface to move body fluids to a container below.

Pepe soaked an old washcloth with ether and placed it over Lorita's nose. He then cut away the flimsy clothes she wore, leaving a rail thin girl, not yet in puberty. Her rib cage prominently displayed.

Her breath remained shallow. Cosmin, well adapted to his job with several months experience, gripped his scalpel and opened the abdomen of Lorita with one smooth stroke. He cut through her abdominal muscles with the ease of cutting through warm butter.

Looking once more at the list provided, he did a very fast nephrectomy, removing each kidney and placed them in plastic bags, then slipped those into a large Yeti cooler half filled with ice. The heart stopped beating when he severed the connective arteries. Her liver was next. The last was both eyes, all going into marked bags and in the cooler. The entire procedure didn't take but ten minutes.

A mesh bag designed to wrap butchered cattle parts found a place at the foot of the table. The remains of Lorita, now ghostly looking with her eyes removed, easily slid into the bag. The foot of the bag was tied and placed in the heavy plastic tray on the floor.

The boy was next. His tag indicated his name was Alvar, written in black magic marker on the tag that could have been on a suitcase at any airport. Alvar was smaller and considerably lighter. Pepe carried him to the steel table by himself.

Except for the eyes, the same procedure was performed on Alvar. This time, when Cosmin severed the Aorta artery on his heart, Alvar's body convulsed in his final death throws, splashing Pepe and Cosmin with a sample of his blood. The lab coats would have to go in the body bag with Alvar.

Pepe finished tying the mesh bag of Alvar just as the Beneteau sailboat started an increased motion with the bow going up and down. They were entering the channel taking them out to sea. The inlet was always considerably rougher than the sea, and continued so, until past the mouth of the inlet itself and into the ocean.

In a minute, the bow rose and fell six feet. The heavy chop tossed the Beneteau with the ease of a child playing catch with a ball. Operating in conditions like this was impossible, which is why they performed the procedures in the smooth water before entering the inlet.

Fishermen lined the rock jetty on the left, casting a variety of baits, often going home with dinner. The boat traveled the mile of the inlet, fighting the sea until they reached the mouth and the Atlantic Ocean. When they were about two hundred yards beyond the inlet, the ocean settled down considerably. Below deck, the trip felt typical every time they made the passage. Cosmin lost track of how many times he did this.

With bright sunlight and cobalt blue seas around them, the Beneteau rode the two-foot seas with ease, heading north. Hector at the helm held binoculars to his eyes and searched north and west, toward land. He soon spotted what he was looking for.

In minutes, a powerful, sleek Cigarette boat, 52 feet long, propelled by dual engines over a thousand horsepower slid next to the Beneteau on the port side. The sleek highly graphic boat rumbled its bass sound as the Yeti cooler containing body parts was transferred from the sailboat to the fast runner.

The cooler barely settled on the deck when the captain of the sleek boat pushed the throttles forward to the full stops. A geyser of water spray followed the sleek boat as it turned south and headed for a stop someplace down the line to deliver the cooler.

Twenty minutes later, a Boston Whaler fishing boat, a 35-foot craft with three 300 horsepower outboard motors attached to the transom motored up to the Beneteau. The Captain was on the flying bridge, twelve feet above the boat deck. His eyes searched the seas for anything suspicious.

Bumpers, oversized sausage looking bags filled with air were tied over the side of the Whaler, keeping the boats from hitting each other and doing damage. In half a minute, Doctor Cosmin Phelan, with his suitcase of surgical tools, along with his partner Pepe slid over the rail and got in the Whaler. Three members from the Whaler traded boats. Those boarding were the cleanup crew.

With the transfer of personnel completed, the Whaler turned west while the Beneteau turned slightly northeast. All they needed was a spot to drop the mesh bags over the side. Each now weighted with a concrete block to ensure they would not float. Hector raised the mainsail and with the stiffening west wind, they sailed on in picture perfect weather.

***

The next morning, as the sun barely cleared the horizon, Joe Dombrowski, the owner of Dombrowski Construction in Cincinnati, Ohio and his son Walter, his partner, settled on the back of the charter boat they hired for the day. Joe breathed in the salty fresh air, then took a sip from his coffee mug, and smiled. He didn't often get a chance to spend time like this with his son. Today would be special, he thought.

Charter fishing had become an expensive sport but what sport wasn't expensive now, Joe thought. The captain of the "Happy Hooker," a 36 foot Trojan, thought the boys would enjoy the workout they would get, landing a couple of Amberjack which can grow to over a hundred pounds. On this reef, a sixty pound Jack was big. It's a tough battle to land one and guaranteed to give the fisherman a memory of a lifetime.

Captain Jack Thompson knew the artificial reef well. He was instrumental in getting the reef placed here. That was four years ago. The reef now had some very large fish that lived in the concrete wreckage below.

Hooking a big pinfish bait on the line with a four-pound weight attached, Captain Jack dropped the bait in the water and felt it hit bottom. He took three cranks on the reel then handed the pole to Joe. He rigged up a similar rig for Walter, this time switching to a juvenile triggerfish as bait. The idea was to drift over the artificial reef, drag the bait near the bottom and hook up with an Amberjack. With a southwest wind blowing easy, fishing conditions were ideal.

"Let it hit the bottom boys then crank the handle six times," said Captain Jack as he made his first drift over the reef.

The strategy paid off as Walter hooked a nice "Jack" fighting it for twenty minutes. It was a give and take battle before Walter got a forty pounder to the side of the boat. Walter was 42 years old and in good shape.

As Joe watched his son battle the huge fish, he wondered if he was up to the task himself. He was a few weeks away from the old age of 67. Maybe he would find out on the next drift.

Circling the reef, Captain Jack hooked on fresh bait sure one of them would hook another behemoth. Five minutes into the drift, Joe's pole bent in a severe arc and the fight was on. Captain Jack stopped the boat and stood next to Joe, offering encouragement.

In short order, Joe didn't feel the tell tale head shake or steady pull on his line and said he thought he was snagged. It happened before, plenty of times. The big weight getting wedged between slabs of concrete below. Captain Jack grabbed the pole from Joe and gave it a mighty heave and felt it move a little at first; then seemed to be free to some extent. It was heavy and not fighting, but it was coming up.

With five minutes of heavy rod pumping, a blue mesh bag could be seen just below the surface.  Joe and Walter held the rod, as Captain Jack used his gaff hook to secure what looked like a medical bag. Getting on the swim platform, Captain Jack ran a sturdy nylon line through a few loops of the mesh bag and secured it to his boat. He then went to the helm of his boat and picked up his phone.

***

Diane and I were running this morning and nearing home after traversing an eight-mile stretch of the beach going south. Today was the second day Diane was here, staying at my home, and our first run together. I usually run every other day and just five miles.

This hotshot woman set the pace and ran a very fast eight miles. Was she showing off? I didn't know and would never ask and acted like this was a normal run for me when in truth, I was winded and beginning to get cranky when about a mile from home, my phone rang.

An hour later, the boat that took the two of us to the reef, the 32-foot Sheriffs boat, was tied snug to the Happy Hooker charter. Rocking in unison on two-foot seas, Captain Jack and the deputy, Paul Agar and I lifted the mesh bag and got it into the Sheriff's boat.

In less than an hour, two more boats joined the scene as another Sheriff's boat arrived with two divers in gear.  Next to show up was a Homeland security boat with none other than Floyd Johnson, my boss, with that crew.

With two divers in the water, Floyd Johnson ordered the mesh bag opened which was easily done with my Benchmade knife I always carried. It was a young boy. He had a name tag on him written in waterproof black magic marker. Just a first name that boldly told everybody his name was Alvar.

Sea animals partially ate the body where they could get past the mesh bag.  There was not much invasion from the sea life, indicating this body wasn't here long.  I opened the abdominal cavity incision and could see internal organs missing.

 I stood up now, feeling like wretching and heard one of the divers come to the surface and asked for a long line. They had another mesh bag and yes, it contained another body.

Three hours later, the sheriff's boat with Diane and I aboard, untied from the other boats and headed for home. The beautiful day with clear skies, a gentle breeze and the promise of a spectacular sunset tonight found both Diane and me looking like we lost our best friend.

"They were just little kids Wade, barely more than babies. And some son of a bitch butchered them up for body parts. They cut up live kids for body parts. What the fuck is this world coming to?"

"I know Diane, I know. We've got a helluva job ahead of us. I don't have a clue how to stop this. First, this is in my back yard and now in my front yard. How the hell long has this been going on? And you know, we got lucky they dumped the bodies on the reef. A hundred yards either side or we probably would never know they were there."

"I don't know Wade, but when we catch them, I don't want you anywhere near them. I want them alone. I'll cut their balls off and make them eat them before I slice them open so they can see how it feels to die like that. They were just little kids for chrissake."

*Right, Diane. You would do that but not if I get them first. I got a different look at the tough lady. She was human after all.*

# *Racing's Blue Blood*

The burble from the dual exhaust Ford V-8 motor was loud. The company named this motor its "Coyote" engine, conservatively rated at 435 horsepower and 400 foot-pounds of torque. The exhaust sounded exquisite to Diane this morning as she backed the Mustang convertible out of Wade's driveway at 6:45 A.M., the top down and Wade in the passenger seat.

Diane was a car nut in the truest sense. Born a dozen or so miles north of Charlotte, North Carolina, the home of more NASCAR teams than all the other locations combined, Diane had a front row seat to speed when it came to cars.

Her grandfather was a moonshiner, running the back roads of the Appalachian Mountains going from still to still of his brother, cousins, uncles and even one aunt that was involved in the lucrative business.

Grandpa Cletus didn't make the stuff, he was the delivery man and delivered more "Shine" than anybody else in several surrounding counties. Everybody, even the revenuers said, "that boy can drive." Well, that boy wasn't a boy. He was well in his 50's when he finally had to quit as the stuff became legal once more and the profits were gone.

Cletus was never caught delivering in the hundreds of runs he made. It could have been a record but with the boys, the tales grew to proportions that could win the tallest tale at the liars club they had at the county fair in the summer. Who was the biggest liar? The trouble was, some of the boys began to believe the lies they told themselves. Ha. They all were tall tale specialists. It was all just simple country fun.

Grandpa Cletus and daddy Joe built the cars themselves. There were several cars with modified bodies to hold a hundred or more gallons of shine which required special suspensions to take the load and the sharp curves in the hills. Every motor was hand built.

What came as 120 horsepower would be modified to produce over 200 horsepower, more than enough to run away from the feds which Cletus had to do often.

When the "Shine" business dried up, there was still a need for fast cars as a lot of the boys would go out and race on weekends for something to do.  For a few bucks but mostly, for bragging rights, the boys would race.  Some of these good old boys became superstars in racing later on.

This racing eventually became NASCAR. But before NASCAR, there were a lot of races on race tracks in the fields of farmers who would lease the land for money.

There was a need for fast cars and with the reputation they had, Cletus and Joe continued to build fast motors and modify chassis for cars to run fast on dirt tracks. Just like running from the revenuers but this time it was all legal.

Joseph and Dorothy had one child. She wasn't the boy daddy hoped to raise. Mama named her Diane after some character in a book she was reading at the time she was born.  Daddy wanted her name to be Agnes, after an aunt he always took a shine to as Aunt Agnes made the best apple pies and was sure her nephew Joseph got a special one every year. She would put extra cinnamon in the apple pie for him.

When she was seven years old, if one pulled in the driveway and saw Diane standing there in her bib overalls, very short hair, grease on her face and hands, you might call her Danny or Dave or anything but Diane. Daddy Joe had his boy after all.

At the age of nine, Diane would hurry home from the county school bus stop and run down the dirt path the quarter mile or so to the house, sending up little puffs of red clay dust with every step. Sliding out of her school and Sunday clothes, she would get into her bib overalls, now a size or two bigger every year. Slipping on her work shoes, she would make a bee line for the barn where Cletus and daddy would be involved in something or another.

 Building fast cars fascinated Diane to the point of an obsession. What made this unusual was Diane's report cards from school always came back straight A's from first grade to now.  Mama told her that if she didn't keep her school grade high, the car work would have to stop until they were satisfactory again. One can't do better than straight A's.

Her age of twelve was a big turning point for Diane. For one thing, Grandpa Cletus died, almost four years to the day his wife and Diane's grandma Sally died from some cancer. Grandpa Cletus died because of pneumonia they said. For a while, Cletus had seemed to have a hard time breathing and catching his breath.

One day, Grandpa Cletus just didn't get out of bed in the morning. Mama woke daddy about four that morning when she heard a funny sound from grandpa's bedroom. Cletus was gone. They buried him in the family plot two days later, next to his Sally. Grandpa said he sorely missed her.  Diane hoped he was happy with Sally once more.

The other big thing that happened not long after grandpa passed was the curse hit Diane. Well, that's what some of the girls called it when blood comes out of your private parts. Mama talked to her about it a few times but Diane didn't want it. Maybe if she didn't think on it, it wouldn't happen.  It did and with it came moods she never had before.

Her chest started developing too. Every day it seemed like those two lumps got bigger.  She didn't want that to happen either.

Poor daddy. He just lost his daddy and now he was losing his little boy. Diane was still the best stick welder in the county. Until a mood and those terrible cramps came on to her. When they happened, she just wanted to crawl in some corner and hide. Meanwhile, the competition for fast motors and cars increased tenfold.

Some big companies were now in the game. The new guys were building better and faster motors than Diane and daddy could make. Because of technology advances, they could make those motors cheaper too.

***

It had taken the rest of the year before things settled down with Diane to where her cramps weren't as bad as they were at first. Her moodiness continued to be an issue. Sometimes, she would snap at daddy for no reason then five minutes later; she would have to apologize to him. Daddy would just smile and sometimes hug her a second and tell her it was all right. He understood. She didn't think he did but why argue?

It happened to be August 29th, the day of Diane's thirteenth birthday. Mom, dad, and Diane sat at the kitchen table eating a great ham, roasted golden brown with a side of mama's special sweet potatoes and turnip greens. Mom made this special birthday meal in honor of Diane's birthday today. The sideboard held a delicious looking apple pie mom made from McIntosh apples she picked from the tree next to the road near their drive, the golden crust waiting to be sliced and enjoyed.

Diane noticed that mama became mom and daddy became dad in some of her conversations with them now. Curious, did her vocabulary change with the curse too?

Mama was putting a few candles between the lattices on the pie top. She only had seven candles but that would do for a quick Happy Birthday song and good wishes to Diane.

Daddy wondered if the item mama picked out for Diane's birthday present would be appropriate but mama was a practical woman, a trait inherited by Diane too. A new bra wrapped in shiny silver wrapping paper sat on the corner chair waiting to be opened.

With the seven candles in place and the match ready to be struck, the ceremony was interrupted by a car pulling up the driveway, stopping near the front door. Daddy got up and went to the door and looked at a bright new shiny Cadillac Coupe DeVille, all black and chrome, a tint of red clay dust settled on the rear fenders and trunk.

Two men got out, dressed in dark business suits with wing tip shoes polished to a mirror shine. The two men walked up the three stairs to the front door. Daddy recognized one of the men. He was Robert McIlroy, owner of McIlroy racing, the biggest name in racing in the area.

In all the years after that moment, Diane never forgot a single word spoken that evening. Daddy made a deal to go to work for McIlroy racing in Charlotte, North Carolina. McIlroy was a good talker but what he said made perfect sense. The small time builders like daddy could not compete but daddy's knowledge was worth a gold mine. Four times the money he was making now and regular hours with a lot of benefits they simply could not afford was the offer.

It didn't hurt that Mr. McIlroy and his companion, Mr. Snellinburger were treated to a generous slice of mama's pie and good southern hospitality. It made the talking easy and friendly.

Mr. McIlroy would help them find a nice house and help them secure a loan until his property here sold if he wanted to sell. They would live in the city of Charlotte North Carolina. Their entire world was about to change. And change it did with Diane remembering the promises Mr. McIlroy spoke. Promises kept, just as he spoke them. He was an honest man.

The burble from the exhaust increased as Diane applied just a modicum of pressure on the accelerator, the car speed increasing to a sensible 25 miles per hour on the street. At the corner of the street where it met the scenic Highway A-1-A, Diane nosed the bright red Mustang's grill south, coming to a complete stop. Looking both ways, a glimpse at the beautiful Atlantic Ocean, she stepped on the accelerator enough to move the car on the highway then mashed the pedal to the floor.

The squeal of the tires was heard for quite a distance. The car left two dark streaks of tire rubber for several feet. The transmission shifted into second gear, leaving a small space of no rubber on the tarmac, replaced with another squeal and more rubber and sound until Diane backed off on the go fast pedal.

"Why the hell did you do that?" I asked, a surprised look on my face as I glanced at the speedometer needle rushing past 80 miles per hour in just seconds.

"Because it feels good Wade. That's why."

"Damn lady, you're gonna have every neighbor here pissed at us. I try and keep a low profile and in five seconds it's blown to hell."

"Relax big guy. I'm just blowing off a little steam from yesterday. I want to meet this bridge tender friend of yours," said Diane.

She turned the corner on Highbridge and drove the quarter mile to the bridge itself and parked the convertible on the side of the road behind a beat up pick up truck I knew belonged to Herbie Moncrief. Herb was my friend and the bridge tender that worked the day shift.

*Damn,* I thought, *with her attitude and how Herbie is, this could be interesting*

*A police cruiser came around the corner, Mars lights flashing as he pulled in behind us. Aw, damn.*

# *The Bridge*

"Hello, Mike," I said to the Volusia County police officer walking toward us. Mike stood six feet tall, about 180 pounds with impressive biceps. Mike was a work out guru, taking on the task of working with troubled teens, getting them on the straight and narrow when he could. Exercise was his program and saved more than a few kids from a path they didn't have to walk. Diane and I stood by the Mustang. I worked with Mike on other projects, the latest of which was the murder behind my house. Mike was a straight shooter and a good guy to have on your side.

"Hi, Wade. Is it safe to say you weren't driving this car a few minutes ago?" he asked, looking at the Mustang.

Before I could answer Diane spoke up. She was standing next to me and took a step forward and stuck her right hand out to shake his hand. Mike looked at her but did not reach for her hand. "Good morning officer. I was the driver. Would you like to see my drivers license? I have it in my handbag in the back seat of the car. May I get it for you?"

I was impressed. She didn't shrink away from the problem but met it head on.

"Before we go there ma'am, do you have a reason for the speed you were going? I had my unit on automatic and I have you at 107 miles an hour. Do you have a reason for going that fast?"
"No, sir. No, I don't, other than it made me feel good for a minute. I broke the law officer. I am sorry. Will I do it again? Yes, but not on a road where somebody could get hurt."

"What do you think Wade?" asked Officer Miller. "Is her word good?"

"Milke, you know me better to try and put me in the middle of this," I said. "You have to do what you think is best."

I went on, "Mike, this is Diane Mason. She and I are tasked with slowing down the disgusting Human Trafficking we discovered here last week. Diane is fresh back in the states from England. I read her bio and she's a car nut, if I dare say so. Do you remember the Mason name in racing a while ago?"

While Officer Miller looked into his memory, Diane said, "You had a good man here you might remember. He had an auto shop here. His name was Yunick."

"Oh yeah, old Smokey's place. He died when I was pretty young but my dad talked about him a lot. One helluva wrench I hear. Is that who you mean?"

"Yes, He was Hank back then. My grandpa gave him the name Smokey. He was always lighting up those tires into smoke. I was just a kid back then. I worked on the front end of his Chevy if I recall. He was a fun guy with a great sense of humor."

Mike said, "Ms. Mason, I'm gonna give you a pass this time. Please don't let me see you do that again. Times have changed. Cars from the factory are just too powerful and there are way too many dumb drivers on the road. Not to mention this is a beach community and we have people walking or riding bikes day and night."

This time when Diane stuck her hand out, Mike shook it briefly.

"Officer, you have my word on it," Diane said.

Looking at me, Mike said, "I heard about what you were into last week, Wade. And now yesterday off the Koster reef. I never gave a thought about human trafficking kids with slavery in mind. I hear yesterday involved killing kids for body parts." Mike looked visibly shaken. "What are the plans to stop this if I might ask?"

"Diane is here because she's our specialist with sophisticated equipment to identify people hiding in boats. We're here to take some measurements and set this bridge up as a checkpoint. It's more an experiment I guess but hey, we'll see how it does," I said.

The claxon bell on the bridge rang loud and clear as the gates came down, blocking the roadway. The bridge was about to go up to allow a large cruiser to pass heading north.

Mike drove off making a U-turn as Diane and I walked up to the small building that was the control room, barely big enough for the three of us. We squeezed in with Herb Moncrief, the bridge tender on day shift. He had a troubled look on his face. I noticed Herb continued to sport a nice haircut and dressed a lot better than just a couple of months ago.

Herb was a confirmed bachelor for the past twenty years. He wore his hair shaggy with a rough untrimmed beard all the time I knew him. That was until the party I had a month or so ago on the fourth of July. Herb showed up looking much like now, cleanly shaven, a nice haircut and nice clothes. He brought a lady friend, Millie, whom he met at a church social who obviously was changing his life.

I called Herb yesterday, so there was no surprise. Herb knew a little about Diane from what I told him on the phone.

"Hi, Diane. It's nice to meet you. Wade told me a little about you. It sounds like you've had one helluva career." Herb said, crushed in the corner in the little room. "What the hell was Mike doing here with the lights flashing and all?"

Diane didn't want to get into an explanation now and said, "Herb, I'd like to run something past you and get your opinion. I'm sure you know this area about as well as anybody could. In Europe, we tried something that had limited success in spotting the scum that transport humans for profit."

"Oh, I've been here a while," Herb said, looking somber at Diane who kept a little smile on her lips. "I know pretty much all about this area. I know this old bridge about as well as the fellas that built her back in 1955."

"Most folks call her the Highbridge bridge cause of the road she's on. Her real name is the L.B. Knox bridge.

"She's one of fifty-four bridges in Volusia County. There's only a few draw bridges left but I don't think we'll see a super bridge built here. Just too danged expensive and we don't get the traffic here to warrant one of those monsters. And it would ruin the scenery. Look at this. It's just like old Florida. It's beautiful."

"I'll bet you have her size and dimensions too," said Diane

"Why hell yes. She's 309 feet long and 37 feet wide. When she's closed, it's sixteen feet to the water during normal tide. Anything over twelve feet tall coming through, we raise her. Can't take a chance of damage. Shutting her down is a nightmare. You'd think the world ended for the locals here. I wasn't here at the time but it used to be a ferry crossing before she was built."

"You want me to take notes?" I asked.

"I take notes like I'd bet you take notes Wade," smiled Diane. "Once it's in that gray matter, it's there to stay,"

"What we did Herb," Diane said, "We get a heat sensing camera. The military has been using them for years and are highly perfected now. We mount it under the bridge and mount a television in the control house here. The sensors in these new units can tell how many people are in the vessel. Well, people or animals of any size. You can't always be right but say a sailboat goes through and you count eight or more people inside. That's a good sign to check this boat for illegal transporting of humans.

It's not foolproof as we found out but it usually works for a while. Then they get smart. First, they shoot out the camera. If that doesn't work, they have heated bags they scatter around. We spend a lot of time on false alarms. Another will come through with the illegals hidden under an aluminum space blanket.  And there are other tricks to fool us. They keep trying while we keep learning."

I asked Herb, "When she is fully up, how high is she?"

"Just a bit over forty-seven feet to the road. Add another sixteen feet or so to the water," said Herb, using his hands to show the steep angle of the raised section. "She's near straight up and down when she's raised."

"I see it isn't too wide between the fenders here, so any boat of any size has to go through one at a time. That's how it looks to me, Herb," said Diane.

"That's what it is all right. Usually, it's first come, first serve but in the busy seasons, we sometimes stack them up so we don't keep the road shut down too long. In the fall, they're going south. Spring and the boats go home, heading north.  A lot of boats have private captains that transport these boats for a living. Pretty damned good living too from what I hear."

"Herb," said Diane. "I've done this a lot where I was so when I tell you what I want, I'm not crazy. I need you to raise the bridge for the next boat that comes along. I'm going to be on the top of that bridge, on the locking fingers. I have a camera in the car and a couple of other tools I need.  I'll take pictures and angle measurements from up there, so we get the right equipment here.  I'll be just fine."

I asked, "How in the hell are you going to secure yourself to the top? It's almost straight up and down you know."

"Wade, I've done this dozens of times. It isn't all that hard, believe me. I need accurate pictures for the right equipment, or we are wasting our time with this. If it makes you feel better, come on up with me."

"I don't think I can talk you out of this, can I?" I asked. I wasn't afraid at all, just concerned for her. Did she know what she was doing?

Looking north and south, Diane saw nothing of any size coming down the river from either direction. "This bridge rises from one side only. I want to check her out," Diane said.

I said, "She's different Herb. I had no idea she was going to want to do this on the bridge.  She's smart as hell and her record is impeccable. I guess she knows what she's doing. I don't like it though."

Diane just smiled. "I've done this a lot boys. It's part of what I'm good at."

"Diane, why the hell don't you let me get people here with the proper gear to do this? I can have people here by tomorrow or the next day for sure."

"Wait two days and then what? Spend a day rigging what won't be all that safe?  If an inspector comes with the deal and they always do, a day will be a week. No Wade, I've done this many times. There is nothing to worry about, believe me. If it makes you feel better, I'll check it out first."

They walked the bridge from end to end. She had seen this method of joining many times before. It wasn't long and Herb shouted he had to raise the bridge as a 56-foot cruiser was heading north.

"Perfect," said Diane. "Wade, tell Herb I will be here as he starts raising the bridge. If he can raise it to say five or six feet, I just want to make sure of what I think I see. I'll walk back down and he can keep raising the old girl. Just stop it for ten seconds or so."
The bridge started to rise until Herb stopped it after just a half dozen feet of lift.  He had already called the waiting boat telling them an inspector was checking on something and not to worry.  No sense in having the boat call in a distress call. True to her word, Diane

walked back after a quick look. She popped the Mustang trunk and took out her camera and another tool.

Ten minutes later, dressed in bright red shorts almost matching the color of the Mustang, Diane walked out to the far edge of the bridge, at the finger joint.  She snapped a fanny pack around her waist with her equipment in the pockets.

Before walking out there, she said, "Listen, Herb, blow that horn like you always do and raise the bridge just like you would any other time. If you stop or do something not normal, it could mess me up and get me hurt. I know what I'm doing."

When Diane walked to the bridge divide, I couldn't help but notice. Diane had a chine walk, a swaying back and forth of her ass like an overpowered speed boat will sometimes do. The sway back and forth is called a chine walk. Damn, her ass was swaying back and forth with the best he's ever seen. My girl was Mary. Wasn't she? My girl was gone. I better call her tonight.

I was still looking at Diane's ass when Herb said, "Damn, she's got a nice ass on her, doesn't she?"

"Uh, I didn't notice," I said
.

As the bridge started to raise, Diane was standing on the white center line of the road. When the separation got to be about six feet, she sat on the edge and swung her left leg over the side and rested her left foot on one of the fingers that connected the bridge.  She sat straddling the lip of the bridge.  Now the slow ride up, taking pictures all the way
.

It took about forty seconds to reach its total open height, almost a ninety-degree angle as Herb said. Diane already knew what would be needed but took a few more pictures. Then she looked down toward the control shack and saw Wade standing next to it with his right hand over his eyes, like shielding them from the sun. The sun was at his back. It wasn't in his eyes.

The boat passed and just before Herb sounded the horn, Diane stood up with one foot on either side of the roadway, totally safe but scaring the hell out of Wade and most likely Herb too.

"Are you OK?" I shouted up, walking a bit toward the bridge.

"I'm fine Wade. Just stretching."

*This would be fun but she better not. If she dove off this now, they would surely want to kill her. No need for that. But it sure was tempting. It won't be long and they'll have drones to do this,* she thought as the claxon bell sounded, the bridge is coming down again. *He isn't bad looking from up here,* she thought. *I wonder if my wiggle got noticed?*

# *The Money Man*

Kaieteur Falls in Guyana's tropical Amazon region is a spectacular sight. The water plunges 741 feet to a pool below. The crashing sound is heard for many miles. The falls are fed by the Potaro River, one of the largest rivers in the Amazon.

Near the base of the falls stood a husband and wife, bartering with a man dressed as though he stepped out of a safari hunting book from fifty years ago. The man has dressed in knee-high lace-up boots and a leather vest worn over a cotton shirt. Blossoming cord trousers and a wide brim safari hat finished his wardrobe. Most of the local people knew him by his nickname. He was called The Money Man.

The money man would travel the Amazon buying things. An occasional gold nugget or a gemstone or a rare artifact of some sort. His main purpose for these trips was to buy children. With the changing world, these parents found it difficult to raise their children. Many in the villages were catching on to what the real world was becoming. One less mouth to feed and a chance their child would have a better life was the reason they sold their children to be taken to another world. This is the story the Money Man told them.

The lush green forest framed the water falling, hitting a plateau below, then moving on to another set of falls. In the process, the mist through the sunlight created one of God's beautiful sights. A rainbow. Under the rainbow, the Money Man negotiated the sale of a child he might buy, then sell for a huge profit. He cared not at all that he was breaking one or more of the laws written on stone tablets a long time ago.

Off to one side of the trio stood an emaciated boy, dressed in ragged shorts.  They were worn thin and looked to be two or more sizes too large for him.  A thin rope, frayed at the ends, tied in a simple knot kept his oversized shorts from falling from his frail frame.

The woman's hands articulated, speaking a dialect most didn't know. She was telling the money man how good and smart her boy was and why he must be chosen by the money man.

The money man was Arthur Dalton. Arthur's business was to procure children. His target age group ran from eight years of age to early adolescence. The children he bought were moved out of the country and sold. They might go for cheap labor, the sex trade, or perhaps body parts.  The risks of getting caught increased but the profit margins were huge.

Born in London, England, Arthur learned to care for himself at a very early age. Born into money, Arthur had the best of everything. Home schooled, he had a brilliant mind. From a small boy on, Arthur chose a life of mischief and shenanigans. It was like his life was predestined, bringing him to where he was now.

Arthur knew he would take the boy even though the lad had mental issues. It was just a matter of money now. How much they wanted and how little he wanted to pay.

Arthur spoke the dialect enough to make it clear the boy was not wanted. He had mental issues while his mother, the one negotiating, was touting how smart her boy was.

"Look," she said, calling the boy over to her and handing him a Rubik's cube. She said something to the boy who started twisting the cube in a rapid motion.  In less than a minute, all the colors matched.

"Nice trick lady," Arthur said, holding the cube in his hand. Arthur twisted the cube in several different ways, thinking the cube was a trick practiced by the boy so he would appear smart.
"Try this."

In less time than before, the boy had the colors aligned once more.

"OK, I'll take him. I'll give you one hundred dollars for him."

"No. The price is two hundred dollars. You pay the others two hundred dollars. I want two hundred dollars." His mother spoke in her dialect.

The negotiations continued for several minutes and ended up at two hundred dollars the mother insisted was fair. Arthur handed over the money in the favored American currency. All twenty dollar bills. Two of them were counterfeit.

With his two pinky fingers in his mouth, Arthur whistled a shrill note. From the boat on the river came two very large black men. Each grabbed the boy by his arms, half carrying and half dragging him, kicking and screaming, down to the boat.

Turning to his parents, Arthur said, "He will be going to a faraway place called China. You won't see him for a long time but he will be rich and happy."
It was the same lie he told over, again and again, just changing the country for the fun of it. Arthur had no idea where these kids would go. Nor did he care.

The boy screamed for his parents all the way to the boat while his mother called to him, "Good bye Abbas. I love you."

*I love you too thought Arthur. I love the money I'll make off of him. These people are so stupid. Thinning them out is helping the world. I should get an award.*

# *Bobby Joe*

It felt like walking into the center of a forest fire. The heat so intense, made more so by spending over two hours in the frigid confines of the movie theater. Bobby Joe grew up never experiencing air conditioning. He was raised in the Okefenokee Swamp in Georgia, deep in the backwaters where no such appliance existed. Air conditioning was a marvel to him once he moved away from home.

 Bobby Joe and his girlfriend Sharon Stone, just enjoyed a thriller, a Jason Bourne movie.  Bobby Joe loved the action movie and loved going to a picture show with Sharon. Sharon loved going anyplace with Bobby Joe. She held his hand tight as they felt a soft breeze from the south envelope them in the intense heat and humidity of the day.

Looking at his black plastic Timex watch, a gift from Sharon, Bobby Joe asked, "So, whatcha wanna do now? It's not even five yet. Wanna go up to Palm Coast and get a dinner at Ruby Tuesday's. Dey got dem ribs we both like."  Beads of perspiration formed on thefaces of both as they walked a distance to the side of the theater, then to the west parking lot.

"Well yeah, that's what I thought we were going to do. I have a half off coupon for the second meal I cut out of the newspaper. We both like the food. Then I thought we could rent another movie from the Red Box and go to your place and turn up the air conditioning. Maybe get a soda and just relax and watch another movie. It's too hot to do much else today," Sharon said.

Sharon went on and asked, "What's with that new woman working with Wade now? I saw both of them yesterday in the grocery store and they were laughing and having a good time. It looked to me like they've known each other a long time."

"Nah, she's new. But I gotta say, dey are getting along great. When I met her on da dock, she gave me a big kiss on my cheek and well, I got kind of embarrassed for a bit. She's funny and Wade said she's smart and tough. Dey is doing things to try and stop people smuggling other people. I guess she's an expert."

When Sharon heard he got a kiss on his cheek, she tensed up for a moment. She wanted Bobby Joe all for herself. She noticed now that he was doing so well in her classes, working at fishing, and also working at Niko's, some of her friends seem to be taking an interest in him too. Some of her girlfriends. She told one of her friends to "back off" and got a reply "finders' keepers, losers weepers." She squeezed his hand just a little tighter as the truck came into sight. It had a good air conditioner.

"Slut."

"Fucking Hillbilly"

Two guys strolled toward them, walking between the rows of cars. It was Ted Arbogast, a one-time boyfriend of Sharon's, who is the quarterback at her school. His companion was one of the offensive linemen on the team, Jeff Schultz. Jeff was born to be a lineman on a football team. He was big and mean. Scouts from Florida State and Alabama were scouting him.

Not long ago, Bobby Joe dispatched Ted at a beach party and had all the gang laugh at him. The confrontation followed him to school, a smaller guy kicked his ass. Today, while most likely just a chance meeting, he had the toughest guy on the teamwith him. This was trouble for sure.

"Hey slut, what are you doing now? Blowing this hillbilly?" Ted gestured with his hand and mouth like he was sucking something.

"Hey Ted, I don't want no trouble but I don't cotton to ya calling my girl names. I beat yer ass once and I'll do it again if ya don't take dat back and move on," Bobby Joe said.

"You scared hillbilly?" Ted asked

Sharon, thinking fast said, "Jeff, we know some big schools are looking at you and you have a shot at making the big time. The whole school is pulling for you. If Bobby Joe does a number on your knee, how do you think that will work out for you?"

Jeff was in the mood for a quick fight until Sharon spoke. Now, he stopped and just stood there, working her words over in his mind, wondering if this guy could break a knee. That could be the end of his dream.

The next instant, Ted lunged at Bobby Joe, throwing his right fist, hitting the left shoulder of Bobby Joe. As he threw the punch, he yelled out, "Come on Jeff. Let's kick some ass."

The next fist Ted threw was his left, blocked by Bobby Joe, looking at Jeff, not Ted. Jeff stayed still.

"Come on Jeff, let's get this bastard," Ted said.

"I got no beef with this guy Ted. I take classes with Sharon and I like her. This is your fight," Jeff said as he walked back a couple of steps.

Ted was on his own and he started it. His buddy let him down. He had to finish this himself. Ted charged Bobby Joe who grabbed Ted's shoulders and threw him to the ground. As Ted got up, Bobby Joe slapped him in his face, hard. Then backhanded, slapped his face again. Tears were falling from Ted's eyes. He wasn't crying but it looked like it.

Others walking to the theater came to see what was going on. Unfortunately for Ted, some were students of the school he attended. This story would get out for sure.

Ted kept backing up under the never ending slaps he was receiving from Bobby Joe. Tears streamed down his face, now beet red from the beating it was taking.

"I want you to apologize to Sharon right now Ted, or I'll slap the face right off of you," Bobby Joe said as he stopped he slaps for a moment.

He was humiliated. Now the tears were tears from crying. He had a choice, say nothing and get a worse licking or apologize.

"I'm sorry Sharon. I won't ever say that again," Ted said, his nose now running as fast as the tears fell.

Jeff just looked on, knowing he made the right choice. Had he gotten into this fight, his career would most likely be over. He respected this hillbilly by nodding and smiling at him as he helped Ted back to his car.

The fight over, the people moved on. Some of the students gave Bobby Joe a thumbs up. Bobby Joe looked at his hand, red as the red clay of Georgia.

Looking at his red hand, Sharon took it in both of hers and said, "Honey, why don't we just go to your place and let Niko throw a couple of burgers on the grill for us. We can stop at the red box and get a movie I think you'll like."

"Dat's OK wid me too if it's what ya want."

The interior of the tan Toyota pickup truck had to be one hundred and twenty degrees. The vinyl seats felt like sitting on beds of coal. Bobby Joe opened the windows and turned on the AC to maximum cold, a minute later, the interior was tolerable.

Both were quiet on the ride back to Flagler Beach and the Red Box movie rental machine. Bobby Joe wondered if what just happened would be the end of his problems with that Ted guy. If not, how could he handle it? He didn't want to keep beating up on the guy.

He sure liked the girl sitting next to him, holding his sore hand. He didn't want her upset and he did not want somebody saying bad things about her. He liked her. And only her.

Sharon's thoughts were on Bobby Joe. Getting a kiss from a stranger. Her girlfriends want to hit on him now.

Sharon wanted to have sex with Bobby Joe but he kept holding back. He kept saying he promised his mama he would wait until he married. And, she thought, if we had sex together, he would be committed to her and not dump her for one of her so called friends. She had a plan.

Bobby Joe turned the room air conditioning to max cold on the knob. He went down to the restaurant and talked to Niko as he threw on two burgers to bring upstairs. They sizzled on the hot grill as he prepared the buns.

Upstairs, Sharon's plan was working better than she expected. She slipped the DVD into the player and played it to come on at the very beginning of the video then pushed stop. The video was not the silly movie she chose from the Red Box dispenser but a movie she took from her dad's hidden box in the garage. The footlocker he kept locked, the key hanging from a nail on the wall, hidden from sight until a year ago.

The movie was called "Behind the Green Door." A classic pornographic video from years ago. If this didn't turn on Bobby Joe, well, what would, she wondered.

Ten minutes later, Bobby Joe bound up the steps and walked in with the pleasant aroma of freshly cooked burgers with French fries. Two tall sodas with straws were in the food carrier too.

The food passed, a hank of paper towels for each, they settled in to enjoy the movie.

Sharon hit (PLAY).

# *Wade and Mary*

The clock on my office wall showed it was exactly seven when I picked up my office phone.  I checked my Rolodex file, then dialed the phone number I had for Mary. It was an hour earlier in Paducah, Kentucky where she was, helping her sister who was in a bad auto accident. I hadn't called for a few days. Yes, I was busy but that wasn't the reason. Now, I felt I had to call. I kept thinking the lines run both ways. Yes, I knew they were not lines any longer but signals sent by transmitters. Mary could have called me. But she didn't.

"Hi, Wade. I just knew you would call. I hurried with the chores here after I got back from visiting my sister in the hospital. Bill helped me, so the chores went twice as fast. I think I told you about Bill, didn't I? How are things with you?" Mary asked.

"Oh boy, things are jumping over here. We are setting up a system checking boats that may carry illegals.  While all illegals are not involved in human trafficking, a good percentage are. Last week, a fishermen not far off the coast pulled up a body bag with a kid in it. We sent divers down, and sure enough, there was another bag and another kid. They were killed for body parts."

I went on and said, "This is disgusting, Mary. Uh, you never mentioned a Bill that I can recall. Is he a friend?"

"He's my next door neighbor Wade. Well, my sister's neighbor I should say. He's Bill Hastings, a retired Oral Surgeon.  He has the adjoining ten acres next to my sister. He had a mini farm too but his wife died and he sold everything off. All but his old dog, a collie they called, guess? Yes, Lassie. How original. He said his wife named her."

Mary went on, "Julie, Bill's deceased wife, was so much fun. When I got here, we all played cards and went out to dinner. Julie always knew of things to do and where to find them. She was a gourmet cook and cooked from scratch. She would brag about her cooking and with good reason. She died from lung cancer almost five years ago. I always thought my sister and Bill might get together, but there's no spark between them. He's such a nice guy too."

"So, how is your sister?"

"It's going to be a long road to recovery for her. The doctors hope she can leave the hospital in a few more days. Then weeks or months of physical therapy. I'll have to drive her for that three times a week."

"You must be under a lot of stress," I said

"You know Wade, not at all like I thought on my drive here. I was born in the Midwest, and those roots don't leave a person I guess. I love the green trees and the smell of fresh cut fescue. I love the mini farm too. Bill even took me riding in the fields here. I haven't been on a horse in years. It felt relaxing and good. I loved it."

Bill again, I thought. I noticed I didn't say anything to her about Diane. Why not? I asked myself.

Even before this came up and Mary left to take care of her sister, I began to have doubts about the relationship she and I had. Mary was fun, but something was missing. Or was it just me? The spark that got us together was fading fast. I'd go to bed thinking of Diane and wake up with her on my mind. Hey, we were hitting it off great but Diane would be leaving before too long.

"Bill took me to breakfast on the way to the hospital this morning and we haven't eaten since then. I'm putting together a couple of beef sandwiches we picked up on the way home. I picked up a container of potato salad, and with the fresh tomatoes Bill has grown behind his house, I think it will be a good meal. I love fresh homegrown tomatoes.

I thought I'd better have this Bill Hastings checked out.

"Uh, Wade, Bill is coming over with the tomatoes. I have to let you go. We're hungry. Thanks for calling and don't be a stranger, OK?"

 "You got it Mary. Have fun when you can and sleep well." I said, hearing the tinkle of an old fashioned store bell they must have had on the screen door.

I also thought I'd add (and sleep alone) then thought, I didn't care. What was this?

# *Mysterious Jill*

GOD WORKS IN MYSTERIOUS WAYS LESTER. He heard his mama tell him as he woke up from a sound sleep. Where did that come from, Lester wondered? He guesses it was a dream but it felt so real.  There I was, I was sitting on mama's lap, as she read the Bible to me, combing my cow lick hair down with her hand. I haven't dreamed of mama in a long time, he thought. Yes, mama, I remember what you told me about God working in mysterious ways but I never saw that happen. It was such a vivid and real dream, he thought.

In his dream, it was just past 7:00 A.M. Saturday morning when Lester walked back to the pen he built, holding two dogs he was waiting to sell. One, a very young black Labrador retriever. The other, the little shit that bit him, a Yorkshire terrier. He was still a beast. Just seeing Lester he showed his teeth and growled. He wouldn't be worth much injured as he was, so why bother with him? I should put him out of his misery. Lester was about to open the gate when he heard a soft voice call his name.

"Lester? Lester Frabill? It's me. Jill Douglas. Do you remember me?

The soft voice right behind him had Lester almost jump out of his skin. He whirled around and stood face to face with an angel.  Not a real angel, but a woman that almost looked transparent in the early sun.  He was startled.  He did not hear her approach and he made his living on having a keen hearing as one of the traits he needed to survive.

He stood looking at this beautiful woman, about his age, wearing a flowing white dress with yellow flowers printed on it. A wreath of yellow flowers of some kind rested in her golden hair, cascading longer than her shoulders. She stood barefoot on the shell driveway.

"I don't know you. This is private property and you got no right to be on it," said a startled Lester.

"Lester, I'm the daughter of Bob Douglas, the history teacher from our school. Well, I'm his stepdaughter but he's my dad you know. I was a grade behind you. I always liked you but you never paid any attention to me."

Shifting from one foot to the other, the sun at his back, he said, "I don't remember you." He wanted to reach out and touch her but was afraid. She radiated a bright light around her. She had to be an angel he thought.

"Lester, I am here to talk to you. Your mother sent me to help you get back on the right track. I can help you lead the good life your mother wanted for you," Jill spoke her words soft, her voice captivating Lester.

"My mama's gone. She ran away when I was a little kid. My daddy said she did."

"No, she didn't run away from you Lester. Let's let that go for now. I'll tell you more about your mother another time. Just know she loves you and always did. It wasn't the time for you until now. I'm here to help. Will you let me?

Lester squinted at the girl in the bright sun. He couldn't think of a thing to say.

"You know Lester, sometimes things are not what they seem to be," said Jill. "You see the sun rise and set every day. Of course, if it's not cloudy. But that's not true you know."

"Like hell you say," Lester said, now gathering his wits about him in the early morning light. Marshmallow clouds scattered in the blue sky. "I see it coming up now. You blind or something girl?"

"Lester, do you remember the class we had about the sun and the moon? That was fifth grade. Think back. I'll help you. What do you see? Think."

Just like opening a door, the vision suddenly came back to him like it was yesterday. The demonstration they had. The sun, a yellow ball, hanging from the ceiling and the earth, a smaller blue ball tied to a string on a stick with somebody holding the stick as he walked around the sun.

It was him holding the earth and telling the class how the sun stood still while the earth revolved around the sun, the earth spinning too. The question was, does the earth spin clockwise or counter-clockwise?

"Lester, your mama helped you with that one and much more. She was so proud of you. That day, you were proud of yourself too, but you had nobody to tell."

"So," said Jill. "We all say the sun rises and sets when in fact it's the rotation of the earth moving, not the sun. Do you see what I mean about some things not being what they seem?"

Lester just stood and blinked. Memories from his past flooded into his thoughts. Now he understood what she meant.

"You've been in trouble. You've done plenty of bad things in your life. Now is the time to straighten your life out. Turn the bad into good. Do good for people. Make your mama happy. It won't be easy but you can do it if you want. You have free will, so it's up to you Lester."

Lester was totally beside himself. This must be a dream. A nightmare. He held on to the to the dog pen gate with his left hand, feeling physically weak and light headed. His stomach churned, bile coming up.
"OK," said Jill. "Now that I have your attention let's see that little dog you have here. Come here, fella."

"He bites lady. He'll bite you I tell you."

Jill walked to the fence while Lester backed away from her and watched her bend down and speak to the little dog calling him Max. *How the hell did she know his name?*

Max limped over to the gate. He licked the fingers on Jill's left hand. She opened the gate just a little and let Max limp out, then pick him up.

"Oh, poor boy. You're hurt," Jill said. She gently massaged his right front shoulder. A minute later, Max was licking her face, making Jill laugh and smile.

"It's been a long time since I've felt that," Jill said. She set Max down, opened the gate and watched Max walk back in the pen, walking without a limp.

"How did you do that?" Lester asked, a stunned look on his face.

"Lester, I want you to go and sell Max at the flea market as you planned. Ask for a fifty dollar bill for payment. Yes, he's worth more but take just a fifty dollar bill. If he doesn't have one, let him get one from somebody. Then come home and hang that fifty dollar bill on the wall where you can see it. Every time you think of doing something wrong, look at that bill and think of today. Then take Scooby Doo, the other dog and bring him home. The kids have been up all night crying, looking for him."

"You do this Lester and you're on the right track. If you don't, well, I won't be back. It's all up to you."

Jill turned, gliding more than walking, and headed down the driveway. Her bare feet seemed to float over the sharp shell driveway.  When she was about twenty feet away, she turned and said, "Remember Lester, God works in mysterious ways."

The Labrador barked behind him. Lester turned to see what was going on then turned back quickly and looked at an empty driveway.

***

Damn, he overslept. What a dream he had last night. It felt so real. He only had three beers last night. It was past 7 A.M., and he had to get that black lab to the market and sell him and probably kill that little shit that bit him. He turned on the coffee pot sitting on the stove, the old aluminum percolator had yesterday's coffee in it but day old coffee was OK with him.

Guess I'll go out and kill the little shit while the coffee gets hot. Something was nagging at him. Not his stomach and not from the beer. It was Coors beer which he liked. He couldn't put his finger on it. Something just didn't feel right.

He walked to the pen and saw the black lab wagging its fool tail off. A new home for you today buddy. Hell, you might like it better. And there was the little shit running in circles. Not a thing wrong with him. He even looked friendly today.

Then he remembered the dream. What a crazy dream it was. Where did that dream come from? Well, now he can sell both of the dogs and make a lot more money than he expected.  He looked down into the dirt and saw a set of footprints that just didn't belong. Small, like a girl's size maybe. And barefoot.  And the dream came back to him.

***

Two hours later, Lester was at the flea market with little Max under his left arm, calm as could be.

“Fifty bucks John. That’s what I want for him.”

“Hell Lester, he’s worth a lot more than that. I’ll give you a hundred. I don’t want to cheat my supplier,” John said.

“Nope. Fifty bucks and it’s gotta be a fifty dollar bill. You got one?”

“Sure do.” John pulled out a roll of money wrapped with a rubber band and handed over a fifty dollar bill to Lester. “See you next week huh?”

“No. I’m done with this. I gotta go. I got one more delivery to make. Some kids need me. And I need somebody to come back.”

# *Sharon and Bobby Joe*

Bobby Joe's room had a new air conditioner. Niko had it installed after the old one gave out. Sea salt has a way of playing havoc on appliances on the beach, cutting service time in half. The new unit was very welcome.

Bobby Joe made it a habit of setting the thermostat on the unit to 80 degrees when he left for the day. Now, Sharon twisted the knob to 68 degrees, a temperature too cold for Bobby Joe, but not too cold for what Sharon had in mind.

The cold air hit Bobby Joe as he entered the apartment with their food. He handed Sharon her burger and fries and passed the soda cup as he shivered involuntarily from the blast of cold air coming from the air conditioner. He kicked off his shoes and settled in on the sofa next to his girlfriend. Looking up, the TV screen was blank until Sharon hit (PLAY).

He took a bite of his fresh burger, a little juice escaping his mouth, sliding down the left corner of his lips. The taste of the burger pleased his palate, as he looked at Sharon to see if she too was happy with her burger. The TV screen came alive as he looked at it.

He choked on his food. His mouth didn't work. He couldn't talk. His mouthful of burger stuck in his throat. With eyes like saucers, his mouth opened, letting particles of his meal fall from his mouth, on his shirt. He was in total shock.

The TV screen showed a woman sitting on a high back chair with wooden arms. She sat with her right leg over the right arm of the chair. She was nude, her private parts exposed to the camera. There was no hair here where Bobby Joe knew hair should be. She stuck one finger in her mouth, sucking suggestively. A moan came from her just as Bobby Joe moaned too.

Sharon turned to Bobby Joe, hearing him moan, thinking this finally did the trick. Her smile turned to fear in a second. His eyes did not show the excitement she hoped to see. Instead, his face expressed incredible sadness, grief, and shock.

Reflexes forced him to chew a moment and swallow hard, the burger now leaving a bitter taste in his mouth. He could not believe his girlfriend would do this to him. He told her how it was. He thought she understood. At that moment, he felt betrayed and so alone.

He jumped up, his burger and fries flying off his lap and on the floor. Rushing to the door, he took the stairs down three at a time. He ran across the highway dodging two cars that honked at him with good reason. He ran down the walkway to the ocean and headed south. He walked ankle deep in the hot sand, his feet hot and his mind on fire. How could Sharon do this to him? He thought she understood.

Growing up in the backcountry had its disadvantages but it wasn't as backward as some might think. One thing that seemed to be a common trait was the folks in the backcountry seemed to have better morals than a lot of town folk did. Men just didn't cuss in front of a lady. Yes, Ma'am and No, Ma'am were common words spoken by all men, young and old.

In most households, Daddy was the boss, but Mama ruled. A tree switch to the behind of a youngin' was a lesson learned and not forgotten. Respect for women was a natural rule of backcountry people. What mama said was the law.

Life is the same for a boy in some ways no matter where or how they live. No difference the color of their skin or whether they were big or tall, fat or skinny. Some things were just the same.

Most young boys, from a toddler on, experience the same situation. They would occasionally get an erection. Erections just happened. The first time Bobby Joe noticed his erection was when he was about five years old. Mama was giving him his weekly bath in the laundry tub in the cabin on a cold winter day.

Lathering up a washcloth after his hair got washed, Mama scrubbed his little body from head to foot. It was when she got to the middle of his body that he noticed his erection and how it felt good when she washed it. Mama noticed his excitement and just said, "Leave that thing alone son. Time for that later." That was the last mama ever said about his "thing."

He was twelve years old and at one of the clan shindigs. The community got together, making music the way they did, playing banjo and the flat top. One uncle is playing the washboard, strumming and making fine music, the backcountry way. He never dreamed his older brother Boyd would take up playing the washboard and be very good at it. A fever at a young age made Boyd a little slow in his head but he sure could strum out tunes.

The ladies prepared the food. Men folk pitched horseshoes or threw knives at a target, boasting about their skills. Bobby Joe's cousin Raymond, everybody called Ray Ray, and another boy, Billy Bob who lived over the ridge a couple of miles behind his house,thought it would be fun to go to the creek they called crick.

They would catch some frogs and throw them at the girls who would scream and run away. In truth, those same girls thought nothing of catching frogs, skinning them and frying them up for a tasty dinner in the summer. Girls were taught that skill at a very young age. The screaming and running away was just a ritual they played.

The flour sack held seven or eight nice green frogs, all looking to find a way out. Billy Bob said, "Hey guys, one o ya all hold dis sack. I gotta pee." Bobby Joe was nearest and got the sack.

One never pees in the water. Water was for drinking or bathing, not to pee in. Billy Bob, a husky lad, built much like his daddy, stood next to a Cyprus tree and let go a stream four feet in front of him. Like his daddy, he liked to brag, so it was no surprise to the other two when his urine flow stopped, Billy Bob started shaking his "thing" which caused it to swell and stand out in front of him, pointing skyward.

"Don't ya all wish ya had a nice tool like dis to play wit?" Said Billy Bob shaking his tool at the other two.

"Ray Ray, ya all ain't never gonna be as big as me, and I got some growin ta do yet. How bout you, Bobby Joe? Watcha got for a tool?"

Embarrassed, Bobby Joe stumbled out the words, "Well, I guess like you maybe."

"Well, bull sheet I say." Said Billy Bob. "Let's see it. Ya all are too skinny ta have a tool like I got,"

Ray Ray got into the mix, encouraging Bobby Joe to show his tool to them. If he didn't, the whole clan would soon know he was strange. Young guys liked to show what they had. It was more important than showing off a prized pocket knife.

Ray Ray opened his pants fly and took out his tool. It was considerably smaller than the one attached to Billy Bob. Ray Ray's tool was not only skinnier than Billy Bob, but his tool was also severely curved up, almost like a circle. Sometimes, Mother Nature was strange.

Bobby Joe had to do it. He had to take it out and compare his tool with his two friends. The past few months his "thing" got a lot bigger, hair growing all around it, even growing on his egg sack. He was getting a lot more erections, sometimes three or four a day. The past few months had him play with it. It just felt so good. He would pump it until the tickle feeling made him quit.

Taking his tool out was a bit of a problem as it grew to almost its full size. When he finally freed his tool for the other two to see, both were pumping their tools, going faster all the time. Pumping their tools had the boys into their own world. Both wanting the release of tension and the pleasure it brought. Looking over at Bobby Joe seconds later, Billy Bob stopped pumping.

"What da? Where'd ya all get a ting like dat? Damn, it's a monster. Hell, ya alls bigger den me. Lots bigger. How far kin ya shoot dat ting?" asked Billy Bob.

"I don't think I kin shoot yet." A look of concern on Bobby Joe's face. "I sometimes tried, and it jest tickles and I gotta stop."

"Watcha gotta do is keep pumping when it tickles. Da first time is da hardest. It don't tickle so much after da first time," said Ray Ray who never stopped pumping his half-circle tool. "Man, it gest feels so good when ya all shoot. Not only da first time but every time. I shoot two times a day. Sometimes more.

The three friends continued to pump their tools. Ray Ray shot in less than a minute. They watched him as he had to hold his tool way to the left so as not to shoot on himself. His face looked like pain and pleasure wrapped up into one.

A minute or so later, Billy Bob started grunting like a hog in search of fallen acorns buried in a bed of leaves. He ejaculated several feet in front of him, each squirt just a little less. Two pairs of eyes now watched Bobby Joe whose tool looked angry, the head swollen and a deep purple color. The tickling was on him again.

The three boys were standing next to a small pool, perhaps a dozen feet wide and twice as long, maybe a foot deep. Water in this pool came from God's green earth, a spring not far from the pond. Water trickled over shiny granite rocks, polished from centuries of water passing over them into the pool, it was a miniature waterfall.

Bobby Joe could see little fish swimming along the bank of the pool, lazily, in a constant search for something to eat. The sunlight is peeking on and off through the tree branches, reflecting on the water.

He could feel his breathing increasing, his muscles tense. His vision blur as his right hand slid up and down his tool. The tickle was intense. He wanted to stop but knew he couldn't. From deep inside himself, he felt a molten mass rise to the surface. His hand is moving at an incredible speed. A primal sound came from deep within him as he reached a point he never felt before.

It was here, in Gods home where Bobby Joe became one with nature. Another person to carry out Gods wish to continue the survival of man. Surrounded by the beauty nature gave everyone, Bobby Joe had his first orgasm. One he would never forget.

Does a mother have a sixth sense? Bobby Joe didn't know what that meant at the time, but somehow, his mama knew he changed. Not long after his first time, sitting on the front porch on a rainy afternoon, Bobby Joe was shucking oysters he gathered earlier. Mama came out and sat next to him, then gave him a little sermon.


"Bobby Joe, yer a man now. I know dis. I want ya all to promise ya will always respect women. I don't want ya to be chasin women fer the fun of it. If ya got a good girl, ya would treat her right. Ya leave her be until ya all gits married. Will ya promise me dat son?"

He promised his mama he would. How did she know about him? He was quiet as a mouse at night. In bed, when those feelings came on to him, he had to do himself again.

That was a long time ago. Many times he felt strong urges inside him to relieve his sensations and pent-up feelings. His hand worked magic to relieve himself. As he got older, he found out most boys did the same thing. Some talked about it. Some bragged about how often they did it. He never said anything.

He liked Sharon a lot, but he just couldn't do what she wanted. He promised his mama he wouldn't. A promise from him was like a promise carved in stone.

He was a quarter mile down the beach when he sensed somebody running behind him. Turning his head, he saw it was Sharon with tears in her eyes, sobbing as she ran toward him. She caught up with him and reached for his hand. Bobby Joe shook her hand off. Sharon sobbed louder.

Throwing her arms around him, she squeezed him tight enough to take the breath out of him.

"I'm sorry Bobby Joe. Oh God, I'm so sorry. I wanted o make this a special night for you. I love you so much and I wanted this to be a happy night for us."

"Aw Sharon, don't cry like dat. I tole you I gest caint do that yet.  I got lots of feelings for ya, and I really wanna do it but I promised my dead mama, and well, I gest gotta keep my promise. I got so excited seeing dat and well, it made me feel real funny to getting like dat with you right next to me.

"And I gotta tell ya," said Bobby Joe, brushing the hair out of Sharon's eyes, damp from her tears, "I love ya and wanna do what ya want but I gest caint yet."
They joined hands and walked the beach in silence for about a mile, passing groups of people now packing up to head home wherever they had to go.

Soon they had the beach pretty much to themselves. Sharon's tears stopped. Their emotions settled down. The pace slowed and Bobby Joe stopped. He lifted Sharon off the sand and kissed here harder and longer than he ever did before. The warm ocean water rippled over his ankles as he held her tight.

When they parted, Sharon spoke. "You know Bobby Joe, there's more than one way to make each other happy. I've been reading about this in some books my dad has in his old army footlocker he has in the garage. It's where I got the video. He's got a bunch of stuff in there. I know they are married and I know they use the stuff sometimes and well, they are toys for sex. But it ain't real sex. Do you think we could try that?

"No."

"But it ain't real sex honey."

"It's messin with yer private parts and I promised my mama. She's lookin down and would be sorely unhappy with me."

"OK, sweetheart, I guess I can wait, but it's hard on me. I love you." *I just have to keep trying, though. I just can't help it* she thought.

# Two's Company

As Bobby Joe and Sharon walked hand and hand along the sand, heading back to his apartment, Diane was ending her final phone call for the evening. Her left ear was sore from talking so long. After her stint in England and Spain, she found American security a step or two behind her last assignment. It just seemed like so much red tape and unneeded checks and rechecks to get something done.

Diane knew the exact equipment needed for the bridge, yet had to argue the point not to take something else. Something less. A phone call later and she had her items on the way.

Another issue was the boat to be used here. Wade worked for the government but his boat was personal. And it might not be fast enough to do the job. Like in Europe, some boats would be the Cigarette style and very fast. Yes, they could be stopped on the waters here but they would probably dump the cargo before they were apprehended with the additional speed the sleek boats possessed. How they might be set free was the question.

The sun was setting, a beautiful sight too. Diane walked out to the pool where she found Wade reading an article on a new weapon designed to stop watercraft without using explosives. Blowing up a boat could not be used when humans were involved.

"I'm done, Wade. I can't take another minute of the bureaucracy today. Where are their brains? Why in the hell do they make simple things so complicated?" Diane sat at the table by the pool, next to

Wade.  A tall insulated mug, palm trees imprinted on it, filled with ice and water, sat in front of Wade.

Diane reached over and grasped the cool mug, brought it to her lips and took a generous drink. Without asking.

I looked at her. She is just taking my glass without asking. Hmmm. I liked that.

"I'm ready for a beer. What would you like? I make a decent Margarita."

"That would be nice," Diane said.  "Making a Margarita takes time. How about you get your beer and I work on your ice water?" Lifting the mug again, she drained it, swallowing several times.  "Maybe you can massage my neck? It's sore as hell." She swiveled her head a few times then rubbed the back of her neck with her right hand.

I grabbed a Bud Light from my fridge in my tool room, off the garage.  A lighter beer was what I had a taste for now. On my way back, I stopped in the kitchen and grabbed a plastic water pitcher and hit the "cube" button on the refrigerator, listened as ice cubes rattled into it. Hitting "water" I filled it most of the way. Opening the pantry, I grabbed a bag of Snyder's pretzels. The ones with a mustard flavor then headed outside.

I stood behind Diane and took my hands and placed them on her neck, causing her to jump forward. My iced hand, cold from carrying my beer shocked her.  I worked my fingers over knotted muscles, feeling them relax after a minute. Mission accomplished, I thought.

"You give a great massage Wade. Thank you," she said as I sat down and grabbed my beer, bringing it to my lips. Her smile was genuine. Her eyes seemed to shine now. My dirty mind thought: *I wonder if you would like a total body massage. Stop it.*

"Here's the deal. Only if you approve of course," Diane said. "The bridge gear will be installed Tuesday. It should take just a few hours but expect it to take all day.

Now here's the stuff that involves you. First, you did say I could stay here, right?"

I answered, "Yes, of course."

"Good. I got you two thousand dollars a month. It's what they were going to pay for the short-term rental of the house they were going to rent for me. Next, we talked about this. Your boat may be too slow for what we need. I have a Donzi speedboat coming up from Miami. We just got it on a drug bust.

As you said, your boat lift is too light for that kind of boat, so they are sending a local crew here Monday to add ten feet to the length of your dock and change your lift to a ten thousand pound unit. The lift has special features you will probably like. It has a quick release. It will get the boat in the water in seconds, not minutes."

I just sat there and took this all in. OK, I was smiling too.

"Then there is the fact you will be losing the business of the ecological tours you do. They agreed to three thousand a month for the first month. What do you think of that?"

Before I could answer, Diane hit me with her thousand-watt smile. "There's my company. That should be worth ten grand a month. What  do you think?"

I just smiled.

Diane had been here for a week now but it seemed more like a month. I tried to explain my feelings to myself but I was at a total loss as to why I felt so comfortable with her.

Diane cooked breakfast every morning. One day, just oatmeal and juice. The next, a special bagel, toasted, buttered, a slice of cheese, a scrambled egg cooked with dollops of cream cheese and topped with a slice of ham, or two strips of crispy bacon. Every day was different. The bagel was my favorite. I did the cleanup.

On the two mornings we didn't have to rush off, she cooked in her purple robe. We usually took our food to the table by the pool, watched dolphin swim past and boats going on a mission as we relaxed. Life felt good.

Lunch was on the fly. Dinner had me over the grill or we went out. Like I just said, life felt good.

Today, I bought a salad from the store. It had strawberries in it with nuts and an assortment of delicious mixes. It was more than big enough to split. I threw a couple of minute steaks on the grill as I toasted two buns. A package of red style potato salad made the meal tonight. Served on paper plates.

We sat by the pool and talked. Not so much about work but about our lives and the things that were part of making each of us who we were. We had a lot in common and yet, we were so very different. The two of us talked and felt so comfortable until well past the dock lights on a timer kicked on.

A crescent moon, like the one a movie producer featured at the start of a movie, made its way across the star-studded sky. I couldn't help but think of a Van Morrison song I liked. *Moondance*. It wasn't October nor were the leaves falling yet but it was a perfect night for romance.

We carried our plates to the kitchen when Diane turned and hugged me gently. She then said, "Thank you. Sleep well." Diane turned north and I turned south to our bedrooms. Yes, life felt good indeed.

# Abbas and Company

While life was good for Wade Nash at that moment, it was anything but good for five boys in the bowels of The Money Man's boat, chugging its way north through a tributary in the Amazon jungle. They had been on the boat for one night and one day already. The second night was falling fast.

The boys were not restrained in a physical sense, just told they had to stay below deck at all times. The thirty-two-foot wooden boat that looked like a big row boat, with a cabin on the deck was typical of many boats that traveled the rivers here. The boat looked old but was in top condition in every way. The owner made his money with the boat. He wanted it to look old which it did. They blended in perfectly.

Food for the boys was bread acquired along the way from a village. Accompanied with a bowl of weak soup, they were fed two times a day. Tonight, it was just bread. Already stale. Four of the boys huddled in one corner, one next to the other, crying at first, now just miserable and wanting to go home. The fifth, the bigger boy, the one who could work the Rubik's cube, sat alone. His crying stopped shortly after the boat left his home. He kept a close vigil on where they were, looking out a porthole window.

One of the huge black men saw the boy watching and told the Money Man. Arthur Dalton just smiled and said, "Not to worry old boy. He will never find his way back here. Let him look. At least he's quiet."

The single cylinder diesel motor chugged away throughout the night. The boy, Abbas, studied every turn they made. He would find his way back one day. He hoped.

## *Marco and Vickie*

The sunrise took my breath away. It often did when it came up displaying spectacular colors like this morning. I had been running since five-thirty A.M. accompanied by the same crescent moon I witnessed last night. The moon now on the western horizon looked to be on a velvet blackboard, with thousands of diamond stars surrounding it. With the rise of the sun, the diamond stars disappeared into infinity.

I ran eight miles this morning, the distance I ran with Diane the first time we ran together. I didn't feel so bad today, running alone and knowing what I was going to do. I knew I could run farther if challenged. I felt good on this run as I headed down the road to my house, slowing my pace, cooling down.

Before I got to my driveway, I could see Marco Rodrigues's Chevy Silverado pickup truck sitting in my drive, backed in, the nose facing the street. Marco never parked like this.

I knew Marco got back to town last night after a four-day seminar in Atlanta on human trafficking. Marco was sharing a home with Vickie Asher now. I was surprised to see him so early.

Vickie Asher was the lady I helped in the case I just finished, the murder in the mangrove swamp behind my house. Vickie was pursued by mobsters from Miami. As it turned out, she was guarded by my friend and working partner, Marco. The two of them hit it off well enough that they were now an item. I guess that's what they call it when two are living together. They liked each other a lot.

I walked in my garage and the side door, past the laundry room and saw a pile of Marco's clothes on the floor of the laundry room. The washing machine was chugging away. What was going on I wondered. Did Vickie and Marco fight? Did she throw him out, and he's here washing his clothes? Then I saw a small pile of clothes women wore under outerwear.

The wonderful smell of coffee and freshly baked cinnamon rolls hit me before I got to the kitchen. Diane and Vickie sat at the table, a cup before each, steam rising from the cups of Costa Rican coffee I favored.

On the stove top was a cookie sheet lined with tin foil, holding four cinnamon rolls, smelling great. Two were missing and I knew where they went, as I watched Diane lick her fingers. Vickie had a partially eaten bun on a paper plate in front of her. I grabbed a roll and a paper towel and sat down.

Diane got up and grabbed my favorite coffee mug and poured a cup for me, smiling all the while. Like they had a secret or something. Vickie just smiled. What the hell were they talking about I wondered.

I said, "Hi Vickie. It's nice to see you this morning. Where's Marco?"

"Marco didn't get home until after dark. As you know, he was gone for a few days and we had some catching up to do. I let him sleep in this morning. Our washing machine is broken. I called the landlord yesterday and a guy is supposed to come out tomorrow and fix it. Marco needed clothes washed and well, I needed to let him sleep. So, here I am. I hope it's OK?"

"No problem. Just don't mix your clothes with mine. I don't want anybody to get any funny ideas," I smiled.

"So, how is Mary? Have you talked to her?" Vickie asked.

I think I knew what they were talking about when I got home.

"Oh, I guess she's fine. She has a neighbor who is helping her with the chores.  She told me her sister would need help for a long time. I would not be surprised if she doesn't extend her leave of absence." I took a bite of the bun and a sip of coffee. Delicious.

"That kind of puts a kink in your relationship, doesn't it? I know it's none of my business, but…."

"My relationship. Uh, well, we were two people who lost their partners, lonely as hell and well, we got together and dated a bit. I'll be honest," I said. "I thought maybe it would move up another level, but it never did. I like Mary, but well, I like Mary. That's it."

"Wade, I owe you my life. I have no right to say this, but I think so much of you, I just have to get this off my chest. Mary was not the right woman for you. And you were not the right man for her. I could tell this from the start."

"Now, that crazy Puerto Rican living with me, he and I are made for each other. And if you don't mind doing me one more favor, you can tell him that." Vickie said with a smile on her face that would charm the devil.

Diane sat, looking between Vickie and me and didn't say a word. Her sore neck must be OK as her head swiveled between the two of us. Her face showed no expression. I didn't get pissed at what Vickie said. I was almost relieved somebody other than myself could see Mary was not the girl for me.

"OK, that's over and you didn't pop me in the chops. I'm making breakfast. Pancakes and eggs with a side of bacon." Vickie said, as she got up and started grabbing refrigerator items, putting them on the counter.

The pancakes were bubbling around the edges as they cooked on the grill. Vickie was about to flip them over when my phone rang. I answered, listened and asked a couple of questions then said, "We'll be there in half an hour. Thanks, Herb."

"Got to hurry ladies. We have another problem. Herb just got to work and saw a gator eating something below the bridge. He said it looks like a child."

We lost our appetite.

## *Arthur Dalton*

On the Essequibo River, a few miles south of the town of Bartica, Guyana, a beat up looking trawler, coming out of the dense jungle, chugged its way towards town. Each chug produced a puff of black smoke as the trawler moved at a snail's pace.

This boat glided past several other similar looking boats that were tied to the long dock, along the shore for several hundred feet. Entire families were known to live on many of these boats. This boat coming had a reputation. A couple of people looked up then averted their eyes. This was a bad man's boat and a bad man was standing on the bow, watching for entrapment of some kind. Arthur Dalton was nobody's fool.

As the boat followed a bend in the river, the vee wake the boat created became less pronounced. The boat was home again. Before securing to the dock, the boat motored to a new sailboat anchored in the bay. The sailboat belonged to Arthur Dalton. He had a fleet of seven in service now. His business was expanding.

Arthur directed his boat captain to pull on the far side of the anchored sailboat, shielded from the eyes of those on shore. When they got in position, his boat tied to the sailboat, the five boys were transferred rapidly from the river boat to the sailboat. Five boys, between ten and twelve years of age, looked to be in good condition. They would fetch a premium price. Young boys were getting more difficult to obtain.

Arthur talked to the sailboat captain then stepped back on his trawler which backed away. The sailboat started its diesel engine, pulled anchor and was heading out to sea before Arthur could dock his river trawler. He had a phone call to make. He decided the phone call could wait for a few more minutes. As the two black workers secured the boat, Arthur opened a cabinet and removed a jug of rum he passed to the two men. Opening the small refrigerator, he took out a Red Stripe beer for himself. As his men hosed down the boat, Arthur sat on a piling and thought back in time.

Arthur Dalton was thirty-seven years old. He had an expanding empire with no end in sight.  He liked what he did. It was challenging and exciting at the same time. He was breaking the law with every move he made and that excited him. His business was large enough now that nobody could hurt him. He hired muscle. Good muscle when it was necessary.

Arthur was born in London, England to William and Abigale Dalton. The Dalton family was on the rise there. William, not Bill, worked his way up the corporate ladder to head engineer for the British Petroleum Company. William had a knack for finding oil in the north sea, most often off the coast of Norway. To do his job, he spent most of his time at sea. Arthur rarely saw his father at that time of his life.

Abigale, his mother, was a stranger to him. She was a socialite who had little time for Arthur. He had contact with his nanny more than anybody else. It was with joy when his father came home and announced the family would be moving to a tiny island called Grenada. South and east of Venezuela, they had vast resources of oil to find.

The island was a joy.  Warm, lush and fragrant, it is the spice island after all. Beautiful flowers and later in his life, pretty young brown bodies to enjoy.  It was paradise until the war broke out not long after they settled in a mansion in the mountains. The war started on October 25th and lasted a couple of months. He remembered seeing soldiers walking up and down the road by his house. His father hired guards to protect their property.

The more things change, the more they stay the same. Soon, father spent most of his time at sea again. His mother suffered, lacking the social activities she had in London. Soon, she started an art club and a book club. Then one called "Fifty Women Who Care." This group would somehow persuade others to give money to charity. Abigale was most proud of this group. Arthur was on his own.

The Dalton's had a full-time gardener who was much more. Frank kept his mother's Mercedes spotless and shined. Frank also fixed things, a broken hinge or a cracked window pane and much more. Frank lived in the little house at the back of the property. His wife Jesse worked for the Dalton's too.

She was cook and housekeeper for the family. They had a son they named Winston. He was a year older than Arthur. Mother tried to keep the two boys apart but that was never going to happen. Over time, and not much time either, both boys became like brothers.

Arthur had tutors and was wise in many things not known to Winston. Winston was street smart. He also had a lot of relatives. He counted sixteen cousins, six aunts and uncles and countless half relatives. Winston counted almost all that lived on the spice island a relative or almost one.

Arthur was nine years old when Winston took him to see his first cockfight. Cocks are roosters bred and trained to fight one another, usually to the death. Sharp blades are taped to the legs of each cock, then two are put in a round ring. The handlers of each push his cock at the other. When both cocks are angry, they are turned loose to slash at each other until one dies. Wagering amongst the spectators is done before the fight starts. Much later, Arthur read that cockfighting was a sport for over six thousand years. It continues today.

"Give me five dollars Arthur. I can make us some money." Winston said.

When the fight ended, Winston gave Arthur nine dollars after pocketing two bucks for himself. Arthur was hooked. In no time,

Arthur could figure out how to bet and how to win. And how to lose. It wasn't the cock or the blood that excited him. It was the money.

Sometime during his twelfth year on earth, Winston taught Arthur how to masturbate. A day after Arthur's thirteenth birthday, a day later because his mother had a party for him at home, Winston took Arthur to see a "friend" who let him do it to her. He was in love with Lisa for a few days after their meeting. It felt so good.

He walked out of her house and saw Winston, sitting on his haunches near the door, a cold can of Coke in his hand.

"Thanks for the present Winston. I liked it a lot." Arthur said, beaming.

"I know mon. I hear you good. So lets go mon."

"Go where?" Arthur asked.

"To da cock fights mon. We gotta make some money. I like da ladies too and dey charge tree dollar to do it to dem."

That was another reason Arthur liked cockfighting. He could make money to spend on the ladies.

Age seventeen was a bad year for Arthur. His father was recalled back to London. His mother was happy. He begged to stay. His pleas fell on deaf ears.

Two years in London had Arthur dodging coppers most of the time. He didn't attend school as he found it boring. He got a girl pregnant and was being hounded by the police for stealing a truckload of appliances.

Winston called. He sailed two days later.

***

It was time to make that call.

105

He got the answering machine. There is a seven-hour time difference to London. She must be at her mother's house.

"Hi, honey. It's me. I will be home in two days. I can only stay for a week but hey, kiss the kids for me and tell them I love them. Bye."

## *Max Finds a Home*

"Can we keep him daddy, pllleeezzz. I'll take care of him. I promise. Look, he loves us. Please daddy. Mommy will love him too," said six-year-old Danny, the boy with the cow lick blonde hair, holding little Max at the Daytona Beach flea market Saturday morning.

Max, the Yorkshire Terrier hadn't been 'for sale.' an hour and already several people took an interest in him. It was certain he would go home with somebody today.  That was OK with Max, glad to be with people who liked him. Someone to hold him and pet him. He would have to admit the guy who stole him became nice at the end. He just felt this little boy would love him to death.  He wiggled and squirmed and licked the little boy as much as he could, deep inside saying "Please take me. I'll make everybody happy."

"Oh daddy, please," said the little girl standing next to Dany, doing her best to pet the little dog.  Max continued to lick the skin of her brother's face. The girl was Debbie and she wanted some of his attention too. "Please daddy, please," begged Debbie.  There were other dogs in surrounding cages who begged for attention, barking and jumping up and down. Danny and Debbie had their hearts set on little Max.

Brian Walsh, "Daddy," was torn. He promised the kids another dog after the family dog died two months ago. The Chesapeake Bay retriever who was with him for over twelve years, "Bear" was in the family a lot longer than his kids.  He died from cancer, his death sudden.  Treatment was not an option. The kids loved Bear and he loved them. This little runt was not much bigger than the size of Bear's head.

The kids begged. Brian thought, his food bills would be a fraction of what it cost for Bear. This little guy seemed to adore the kids, plus Bonnie would probably feel better with a small dog in the house. And one that did not shed.

"How much for this little guy?" Brian asked the owner of the booth.

"Tell you what friend," said John, "A guy just walked in here as soon as we opened and well, he said his kids were allergic to dogs. He just bought him and now had to sell him. He's got papers and said he would bring them around next week, but well, I don't know."

"I gave $150 for him. His breed with papers is worth at least $600 bucks. I want $300 for him, but I see the kids love him so much and it makes me happy to see happy kids. I'll let you have him for $250. You can stop by next week but I can't guarantee I'll ever get his papers, so you are taking him as is. You can see he's healthy."

Brian did some quick thinking, knowing another Chesapeake would cost him double or triple the cost of this dog. Then there were the months of training. This guy seemed ready to go and fit right in. Reaching into his wallet, Brian said, "Will you take two and a quarter for him?"

"No, the price is low and you know it. But, I'll tell you what, I'll throw in a nice collar and leash with him." John watched two little kids scramble over each other to the rack with collars and leashes. Debbie cried out it had to be pink while Danny made a face at her, grabbing a camouflage leash.

Ten minutes later sporting his pink collar and a camouflage lease, Max sat between Danny and Debbie in the back seat. *Well, wonders thought Brian. The kids always fought for the front seat.*

Driving down Beach Street which ran on the west side of the intra-coastal waterway, Brian pulled into the parking lot of a friend he knew for years. He and Jeremy went to college together, both on the track team. Jeremy went on to become a veterinarian, Brian, an electrical engineer.  Dr. Jeremy Higgins opened the clinic about ten years ago. Brian used his services for his dog exclusively.

Brian called Jeremy as they left the flea market with Max. Jeremy said he would check Max as soon as they got there.  He wasn't busy this morning, and a checkup would be wise.

As soon as the car stopped, Danny hopped out with Max tugging on his new leash.  Max hit the ground, his senses overloaded, dog smells were all around him. In the back of his little brain, he remembered his brother Rambo and knew his scent. He was pretty sure he smelled Rambo. Max ran in little circles as if he were wound up. If they would take him inside, he might just see his brother again.

Max stood on the examination table made of shiny, cold stainless steel. His little feet didn't get much purchase, slipping on the slick surface. His nails clicked with each move.  Little Max had no objections to the doctor looking at his eyes and ears and opening his mouth to check his teeth and other parts in there. He ran his hands along his flanks and each leg.

Dr. Higgins removed the new pink collar Max wore and felt his neck, stopping at one spot in particular. He felt the spot again and walked over to a stainless steel chest of drawers that matched the table Max stood on.  He picked up a device that looked like a portable telephone, then took it to Max and ran it over his neck.

"He's got a chip in him, Brian," said Jeremy Higgins. "Let me take this to the computer." With the touch of a few keys, seconds later, a reading came on the screen. Max was stolen three days ago. His owner didn't live far from the clinic.  Max belonged to somebody else.

*Damn thought Brian. How the hell do I tell the kids we have to give him back to his owner? And I'm out $250 and this vet bill. Bonnie's gonna kill me.*

# Abbas's Nightmare

The pain was like nothing he ever felt before. He was the first boy they did this to. Before this trip ended, all would be subject to this treatment. The guy came down the morning after they were transferred to the new sailboat. He grabbed Abbas, jerked him off the floor and backhanded him on his mouth. Abbas could taste blood. His lip  was cut.

The guy grabbed the wrist of Abbas and tied a short rope around his hand. Then the other wrist, each rope cut into his skin.  He pushed Abbas face first over the table and tied each wrist to the table legs. Abbas was bent over. He thought he would be whipped.  A sharp knife cut the rope used as a belt by Abbas and his shorts yanked down to his ankles.

It was like a hot poker shoved in him. Each time he pulled it out and pushed it in was total agony. *God, I've been good. Why are they doing this to me* he thought as tears flowed from his eyes. With agony on his face, he could not hide, eyes clenched tight, he tried to shut out the pain and humiliation.

He refused to cry out in pain and anger. He thought that was what they wanted him to do. He didn't cry out but he could not hold back the tears as the guy standing behind him forced his cockey into his push hole. In and out. In and out. He could feel blood running down his leg.

"Grasshopper" Port Arthur, TX. was the name painted on the stern of the Catalina Ocean Going sailboat, purchased just a few months ago. The plate on the side said it was a Catalina 445, forty-four feet long.  Grasshopper looked like it was the property of a couple that wanted to see the world. That was exactly the look the true owner wanted.

 The stocky man had several days growth of whiskers on his face. An unfiltered cigarette dangled from his lips.  Gustav, the captain of this boat, set the cruise control for north by northwest into a ten-mile per hour breeze out of the west. The seas were mild and the sun brilliant today. It was time.

Gustav Fletcher was a gypsy and grew up traveling Europe with a band of gypsies.  When he was twenty-three, serious trouble in Paris had him flee the country or face incarceration for a very long time. Murder can have that effect even though it wasn't his fault.

Gustav found his way to Brazil and eventually ran into Arthur Dalton. Arthur taught Gustov to sail.  Soon Gustav became an intricate part of Arthur's business. Time together had Gustav teaching Arthur a thing or two.

His partner for this trip was Polo. Hipolito, called Polo for short. Half Hispanic, half African, Polo was the muscle needed at times on trips like this. Gustav sailed with Polo many times and while he never thought about it, he knew very little about him. Not even his last name. He just did what he was told and he did it well.

It was time to start the training. Gustav needed those young boys to jump when he spoke and follow directions to the letter. What better way than putting total fear in them and the best way was to take away their dignity.  It happened to be a good way to make him feel better.  No women, no problem. Not with young virgin boys on board.

"Let's start with the quiet one," said Gustav, picking up a couple of hanks of rope to bind the hands of the quiet one to the table. "We get him, the others will fall in line and won't give us any shit. Well, they might" he chuckled "but we can wash that off."

*Why? Abbas asked God. Why do you let this happen?"* Tears formed a puddle on the floor, between his hands tied to the table legs. He gritted his teeth as hard as he could. He did not scream. The white guy behind who was hurting him picked up speed. The agonizing pain became a white-hot blaze to where he thought he could not hold back screaming any longer. With a final burst of speed, a grunting noise from the white guy, he suddenly stopped, then took his cockey out of him.

Humiliated, sore, and bleeding, he was proud he never did cry out in pain. The big black guy untied his hands and picked him up like a sack of rice and flipped him on top of the other boys trying to hide in the corner. Walking over to the boys, Polo chose the little skinny one. He would be next. This one would scream. He liked them to scream.

Bleeding from his push and no clothes on his bottom, Abbas made every effort to burn the faces of these two men into his memory. He would never forget and hoped one day they too would remember.

# Diane's Big Thrill

While the girls cleaned the kitchen, I went into my office and shut the door. Secret stuff was going to be spoken. I punched a number on my cell phone heard it ring and answered on the third.

"Hey Marco, are you awake?" I asked, looking at the wall clock showing it was five minutes to eight. I heard his sleepy reply.

"Yeah. I am now. I guess I was more tired than I thought. What's up?"

I asked, "Don't you have a friend at the track, the NASCAR track?"

"I do. It's Jerry Wood. Jerry ran the circuit for two years then couldn't get enough sponsors to support his effort. He's an instructor now and he takes people looking for some excitement in their lives for a spin. What's up? Is he in trouble?" Marco asked.

"No, not at all. I was wondering if you could call him and see if you could arrange a ride for Diane, today, if possible. Today is August 29th and her birthday. She doesn't know I know but it's in her bio of course. I'd kind of like to surprise her with a thrill ride."

"Hold on a sec Wade. I'll call him on the other phone."

I put my phone on 'speaker' and started going through my e-mail on my computer and got half way through when I heard Marco speak.

"It's all set. Go to the ticket office at eleven. Ask for Jerry Wood and tell them he is expecting you. He will do you right."
"Thanks, Marco," I said. "What will I owe him?"

"Nothing. I did him a big favor. This one is on the house. Have fun. Hey, it's Diane's birthday?  How about we go out for dinner? How about the salt flats? The girls will like that. I don't see Vickie here but when she comes back, I'll tell her."

"I'll tell her. She's here, washing clothes and made breakfast. Sorry, you missed out. When she gets home, maybe she'll put your sleepy ass to bed," I said, laughing as I hung up the phone.

At five minutes to eleven, Diane and I met Jerry.  Jerry stood about five foot ten and weighed perhaps 160 pounds but it was hard to tell with the baggy Nomex suit race drivers wore for fire protection. Nomex fire retardant coveralls is the business suit of his profession. Light brown hair and a complexion of granite aged by time. If one met Jerry on the street, you would think he was a NASCAR driver before you picked any other profession.

Jerry was good at racing. Very good in fact but just not quite good enough to run with the elites. It was a matter of money and sponsors he thought but knew deep down he was a fraction of a second too slow.  That fraction had you win a race or sucking tailpipe fumes from guys ahead of you.

His gig of driving tourists was far safer and a steady paycheck. With three kids and a wife, he opted for this job and loved scaring the hell out of brave men. A few weeks ago, he had a real hero in the car. A three tour war vet who was wounded twice. When the thrill ride was over, the ashen soldier said, "Fuck this man. I'd rather face those fucking bastards overseas then drive one of these things. This is certain death. At least I get a chance to shoot back."

Jerry had us settled fast. Diane would ride shotgun in the car while I watched from the pit. I hoped to take a picture or two as they flashed past me. Jerry fitted Diane with Nomex racing coveralls and a helmet. The racing helmet was set up with a microphone and speaker, the driver and passenger could communicate as they navigated the 33-degree banks of the two and a half mile Daytona International Speedway.

NASCAR cars have no real doors. The driver climbs in the car through the window. These cars had one real door, on the passenger side. The body of the shell of a car was built with tubing around the interior and called a roll cage for obvious reasons. Diane slid in and buckled up the six-point racing harness.

As I watched, Jerry shifted the transmission into first gear and eased the clutch pedal enough to engage the transmission to the engine. As the car moved smoothly forward, Jerry started the speech he gave every time.

"Diane, this is not a true NASCAR race car but very similar. It has a small block Chev motor making a bit over six hundred horsepower." Jerry was in third gear, sweeping past turn two at over a hundred miles per hour. "The top speed on this baby is close to one eighty but most people are happy at one sixty, or less.  If you feel uncomfortable, just let me know and I'll slow down."

The back straight had the tach needle pointing past five grand.  The speedometer close to one fifty. The thunder from the engine is booming and echoing off the walls.

Their number 88 car took the thirty-three degrees banking in turns three and four, glued to the track. Jerry mashed his foot down to the floorboard as they zipped past the pit entrance, passing Wade half way down the straight away leading to turn one.

Jerry took a peek at Diane for a second, expecting to see startled or frightened eyes.  She might have been having her fingernails filed and polished. A slight smile seemed to be on her lips. OK lady, let's see how you feel about this lap.

The roar from the open exhaust tore up the walls of the speedway as the multi-colored car flashed around turns one and two and down the back straightway. Jerry eased off the throttle for turn three just a fraction. Turn four was seconds away.

Jerry backed off a little then mashed the throttle to the floor once more. Flying past Wade at near one eighty. He backed off again and looked at Diane who looked positively thrilled, smiling a brilliant smile. The excitement was all over her. *Was there no fear in her,* Jerry wondered.

"So, what do you think Diane? Fast enough for you?"

"I think if you took turn four one lane higher and flat boarded the throttle a few hundred feet sooner, you could have picked up four or five miles an hour and maybe passed a car or two. Take a higher apex then bring her down sooner. "

"Do you know racing? What the hell do you know about racing?" Jerry asked, upset after one of his best runs and this woman is critiquing his efforts.

"Son, I've been racing cars since before you were a gleam in your daddy's eye. Ever hear of the Mason car builders from Carolina?"

"Well hell yeah. They were a legend back when Big Bill France started all of this. Are you related to them? I never caught your last name."

"Diane Mason. I'm the daughter of Joe and granddaughter of Cletus. Can I drive?"

The pit stop was fast. Diane stepped out, as Jerry climbed out his window in front of me. I smiled, thinking this finally got Diane. She just marched around the car with a determined look on her face then put her right leg through the window followed by her left one and slid through the tight space. *What the hell are they doing,* I wondered.

Diane settled down in the custom built seat made for Jerry, her slightly bigger bottom was a tight squeeze but it would only be a short ride. She overrevved the engine a bit as she eased the clutch, engaging the rear wheels, then mashed the throttle engulfing me in a cloud of bluish gray smoke from the tires.  Take that officer Mike Miller.  She didn't hear me swearing at her.

On the second lap, an old song grandpa and daddy blasted all the time, was ringing in her head, Nervous Norvus, singing "Transfusion." "If it were me, I'd ask for two turns in the right rear and I'd add a pound of air in the left front. I think that would balance her a bit better but this baby is good." Diane hit turn one flat out for one more fast lap.

Like she said to Jerry, she took turn four higher and turned down sooner, the speedometer showed 188 miles per hour. The sound was intoxicating to Diane. The vibration went down to her soul. This speed and time were faster than Jerry ever had this car around the track.  The fun was over but damn, it sure was a blast.

I slipped Jerry a crisp one hundred dollar bill as a tip. This was a big deal for Diane. I said, "Happy Birthday" as she was getting into the car the first time. Now, as I looked at her as we walked to her car, I was very surprised to see how she looked after the drive.

Her eyes were shining like they were wet and yet, there were no tears. Her smile was almost like a grimace in a way. Like she was trying to suppress it. I didn't know quite how to take her as we walked. Finally, Diane said, "Thank you, Wade. That was one helluva birthday present. I missed the speed and the noise and the excitement. It all came back on that first lap. This is the second best birthday present I could have gotten from you. Thank you again."

"The second best present? What do you mean?" I asked.

Diane took a half step in front of me and stopped. I felt her right arm around my back and her left hand behind my neck, pulling my head down to her as she reached up and kissed me. Kissed me is far too weak to explain.

Her tongue darted into my mouth and in seconds, I found the two of us thrashing our mouths and tongues like a war was being waged inside us. I never kissed like that before. Diane told me later she never did either. It was spontaneous. I guess. So was the bulge in the front of the casual shorts I wore.

"Take me to bed Wade. I've never felt like this before and I want you. I need you."

Did I hear her right? I looked deep into her eyes, now a fire behind them. I guess I did hear her right and boy, was I ready.

"Ok, let's go home.

"No," she said. "Across the parking lot, over there, is a Holiday Inn Express. We can walk."

And we did. Well, it was a fast walk. Kind of a run.

## *Birthday Dinner*

Saltwater Cowboys is a rustic fish camp style restaurant south of the city of St. Augustine. Drive the half mile down the tree-lined road and find the salt marshes and the restaurant. The name alone has people curious. What is a Saltwater Cowboy? When they arrive and see the restaurant built over the salt flats, most people are interested enough to try the food. Hopefully early enough and lucky enough to find a table. The views looking at the salt marsh are incredible.

Vickie and Marco sat across from Diane and me. We had a great view of the marsh looking west. As it happens, we would be gone before the sunset and miss the spectacular views photographed thousands of times from where we sat.

Four iced teas sat in front of us. Two sweet for the girls while us guys opted for unsweetened tea, all served in pint size Mason jars. All the jars dripped from the iced product inside and the high humidity in the air.

Yelp rated the restaurant four stars out of a possible five which I thought was probably right. The restaurant specials always include fantastic white shrimp, all caught local and fresh daily. All the meals I had over the years here were good. It was the name and the atmosphere that brought people back again and again. In this case, this was a new experience for Diane. Another birthday treat.

I sat with the palm of my left hand on my chin, my elbow on the table, looking over the salt marsh at nothing in particular. The three of them talked while I let my mind slip back to a few hours ago.

That time was a game changer. That time and what happened changed my life forever.

We walked in the hotel, arm-in-arm, like a couple that missed their flight. We were less than a mile from the airport. I did my best to keep the grin off my face. I gave the girl my credit card and in a minute, she handed me two plastic cards that were keys for room 309. "Take those elevators over there sir," She said.

I opened the door and stepped in. The room smelled a bit musty and it was too warm. I found the thermostat and set it to 70.

*Now, Wade, I'm thinking, she asked you to take her here. Don't be an ass and ask her if she is serious about this. You know the two of you hit it off from the first minute she got out of her car. Like you two think alike. And you know you want to take her to bed. So now, Mr. world beater, what's next?*

"What are you thinking about Wade?" Diane asked, bringing me back to the present.

"Oh, just this case we have. I seem to have it on my mind this evening."

Vickie asked Diane something, and my mind slipped back to the hotel.

I put my arms around Diane and the kissing started again. This time, we ended up falling on the bed clumsily. After a bit, I pulled back and looked into her eyes. Once more, they were wet, like she was crying. Her hands were on my back. They seemed to be trying to tear through my shirt. My right hand found her left breast, and we kissed again as I rolled her nipple between my thumb and finger.

"And that's what it looks like to me. What do you think Wade?" Marco asked me.

"Huh? Uh, I was thinking about something else. Sorry, Marco."

"Man, you look beat. Are you getting a cold or something?"

"Nah, I ran a little farther this morning than usual and I didn't sleep all that well last night, and well, it's been a busy day. I'm just a little tired." My excuse sounded lame to me. I held back a yawn and tried to cover it, moving my hand from my chin to my mouth.

An egret landed on a post outside, in front of our window. The girls were talking about the bird while my mind slipped back again.

In a minute, we had each other undressed. I got on top of her and the kissing started again, this time I felt her darkly painted fingernails dig into my shoulders, turning me on even more. Moving from her mouth, I moved to her neck and felt she didn't want her neck kissed, so I worked lower.

I kissed one breast and then the other for a minute or so. Time wasn't relevant at all. Time stood still for us. I kissed lower and when I got to her belly button, she took my head with her hands and pulled me up.

"Not this time honey." She said. "I'm far too ready already. Next time. Come here, baby. I need you."

I found her and became one with her, as we moved in a ritual as old as man himself. This wasn't sex. Of course, it was. It was love. Of course, it was. But it was sex after all and so much more.

Was it a minute? Was it two or three? I had no idea when Diane suddenly stopped her motion, squeezing me tight where it mattered. Her eyes rolled back in her head and a scream escaped her mouth. A scream so loud I was concerned for a second the desk might call 911. And then I didn't care. Her clenching had me over the top too. We screamed together. But hers, louder. Much louder.

After sex, I've been known to roll over and fall asleep. Not with Diane this afternoon. Talking about nothing and making promises about everything, we were both ready again in time. Diane on top made it easier for the old man I was but I felt like a teen this afternoon.

In that elusive time, however long it was, Diane had her second orgasm, another screamer, while I was just happy to be part of this. And more than that, I liked this lady. A lot.

Marco asked me something, and once more, my mind was on a bed, by the racetrack, with a beautiful woman, now sitting next to me.

I said, "Huh? I didn't hear that."

"Bullshit," Vickie said, in a loud voice. "I smell a lie and I smell sex a mile away and you too reeked of it when you came home this afternoon. Look at the two of you. You both look beat but so damned content. You don't have to tell us, but don't lie." Vickie sipped her iced tea before setting it down on the wet coaster.

Vickie said it loud enough that the surrounding tables stopped eating and looked at us. I wondered if I would look funny crawling under the table.

"OK," Diane said, in almost a whisper. "I guess it was bound to happen. I don't know. This guy just hits all the right notes with me. I've never felt like this before. The speed ride on the track set it off for me. It was something else and well, hey, I know this is so sudden but hey, I really like this guy.

The food arrived, steaming hot, and the conversation stopped. The two girls and I got some variety of shrimp. Marco opted for flounder stuffed with crab meat. All the food was good but none was memorable. Perhaps because I kept flashing back to a few hours ago.

Diane had flashbacks herself on the way to the restaurant, she told me later. She wondered what I thought of her now. Was she just some girl to have sex with? Was he just a guy giving her what she wanted? She didn't think so. Not after they were done with sex that afternoon and the two were clinging to each other, all the way out the door, across the parking lot, and to her car. She felt what he felt. There was something special between them.

"We have great Key Lime pie. Lots of folks say it's the best. We also have a raspberry tart with vanilla ice cream. The tart is made fresh here. Of course, we have vanilla and chocolate ice cream. Anybody for dessert?" said the waitress in the gingham apron.

Diane and I shared a slice of very good Key Lime pie while Marco and Vickie tried the tart. Then we shared across the table. The bill came and was paid. It was time to go.

As we got up, the near tables got a good look at the four of us. Curious, as they heard much of our conversation, one of the guys gave us a thumbs up.  Diane gave him one back. People were lined up outside, waiting for a table. The wait staff would do well today.

I drove, so we took my Audi. I dropped Marco and Vickie off at their house. Diane thanked Vickie for the book she bought her for her birthday. Fifty Shades of Grey. Must be a decorating book, I thought. We drove the three miles to home.

We were no sooner in the door when Diane turned around and kissed me. This time, just lips.

Diane said, "Wade, I don't know where this is going but I'd like to find out. How do you feel?

"I'd say we have another guest bedroom in the house now." as I picked up ten stone two and carried her to my bed. Love was in the air.

# The Morning After

"Good morning Diane. Did you sleep well?" I asked, carrying a tray holding steaming coffee in a blue ceramic mug. The coffee shared the tray with a napkin, and the brand sweetener she liked. Diane yawned and stretched in bed. She rubbed her eyes, waking up.

"I don't know when I've ever slept better," Diane said with a morning yawn. "Look, Wade," as I did, and saw a sleepy woman whose short hair was not combed yet nor did any makeup touch her face today.

"I woke up sometime in the middle of the night and took a sleeping pill, or I wouldn't have gotten back to sleep. It knocked me out pretty fast but before that, I felt like wow, how the hell do I say this? I just don't know what the hell to say about yesterday and how I acted. Damn, I've never done anything like that, ever."

"Please, let me give you a little background you didn't ask for and probably never would. You won't find this in my bio either. I was never married, but I went with this one guy for seven years."

"We talked about marriage but our schedules had one of us going someplace when the other was home. I thought we could make it work but then what? Kids? Then I would have to quit and I love my job. You know, if you love what you do, it isn't a job."

I sat on the edge of the bed, near her head and listened. Now I was curious.

"One day, I found out he had another girlfriend in Paris. Oh, I was so smart. I gave him a choice. And he moved out. I was so sure, so damned sure he would stay with me. I loved him. But, when I finally got over the fact he loved somebody more than me, well, life moves on with or without us. I never got serious about another guy since."

"It's Sunday Diane. I always treat myself on Sunday to what I call a forbidden breakfast. How about a big stack of pancakes with lots of butter and maple syrup?" I changed the subject. I didn't want to know her story. Did I?

"I'm not a good cook but I can make pancakes. Let me get this first cup of coffee down and I'll make them. As you know, pancakes come out of the box practically made. Add an egg and some milk and mix it and that's all it takes. Oh, don't mix it too much or the pancakes will be tough. I learned that from Vickie," I said, trying to change the subject again.

"So," Diane said, "I never really dated after that but hey, I'm human, and I have needs too. Sure, girls have their ways. But it's not the same."

"I don't pick up guys. There has to be some connection for me. Yesterday was the exception. I guess it had something to do with the thrill of the ride. How did you know I'd love something like that? I've never been that turned on in my life and now that it happened, well, it was the absolute best sex I've ever had. I had no idea it could be so, so great."

"Ha, so now you've seen me at my best and at my worst, all in a room near that racetrack. What do you think of that?" She blew on the rim of the blue ceramic mug before the sip. Her eyes looked over the rim of the cup at me, burning into mine.

I could see the sincerity in her eyes and her face as she looked both terrified and excited at the same time. Her eyes are giving away her emotions. If you asked me later, I could not tell you with any reasonable certainty why what happened next happened at all.

I set my coffee mug, my old stainless steel one with half the copper color peeling off, on the dresser. Taking the tray from her lap, I bent to Diane and put my arms around her as my lips found hers with a tender kiss. No fiery urgency at all. The night clothes she wore almost fell off without her help.

The first minute or so, we had sex. A pounding urgency Nature demanded.   Then, we made love. A tender, caring, sweet love neither of us felt in a very long time. We took our time, pleasing each other until it was over, both climaxing in a vocal outpouring, thrashing on a bed with sheets in a shamble.

"Oh God Wade, what brought this on? We're working partners and now, wow, this felt so right. I've never..."

"Shhh. It's OK. I don't know why this happened but it feels so good to me too."

"Uh, right. But we might have some splainin to do Ricky. We have company. Somebody is in the kitchen."

"What?"  I sat up, found my shorts and slipped them on and walked into the kitchen.

Bobby Joe sat at the table with a half empty coffee cup in front of him. A cookie perched half eaten in his left hand. He had a smile on his face as I walked into the room.

"I knocked boss but the door was open and well, I always gest walk in. It sounded like you musta bin doin some work in da other room so I gest grabbed a cup of coffee."

"Yeah, Diane saw a palmetto bug and wanted me to kill it. The damned thing was hard to catch."

*Oh, damned straight boss. I can buy that. Especially after I've seen her pick one up on the dock, pop it's head off with her thumbnail and throw it to the fishes.*

"What I come fer is the message we got early dis morning. About da new boat an all." Bobby Joe said.

"What about it? I didn't read my messages yet."

"The guy deliverin it lives in a place called Boynton Beach and he picked da boat up yesterday late in Miami. Sez he went home and dropped it in da lot next to his house den takes da family out to eat. Comes home and da boat is der. When he gets up dis morning, da boat is gone. Somebody stole it." said Bobby Joe as he took a good swallow of the excellent Costa Rican coffee I always bought.

"Da police an all are lookin for it but dey say a boat like dat can be painted in a half hour and da yellow one might be a blue or red one today."

I could hear the shower running in the background as I walked to my office and called my director, Floyd Johnson. A fifteen-minute conversation and I was back in the kitchen with news for Bobby Joe.

"We're gonna use our boat, the Hurricane deck boat. He's having a bar light shipped. One that we can just hold up or somehow mount on the bow. Hell, with that 250 Yamaha, it'll do close to 50 with four on board and no sailboat or big rig can run that fast. The radios are a helluva lot faster than any boat we have running here. Now we have to wake up Gordon at the boat shop in town and get our boat back here." I sat down at the table while Bobby Joe poured coffee for both of us.

"Any coffee left?" Diane asked. She walked in with her hair freshly washed but not dried yet and no makeup. "Did Wade tell you about the electrical short he had to fix in my room a while ago?"

# Herb and Diane Talk

The heat sensors and camera for the Highbridge project didn't arrive until late Tuesday evening. Diane sat on the bridge rail before sunrise the following day.  She would be here the entire time of the installation, making sure the items were installed as she demanded.

As usual, Herb Moncrief, the daytime bridge tender arrived early.  It was six thirty-five when he parked on the roadside.  Getting out of his truck, he carried a container holding two coffees and a paper bag with donuts.  One for him and one for Diane.  Her coffee contained milk and two artificial sweeteners. He talked to Wade yesterday and found her coffee preference.  The sun was just breaking over the horizon.

Diane got down from the rail, meeting Herb half way, then leaned on the left fender of her car.  She gladly accepted the coffee, her first of the day. Even without her morning coffee, she was fired up, wanting to get started.

"Why thank you, Herb. That was very thoughtful of you" Diane said as she slid a fingernail under the lift off portion of the lid and took a careful sip.  The coffee was hot but drinkable.  And it was very good.

"Mornin Diane. Where's Wade? I thought he'd be here what with all this going on this morning."

"I heard the garage door go up as I walked into the kitchen. I guess he's running this morning. He runs every other day, and sometimes more. I didn't push the coffee maker button. He's very particular about having hot fresh coffee. I've learned that already and whatever you do, don't touch his coffee mug." Diane smiled, taking another sip.

They both looked east. The sun was making its presence known, as it lit up the sky with coral streaks radiating to the heavens.

"You know Herb, he's not such a bad guy. I read his bio before I got here and thought he was just some hard ass Marine with an attitude and then I find I was way off base."

"That would be way off base. Hell, I've known Wade for all the time he's been here. I knew his wife Catherine too. A sweetheart and the love of his life. Her death just knocked the hell out of him for quite a while. Then he somehow got on the proverbial bike and he's living again."

"Maybe I shouldn't say this cause we are friends but he seems to be kind of sweet on this one gal, Mary Connors who works for the same folks he does. Now Mary's run off to Kentucky to help her sister who was in a bad accident. Kind of looks like she will be gone a spell too. I don't know how Wade will handle this. They seemed pretty tight before she left."

"To lose Catherine and now Mary, that's a lot to put on a guy. I hope he can manage all of this loss. But you know, he stopped by yesterday and damn, he sure looked happy."

Herb was looking down and had seen this a million times. He pointed down to the river below them. Diane looked and shared the sight with him. Swimming along the edge of the river, a female manatee with a baby swimming by her side skimmed the surface. Manatee was new to Diane who watched with keen interest.

A movement above caught her eye. A bald eagle glided in graceful circles not fifty feet above them. Two fishermen in a bay style boat idled under the bridge heading south, while on the far side of the river, moving north, a "crabber" was setting out crab traps he would check in two days and harvest the succulent blue crabs that were abundant in these waters.

 Diane looked around, thinking this was indeed a fabulous place to live. No wonder Wade liked it here. What was not to like. Her stint here would be up in a few months and she would move on. She never stayed in one place too long. If she had a choice, this just might be the place she would plant herself.

"Oh, I think he'll manage," said Diane as a flatbed truck pulled behind Herb's, followed by a four-door pickup truck with a crew of six men, all decked out wearing chartreuse work vests. Time to get this project going.

"Not to worry Herb. Wade won't have time to be lonely very long. We're going to be very busy soon."

# *Sandbar*

As Diane and Herb waited for the thermal imaging system to arrive, the bow of the sailboat "Grasshopper touched a sandbar a hundred yards off the shore of Guardalavaca, a town on the east coast of Cuba.

The name "Guardalavaca" translated to "Guard the Cow." Gustav Fletcher, the boat captain, saw no cows on the beach. The only life was a pair of blue heron walking the shore, searching for food in the brilliant white sand.

Gustav had been here several times in the past. The sandbar he was touching was not new to him. The tide was just starting to roll in, so he knew he would have no trouble backing off the bar.

Polo went below deck and rousted the kids, kicking their legs, chasing them up on deck. Gus handed the quiet one a bar of soap and told all of them to get into the water and bathe. All the boys were filthy, smelling of sweat, feces, and dried blood. Each boy had been raped at least twice. Blood trails were seen on their legs as they climbed over the side of the boat and into the clear but salty water. The salt stinging each boy from the cuts and abrasions each had, but the clean water was welcome.

Polo stood on the bow with an AK 47 rifle, telling the boys he would shoot and kill any that tried to escape. Abbas was a good swimmer and estimated he could get perhaps half way to shore underwater but that was not enough to get out of range of a rifle bullet. He started lathering his hair.

Ten minutes later, the boys were helped back aboard the boat and ordered to bring buckets of water below and clean the cabin floor. The last bucket held a portion of pine smelling liquid. Ten more minutes and the Grasshopper pulled anchor and backed off the sandbar. The two blue heron was still hunting for food.

Gustav sailed under diesel power and picked up the satellite phone, punching in a number he had in his memory. A half hour later, he cut the power on his engine, watching a small fishing boat coming toward him at an intercepting angle.

When the fishing boat reached them, the man in the fishing boat slipped his motor into neutral, then handed up two large seabags, just like the Navy once used. Then a smaller attaché case made of aluminum. Gustav handed the fishing boat a package. The two seabags belonged to The Money Man. The case was his. What the Money Man didn't know wouldn't hurt him.  One more trip and he could retire.

As the fishing boat chugged away toward the mainland, Gus and Polo raised their sails. The next stop, Florida.

# Max Goes Home

Bob and Myra Masters were on an extended weekend trip visiting Myra's sister Nancy in Bluffton, South Carolina. Nancy and Ted, her husband, lived in a gated community with all the amenities one could ask for including a pontoon boat and good fishing.

They planned just a two-day weekend visit, having fun as they always did. Nancy asked them to stay longer. It was a pleasure to stay another day, especially since Sunday afternoon, Bob snagged a seven plus pound, Largemouth Bass. Pictures were taken and the bass released to fight another day.

The clubhouse was buzzing about the huge bass Bob caught and of course the skill of the angler, able to land the monster. As the cocktails flowed, so did the angler's tale grow. The girls loved the extra time too. Sunday's newspaper had a bevy of sales in stores they loved to shop.

The four-hour ride home left them tired. They told Ted and Nancy about Max and their search for him, feeling a bit guilty they took this planned weekend away. The great weekend helped heal the hurt of their loss.

The message light on the phone blinked. Myra listened to the message. The recording was a huge surprise. Max was found. Calling Bob over, they listened again as Myra jotted down the information then called Dr. Jeremy Higgins, the vet who left the message.

It was already past seven, too late to do anything tonight. Arrangements were made that tomorrow at ten A.M. they would meet at the vet's clinic and get Max back. Dr. Higgins briefly told the plight of little Max.

He then called his friend Brian Walsh and told him of the meeting and offered to take Max in either that night or early tomorrow if the Walsh's would rather do that instead of seeing Max's owners. Brian declined. He would be there.

Next week was the start of school for both Danny and Debbie. Danny was starting second grade while Debbie would have four hours of pre-kindergarten. Lucky for the Walsh's, both kids were excited to start school.

The start of school would be a big help as both kids fell instantly in love with Max and he with them. The school would help ease the pain of the sudden loss they should never have had. Kids don't understand things like this in spite of Brian trying to explain how this can happen.

The Masters got to the clinic a few minutes before the Walsh's and were waiting in Dr. Higgins office when Brian and the two kids walked in. Danny carried Max who had not a care in the world, his little tail wagging a hundred miles an hour.

It was regular hours for Dr. Higgins who offered them his office as other customers were bringing their pets in to see the doctor. The little office with degrees framed and hanging on the wall had one small window looking out at the parking lot. The room was crowded. Brian explained how he bought Max and how the transaction transpired leaving no thought he somehow stole their dog.

As he explained, Danny and Debbie started crying. Sounding almost like a sobbing hiccup at first, Danny couldn't control the emotion and love for his newfound buddy. Debbie cried out loud, no hiccup cry for her. Just a steady loud cry. Both clung to little Max who didn't understand all the attention he was getting.

"Danny, son, I explained this to you already. It isn't our dog. Give him back to these nice people. Go on now." Brian's hand gently on the back of Danny's head nudged him toward the Masters.

Looking up with saucer eyes brimming over with tears running down both cheeks, a sobbing Danny held little Max out to Myra Masters, now crying herself looking at the kids while her husband Bob looked away, checking something outside the window.

Of course, Max knew Myra. She was very nice to Max all the time. He snuggled in her arm for a few seconds as he watched the two kids back away from him. His new camouflage leash drug on the floor. He wanted to be with the kids. Danny snuck him into his bed last night and he liked that. He did what any dog would do. He tried to jump out of Myra's arms as he barked frantically, something he rarely did.

"Thank you, folks," said Brian. "Come on kids; we gotta go." They walked out of the office with Danny crying as hard as his sister. People who waited with their pets to see the vet had to think this family just lost a pet to a disease or accident and felt instant sympathy for them. This showed in the looks on their faces. Pet owners are special people. Well, most of them are.

"Buckle up kids. When we get home, we can talk about getting a dog," said Brian, closing his door, inserting the ignition key ready to start the car. Both kids continued crying. A twist of the key had all the functions working on the car again, a warm blast of air blew from the vents, quickly getting noticeably colder.

A sharp tap on the passenger window got his attention. He saw it was Myra and her husband with Max on her arm. A push of a button on his door panel lowered the passenger window.

Tears flowed from Myra's eyes as she placed Max through the window and on the empty passenger seat which was instantly vacant again as Max jumped over the seat to the back and between the kids, hopping up and down for all he was worth.

"Mr. Walsh, Brian, please let the kids have Max as a gift from us. We love him but it's easy to see the kids love him more and he loves them more too. Here is my husband's business card which has our home address on it. Please call. We would like to get together this weekend if you can make it and we will sign his papers over to you. Max can see his buddy Rambo once more."

"I – I don't know what to say. I mean. Oh, wow. What can I say," Brian choked out the words.

"Kids, what do you say." Brian turned to the kids, his eyes glazed. "These nice people are giving Max to you. To us."

Thank you shouts, and the Glee could have been heard a half mile away if they weren't in the car.

"Folks, you made our day. No, you made our month or more. Thank you," said Brian.

As mascara ran down her cheek, Myra smiled and said, "Brian, this is Christmas in August for us. You have no idea how happy we feel doing this. It's not what we planned but a thousand times better. Good luck and God bless. Tears that fell from Myra were tears of joy.  The Masters walked to their car holding hands. Brian had no idea they could not have children and seeing this indeed made them very happy. The sun was especially bright today. The world was right.

# Moonlit Talk

The atomic clock hanging above the sliding door leading from the garage to the house showed it was 10:07 P.M. I followed Diane through the garage, and out the back to my dock. My left hand held a bottle of Michelob Amber Bock beer, one of my favorite brews. My favorite list seemed to be expanding.

When I reached the first dock piling on the right, I bent down and tapped the control button on the transformer once, shutting all eighteen, seven-watt low voltage lights, immersing the dock in near total darkness. The quiet was intense, until a fish feeding on the far bank broke the surface of the water with a splash in pursuit of its prey.

On military assignments at night, I learned to close my eyes for a while, aiding in the transition from light to dark. That was on a combat mission. This was a mission in a way as Diane insisted we talk and wanted to talk outside and on the dock.

With a waxing crescent moon tonight, sitting at the two o'clock position, the glimmer on the mirror surface of the water gave enough light to see each other. The soft light the moon provided enhanced a romantic setting, as our eyes adjusted.

My dock has two Adirondack chairs of a sort sitting on the end. Adirondack chairs have long legs making for a comfortable seat, easy to get in and out. Catherine picked the chairs, one lemon yellow and the other lime green. Diane sat in the yellow one on the left while I angled my chair forty-five degrees, toward her. I had a feeling this was going to be a very important conversation and I thought I knew which direction this talk would go.

"Wade, my mind's a mess. How in the hell did I get this way?" Diane said. "I came here to do a job and all of a sudden I'm in bed with you and enjoying the hell out of it. I can't blame you if you don't believe me but it's the gospel truth. I've never done this before. How the hell are we supposed to work together now?"

"Yeah. Beats the hell out of me how this happened but well, I have this strong feeling for you and it's not so much about sex although wow, it's been something for me. I never…uh, well, I never. Uh, you know."

I looked into Diane's face, the ribbon of white light the moon laid on the surface of the river reflected off her glasses. The light shimmering ever so brilliant, making her face glow, her expression pained. I looked at her with an honest blank look in my eyes that spoke sincerity. How the hell did we get into this? Now what?

"Vickie said you've got a girlfriend who's out of town with a sister who needs her for a while. You know Wade, I'm the cause of all of this. If I didn't get so freaking turned on with the cars, this would never have happened. I sure can't blame you for that. Hell, I never knew that a ride like that would turn me on. How the hell would you know? Of course, you didn't. I didn't know." Diane grimaced as if in pain thinking back on what happened.

"Well, I guess I could have said no and I wanted to. Until I looked at you and said yes. Hell yes. And I've got to say, Diane, I don't regret it. I'm sixty-three years old and never had sex like that, ever. I feel it's far more than sex. I can't explain it."

"Yes, I had a thing going on with Mary Connors, a widow who works on our team. I don't know, hell, I got pretty lonely and well, Mary was there and lonely too. I thought I loved Mary at the time but since she's gone, I've been thinking a lot and well, maybe this was just a knee-jerk reaction to her for a glimpse of love."

"You know Diane, we all need love if we are normal people. I've been missing love since Catherine got killed. Mary was there. Oh, I still like her a lot but it's not the same anymore. I'm not making excuses. It's just the way it is."

"I can move out Wade. I'm sure they can find me a place, or if nothing else, I can stay at a motel until they do. I turned down the house and at the time, I thought it was the right thing to do."

Diane moved enough to set the river moonlight reflection switching from her right eyeglass lens to the left one. The hurt still showed on her face. Looking at her, I could feel her pain deep inside.

"If I move out, we won't have the same pressures on us."

I took another swallow of beer and said, "Is that what you want to do? Do you want to move out? I guess I don't want that but it's your choice. Mary. Damn, what can I say? I guess I don't feel the same way about her as I do you. Not at all. There's just something different in how I feel about you. Like we belong together. Damn but if I don't feel like a teenager again and it feels so good."

"Not only that, I think Mary might have found somebody herself. There's a neighbor of her sister helping them. He's a widower himself. Mary has known him for a while. It sure seems like it to me anyhow. I'll admit, I was a little jealous at first but I soon realized I didn't care so much after all. It's funny, I thought I was in love with her but now I can honestly say, no. I'd just like to stay friends."

"You know Wade, I have feelings for you I've never had for anybody else. We can't let that get in the way of our job here. It's been so damned fast coming on to me too. I feel like… I guess I feel like we belong together. Stupid huh?" said Diane looking deep into my eyes. "I know your bio but I don't really know you. And yet, I've known you all my life. No, I want to stay if you think we can work this out together. I think we can. Maybe I won't have that hollow feeling when we are apart now and know you care for me as I care for you. Falling in love at our age is almost like a miracle."

"Then it's settled," I said. "Let's go with the flow."

A whoof sound followed by another a second later came from the water near us.  A pair of dolphins blowing air swam past us on a journey to who knew where.

"Do you know Diane, dolphins, and humans are the only species that have sex for fun?"

"I think I read that somewhere. And they mate for life. Isn't that what we are supposed to do?"

My phone vibrated. I had the ring tone shut off. Who would be calling me at this time? It has to be trouble. I looked and saw it was from my boss, Floyd Johnson.

"I'm sorry to bother you Wade but we had a little snafu here with our computers and I see you didn't get the message on what looked like an alligator with a child. Well, the dive team found a half-eaten hog under some mangrove roots across the river and down a couple of hundred feet. We feel sure this is what the bridge tender saw."

"That's good news for sure," I said. "Everything is a go here."

"So tell me, how is Ms. Mason working out? Is she busting your chops? I hear she's hell on wheels."

"Actually, Floyd, we're getting along fine. She's smart and ambitious and she isn't afraid to say what's on her mind.  We aren't having any problems at all."

"Ooooooo Kayyyy. Wade. Do I hear something I shouldn't?

"What? Because we are getting along, you think it 's something else? Get real Floyd. Good night," I said, disconnecting our phones.

"Did I sound different to you when I talked to Floyd just now? He somehow picked up something I said or how I said it."

"Or what you didn't say maybe?" Diane said. "He's the director for a good reason,"

Standing together, I found my lips on hers. Her left arm pulled us closer together. If neighbors were out, they would see two people holding on to each other as their very lives depended on it. This would indeed be one helluva ride. And he thought the Herdy Gerdy was strange.

## *Last Encounter*

 "Hey boss, I can see da lights ahead over dere," Polo said, pointing ahead of him with his right arm extended. "I think we be maybe three hours to make da land. You know boss, I tink we should kill da quiet one. He scare me wid all the lookin and never talkin at all. He is evil for us. Maybe I should break his neck and we sink him out here for da crabs to eat up."

"He's worth eight hundred dollars to us," Gustav said as he stood at the helm, a warm tropical breeze in his face, a half burned cigarette dangling from his lips.  With cruise control set, the boat would soon be on the Miami River and on their way north. "Do you want to take eight hundred bucks out of your pay? It's all on you if you do kill him. Go ahead, kill him but it's out of your money, not mine. He can't talk and he's a long way from home. How the hell can he hurt us?"

"I jus don't like him. He scares me. I tink I go down and fuck da little one again. I like it he screams so loud. We get to land we can no more do dat. Dey all makes too much noise.  But not da evil one. Maybe I no kill him because if Sondra find out I trow away eight hundred American dollars, she be pissed and she be no fun. Sometimes I tink I should feed her to da crabs."

"No, she sometimes makes me so happy and she a good cook too." Polo moved to the hatch leading down to the cabin for one last encounter with the little one.

As he reached the deck below, his eyes settled on the quiet one who was burning his eyes into him. I *tink he be a bad for us thought Polo,* grabbing the little one who was already crying, knowing the pain and humiliation in store for him again.

# *One Step at a Time*

The clock on the old dresser across the room showed Lester it was 12:42 A.M. The light in the room from the face of that old clock joined the light of the sliver moon, shining through the window on the wood plank floor. A gentle breeze fluttered the curtain, changing the light patterns. Lester woke up with a sheen of sweat on his face. He sat up, awake for no reason. His bed linens, such as they were, old and threadbare, once white, now a pale yellow from age, now damp with sweat.

Sitting up, he felt frightened. He felt like he wasn't alone. As he looked around in the dim light, his eyes settled on the corner, resting on Mama's old rocking chair. As he looked, the chair started to rock back and forth. There wasn't enough breeze to move the chair, yet it was rocking. He had the feeling it was years ago. His mama was holding him in her lap singing a song about Jesus and stroking his hair.

"Mama? Mama, are you here? Did you come back to see me? Mama, I miss you so much."

A scent came upon him filling the room. The scent of Lilacs in the Springtime. Mama loved lilacs. During the short life of its flowers, she would cut a bunch and put them on the table in the cracked white vase. The scent filled the house with the same odor Lester was sensing now. It was far too late in the year for Lilacs he knew.

A noise on the front porch diverted Lester's attention. It sounded like an opossum or an armadillo scratching, in search for something to eat. They visited most nights. He turned back to another noise and looked at mama's rocker again, then cried out with a sudden start. Sitting in that rocker was Jill Douglas. Jill, the daughter of old Bob Douglas, a teacher he had years ago. He bought the faded old Dodge van sitting under the carport from Bob not long ago.

Jill was the same person who came to visit when he had the dogs. The same person he said a prayer for each night, hoping to see her again. Now, here she was and her visit upset him.

Jill radiated in a glow as she smiled at Lester. Dressed in another flowing summer dress with pink flowers printed on it, she again looked like an angel to Lester. Her hair appeared as spun golden silk resting on her shoulders. Even in the dim light, Lester could see her blue eyes shining. Her look gave him a calming feeling.

"Hello, Lester. This is just a dream, so don't worry. Mama sent me to see you again and to tell you she is so proud of how you handled the dogs. And how you are changing your life around. I'm proud of you too. I see you tacked that fifty dollar bill on the wall as I asked. As long as that bill is there, look at it whenever you feel you want to do something not so nice. That bill will help keep you on the right track."

"Uh Jill, this ain't no dream. I can pinch myself. I can rub my foot on the floor. I can even feel grit on the floor. This is for real ain't it?"

"Lester, when we are done talking, you will go back to sleep. When you wake up, you will feel so good inside. You will feel calm and rested. Then you will hear a hoot owl calling out. You will know this was a dream, but a good one."

Jill added; "You're doing great. Mama and I want to help you move forward to bigger and better things. You can't just sit here every day and piddle around. You're far too smart for that, but you need a little boost.

You have forty acres of land here, and you will need most of it for what is coming. First, to get there, you need to sell a couple of acres. You need money to do what you have to do. Let's just take it one step at a time. "

"You need to sell two acres of your land. The land on the river, where it juts out on a point.  Its high enough it never floods. A woman will buy it to build her house. She will offer you a lot of money for that property and you will sell it but you will sell it with a promise we will talk about later.  She will be a good neighbor and together, you will be successful."

"She is a pet person herself.  This lady and her pets and her business will change your life forever. Her name is Lynn Olson. You will know her right away. She is about the same age as your mother and looks strikingly like your mother too.  Do you understand this?" Asked Jill. She leaned forward in the rocker as she spoke softly to Lester.

"This ain't no dream Jill. I can see you, and I can smell you or flowers or something. I can walk across the room and touch you. " Lester stood up and took one step toward Jill who smiled at Lester. He got no closer than that step and she was gone.  Things got hazy for a moment then he opened his eyes and found he was back in bed. It was just a dream.

The next sound was old Brewster the rooster crowing, calling for the sun to arrive on time. Stretching, as he lay in his bed, the dream came back so vividly. Like it really happened. He sniffed the air. There was no scent of lilacs now.  Mama's rocker was sitting just where it always did.  Lester swung his legs to the floor, getting out of bed. He stood and heard a sound.  He suddenly remembered Jill's words in that dream. Whooo, Whooo, Whooo from an owl on a branch in the live oak tree next to the open window.

*Whoo, thought Lester. Who is doing this to me?*

# *First Alert*

The bell on the new system in the control room of the L.B. Knox bridge rang without a pause. Its tinkle sounded much like a bell she heard every Sunday in church. Wanda, the night tender reacted as trained. It was 02:24 when she picked up the phone and made the call. Called the Highbridge bridge by all the locals, this bell sounded a warning that the 46 foot Viking cruiser passing below showed a HOT or "not normal" amount of body heat radiating from below deck, thus setting off the alarm. It responded the way it was designed to work.

Wanda Freeman was the night tender tonight and worked five nights a week on a weekend rotating basis. Wanda and all the tenders working this bridge just completed training on the new system. That wasn't the problem. The system was to be "active" today. Did that mean from midnight two hours and twenty-four minutes ago or did the active time start at 7 or 8? What Wanda knew was it started today. Wanda was fifty-four years old, with twenty-one years on the job. She wasn't about to lose this job because she messed up big time. It took Wanda all of three seconds to pick up the red phone on the crowded desk. Three rings later, a sleepy voice answered, "What?"

I had been in one of the deepest sleeps I could remember ever having as I later thought about it when that alarm on the red phone penetrated my sleep.

The first ring woke me but it took two more rings to get untangled from the sheet and Diane's arm draped over my body, spooning next to me. Diane didn't wake up until I was sitting on the edge of the bed reaching for the phone. I guess we both were tired after our love fest last night.

"What? What is it?" I asked into the phone. I tried to focus my eyes on anything that made sense.

"Sir, this is Wanda Freeman, the tender on the Knox Bridge. I just had a 46 foot Viking powerboat pass with a very hot reading from below. It's heading north, and the camera is showing eight or nine people below deck but I'm not positive of the number."

"I know this process starts today but I didn't know if it was starting at midnight or later. If it's later, well, I'm sorry I woke you."

"No Wanda, you did well. It's eight this morning but this will give me a good shot at seeing what the hell we are doing in the middle of the night. Call both county's and get those boys out too. I should have the boat stopped near my house by the time I get on the water. Thanks."

Both of us dressed and were out the back of the garage in less than three minutes, I handing Diane a Smith & Wesson AR-15 with a thirty round magazine while I grabbed my Glock 9 MM holding fifteen rounds with two back up magazines.

I had gone through this drill several times yesterday with the nine men who would man this boat, three crews of three men each. It was now second nature to hit the release on the custom boat lift having the 23 foot Hurricane floating in less than five seconds instead of the normal forty. When the boat bottom was wet, I found the ignition switch and inserted the key, fired the motor and backed into the channel.

Diane snapped the flashing red and blue light on the improvised bow mount and set the strobe light in action.

In the fading moonlight, the moon falling below the tree line to the west, I could barely make out the vague outline of a large boat coming toward us at a slow speed.  The boat shut off its running lights, sneaking its way up the intra-coastal.

I grabbed a powerful two million watt hand held search light from the compartment under the helm.  I flicked the switch ON, casting the oncoming boat in a brilliant white light that startled me in its intensity. As I did this, Diane removed a power bullhorn from under the Starboard seat and hailed the cruiser with the speaker.

"Captain, stop your boat. Kill your engines now. We are Homeland Security. Stop your boat and prepare to be boarded."

The sound of the twin diesel engines slowed to an idle. We expected the next sound would be silence from the boat.  Diane and I were surprised when the captain pushed the throttles forward, raising the bow of the big boat, aimed at us.

I hollered to Diane "Hold on," as I pushed the throttle forward, turned the wheel sharply right, and cleared the port side of the big boat by a foot or less. The force of the wave the big boat created had our boat almost on its side. In a couple of seconds, our deck boat was amidship of the bigger boat which was blasting its way north past us.

A three round volley erupted from the barrel of the AR-15 Diane held, smashing the radar antenna on the roof of the cabin of the cruiser. The sharp report from the bullets and the shattering of the radar unit above his head changed the captain's mind about running. He pulled back the throttles and shut off the ignition.  We were three houses south of my home. Lights came on in two of the homes nearby, one was my neighbor George who walk out to his dock.

"George, it's me, Wade," I shouted. "Do us both a favor and go back in your house now. Help is on the way. I'll talk to you later."  I had my sidearm drawn, not knowing what to expect from the boat, after his attempt at getting away.  I now knew a sidearm and AR-15 wasn't enough for this kind of operation. I would have to talk to Floyd Johnson, before this was over today.

The megaphone carried Diane's voice saying, "Captain. One more stunt like that and the next volley will cut you in half. Do you understand? Now raise your hands above your head and walk out, away from the helm."

It was ten minutes before backup arrived. During this time, the Viking captain, stood with hands on his head, silent, and not moving.  Both boats drifted south at a slow rate, moving with the incoming tide.  A police boat from the sheriff's office of Flagler County arrived followed by the wildlife officer's boat with two officers aboard.

"Captain, we are boarding you. We are armed and any sudden move by you may be your last. Do you understand me?" Diane spoke over the rumble of three outboard motors at idle.

Four men from the two other boats trained their guns and flood lights on the captain.  I stood on the gunnels of my boat, grabbed the side of the Viking and climbed on the deck of the big cruiser. Diane handed me a line to secure our boat to the bigger vessel then climbed aboard the bigger boat herself, using the swim platform on the Viking.

When I had my boat secured to the cruiser, two sheriff's deputies, Justin and Chris boarded the big boat too. Once on board, Chris handcuffed the captain behind his back then sat him down in the lounge seat.

I said, "Captain, we are going to search your vessel. I'm only going to ask you once so pay close attention. Is there anybody on board that has access to a weapon? If you say no and we find out different, it's going to be very rough on you."

"No Sir. There are two families below. They are my cousins and they are escaping almost certain death. They are from Syria. From

Aleppo. We have family in New Jersey and I want to get them to safety."

"Tell them to come up here with their hands on their heads and walk slowly. No sudden moves," I said. "One family at a time."

Speaking rapidly and in what sounded like an encouraging tone, the captain called down into the cabin below. The first to come up was an adult male, followed by two young boys, both pre-teens with an adult woman carrying a little child. They were patted down by the two sheriffs.

After their search, I had the captain bring the other family topside. The first to come up was another male about thirty-five years old followed by three girls, two could have been in their early teens, the last, a few years younger. As the captain said, they appeared to be families. All had a scared to death looks on their faces.

"Sir," from the captain, "My cousin Sophia is down below. She is to have a baby soon and she cannot climb the stairs up here. I vow my life she has no weapons." He spoke rapidly to the second adult male that came up and got a quick response.

"Sir, her husband Adar just told me her water broke. She will have the baby soon."

*Just what I need, I thought.*

"Come on Diane. Let's go check this out." I descended to the cabin below followed closely by Diane. I switched the lights on for both the forward cabin and the one below the helm. What I saw, I wished I didn't see.

Sophia lay on the bunk to our left, below the helm. Her legs splayed apart. I could see the partial head of a baby, making its way out to join the world. Sophia's face showed pain as she bit down on the handle of a wooden cook spoon. Her face was glistening with sweat as she breathed rapidly for a few seconds, then did her best to push the new life out of her body.  Sophia looked at us, pleading in her eyes.

Forgetting everything else, Diane climbed on the bed between Sophia's legs and cleared the way moving bedding aside to make room for the baby on its way. Diane spoke softly to Sophia, not knowing if the woman knew a word of English. Her soothing voice is telling Sophia what she had to do, recalling a class she had on child birth so many years before.

I holstered my gun and just looked, not knowing what I could do or what I might say. I too had taken a class on childbirth years ago, but the lesson was so far in the back of my mind, all I could remember is the mother had to push.

"Wade, I'm going to need something to cut the umbilical cord soon. A sharp knife or scissors will do. I'll need some cord to tie it off. See if you can find something fast." Diane said, never taking her eyes off Sophia.

I always carried my Benchmade knife that was sharp enough to shave. I scuttled toward the front of the cabin and found just what I thought we needed. A fishing rod with a stout line on the reel.

Cutting several feet of line off the rod and reel was a snap. I hurried back to the cabin behind me, just in time to see the baby's head fully clear of Sophia's body.

"Wade, the baby's blue. The umbilical cord is wrapped around its neck. I have to cut the cord now. Get next to me and help me or this baby won't make it."

In my youth, I gutted a deer I shot while hunting in the beautiful Shawnee National Forest in southern Illinois. Those memories flashed back.  That umbilical cord reminded me of the intestines of the deer I field dressed.  I kept that thought in my head for fear I would get sick and really make a mess of things.

"Give me a foot of line Wade."

I cut a foot from the line I had.

"Now, slip your finger under the umbilical cord and do what you can to give me enough room to get this line under, so I can tie it off."

*It's just a deer. It's just a deer.* I kept saying to myself as I worked the index finger of my left hand between the cord and the baby's neck. Diane made quick work of tying the line tight and none too soon as this deer was alive.

"I'll hold the baby as still as I can. You've got to cut the umbilical cord and make sure it's just the cord you cut. Hurry. This baby is blue and dying."

I slipped my knife under the cord and with no effort, the umbilical cord was severed, allowing the baby to rush out of its nine-month incubator and into the real world.

"It's a girl and she's not breathing," said Diane who held the baby upside down and smacked it with a few good but loving blows to its behind.

Lying the baby down in front of her, Diane took the index finger and thumb of her left hand and pinched the tiny nose of the blue bundle before her. She then breathed a breath into the baby's mouth, ignoring the slime covering the infant. Once, twice, three times. On the fourth breath, a scream came from the baby, laughter from her mother, and a collective sigh from Diane and I. The little bundle joined the world. God's gift.

Smiling now, I looked at Diane and thought, *This is why I love this woman. I just know she's the one for me. She saved this baby and she will save my sorry ass too.*

Bending over, I kissed Diane through the slime and sweat. It was the sweetest kiss we ever shared.

# Bobby Joe, Restaurateur

The sun was peeking over the golf course east of my house when we idled back home. The distance was short, the action, lively, all of it less than a quarter mile from my house.

Bobby Joe Green loaded several fishing rods on the skinny water boat, preparing to take a customer fishing into the shallow backwaters on the west side of the intra-coastal. These waters were fished very little as it was difficult to get into the area. The water is very shallow and home to some whopper Redfish and "gator" sea trout. Gator size trout were 24 inches long or longer.

As I idled to the dock, Bobby Joe had his hand on the lift control and toggled the switch, lowering the lift for me. Bobby Joe had been working for a half an hour and saw what was going on.  He thought the plan to catch human traffickers was paying off fast. It must have been happening the better part of the night, he thought as he looked at Wade and a very tired Diane. Even her pixie salt and pepper hair were messed into a birds nest.

With just a simple "HI," I looked at the Rawbone lean man, my partner now, realized this too will end and not too long either. I started this business just for something to do and it flourished and expanded to where I needed Bobby Joe. Now Bobby Joe was taking over a restaurant in town.

In Bobby Joe, Niko saw a way to retire and be proud of the business he built. He would train Bobby Joe and when he knew enough, sell him the business on a payment basis, so much a month for so many months. Of course, Niko would stay as a consultant for as long as he was needed.

Bobby Joe already gave up the crabbing business he and I started. It took too much time away from the restaurant. Raised in the swamp, Bobby Joe was far from dumb. He introduced "Crab Cake Sandwiches" at Peppers Restaurant. The recipe came from Old Cyrus Winkleman, an old man who lived in a little shack of a house on the river up in the Hammock area

Bobby Joe was fishing near Old Cyrus's place a while ago and saw the old man trying to move a tree that fell on his property. Bobby Joe stopped and helped. The two became friends in short order. The recipe was from Old Cyrus's Mama Clara.

When the delicious sandwich was introduced at Peppers, it was called Clara's Crab Cake Sandwich. It sold out daily and the naming made Old Cyrus very grateful. So much so that he and Bobby Joe became very good friends. Old Cyrus didn't have many friends. His friends all died. He would tell those that would listen, his friends must be thinking he went to hell by now. He laughed a cackling laugh, telling his story.

Another innovation was advertised as the best Key Lime Pie in the state. And it probably was. The widow Sally Kayton lived on Daytona Street in town, a quaint two bedroom home well kept. Most of the work around the house was done by the widow. Everybody called her Ms. Kay.

A month ago, on his way to see a guy who made fishing lures, Bobby Joe went down Daytona Street and saw Ms. Kay pulling on the starter rope of her lawnmower. Bobby Joe could see her from a distance and by the time his truck got to her, Ms. Kay must have pulled that rope a dozen times as she was plum tuckered out.

Bobby Joe stopped and soon found the problem. A loose ground wire was shorting the system out. He fixed the wire and on the first pull, Old Reliable she called her mower, roared to life. He had time, so he started pushing Old Reliable back and forth across the lawn and in ten minutes, the wiry Saint Augustine grass was cut short again.

When he was done, Bobby Joe saw Ms. Kay go in the house. *Oh, I'll bet she will want to pay me. I don't want nuttin. Jes helpin.* He thought.

It wasn't money Ms. Kay came out with and yet, it sure was. Her hand held a plate with a slice of the very best Key Lime Pie Bobby Joe ever tasted.

In the back yard, sitting on the hanging wooden bench swing, suspended by sturdy ropes, Bobby Joe made a new friend. Sipping on an iced tea, the two talked long enough Bobby Joe forgot about the lures. They talked of a deal and shook on it. A concrete contract .

Ms. Sally Kayton would bake five Key Lime pies daily and sell them to Peppers Restaurant for ten dollars each. Ms. Kay estimated her cost would be about $4.70 a pie plus electric on the stove, say five bucks each and make five dollars a pie times five or twenty-five bucks a day, times five for the week or $125.00 a week. Five hundred a month. She would be rich.

Bobby Joe knew he could sell the slice of pie at $2.50 a slice and as they were large pies, eight slices per pie or $20.00 a pie. Put the slice on a paper plate with a plastic fork and a small napkin and it was still a very nice profit. More important, this was indeed the best Key Lime Pie in the state and maybe the world.

Niko loved the idea and in just a week, the pies would be sold out before four in the afternoon unless somebody reserved a slice, like say Sharon Stone.

The kicker was Bobby Joe, seeing how well the pies and the crab cakes took off instituted a special day for the additions. Two weeks ago this past Saturday, he advertised the event. Meet the people who made the best Crab Cakes and the best Key Lime pies possible.

A regular customer living in town who worked for the Daytona News Journal, the local paper, got wind of the event and did a small piece on it attesting to the goodness of both items. Inspired by the free meal he got two days before the article was published, he swore he would have written it even without the free meal he would not admit to having.

The result was over four hundred people packed the street while Ms. Kay and Old Cyrus sat on the small improvised stage, signing their names on whatever somebody handed them. Both instant celebrities in their right. Ms. Kay would have baked for free and Old Cyrus, he was just proud as punch his mama's recipe would live forever.

*No Wade,* he told himself, *this will all change and change fast when it happens. Maybe it's time to retire. Maybe.*

"Was it dat people smuggling ting Wade?" asked Bobby Joe who sometimes called Wade "boss" just to piss him off. He saw Wade was worn out and felt no need to make matters worse.

"No, well, kind of I guess. This guy is sneaking in two families from Syria. They are cousins and could be killed over there. Wanda, with the new setup Diane installed caught them. She called me not knowing the deal was to start today at eight but Diane and I took the call. It turns out the boat, a 46 foot Viking is owned by a guy who has a business in New Jersey.

He's a stone mason and a cement finisher whose last name, get this, is "Portland." Like in Portland cement. He came from Syria over twenty years ago and changed his name from one sounding like Syria to the name on the bag of cement he used. Portland cement."

I continued, realizing Bobby Joe didn't get the (Portland connection), "We stopped the boat a few houses south of us but the asshole thought he could ram us. Diane shot out his radar unit and that put an end to his running on us. We board and find out the story and of course, nothing is that simple as there's a woman below having a baby.

"Of course, even that can't be simple. The baby has a cord wrapped around its neck and is sure to die but Diane delivered it and revived the little girl. Diane is the hero here."

"Hey, Bobby Joe. That baby wouldn't be alive today if it weren't for Wade's help," said Diane, tired but looking content. "He was great. Never flinched at all and it was a spooky deal for a while. He deserves as much credit as I seem to have gotten."

"Well," I said, "they named the new baby "Diane" after the lady who made her life here possible. And I have to wonder what the hell will happen next. All the alphabets showed up. The CIA, FBI and the rest of them including Homeland Security. The baby is a US citizen as is the captain who did an illegal act smuggling family in who would have most likely been killed had they stayed in Syria. It's a mess. All I could do is tell all of them what happened but I somehow forgot to tell them about how they tried to ram us. Those folks have enough problems without that. The captain was just scared."

"Sounds like you had some night," said Bobby Joe. "You see da weather dis morning? A big storm's comin and dey say it will hit Florida for sure in two or tree days. Gotta get ready jest in case."

"Right now, I'm ready for a few hours sleep. I didn't get maybe two hours. Leave the boat. I'll get it squared away when I get up later." I knew full well when I woke up Bobby Joe would have it ship shape and ready to go. On top of that, the first three-man crew would be here in an hour. They could get the boat washed down and set up.

I following Diane toward the house.  As we reached the garage, a yellow Corvette pulled in the driveway. Bobby Joe's client.

"I have to shower Wade. No way can I just crash."

"Would it be OK if I joined you? Just to save water and all you know. And maybe after we dry off, we can just sleep as we were before the phone call. I'm going to call Marco and have all my calls switched to him for a few hours. Then maybe we can start where we left off at two this morning. Just sleep. What do you say, Diane?"

**"Race** you to the shower."

# Mary's News

Eight hundred miles west of Flagler Beach, about five miles south of the town of Paducah, Kentucky, was a pretty home on a mini farm. In that home, Mary Connors was in bed with her neighbor, William Jennings Hastings. Mary smiled with contentment, watching Bill's penis deflating fast. And well it should. It was the second time that night they got it on. Not bad for a guy his age she thought.

Bill's legs trembled from the thrill and physical effort of the last twenty minutes of sex. He felt exhausted but masculine. He bent toward Mary who reached up and grabbed him behind his neck and pulled his face to hers, kissed him with as much passion as she'd ever felt.

When they released each other Mary said, "Oh Bill, this was incredible. I told you about Wade, the man I've seen in Flagler Beach. I've been honest with you about all of it and I did think I loved him but I know it wasn't love at all. I feel so different about you. I don't know how I'm going to tell him about you."

"You don't have to say anything about me," said Bill Hastings, slipping the condom easily off his well-deflated penis. "Just say you've have different feelings about everything. You've already told me you want to stay here with your sister and help which she will need for a few months anyhow. All of that is the truth, so you aren't lying."

Yes, yes, I will, and it's all true. I just don't know how he will take it. I mean, we got pretty close at the end. I don't know what would have happened if my sister didn't have the accident. What if he says no, I want you? What do I do then?"

"Don't put the cart before the horse, Mary. He must be a pretty smart man to have the position he has and all and I'd bet he will be able to take the news, as a man, and not get crazy. Although I can see how he could with you. Hell, I'm crazy about you, and you know it. "

"Wade is sure to call today. He didn't call yesterday and must have been busy not to call. I'll tell him the next time he calls."

Getting up and walking to the bathroom, Bill dropped the soggy condom in the commode then stood by the appliance for a good minute before he could pee. *Damned prostate he thought.* Eventually, the stream slowed to a dribble and he was done. Sliding into bed with Mary who never added any clothes to her body while he was gone, she turned on her left side while Bill spooned her with his arm around her resting his hand on her left breast. Within a minute, both were sound asleep. Tomorrow will have to wait.

# *Polo's Party Night*

In the part of Miami where even black cats fear to go out at night, a small bar sat in the corner on an old street, next to an alley littered with rotting garbage that hadn't been picked up in ages. This was the third bar Polo visited, striking out at the first two.  This bar had the name "Tecate" after the Mexican Beer of the same name. Polo sat at the bar, facing toward the door.

The old clock on the wall, stained from years of nicotine showed the time. 2:24am. Polo thought he should go home. He hated the thought of striking out. He had his mind set on a woman. Any woman of any look, nationality, culture or persuasion would do.

The "Grasshopper" was safely moored in a slip on the Miami River, in front of the safe house.  The boys were taken off the boat under cover of darkness and into a house set up by Arthur Dalton, the money man. Arthur owned the entire building, although Polo didn't know this.

A big storm was brewing. Boat traffic would shut down by tomorrow morning. The best thing to do would just sit it out a few days in Miami. The building is in an upper middle-class area, the tenants, all friends of the Money Man. They were safe as can be under the circumstances.

Earlier, Polo had taken a shower and slipped into a clean pair of jeans, then put on a Bob Marley tee-shirt that had seen better days.

He slid into his leather boots with the high heels making him look taller than he was.

"Hey man, I'm going out for a few hours," Polo said to Gus.

"Where the fuck you going man? Stay here. We can order out a couple of pizzas and have some beer and chill."

"Fuck that man," Polo said. "I need some pussy. I ain't had any pussy since I left home and man, I need it. Boys don't do it for me."

"Shit Polo, no one would ever know. You tapped every one of them more than once. You go out and it could be trouble. Hang tight man."

"Fuck it, man. I need a woman and I need it bad. I know where to get one too. See you tomorrow sometime. Just handcuff these kids if you have to."

Being smaller and older and not as tough, Gus knew he couldn't stop Polo but said, "You get busted, don't come to me."

"I ain't gonna get busted. I just want to bust my balls into some poontang man."

Sitting with his back to the wall, six shots of Jack Daniels and three tap beers in him this evening, Polo liked what he saw when the chick with the long legs and tattoos up and down each arm walked in with who Polo thought was her pimp. He didn't care. Hookers were expert at fucking and sucking although he never liked the oral shit.

The guy she was with called her Lola. She seemed to know the bartender, nodding to him as he grabbed a glass and started pouring a clear liquid to the brim. The bartender, a fat blob of jelly, didn't talk. This must be the bar she was working, Polo thought. The bartender probably gets a cut of her action. That's what they did back home.

There were five other guys in the bar and not one of them even looked at her, and she was pretty damned hot to look at. Wearing a black mini skirt with a fluorescent pink tight top covering what looked like nice tits, she stood about five nine, long slender legs all the way up to her pussy. Just the way he liked his women.

Her pimp headed for the men's room which gave Polo the chance to get up casually and saunter up to her. The Jack Daniels is kicking in now, making him sexier and bigger. How could she resist?

"Ola mama. You looking for a good time tonight? I got plenty of dinero and I got a big dick to keep you happy all night long. So what you say, mama? We party tonight?"

"Hey, fuck off man. I've been working all night and I'm off and I'm tired and I just want a drink and a good night's sleep. Alone."

It was probably the sixth Jack Daniels that did it. Polo found the courage to put his left arm around her back while his right hand went up that short mini skirt, reaching between her legs.

Hey OK. No panties and shaved as clean as a newborn baby's ass.

Lola didn't seem to like his technique which worked for him many times in the past. She tried to pull away from him, using both her hands, pushing against his chest. He knew how he could get her to calm down. He slipped his index finger in between her legs and started rubbing that slit with some vigor. That turned Lola on. Her efforts to get away doubled.

It was about that time Polo heard a click of what was unmistakably the sound of a gun safety lever. He doubted it was going to the 'safe' position. Polo, from the corner of his eye, saw the bartender reach over and turn a dial and suddenly the music, an old Johnny Cash song, Six Feet High and Rising, blasted out of speakers over the bar.

It was a sobering sound. All at once, the Doors song, "The End" popped into his head. He was about to be shot right in that grungy bar far from home and his woman. He was drunk. It wasn't his fault.

Polo froze. Not a muscle moved for a few seconds, then he released the woman slowly and took two steps back, bumping into her pimp. He heard the guy behind him say "You fucking half-breed. You're fucking with the cops asshole." No wonder nobody looked at them. They all knew.

With those words, Polo dropped to the floor as if pole axed. On his way down, he reached in his right boot and slid out a pig sticker knife, pushing the button, releasing the blade, he spun and rammed the blade into the cop pimp's groin, just as the gun went off next to his left ear. The cop screaming in pain yelled to Lola, "Shoot the motherfucker."

This is where the Jack Daniels might have helped. Partly deaf and dazed, he got to his feet in time to see the chick had a toy gun in her hand. A little Kel Tek 32 caliber pointed at him, as he ran for the door.

He heard three more shots. One clipped his left ear, the second hit his right thigh and the third he felt hit his ass cheek on the right, as he made it out the door.

"I was in dis bar, and some crazy comes in and starts shootin and I got hit trying to run out Gus. I swear."

"The ear isn't a problem but the other two, the bullets are still in you and they'll get infected. They gotta come out man. I fuckin told you to stay here."

Gus called the Money Man and a half hour later, a dark blue minivan pulled up to the complex. It would take Polo to see a private doctor and get those two bullets removed. As he hobbled out the door, Polo said, "Sorry man. Next time I listen to you."

"Right. See you soon."

An hour later, a phone call came on Gustav's private phone. It was the Money Man.

"Why did you let that asshole go off? I told you both to hang tight."

"I couldn't stop him, Mr. Dalton. I tried to talk some sense, but he didn't listen.

"In about five minutes, a guy will ring your door bell. Let him in. His name is Mario Escalante. He's a good guy. He will be completing the trip with you this time."

"OK, I got it. What about Polo? Did you send him home?"

"Oh yeah. He went home with his family."

"His wife will be glad to see him I guess." Said Gus.

"Uh, no. He's with his mother and father now."

"Oh, I thought they were dead?"

"Yeah, that's what I hear too."

## *Hurricane*

"This is going to be a helluva storm, Wade," Floyd Johnson said, over the phone. "All non-essential boat traffic on the water is terminated until further notice. Hurricane Matthew has the potential to shut down the entire east coast."

"I know the experience you just had wasn't human trafficking but it came pretty damned close. Now with the waterways closed, I thought it would be a perfect time to get the major teams together for a few days and brainstorm what we are up against."

"Sure, and make sure you have an Ob- GYN doctor to give a presentation on delivering babies." I chuckled.

"As a matter of fact Wade, we plan on just that. Or, we can save a few bucks, and you can give that lecture. I hear you did pretty good."

"Oh no, you don't. It was Diane who talked me through the whole thing. I have a strong feeling she would rather not give that lecture either," I said, sitting on the edge of my bed, my feet on the floor. The hurricane shutters were down. The room was dark. The phone I held was the biggest light source.

Diane and I managed to get four hours sleep before the phone rang, once more waking us. Diane spooned to my backside. I had my phone calls forwarded to Marco but when the director calls, Marco pushed the call to me.

Floyd said, "I decided Atlanta would be the best location for the meetings. It's far enough away from the storm yet central to all of the east coast. The airline access couldn't be better. Plus, there is plenty to do in Atlanta when you have time off. The twin Beech is sitting in the Daytona airport and will get you there in a couple of hours. Your crew will be Diane and Marco. There will be five crews total with all staying in a different hotel. You know the drill."

"Sure. How about we include Vickie, Marco's friend? I know you're smart and Marco is the perfect replacement for me. Keep him happy. You sure as hell don't want to lose him."

"There you go again. What do you want? More money? I can probably get you another five percent."

"No Floyd. I'm getting too old for this shit. One day I'll be a fraction too slow. I want out, soon." I took my left hand and gently slid it over the ass of the lady lying on her stomach next to me. "I want to enjoy life the way I am, not from a wheelchair or walking on crutches. I've done my part. You know that. Let a younger man have the reins. Marco is perfect for the job. Keep him happy. I'd bet Diane would enjoy Vickie's company too."

Floyd said, "Why don't you ask her? Oh, never mind. OK, you can tell him. I am setting it up for four nights, starting tomorrow night. Get your stuff together. The flight leaves tomorrow afternoon. I'll be in touch.  Oh, you will be staying at the Wyndham Hotel. Two rooms. The girls can share I think. Or,…whatever."

"You know they will shut the barrier islands down. We've got a lot of sensitive stuff here." I said as I continued to stroke my hand over the backside of the lady on the bed next to me.

"I know. I'm going to have a three-man crew stay at your house. How about you pick the three from the nine you have. I want one always awake. I'm also having the coast guard on alert in case it gets hairy. They can get those boys from the water if it comes to it."

"You got it, Floyd. I'll send you the names of the three guys as soon I get them picked. No married guys for this detail. I'll see you in Atlanta."

"Uh, no. You don't need me. You handle it. I'll be talking to you." The connection was broken.

"Well lady, we're going to Atlanta for a few days. Maybe we can play a round of golf. How about that?" I asked.

"As long as you're enjoying yourself playing with my ass, not that I mind, rub here on my right hip. She took my hand, guiding it to the spot on her hip she wanted massaged.  "Yes, that feels good."

Diane continued, "I saw a snip on TV yesterday. Dale Chihuly is wrapping up his fabulous glass exhibition at the Atlanta Botanical Garden this month. We have to see that."

"Chu, who??

***

It was just a friendly kiss. Nothing personal or sexual involved. Just a kiss to a very good friend, saying our first good morning in Atlanta.  My lips brushed the lips of Diane as she opened her eyes in the nearly dark room of the Windham Hotel in the northeast suburb of Atlanta, Georgia. The room had two queen size beds. We used just one. The left one, closest to the bathroom.

In our short time as lovers, both knew we wanted to sleep together. Diane discovered I was far more comfortable to sleep with than her body pillow. With Diane, my nights had me sleeping sounder than I could ever remember.

A faint light shown through the top left a corner of the room darkening drape. The light from the window overlooking the parking lot four floors below. A gas station across the street, open 24 hours, was the source.  A quick glance at my left wrist showed me it was 5:37, twenty-three minutes before I had to get out of bed

170

and get moving. I took my shower last night but needed breakfast, which was downstairs. Then a seven-mile trek through horrendous traffic. This would be my first meeting with the groups involved in human trafficking classes.

Diane headed for the shower as I turned on the TV using the remote. The scene was the east coast of Florida and Hurricane Matthew. It looked like it would be abreast of Flagler Beach by noon. I looked at my phone app on tides. Noon hour would be exactly low tide, which was as good as it could get for my area. The shower water shut off. It was time to get my ass in gear. I wondered how Bobby Joe was making out with the storm soon centered on him.

## *Evacuation*

The bright red fire rescue engine had Flagler Beach, Rescue 9, painted on its sides. As it passed slowly down the street, it blasted a very loud horn. This was followed by a fireman sitting on top of the fire truck, a bullhorn to his lips, shouting out his message.

"There is a mandatory evacuation for all the barrier islands. It is highly recommended all personnel evacuate at once. Once the wind speed reaches 55 miles an hour, all access bridges will close. You will not be able to leave, and no help will be available to you in an emergency. We expect the bridge closure in an hour or less. This is your last warning."

The wind was freshening, now forty miles per hour in gusts. So far, only intermittent showers made their way to shore, a prelude to the heavy rains expected as Hurricane Matthew worked its way north, then up the Florida east coast.

The horn sounded once more. Again, the man with the bullhorn, now half a block south, spilled out the same message. Most people in the neighborhood were gone. People are waiting in line for gas and hitting the grocery stores. Necessity items were scarce. Shelves normally holding water were empty, including the gallon jugs which made more sense than the sixteen-ounce bottles. A gallon of water for the price of two small bottles.

Bobby Joe just arrived at Wade's house. He planned on staying here all along. Wade asked him to go along to Atlanta, saying he would pay his way. Bobby Joe declined, saying he was going to stay in

Flagler Beach. He wanted to be close to the home of his girlfriend and her family.  Sharon lived a block west of the intra-coastal waterway, well off the barrier island. Sharon did ask her parents if Bobby Joe could stay with them. Her dad Hiram, went ballistic in his response NO. No way did he want that hillbilly staying with them.

It was bad enough his daughter was dating him even though he seemed polite the few times they met. The last time, just minutes ago when the tan Toyota Tacoma pulled into his driveway dropping Sharon off then politely asking him if he needed any help.

"No. I got it kid." Hiram turned his back on the two and walked away. Sharon just squeezed Bobby Joe's hand and kissed him on the cheek and watched her boyfriend drive away, back across the bridge, on the island and into harm's way.

Hiram's front porch faced east, dead into the wind now. The cabbage palm trees were shaking their fronds violently. Just then, one branch broke free and crashed into the front of the house, not ten feet from where Hiram confronted Sharon. Or was it Sharon who confronted Hiram. It wasn't quite clear.

"Dad, what harm would it do to let Bobby Joe stay here? He would have helped if it came to that. How are you going to feel if something happens to him over there?"

"He's a hillbilly, Sharon. You can do a lot better than him. How about that boy you dated, the captain of the football team. He's got a future."

"Ha, Ted. He's an octopus with hands all over me." No way would she ever admit she let him fuck her. "He's a loser. Bobby Joe will soon own Peppers restaurant, and he has a business with Wade Nash, doing fishing trips and ecological tours. He's done it all himself and he's learning so fast.  Dad, I love him. He's a perfect gentleman, not like that dork Ted Arbogast."

"Well, he ain't staying here. I don't like you seeing him. I don't care if your mama likes him. I don't," said Hiram as he picked up the loose branch and looked around. He had several trees that could put his house in danger. He was Hiram Stone. He could handle it.

Sharon helped Bobby Joe secure Pepper's restaurant. He taped the windows with duct tape in a cross manner. He wasn't sure how that helped, but everybody did it, so he did too.

Perhaps it keeps the glass, if broken, from flying in thousands of pieces? He sandbagged the bottom of the door then took a two by four piece of wood, half of a wall stud, and nailed it across the center section of the door and the other half of the same two by four across the top of the door, about six inches down.

If the wind blew the door down, all would be lost. If the winds were that strong, the entire town would be destroyed. While the wind could be a major factor, the storm surge which came with it was the real problem. If the waves went over Highway A-1-A, the damage to businesses and homes would be catastrophic.

Sharon and Bobby Joe exited through the back door. Bobby Joe piled several sandbags against the door although it made little sense to do this as the door opened inward. As they got into the truck, the wind almost ripped the truck door out of Sharon's hand. They slowly crossed the bridge seeing sawhorse barriers and rolls of tape being made ready to put in place stopping all traffic either way. The time for this was imminent.

Bobby Joe got Sharon to her house, then slowly made his way back over the bridge and back on the barrier island. He nodded at the National Guard troops starting to move barriers across the road. He guessed he was the last to cross back on the island that day.

The three and a half mile drive south on A-1-A showed a beautiful sight to his left, as huge emerald waves with frothing white tops swept on to the shore, crashing against the base of the dune supporting the highway. Beautiful, it was, but trouble was on the way.

The wind butted against the truck, trying to push it off the road.  A quarter mile farther and a wave sent a spray over the road and hit the truck, the first of many waves to breach the highway. He turned on the windshield wipers for a moment. Bobby Joe felt the highway was in danger of being destroyed. Will the homes and businesses survive? Will Sharon be OK?

# *Atlanta Respite*

Four hundred and twenty miles northwest of Flagler Beach, I walked with Diane, Vickie and Marco just as nighttime settled in on the Atlanta Botanical Garden.

The four of us, with several hundred more visitors, were looking at the stunning glass works of art, created by the master artist Dale Chihuly. The beautiful displays were placed in strategic locations along the pathway, each different and each something to remember.

I never was into art. Oh, one time the centerfold of Playboy was art to me. Later, my art appreciation expanded to a Buck deer with a twelve point rack or a Largemouth Bass, jumping, with a spoon in its mouth. I never stooped so low as to like the card playing dogs on black velvet. The past thirty or so years, a beautiful picture was five shots into the red center of a target shot at a thousand yards. Now that was beautiful.

An hour earlier, the four of us finished a fantastic dinner at a quaint Italian restaurant we discovered. Here I was, a new world opening for me and I paused my thoughts to think I should be concerned about my home.  As we rounded the corner of the path, a beautiful display perhaps twenty feet tall, glowed an amber yellow and sat on a hill.

A waterfall is flowing below the tower of glass art set off the display. Perhaps I was getting old.  The display was stunning.  I marveled at the talent it took to create this. My mind went briefly to my home and the storm once more.  There was nothing I could do.

Worry was not in my DNA at this time. Then why was I thinking of home? This was a huge storm on the way.  We walked on to see more wonders.

# Bobby Joe's Rescue

At 4:12 A.M. the power went out on the barrier island. Bobby Joe was happy his phone was fully charged.  Being conservative, he could get more than two days use before the battery would give out. He wanted to maintain contact with Sharon.

Three special op's guys were in Wade's house. Ernie, Brad, and Tim were young but very able in body and mind. They were at the age and stage of their lives they felt indestructible. They were sitting at the kitchen table playing cards, enjoying themselves when the power failed. Brad introduced them to a new card game called 2,500. Bobby Joe joined them. No betting, it was a friendly game they all loved.  A battery powered light was at hand, so the game carried on.

The full fury of Matthew hit them at 9:30 that morning. Sheets of rain flew sideways, in mini bursts. The wind exceeded one hundred miles an hour, with many gusts stronger and increasing. As the wind was from the east now, looking out the back windows, facing west, you would see shingles from homes east of them, mixed with palm fronds and assorted debris blow past them. Lucky so far, Wade's home was not hit with anything more substantial than tree branches. The homes along the intra-coastal are fifteen feet below Highway A-1-A. Being substantially lower than homes along the ocean, they escaped the worst of the heavy winds.

The rushing wind was so loud it was impossible to talk if you were outside.  All of the men took turns in pairs, checking the perimeter every hour. They would venture out during a lull.

The truck the trio came in was driven through the garage and parked on the outside of the garage on the west side. It was protected unless the roof of Wade's house was blown on it.

Bobby Joe's phone rang. The tone was the one he assigned to Sharon.

He walked away from the other three guys, then hit the button connecting the two of them. Sharon was in a total panic.

"Bobby Joe, that big Washatonian Palm tree in our front yard fell on the house. It crashed through the roof and fell into our living room. Daddy was sitting on the couch when it happened and it fell right on him. He's pinned under the thing.  We can't get him out. I called for help, but nobody is answering. Oh, Bobby, what should I do? He's in pain. I think he has a broken arm and his legs are trapped. What should I do?"

"Oh damn Sharon. You can't get through to the rescue crew? They must be swamped with calls. I'm coming. I don't know how but I'll be there. Keep your phone open. Call rescue every five minutes but don't stay on too long. I'm coming."

Bobby Joe walked back to the guys standing in the Florida room and told them what happened and what he was going to do.

"I know you guys won't like this, but I'm not part of your team. I have to try and help. My girlfriend's father is trapped in his house. A tree fell on the house. He's hurt, and he can't get out from under the tree. I gotta help. Do you guys have a chainsaw I kin use?"

"Where the hell is he?" asked Ernie.  "Bobby Joe, we can't leave here. We are under orders and could end up in the brig if we left our post."

"I know," said Bobby Joe.  "They live on da another side of the river, a block in from the water."

"Da water's almost to the top of da seawall, so I'll take da small boat and hug da shore on da east side. I'll be mostly out of da wind. When I get to where I have to cross, I kin go straight across and ride da boat up on to da land. I'll be OK.

"We have a good chainsaw. Two of them in fact. Take the smaller one, it has an 18-inch chain bar. The gas should last an hour anyhow. It's in the toolbox in the truck bed. I'll get it. You know how to use a saw?"

"Oh yeah, I bin loggin wid my brother for a few years. I'm purty handy with a saw."

While Tim got the saw from the gang box toolbox in the bed of the truck, Bobby Joe loosened the tie downs on the flats boat. The boat was so light the front end wanted to fly up as the tie straps were loosened. He tied the chainsaw to a boat rail, ensuring it would stay in the boat. Bobby Joe had Tim lower the lift. As soon as the boat floated, he fired up the fifty horse power Tohatsu two stroke motor and backed off the lift. He turned the boat heading north and hugged the east bank.

He had his life jacket on which could save him if it came to that. He was determined to get to Sharon's house and help. The Ultralight shallow water boat moved slowly over areas it would never see under normal conditions. The hurricane winds from the east pushed water into the intra-coastal, well over the banks in most places.

Gusts of wind and rain played havoc with his sight. The wind carried rain mixed with small debris, tearing into his face and hands. He had the hood of his rain jacket cinched tight, just a slit to see out. In spite of this, his eyes watered, and the shore disappeared at times.

He found that if he knelt on the floor and got the lowest profile to the wind, the boat tracked better than sitting on the seat. The violent wind ripped into him and the boat, pushing the bow toward the west. He had to fight this all the way over the three-mile journey. The normal ten-minute ride took a half hour. The three miles felt like thirty.

It was the third time the super burst of wind and rain hit, almost capsizing his boat when Bobby Joe saw the area he wanted. Turning the boat west, he made ready to across the river. He waited for a super gust to hit again. He knew it was a thousand feet to the west bank as he gave the Tohatsu full throttle. The little boat skipped over two-foot white cap waves, the bow of the bow crashing and pounding hard, all the way.

With one hundred miles per hour winds at his back, the little boat flew across the gap in no time. He had sensed the shore before he saw it as sheets of pummeling rain continued, now helping him cross the water. When he was twenty feet from shore, he killed the motor, then raised the lower unit to a nearly horizontal position. He hit the shore and felt the boat slide over wet weeds and grass, stopping thirty feet in from the shore.

In a crouch, avoiding some of the strongest wind, he grabbed the bow line and pulled the boat another twenty feet to the porch of a house. He tied the trusty shallow water boat to a deck piling. It should be safe here.

Chainsaw in hand, he cut across one street and one more, to Sharon's house. With the violent wind at his back, he stood at the front of Sharon's house in a minute. The house looked different than the day before. A huge palm tree fell through the roof and rested in the living room. The root ball looked to be the size of a Volkswagen Beetle, the tree on its side.

Bobby Joe stood by the opening where the tree crashed through the roof and wall. He called out for Sharon but was answered by her mother, Ethel Stone.

"Sharon, Bobby Joe made it. Bobby Joe, come to the back. Hurry Please. Hiram's hurting bad." Ethel shouted back.

Bobby Joe surveyed the problem. It didn't take him long to say, "Dis is one big tree and if I cut it here like it looks like it should be cut, da weight from da top will crush him. Gimme a hand. We have to shore up the base, jest below his feet. Books, magazines. Anything solid.

Sharon slid a box full of school books to him. Bobby Joe wedged them between the floor and the tree trunk, below the feet of Hiram Stone. Hiram was groaning in pain. His eyes stayed closed, until he heard the voice of Bobby Joe. A look of surprise replaced the pain.

OK Mr. Stone, I'm gonna cover yer face with a towel or a sheet to keep da shavings out of your eyes. Den I'm gonna cut the top of da tree right close to yer head. Now if I cut a little close and give you a haircut, I ain't gonna charge you for it. You understand? Ya gotta stay real still."

A groan was all the response Bobby Joe got but it was enough. One pull on the starter handle and the Stihl chainsaw with the eighteen-inch bar and the new chain, came to life. Homeland Security sure knew how to buy good tools.

In less than a minute, the sharp saw made easy work of cutting through fourteen inches of tree trunk. As it fell to the floor, it eased some of the pressure off Hiram. Hiram was fully awake as the sharp saw missed his scalp by less than an inch. Near bald was a good thing today.

"Now here's da thing Mr. Stone. I gotta reach under da log and see how much room I got between you and da log by your private parts. I ain't getting friendly you know." Bobby Joe tried to keep the serious situation light. His humor fell on deaf ears.

"Can't you just cut the damned log by my feet now?" asked a fully awake Hiram.

"No, sir. Da weight would crush you before it fell free." Bobby Joe slipped his hand between the log and Hiram's groin. He was thinking of making a joke asking if Hiram was a girl as he felt no bulge down there but thought better of it. What he did find was room enough for a comic book or two. Working hard, he managed to get just one comic book between the log and the family jewels of Hiram Stone.  It was a Superman comic from years ago.

"You sure about this Bobby Joe?" asked Hiram, now looking scared.

"Yessir. I shore am. These palm trees are full of water and dey way a ton. But they are easy to cut. You be mighty still now," said Bobby Joe

He pulled the starter rope and once more, two cycle oil smoke filled the room in spite of rain pouring through the open roof above them.

*A quarter inch maybe. That's about how thick a comic book was* Bobby Joe thought.

Hiram watched Bobby Joe come at him with the chainsaw.  What did he say to this kid yesterday? A quarter inch from making him a she. Was his dick right there? He thought so as he could feel Bobby Joe's hand brush over it, wedging the book between him and the tree. His body was getting numb now. His breathing became raspy and difficult. He was running out of time fast.

The clutch engaged with the squeeze of the throttle.  The blade dug into the log sending chips of palm trunk flying back, over both Bobby Joe and Hiram. The log was at least twenty inches thick at this point which meant Bobby Joe could only cut down so far, perhaps a third of the way through the log. Walking around the tree trunk, he then cut about three-quarter of the way through the other side then he shut the saw off.

Bobby Joe said he needed a wedge and used the blades of three butcher knives to keep the cut separated so as not to bind the saw blade.

"OK, Mr. Stone.  Here's da moment we find out if I can cut wood or just think I can. Now you be still, hear?"  Bobby Joe once more fired up the saw and started cutting this side of the log. He took his time yet kept the blade cutting slowly, watching, as best he could through the smoke from the saw and the rain pouring in.

*Bobby Joe, you kin do dis. You did this lots of times. Well, not when somebody was under da blade.* He thought to himself.

With an audience of Ethyl and Sharon, both holding their breaths, hands to their mouths, it was time to get to work.

The high pitch of the saw screamed at them as Bobby Joe guided the blade. The chisel blade removed small pieces of palm wood with each fraction of travel. The engine screamed at its maximum revolutions, doing its job. As soon as Bobby Joe saw paper chips fly out toward him, he released the throttle trigger and lifted the blade up an inch, then pulled the blade and chain bar out of the log. He shut the saw off.

Hiram was sweating profusely but one would not know with the rain falling on him. He didn't say a word. It looked like he wasn't breathing.

"Dis thing is still real heavy and I can't lift it but I kin roll it off of you. It's gonna hurt a lot for a second. Are you up to it?" asked Bobby Joe.

"Let's get er done," said Hiram, now breathing once more. "I can help." The two of them rolled the heavy log off Hiram, watching it roll a few feet across the floor coming to a stop against the door jamb.

Bobby Joe picked up the comic book, opened it and counted seven pages that were cut. Just seven pages.

"Mrs. Stone. I think yer gonna want to keep this for a souvenir to remember dis day.

Bobby Joe helped Hiram, lifting him free of the debris. Hiram had a broken right forearm. It was a clean break, the bone was not protruding from the skin. They could have waited for professional help but they had no idea when that might arrive. Hiram's pain was short-lived, as Bobby Joe set the break in Hiram's arm. He used a long wooden cooking spoon and an elastic bandage to secure the break.  Not long after, Hiram was sitting in a chair at the kitchen table.

Bobby Joe called the crew at Wade's house and gave them a quick rundown on what happened.  Ernie and Ted said they knew he could do it.  Brad claimed he was an asshole for doing such a stupid stunt, laughing the whole time. They were very impressed, he knew.

"Tell me Bobby Joe, had you cut too deep, what name should I have picked? Harriet, Helen, Honey?" Hiram asked, with a smile.

"Uh, I don't see Honey Mr. Stone. I knew I could do it. Well, I thought I could anyhow.

"Tell you what. How bout you reach over in the fridge and get us a couple of beers. They're still cold enough to enjoy.  Bobby Joe set two bottles on the table, twisting off the tops.

"I'm glad as hell you came, Bobby Joe. I don't know if I'd a made it much longer. The weight was wearing me down pretty fast. You sure got guts, young man. And a damned good eye cutting wood."

"Well sir, I jest did what I had to do. Glad it turned out good."

Raising his bottle of beer, Hiram said, "Here's to you son. I'll always be grateful, and you'll always be welcome.  I'm damned proud to have you for a friend or however this works out with you and Sharon. I sure wouldn't mind having a son like you. Welcome home, Son."

## *Trouble on the Water*

The 46 foot Grady White fishing boat was passing under the raised bridge. It towed a Zodiac inflatable boat. Connected to the two boats was a half inch Kevlar reinforced line, with a working load of three thousand pounds. The color made the flexible rope look like stainless steel cable.

As the boats approached the L.B. Knox bridge from the south, the captain of the Grady White called the bridge tender, requesting the bridge be raised, allowing him to pass.

Eddie Farver was manning the bridge this night. Wanda had a long weekend off.  He wasn't disappointed to see headlights coming toward him on the road from A-1-A.  It was Herb Moncrief.  Herb pulled ahead of the parked VW Bug belonging to Eddie.  Make it 6:37. Herb was never late for his 7:00 A.M. start.  Eddie and all the tenders always left a parking space closest to the bridge for Herb. They did this out of respect and seniority.

Herb walked in the control room with a paper sack lunch and his thermos of coffee.  Today, as usual, he carried a bag holding two donuts. One for him and one for Eddie or whoever drew duty overnight. Knowing it was Eddie this morning, the donut was a glazed sour cream, sharing space in the bag with Herb's old fashioned donut.

The sound of the warning alarm bell rang loud. The bridge started its ascent allowing the boat traveling north to pass below and move on.

"Good morning Herb. You're early.  One of these days you really will be on time, and we'll all worry," Eddie smiled, as he checked the road both ways, the bridge continuing its upward movement.

Eddie was twenty-eight years old. He was divorced for three years now, with a six year -old son, Gordon, living with his ex-wife. Eddie got to see Gordon on weekends only.  His days were crammed with homework. The bridge tender job was good but Eddie had a strong desire to be a male nurse.

Once he got that degree and some experience, he would work extra hard until he reached his ultimate goal, to be a Nurse Practitioner. Now in his third year of nursing school, Eddie's days and nights were booked to the max.

At least now, Eddie could now see the light at the end of the tunnel. He studied at Daytona University, near the famous racetrack.  He had one year remaining to get his nursing degree.  His mentor, Dr. Rob Goldman had Eddie set up with a part time job working with a friend of his, Dr. Warren Fischer, a highly regarded surgeon. Interning with Dr. Fischer was a huge benefit for Eddie and his goal. Things were working out for him lately.

It was funny too. His ex-wife was taking a lot more interest in him lately. Starting a couple of months ago, he noticed a big change in Karin. A month ago, he went to her apartment to pick up Gordon for the weekend. Instead of waiting at the door as he always did, Karin invited him in. He noticed at once the apartment was spotless, not a thing was out of place.  This was a total change of how things were when they were married.  It was Eddie who did most of the cleaning. Karin had her priorities and they didn't include housekeeping.

Two weeks ago, Karin invited him in for dinner when he brought Gordon home.  It was the first time in years the three of them shared a meal with the family he envisioned when they shared wedding vows. After the meal, as Gordon bathed and got ready for bed, he helped Karin with the dishes. Suddenly, he had a strange but warm feeling inside he hadn't felt in years. *What's this all about he wondered.*

"This guy is off to an early start huh," said Eddie to Herb, nodding to the boat passing under the raised bridge. "He must have spent the night just outside of the Tomoka Basin where it's wide enough to park without blocking the channel huh."

Herb didn't say anything. He just looked at the boat passing below them then grabbed the binoculars and stepped outside of the control room. He glanced at the bridge of the Grady White, where a slim man in his thirties held the wheel. Herb then focused his attention to the Zodiac being towed.

Herb's IQ was probably in the normal range whatever that was, but he possessed a great deal of common sense and knew something wasn't right.

"Eddie, check the sensors. What do you see?"

"I did Herb. Just two people. One at the helm and one on a bunk below, an adult from what it's reading. It looks like somebody sleeping."

"OK, now look at that Zodiac. What do you see with that?"

"Nothing Herb. She's empty."

"Now come out here and take a look at her, the Zodiac I mean. Way back when I was barely shaving, I remember a high school class that stuck, because even back then I was interested in boats. This Greek guy I think, his name was Archimedes, well, he figured out what they call the Archimedes Principal. The amount of water displaced is equal to the weight displacing it. Well, something like that anyhow."

"That Zodiac is light. About 250 pounds I'd say. Add one fifty for the motor and gas, and you're looking at something like four hundred pounds. That boat should be floating in three or four inches of water, but she's half way down the float tubes."

Herb continued, "When you pull something so light, you get slack in the tow line on and off. Ain't no slack in that tow line. That Zodiac is heavy and it's empty. Call it into the boys and have them check it out while I pour myself some coffee."

***

The near silent bell sounded from the box on the south wall of the garage. As it rang, a strobe light above the alarm box flashed a brilliant light just as I walked into my garage. I was rested after my Atlanta trip and eager for action. Three men sat on duty until eight this morning, the night shift waiting for some action regarding human trafficking. Was this it? All three jumped up, looking at Ryan who answered the phone.

The three guys making up this team were Ryan Adams, one time a Navy Seal. Chet Puller, a Marine Force Recon man and Fred Dalyrimple, Freddie D. Another Navy Seal. Everybody gave Chet shit about his name.

Everybody called him Chesty Puller, the most decorated Marine in history. With the last name Puller and his father a lifetime Marine, it was inevitable they would name their first born "Chester" even though Chesty was not the first name of the great General.

Getting off the phone, Ryan relayed the messaged Herb passed. They all respected Herb's word because of his reputation and he took this task seriously.

"I'm going with you boys," I said. "Let's Roll." A statement made famous some time ago.

Punching in a four number code on the safe in the garage, Wade grabbed his duty belt which held his sidearm and other necessities. He trotted out to his Hurricane deck boat, already holding the three man crew. In less than a minute, the deck boat backed off the lift and headed south, already seeing the Grady White coming toward them. I drove and pushed the throttle forward. The Hurricane easily jumped on plane.

189

"Herb said there seemed to be only two people on board. One on the bridge at the controls and another below deck and looks to be sleeping," said Ryan who took the call. "His concern is the Zodiac. It's half submerged and sinking or something is weighing it down a lot. He thinks there could be something hidden in the float tubes."

"Hit the lights, boys. I'll hail her," I said as I grabbed the bullhorn. My voice amplified, I shouted, "Grady White, shut down your engines. This is Homeland Security. Prepare to be boarded."

Sounds carry much farther on water than land. I was sure some of the nearby homes would hear me. I probably woke up more than just a few people. Complaints were sure to follow but it couldn't be helped.

What surprised me was some neighbors had little or no interest in what was going on in their back yard.

As he watched the smaller boat coming toward him off his port bow, the Captain thought he had a choice. He chose to run for it. If he could ram the small boat, he could get up the river far enough to get Sergio into the Zodiac. Sergio could hide in the mangrove swamps that lined both sides of the main channel. He couldn't outrun Homeland Security but he could say he thought he was being hijacked. With his broken English, he thought he could get away with this. Getting caught with the Zodiac was not an option.

There were four of us on board. The added weight had my boat acting sluggish in its turns. I saw the big boat aim for us, so I hit the throttle and turned right. The added weight had us a fraction slow. The larger vessel hit our stern a glancing blow. The collision was enough to knock all of us off balance.

"That son of a bitch tried to ram us, boys," said Freddie D. "Let's see if our new toy works." Fred picked up a black tube that looked to be about four feet long and about four inches in diameter. It was an experimental prototype of which they had just two.

The idea was to get behind the pursued boat, to about three hundred feet.  Arm the weapon and shoot it at the stern but behind it several feet. The weapon resembled a bazooka and stayed with the shooter but an inner tube would be discharged and track the boat ahead. Sonar would guide it and when in range, that tube would trigger and discharge a multitude of thin very tough line and entangle in the drive and propeller of the target.

The line, a quarter of an inch thick was ten times stronger than steel. Once tangled in the prop, it would wreck the transmission drive unit, shutting down the boat. It should do no harm to people on board which was a critical consideration.

I swung the Hurricane around and soon was at the optimum distance from the bigger boat. Freddie had the experimental weapon locked on, a tonal beep coming from within the unit.

He fired the weapon as they all watched. Exactly as advertised, the inner tube quickly overtook the big boat.  Five seconds later, the sound of metal grinding and popping was heard. The bigger boat fell off plane and veered to the left. It appeared the side of the dual drive was now inoperable. Score one for the good guys.

The Captain of the Grady White slowed down to a near stop.  He already gave orders to Sergio. As soon as they were slow enough, Sergio was to slip over the right side of the big boat, away from the pursuers, slide below the surface of the water until the Zodiac was upon him. As the Zodiac passed, he was to grab on to the side and pull himself in, then cut the Zodiac loose and haul ass out of there. If luck were on their side, they would meet up later.

I kept our boat half way between the big boat and the Zodiac. The big boat angled toward the east shore, slowing to a crawl. The left engine was shut down.

"I saw somebody get in the water on the other side," said Chet. "He went under as soon as he hit the water."

"Go get em Chesty, said Ryan, his partner, followed by Freddie D chiming in.

"Let's see what you're made of Jarhead."

"Hey assholes, you guys are Seals. That's your specialty. You get him. I spotted him you blind bastards."

"Aw, come on Chesty. Can't you swim? You want some water wings?" Ryan chided.

"Fuck you. Both of you assholes." Chet dropped his belt holding his sidearm, and other gear then took his trusty K-Bar knife made popular during the second world war by the Marines. He slipped it in its sheath, under his belt behind his back.

Sliding out of the deck boat, he slid under the surface and stroked toward the Zodiac. The water was cooling down this time of the year but still far warmer than water in his stint in Alaska last year. It had a fishy smell here, the salt water burned his eyes as he swam.

In less than a minute, Chet was next to the Zodiac on the port or river side, then easily pulled himself into the small boat, keeping a low profile going over the top. He lay silent on the aluminum floor. His hunch paid off as less than a minute later, a hand and then an arm came over the right side. They pulled a body behind it into the boat. The intruder landed next to Chesty Puller.

"Howdy Partner. Nice to meet you," said Chesty. The new arrival looked in shock for a second or two, then decided to kick Chet in the groin. Chet turned his body a fraction before the kick landed, catching the blow on his upper thigh. As both men were wet, the kick had little power, but it did piss Chesty off.

"See here. I try and be nice to you and look what you've done." Chet backhanded the intruder on his mouth, splitting his lower lip. Blood flowed instantly, running down his chin.

Chet glanced at the big boat, seeing his two partners board her. Nobody was going anyplace soon.

Chet looked at the guy next to him, thinking, should he handcuff him or cuff him around a bit. Before he could decide, the fool came up with a knife. It wasn't a bad knife. It had a four-inch blade with a decent handle, but it was no match for Chet's K bar which he slid out of its scabbard.

Sergio lunged at Chet. Going high, for his neck. Chet didn't want to kill the guy, but he also didn't want to get stabbed. His left hand deflected the guy's knife arm while he took his K-Bar, raised it over his head for an instant, feigning a left jab keeping Sergio's eyes on that hand. He plunged his K-Bar in the top of Sergio's left foot, completely through his foot, pinning him to the aluminum floor of the Zodiac. The knife went deep into the quarter inch aluminum floor of the boat, holding the intruder in place.

Sergio's scream pierced the early morning. A flock of white Ibis birds took flight from the mangroves behind them. The scream got louder when Chet took Sergio's right arm, which still held the knife and tore the arm out of his shoulder socket. His scream sounded like an animal being killed by a predator. A good doctor would set it back in place for him but until then, it was awfully painful. He wondered if the dirty water along the shore would cause Sergio to get an infection. Then he wondered why he even thought of that.

# Boat Contents

The following day, Diane and I walked into this huge building that once was the birthplace of many large ships now roaming the waters of the world. The building was in the Hammock, on the intracoastal, abandoned for several years, now rented for our work. We were going out to dinner shortly with my boss, Floyd, who was in town. Thus the occasion for our somewhat fancy dress.

Diane wore a stunning top. A silk-like material, the color purple, her favorite color. The style was three-quarter sleeves, slit from her shoulder to her elbow. Her skirt was black and tight, very sexy. Me, I had on khaki dress shorts with a bright green fishing style shirt that was pressed. Almost my maximum dress.

Eric Clapton's voice blared over two huge speakers hanging from the rafters of the giant shipbuilding facility. His voice backed by twangy guitars, he sang:

"If you want to hang out, you've got to take her out, Cocaine".
"If you want to get down, get down on the ground, Cocaine,"
"She don't lie, she don't lie, she don't lie, Cocaine."

The metal building had been vacant for several years. Weeds grew around the foundation. The building was just over two hundred feet long and open at both ends. It had a metal roof with metal panel sides, now rusting to where a coat of paint was no longer an option. The steel beam structure was solid, making it a perfect place for what we needed. A place to take apart boats and look for contraband.

"Hi, Ted," I said, shaking the hand of a friend I had known for years. Ted Sizemore was near my age and was once a naval officer. He held the rank of Lieutenant Commander, pulling the pin after twenty years. An Annapolis grad in nautical engineering, Ted loved his work which had him move many times in his career. His wife was tired of the constant moves and very vocal about it. As is often the case, Ted had to make a decision, hang up the career he loved or go it alone without Carrie, his wife of seventeen years. He chose Carrie.

I looked back at what I knew of Ted. After his military time, Ted worked in Baltimore for three years as an engineer, building ships. He enjoyed the work but missed his naval career. It was Christmas Eve. Ted enjoyed a gathering of the staff with a little party his boss held. Business was good and today was the day bonuses were given out.

Ted was happy to see his bonus this year, a very substantial twelve thousand dollars. He couldn't wait to see the look on Carrie's face. Now he could trade up her Pontiac for a Buick or maybe even a Cadillac. That would make her happy, he thought. He hoped.

The surprise was on Ted when he got home that day, one cocktail in him and a very nice check in his pocket. He walked into an empty house with a letter on the table. Not so much of a letter, more a note.

Ted:

I've had all I can take. I'm out of here. By the time you read this; I will be well on my way to Hawaii with a friend I met in my Art class, John Sizzle. Yes, a funny last name but he makes me sizzle. Something you never could do. All I want is half of everything. I'm entitled to that after living with you for so long. My lawyer will contact you.

Carrie.

He hung his coat in the closet, then sat down and read the note again and then once more. The words didn't change. The rational side came out as he picked up the phone and called Charlie Walker, his boss.

"Charlie, Ted here. What a great bonus. Thank you very much.

"You earned it Ted. Every penny. I'm glad I could get that to you. Thank you for your dedication and helping us grow."

"You are very welcome sir. Now, I'd like to ask you for a big favor. Can you take that bonus back and give it to me next year?"

Ted went on to explain the reason for the request. The conversation soon ended. Ted looked once more at the check then tore it up. This amount would be added to next year's bonus.  He had to get cleaned up. He was meeting an old friend for a Christmas Eve dinner in two hours. It will be good to see Wade Nash and his lovely wife Catherine again.

That was a long time ago. Ted eventually started his own business working on ships.  He specialized in troubleshooting problems others could not fix. Many people were buying boats from China. It wasn't that they were badly assembled, they were not as stable as boats built elsewhere.

Most Chinese builders used rocks for ballast. Rocks had a tendency to shift, causing the boats to ride and handle poorly.  The boat hull had to be separated, and the ballasts corrected. The "cheap boats" weren't so cheap after all.

It was a good business for Ted. It was Wade who suggested Ted for the job at hand. A fill in for Ted and his company and a way to reunite with the government.  Sometimes friends can help friends and it's beneficial to both parties.

I introduced Diane to Ted who led the way saying "You got to see this." Ted walked them toward the back of the building.

Stacked on the catwalk in bricks approximately six inches thick, a foot wide and about eight inches deep, each brick wrapped in a different color visqueen film, the pile was probably eight feet long and three feet tall. The vivid colors made the pile look festive.

"You are looking at a rainbow of three hundred pounds of high-quality cocaine. The DEA are here and weighed and tested the stuff already and sent for a pick up." Ted said smiling a huge smile. "You boys did fine. The tester of the stuff said it had a street value of about eight to ten million bucks. Now it's off the street. I hear it was a bridge tender that spotted the possibility with the Zodiac. This was in the float tubes, sealed up just like factory new."

"That's our Herbie," I said, looking at the pile of broken dreams. "Herb is one of a kind."

"If he ever wants a job, have him give me a call. I know I can get him on with one of the alphabet agencies." Ted said.

"Nah, that won't happen. Herb is like me but a little older. We've both had enough of this life. I'm ready to pull the pin. I've found me this lady here who just does it all for me," as I slipped his arm around Diane. "I never looked, but life found out I was hiding and sent me Diane" Who at this point found interest in her shoes, blushing, and smiling.

"I know what you mean buddy," Ted said, with an ear to ear smile. "You remember back a long time ago when Carrie left me. What you and Catherine said to me? God works in mysterious ways. He sure does."

"I found my April on the side of the road," Ted spoke to both of us but looked at Diane." It was a rainy late March day. She had a flat tire in not the best neighborhood, so I just stopped to help. Nineteen years later, our adopted daughter Soo Lin is graduating from Harvard. We couldn't have children of our own. Not that it matters, but it was me, not April. I was working on Chinese boats and we adopted Soo Lin. Back then, the Chinese were killing baby girls. What a joy she brought to our lives.

Diane smiled and felt the warmth Ted generated telling his story to them. She would have liked to tell Ted how she felt about Wade. A story she wanted to be with in him every waking moment. To go to sleep with him at her side. Wake up in the middle of the night and have to remove his arm from around her with reluctance as she used the bathroom. To return and put her arm around him, feeling so much love between the two of them. She had no idea how this love thing happened but she was so glad it did.

# *Dreamer*

As it happened many times before, just before dawn, Wade woke up trembling and in a total sweat. His side of the bed was wet with his nightmare sweats. The nightmare was back. It had been a while since he had that terrible dream. Long enough he thought it was gone forever. This time, the dream went deeper.

Wade was on a mission. The point man for his unit. In charge of the mission, Captain Nash always took the point. On point was the most difficult job as one had to be virtually invisible. If he was spotted, the mission was a bust and the possibility that several of his unit would be in grave danger ran high.

Wade just dispatched a guard in front of the building they planned on entering and securing before its contents were taken or destroyed. Word was the building was fixed to explode if breached. This would not only destroy all the critical data they wanted but would kill or maim many in his unit.  There was nobody better than him for this mission.

They were within moments of entering the only door when a woman walked out, holding an infant in her arms. One scream from her and it was all over. Wade drew his side arm. A 9 millimeter Heckler and Koch with the long tube silencer on the barrel. He aimed his handgun. This is where his nightmare always ended. Not this time.

"Wade, are you all right?" Diane asked. She sat up and saw him, eyes clenched tight, his lips in a grimace, two fists on his face, trying to chase away the demons.

He didn't hear her. He was in another place and time. In a world he hated.

Wade took careful aim in the fraction of a moment he had. It was the woman's life or the mission. Her life or the lives of several of his men, probably his life too. An infant. Was the baby real? Yes, it made a noise as it began to suckle his mother. It was two lives against how many. This wasn't like shooting rats in the Chicago garbage dump with his dad where he learned to shoot.

He could shoot well enough. He could clip the nose of a scampering rat, or shoot its tail off. Then follow up with a killing shot. No, this was a human life. Two of them. He aimed. He had no choice.  And he fired.

# *Sailboat in a Storm*

Dark rolling thunderheads, spit flashes of lightning. This was followed closely by the deep baritone booms associated with storms like this. The storm was catching up to the sailboat heading north.

The boat approached the bridge Gus was anticipating. Central Florida had its share of storms off the ocean. The most typical and strongest thunderstorms came from the west, over the peninsula, building up all day in the heat and humidity. This storm was more than welcome as Gustav Fletcher watched his radar screen in front of him.

Gus was happy to see the storm at this time as he would soon cross the L.B. Knox Bridge just a mile ahead of him this afternoon. About this time yesterday, Gus got a call from a member of the group telling him this bridge had been set up with special detection devices to pick up people hiding inside the boats. What they had was the very latest in personnel detection devices. The money man had a lot of good inside connections getting this information.

Gus called Mario topside with a yell down the hatch to come up for a minute. Mario proved to be a good hand, spelling Gus for breaks now and then. He had no interest in those boys in a sexual way which seemed to put the boys at ease and calmed them down. The only negative about Mario was his incessant talk of his conquests with women and the sex they had.

It was like he invented sex. He would pick up girls and have sex with them. For many, it would be their first time. He was drop dead gorgeous to look at and had a charm most females could not resist. Once he had them, he would then turn them over to others to be part of the sex trade. It was just sex.  He never induced drugs at all. He never had to.

Mario bragged about his specialty for the company. The girls made a lot of money for the business. He picked up very young girls whenever he could.  His favorite being fourteen to sixteen-year-old kids. He even said proudly he had one girl who was just eleven and just had her first menstrual cycle. The younger they were, the more they were worth, although girls in their late teens seemed to be the easiest to acquire. Most had no idea what they were getting into until it was too late.

Gus said to Mario, "In a few minutes, we're going to go around a little curve up here and be at that bridge we talked about last night. This is the bridge with those special cameras. What I want you to do is get those boys in the front V bunk and cover them with that special heavy blanket that has the metal sewn into it. You can just sit at the table and make sure they stay quiet, under that blanket."

"OK, Gus. This storm is gonna hit hard any minute. Can you smell it in the air?"

A flash, followed by a boom exploded seconds later. The storm was close.

"Yeah, and it's a good thing for us. The rain will cool down the whole boat, and those fancy cameras won't pick up a thing. We're lucky."

Mario slipped below just as the boat rounded the curve in the waterway. Gus picked up the phone to hail the bridge tender of his arrival and request to pass. One was always nice to the bridge tender lest they have you sit for a long time for reasons that made no sense.

"OK boys," Mario said, "Here's what we have to do for a little while. All of you have to get up in that front bunk and I have to cover you with a special blanket. It's only for five minutes maybe. No big deal. Come on now, hop up there."

In the four days ride up from Miami, the boys got to where they trusted Mario when they found out he had no intention of tying them over that table and doing those cruel things to them, making them cry and want to die. Two of the boys shook their heads in acceptance, mumbled something to the other three.

They all climbed into the forward bunk. The bridge horn and bell sounded as the bridge started its ascent. Mario covered the boys with that special heavy blanket just as the first drops of rain hit the roof above them. The first few drops were unusually big were hitting the skylights with loud pings.

Gus timed the approaching storm but was off by a couple of minutes. The storm was slow. The bridge opened fully, the bell chime stopped ringing and the tender told Gus to pass. Gus just sat still for a minute until the tender asked if something was wrong. Gus answered he was having trouble getting the boat in gear. The shift lever was stuck. He would have the linkage checked that evening.

"I'll give you a minute buddy then I have to drop the bridge. I've got cars backing up here," Herb responded.

Gus waited another thirty seconds then had no choice but to slip the transmission into forward and nudged the throttle. It was just enough of a delay to allow the storm to catch them. Waves of water washed over the boat, making it almost impossible to see, in spite of the windshield wiper moving full speed. Gus was one happy man.

The problem started because one of the boys in the forward bunk was claustrophobic. With the heavy blanket over his head, he started to hyperventilate. He never could take something over his head. He had to get out from under that blanket, throwing the blanket on the deck.

Mario yelled at him and quickly threw the blanket back over the boys, only to have the same boy, the quiet one they called Abbas, throw the blanket off again, and climb out of the bunk.

Frustrated, Mario was fighting a little kid and got angry and slapped Abbas hard on his left cheek.  The loud snap heard clearly by the other boys, reminding them to behave. Instead of calming down, Abbas went into a frenzy and started kicking and punching anything in sight, including some of the other boys who jumped out of the bunk trying to get away from Abbas.

*Mario, you stupid ass. You should have let that quiet one stay next to you at the table. Nobody would have thought two below was unusual. He thought to himself.*

Mario quickly got the other four boys back on the bunk and covered with the blanket just as the boat passed through the bridge fenders. All he could do was hope he was fast enough.

In the bridge control room, Herb Moncrief watched the sensors that were quiet. They picked up no unusual heat sources.  As the boat slid by below him, Herb watched the TV monitor and noticed the front V bunk.  While it had no heat indicator, the area was moving. He could see what looked like something under some cover.

Soon, that part of the boat was past and the remainder of the boat appeared to be normal. Something about that movement bothered him. Should he call it in? Hell, he was off in a half hour or so and if those boys went out in this weather and found out it was a dog under the bunk or something like that, he'd be in for a lot of grief. But then again, he was off soon. Picking up the phone, he pressed the red button connecting him to the phone in Wade's garage. It was picked up on the first ring.

***

"Wade, Ryan Adams here. We got a call from Herb about a suspicious activity he thought he saw on a sailboat, so we ran out and stopped the thing just down the river in front of the townhouses. The boat didn't want to stop until we shot a flare across the bow."

"The captain doesn't speak English I guess and when we told him we were going to board his boat, another guy comes out from down below and fires a shotgun up in the air, yelling he'd kill the kids if we got any closer."

"I just now pulled in my drive from a meeting with the bosses who want to know why nothing is happening.  Who did you call Ryan?"

"This just happened. Just you. What do you want us to do? The guy that shot the gun said he would kill the kids if we got any closer. Who do you want me to call?"

"Huh, are they in Volusia or Flagler County?" I am talking more to myself.  "Call both counties and tell them to get their asses out there but stay a couple of hundred yards away from the boat. And keep those damned news people the hell away from there. Diane is with me and she speaks a few languages.

Maybe she can talk to the captain. I'm going to jump in my fishing boat and be there in five minutes."

Jumping out of the car, Diane said, "Wade, while you're getting the boat ready, I gotta pee real bad. I drank way too much coffee listening to our bosses bitch we weren't doing any good. Grab my belt with yours."

It wasn't five minutes before the skinny water fishing boat was on the scene. I nudged the little boat next to the bigger deck boat and tied the two together. We had no time for bumpers to separate the two boats. Hearing the story again and who Ryan called, I could hear a helicopter overhead. It couldn't be, I thought as I looked up and saw a big number "2" on the side of the chopper. The news was here.

With the deck boat no more than thirty feet from the sailboat, Diane called over to the captain who said he spoke no English. Just Portuguese. So, Diane answered in Portuguese.

With Diane's answer in that language, the stunned captain started speaking English, knowing he could not get away with the plan he had in the back of his mind since starting this trip.

Diane said, "Captain, if you have children on board and any of them get hurt, it will not go well for you or your partner. If one of them is killed, Florida has the death penalty, and I can assure you, Stark prison is not the place you want to spend the final days of your life."

In the background, several boats could be heard coming on the scene.  The shore on the east had several armed officers running between the townhouses to the river's edge.

"Let me try please," said Gus to Diane and then called down to Mario. "Mario, it's over. We got caught. You heard them. If one of those kids gets hurt, we will be in worse shape than just giving them a free ride to freedom." Hoping Mario would get what he was saying to him.

This was not human trafficking, just being a good friend to kids that want freedom. Polo abused those kids. Well, he did too but not as much.

"Do you know what they will do to me in prison, Gus?" I'll be bent over a bench ten times a night if not more. I can't do that Gus. They gotta let me go or I'll kill these kids and then I'll kill myself.  Tell them that Gus." Mario said with a trembling voice, almost tears in his words.

Diane and I listened then she said; "Gus, you seem like a smart man. Let us tie up to your boat and you come on board here with us.  We will see about your partner. What do you say? You don't want any part of hurting somebody, do you?"

Gus was smart enough to know he was knee deep in shit no matter what, yet it would be a lot worse if Mario killed a kid or a cop,

"Listen, I'll cooperate with you but you got to put it on my arrest sheet that I did cooperate. I don't want to hurt anybody."
Gus climbed aboard the deck boat as I called in the Flagler sheriff, asking him to come alongside and take Gus from us in five minutes. That was all it would take to get the lowdown on what we faced. I wanted Gus close for now.

"It'll be dark in a couple of hours. I'd sure like to get this wrapped up before then," I said. "Chet and I will go aboard and see if we can't talk some sense into him."

"You will like hell," Diane burst out. "Don't start this crap now Wade. We are equal partners in this. You sit here and I'll go with Chet or Ryan or Fred."

"This is dangerous Diane. Things have changed and you know it."

"I do know it. Either we go together or neither of us goes. What's it going to be?"

Diane grabbed the rail of the sailboat and vaulted on the deck, then drew her gun and looked down at me. I think I had a look between shocked and shook up.

"Come on up Wade. I got you covered."

A quick vault had me next to Diane, feeling like I wanted to strangle her but maybe kiss her first. Damned love. What's love got to do with it? So sang Tina Turner. Everything.

Not waiting for advice, Diane walked closer to the hatch leading down to the cabin below and called out, "Mario, my name is Diane Mason. I'm a cop,, and I'll tell you, the last thing I want is for anybody to get hurt here. So far, nobody's been hurt. If you are giving those kids a ride to freedom, you still broke the law, but that isn't so bad. Not as bad as hurting somebody. Come on out to where I can see you and talk to you? How about it Mario?"

"Lady, you know damned well these kids didn't ask for a free ride. I know it's prison time for me, and for a long time. I can't go to prison. It's that simple."

"Stark is a son of a bitch but if you cooperate, I think we can get you to Raiford which isn't nearly as bad.  You probably won't get a long sentence if you cooperate. How about it Mario?"

"I'll tell you what lady. How about you come down, unarmed and we talk. How about that huh. You want me to trust you, how about you trust me."

"No way Diane," I said. "He could be some loon and take you out just for the hell of it. I'll go."

"He said me, Wade. I'll take my 9 and tuck it under my vest. My holster will be empty and he won't know. If he kills me, big guy, this thing between us just wasn't meant to be but I just damned well know I'm gonna be OK and give your ass a hard time for lots of years to come. I'd kiss you but it would be on national TV before we broke apart. Love you, darling. It's me."

"We gotta try and save those kids. If we don't at least try, we will regret it forever. You know that too."

There are five steps down the hatch ladder to the cabin below. When Diane was at number four, just one to go, she got a good look at the cabin.

There were kids up front in on the V birth and one kid sitting at the table. As there was five kids total, that made four in the front birth. Diane called up to me, relating what she saw.

Standing on the other side of the cabin stood this drop dead handsome guy, smiling at her with something in his hand that she knew was not a gun. It was far more lethal at that moment.

It was one of those long nose lighters one uses to light a furnace or a camping stove or maybe some scented candles. The scent she smelled was LP gas. LP settles low to the ground and builds up higher which is why she didn't smell it until that last step. Looking down to her right, she saw a five gallon LP gas tank with a sister one next to it. Both valves open, pouring the pungent odor of rotten eggs, LP gas odor, filling the room.

"This is how it's gonna end lady," smiled Mario. "Do you know what they'll do to me in prison? The way I look? I can't take that. I'd rather die. I was good to these kids. I didn't do anything bad to them. This isn't what I do for the company, but I'll get the blame. I can't do that."

With those words, he pulled the trigger on the lighter. Diane saw the flame, turned her face away and did her best to tuck her face under her left arm pit as the explosion flared up violently. The LP gas didn't have time to fill the room, or the explosion would have ended the lives of all at that moment.

Ingesting flames will sear the lungs inside which cuts off all oxygen flow. If you don't burn to death, you suffocate. Diane held her breath as she tucked her face under her arm and only took a breath after she climbed three steps and yelled at me to break the front skylight and get those kids out and then slid back down the steps to a flaming inferno below.

When the gas exploded, I had my face over the hatch and caught a face full of LP flames but only for a second or two. The force of the blast pushed me back a step, saving me from more damage.

I yelled for help then ran to the bow of the ship. I used the heel of my right foot and I smashed the Plexiglas hatch. I then reached down and grabbed the metal lined blanket that saved those boys lives and pulled it off of them, dropping it into the cabin. I looked at four pairs of petrified eyes. I grabbed the nearest boy and hoisted him through the hatch as smoke billowed out with the child. By now, Fred was by my side. The two of us snatched all four boys through that hatch in just seconds. The fire's intensity increased rapidly. The Sheriff's boat just left, taking a handcuffed Gustav Fletcher into custody as the four boys were transferred over to the deck boat and safety. Ryan flipping each boy through the air to Chesty, who sat them on the bow cushions.

The original blast set the curtains and bedding and other items on fire. The cabin was full of smoke until Wade kicked in the skylight which vented much of the smoke hanging below the ceiling. Diane could see Mario lying on the floor where he stood when he struck the lighter. The other boy was lying face down on the table showing no signs of life. When Wade kicked the skylight out, the smoke cleared a great deal but the draft increased the fire tenfold as now it started burning intensely.

Diane thought she had but one chance and ran as fast as she could to the front of the cabin, grabbed that very heavy blanket and threw it over the boy at the table.

She then picked him up and carried him back to the ladder to take him up and out of the blazing interior. All of the sudden, the intense heat and smoke started to overwhelm her. She suddenly had doubts she could save herself let alone get this kid out of here. This feeling was a shock to her. She was always tougher than any assignment.

She barely got to the ladder when she saw me hump down the hatchway. Seeing what was happening, I grabbed the boy and threw him up the ladder and half way out of the opening where Fred Dalrymple was waiting. He grabbed the boy and ran with him to the Hurricane deck boat to an anxious Chester Puller and Ryan Adams.

"Let's go, Diane," I said, my right hand under her left arm.

"One more Wade. We've got to try and save the son of a bitch." She was fighting for breath, her lungs choked with foul smoke. Her strength fading.

"OK, I'll go. Please, please get the hell up this ladder before I have to knock you out and drag you up myself. You're done. You'll never make it. Get out of here. Please baby."

Fred was back and helped Diane out of the hatch. He half carried her to the side of the boat and on the Hurricane deck boat where Ryan and Chesty grabbed her and lifted her on board. They settled her on the front lounge of the deck boat, next to the boy she just saved.

Tears ran down her cheeks, leaving wet trails through soot crusted skin. She gasped for clean air into her lungs, filled with fire burnt soot. The Coast Guard showed up and had a tank of oxygen. She shared her mask with the boy she pulled out of the fire. Soon, that boy clung to her like his life depended on her.

It wasn't more than thirty seconds before I asked Fred to grab the guy on my shoulder and get the two of us out of the blast furnace. All the while, Diane prayed a silent prayer that was answered when she saw a beaten man that minutes before looked like her Wade Nash. Now, his short hair much shorter with a fire-induced haircut and smudges of soot making him look more like a Halloween costume than the man she loved.

If Diane could look in a mirror, her short hair was curly on the ends where the fire touched it. Her complexion, under the soot, looked like she sat in the sun far too long without any protective cream. She showed blisters on her cheek and the backs of both hands.

Mario Escalante was just coming around when they transferred him to the Hurricane deck boat. They quickly untied from the sailboat and pulled away, just as the mast of the once beautiful sailboat lit up like a tall candle, burning all the way to the light on top. They weren't a hundred yards away when the diesel fuel ignited. Just then, the fire boat arrived and went into action. Streams of water soon had the flames out, but smoldering.

Groaning, his face a mass of blisters as were his hands and legs, Mario was in terrible pain. Kneeling down in front of him, Diane looked at him and said, "Well, the least you can do is say thank you for saving your life, Mario."

"Why? Why didn't you let me die?"

"Oh no, no, no. I want you to share all the good times you will have in our prison system, Mario. Ah, but don't worry. You don't look so pretty now. I bet Bubba will find that nice ass just as pretty as before." Mario shrunk back in horror.

"No Mario. You were worth saving. Look above you. See those helicopters? You'll make all the news stations tonight. You'll be a Hollywood celebrity when you make the big jail. I can't wait to see the fun you'll have you piece of shit."

Moving to the back of the boat, Diane sat next to me and said, "We gotta talk big guy. This was too damned close. I think I'm gonna pull the pin soon too. What do you say? Oh, are you ever going to buy me a ring and make me a legal person or we just going to shack up forever?"

Through cracked lips and a burn on the top of my left hand, the tips of my fingers just touched Diane's right hand tenderly and I said "Oh yeah sweetheart. This is it. After the job is done. We aren't done yet. We have to find out the source and cut the head off the snake. Then I'll make you a legal woman and we can move on to the life we both deserve. Just a little more to go, honey. Stick with me.

Smiling, Diane knew she would go through hell if she had to just to be with her man. *Let's go snake hunting she thought.*

## *Meeting Abbas*

Flagler Florida hospital is located off state road 100, a quarter mile west of Interstate 95. Traffic at the hospital slowed down just before five P.M., dinner time. Today was a bit of an exception as a steady stream of emergency vehicles and police cars drove under the new canopy at the emergency entrance. The hospital had new construction on the west end. The relatively new hospital was gaining several much-needed beds.

Three emergency vehicles pulled under the canopy within minutes of each other. The first ambulance held Mario Escalante, a burn victim. Mario had the most significant burns. His face showed the most damage with second and third-degree blisters all over his once pretty face. Both his hands and arms had second-degree damage. The pretty boy would be pretty no more. His days of picking up teens and pretty girls would be a challenge after today.

That challenge would likely be far down the line after prison time he would see. The charges of transporting humans and a participant in human trafficking would be enough to send him away for a long time. Adding attempted murder to the charge would insure Mario would be an old man before he had a chance to see freedom. In the bus with Mario were two armed guards, even though Mario was in no condition to offer any resistance. As soon as the ambulance stopped, Mario was whisked into the emergency room, his two guards by his side

The next ambulance three minutes later held Diane and the boy. As soon as Diane got on to Wade's Hurricane deck boat, the boy clung to Diane like his very life depended on her. She did save him on the burning boat, covering his frail body with the heavy blanket, and carried him to the hatch. The boy suffered minor first and second-degree burns on his hands and arms while his hair was singed short on the right side of his head. His face resembled someone who spent far too much time in the sun without sunscreen.

His thin, dirty arms clung tightly to Diane. He continued to hold tight all the way to the hospital. They were transferred to wheelchairs and pushed into the emergency room, side by side. His left hand squeezed Diane's right hand with a force she was surprised he had.

The third vehicle to arrive was the Fire Chief's Suburban with Chief Duane Rawlings driving, Wade, in the passenger's seat. Wade held a portable oxygen mask over his face, not too unlike what one might see on an airline demonstration. Sucking in the oxygen during the ten-minute ride to the hospital had Wade feeling much better.

He had what appeared to be another case of severe sunburn on his face. His right hand had second-degree blisters on the back. Wade replayed the memory of the past hour and felt truly lucky how things turned out as well as they did as it could have been far worse.

Mario suffered the worst burns because Liquid Propane gas settles low, close to the floor, then builds higher with additional gas added. The explosion knocked the slightly built Mario to the deck where the greatest concentration of LP was heaviest. He had two IV tubes dripping medicating fluids into him. The pain meds were working. The hospital was notified in advance of burn patients coming in and called in Dr. John Longton, a dermatologist. Dr.Longton arrived at the hospital as Mario was wheeled into room three.

The two wheelchairs occupied by Diane and the boy sat in room four. The smell of an antiseptic surrounded them, masking the scent of burnt hair and skin. Bright lights lit the pale green room. A young male orderly and a female nurse struggled to pry the slim fingers of the lad from Diane's hand he squeezed.

They carried him to the bed, in the room, with him fighting all the way. The nurse said they would have to restrain him with straps but before they could, he jumped off the bed, escaped the orderly, and lept into Diane's lap.

Animal like sounds was came from him, with a grunting uh ha uh ha over and over as he wrapped his little body around Diane who held him tight. She told him over and over he would be all right. She watched streams of tears fall from his eyes, leaving streaks down both cheeks of his dirty face.

Diane asked the staff just to leave him and let him calm down for a few minutes. It would be difficult to treat Diane with the boy clinging to her and yet, that is just what they did.

Dr. Longton stepped into the room and gave a quick cursory exam to both Diane and the boy. He gave instructions to the staff on how to move forward with the treatment for both.

Speaking to Diane he said, "The burns both of you have are not what I would call serious. Although painful, we need to clean the areas. Our skin is our largest organ. Debriding, uh, cleaning and antibiotics will have you fixed fine in a short time. Our skin is our first line of defense against attacks on our body."

The young boy was treated first while sitting in Diane's lap. The little guy didn't make a sound. Clean surgical dressings were applied on his forehead and his hands while his left foot wore a surgical looking white boot. The bottom of that foot suffered blisters. In the process of treating him, the attending nurse managed to get much of his body reasonably clean using antiseptic wipes.

With the boy in her lap, Diane received her treatment. Her burns were not nearly as significant as those on the little guy. Cleaned and the wounds dressed would allow new skin to grow under the burn was the best solution in her case.

Her hair was singed slightly on the back of her head but nothing serious enough a good beautician could not fix. All the time, the skinny little boy clung tightly to Diane, his arms around her while his head rested on her breasts. His sobbing stopped but tears continue to trickle from his big brown eyes.

I walked in just as the nurse finished working on Diane. My left hand was wrapped in white gauze taped in place. It was all Diane could see and yet Wade looked like he aged ten years in five minutes on the burning boat. Haggard stress lines on his brow and a wheezing coming with each breath had Diane worried.

"Well, you look like hell for a knight in shining armor Wade," Diane said.

Following Wade in the room was a man in blue scrubs who said, "I want him to spend the night with us and get a little respiratory therapy.  We've got a cutie on tonight. Renee will take good care of him but no. Mr. Macho won't hear of it. He ingested a bit too much toxic smoke. The faster we get that out, the better he will feel."

Shaking my head no, I sat on the edge of the bed which now had Diane square in the center, her legs hanging over the edge. The boy still held her tight.

I looked at Diane after I covered my mouth and coughed my lungs up. I felt like I had sand in my lungs. If only I could cough it up, I'd feel better.

I said, "The other four boys are OK.  They're in the Hospice building behind this hospital. They have room tonight.  The four boys are sharing two rooms. They have a psychologist there and a social worker is talking to them. The first report is these boys are so traumatized they simply cannot remember much. Or they were taken from deep in the jungle and are uneducated.  They have no idea where they came from."

"All of them were sexually molested over and over." I started coughing again. "Did you get anything from this boy?" I asked.

"No Wade. We just got finished. I'd like to spend some time with him alone. I'm sure he is no different than the other boys and was molested too. Come on Wade, look in the mirror. You look like hell and we can't do a damned thing until tomorrow anyhow. Why don't you listen to the doctor for a change and spend the night. Take the breathing therapy. I'll take this boy home with me. I'll call Marco and Vickie and see if they can come over and watch the door so he can't get out."

"OK, ok. I know you're right and the doc said I'd feel a lot better by tomorrow. Anyhow, I'm anxious to see a sexy woman tonight. Not one bandaged up with a clinging kid hanging on her. OK Doc. Get this sexy Renee chick here and fix me up. Fast." I stood up and gave Diane a quick kiss on her forehead. That's all the energy I had left in me.

It was just after 9 P.M. as Diane sat with the boy at the table in the kitchen, across from Marco and Vickie. The boy just finished his second bowl of quick cook oatmeal with raisins and other goodies mixed in. It would seem the boy was starved and looked like it. This must have hit his palate just right as two bowls made with whole milk vanished very fast. Fearful of giving him too much food too fast, Diane thanked the other two for the fifth time then said she was going to bed and taking the boy with her. Not that she had a choice as Abbas clung tightly.

The three of them tried to get the boy to talk but got no response at all. Even speaking Portuguese to him had no effect. They just got a blank stare back, almost like he wasn't there. He was somewhere else deep in thought. Somewhere else in this world.

The dilemma started in the bedroom. Diane could not sleep in clothing. Well, panties were all, but anything on top and she simply could not sleep. She couldn't even fall asleep let alone get any significant down time wearing something over her breasts and shoulders.

*Come on Diane. He's just a little boy. Probably from the jungle and slept sans clothing too,* she thought.

The lamp lit on the nightstand next to the bed. A fluorescent bulb equivalent to a 60-watt incandescent bulb cast shadows on the left side of the bed. In this shadow sat a boy, his stare transfixed into space. He sat on the left side of the bed, where she always slept.

Diane unbuttoned the soot-stained and slightly singed long sleeve blouse she wore that day, grateful for the sleeves. Next, she unbuckled her slacks and let them fall to the floor, kicking them to the side. Tomorrow was soon enough to deal with those clothes.

She looked at the boy who had his vision fixed on something straight ahead of him. He never acknowledged Diane at all as she undid the clasp on her bra facing away from him. A thought came to her, as she opened a dresser drawer and removed an item Wade got her a week ago, just for a laugh. She slipped on the sleeveless tank top shirt that was two sizes too big for her. On the front was printed a huge "S," in red on the bright blue shirt, the Superwoman insignia.

Wade got this top for her as a joke. She never had a chance to wear it yet. The top was long enough to come down to her knees, covering her black panties and loose enough to barely stay on to her shoulders. She would give it a try.

Sitting on the bed, Diane pointed to herself, thumping her breast and said "Diane." She repeated this again and once more, a third time.

Turning his head, looking at her, the frail little boy looked deep into her eyes and smiled and pointed to his chest and said, "Abbas."

Abbas. Oh, my God. He spoke. A smile broke over her lips. Deep in her memory, that name came back to her. She had a friend who had a brother named Abbas. What was it about that name?

Diane looked at the boy. She let out a very loud GRRRROOOOORRR. Abbas was the name they called The Lion or something like that.

The boy beamed and with his little right fist, he thumped his chest over and over and repeated, "Abbas, Abbas." The boy had a name.

In seconds, the bedroom door flew open and Vickie charged in with a worried look on her face. Marco followed a step behind her and suddenly had no idea where to look. Diane sat in bed, beaming, oblivious to the fact her left breast was totally out of the oversize top she wore.

"Is something wrong?" Vickie asked, a question on her face. "We heard this roar and well?"

"Oh no," said Diane. "Everything is great. Our little boy has a name and its Abbas. That means lion in another language. No, we have a start now."

Diane hugged Abbas to her breasts, tears streaming down the faces of both she and Abbas. This was a start. A very good start.

Pushing Abbas away from her several inches, she looked at him and smiled, and said, "Abbas, we are going to find a way to get you back home. Don't worry little man. We will do it. I promise." Then she hugged him tightly to her breast, the tears were tears of joy rolled from her big blue eyes.

## *Hiram's Revelation*

The crunch sound the tires made from his Chevy pickup truck made a little noise and yet the sound was a comfort to him as Hiram Stone pulled in his driveway.  The root ball from the big palm tree that fell on the house was gone. Bobby Joe cut it up into manageable chunks and hauled it away. He was a big help and with Hiram disabled now, he was a welcome guest. The house roof was covered in two blue tarps. After a storm like they had, blue tarps were all over.

The entire crew from the boat factory was sent home this morning. The crew put in two hours into a scheduled overtime day.  The plant was that busy.  A leak in a line transferring a chemical thought to be a possible toxin caused the entire plant to shut down. Hiram was grateful for the good job he had for over twenty years. *Shit happens,* he thought. With his broken arm, the plant manager found easy work for Hiram.  He needed the paycheck.  Stan and Hiram went back a long way.

Ethel, his wife of twenty years, was out shopping. Her Chevrolet Equinox was missing from the garage. Ethel said she was going shopping this morning with a neighbor friend. Some huge sale at Kohl's or someplace where they had a real bargain on towels she said they needed.

Bobby Joe's tan truck sat next to the garage, off the driveway, not blocking access to Hiram's side of the garage. It appeared Bobby Joe was home alone with Sharon. Oh boy, what to do. What are they doing? He thought.

After hating the kid for months, the kid came through, and truth told, Hiram felt the kid saved his life when the tree fell on him. After that, he liked the hell out of Bobby Joe.  He set Hiram's arm as good as any doctor could and was very respectful to everybody. He came around a lot and helped clean up the mess the storm caused, without being asked.  Of course, he was sweet on Sharon. It was obvious she was crazy over him. Suddenly, his hillbilly ways vanished to Hiram. But now what. He wished he was back at work.

Hiram had been down this road before. Heck, twenty or so years ago he could have been Bobby Joe himself. He remembered high school dating. Going to the drive-in with half his high school classmates parked around him. Sneaking in beer and trying to get your date to drink a couple.

Get her feeling tipsy and hopefully take advantage of her. Cop a feel was for sure. Getting a breast in your mouth was a bonus and about as far as most guys got. Get real lucky and get your hand between her legs was the ticket. Play it right and get her hot.  If she had clothes loose enough, get your hand under her panties and try to rock that little man in the boat.  Rock it just right and she was yours. The least you'd get was a blow job.  That's how it worked with Ethel anyhow.  He remembered, thin as Ethel was, she often wore a girdle when they went to the drive in. And that darned gold cross around her neck.

Now he had to go in the house and then what? He guessed he'd have to yell at Bobby Joe and throw him out of the house. But not so that he wouldn't come back. Just not take advantage of his sweet little girl. She was still "daddy's girl" to him. If they were gonna fool around, at least don't get caught. He'd have Ethel talk to Sharon.

He closed the screen door quietly but he didn't need to. The voice of Bobby Joe was loud enough to hear from outside. They were in the living room.

"Please Sharon. Don't do dat." Spoke Bobby Joe in a strained voice.

He must be trying to get into her pants, thought Hiram.  She must be fighting him off.

"Come on Bobby Joe. You promised. Are you gonna break a promise to me?"

Ah, his little Sharon had Bobby Joe promise not to do this. Boys will be boys he remembered.

"It's gest dat I cain't help it. Didn't we promise last week?" said Bobby Joe, his voice an octave higher now.

Oh sure, thought Hiram.  Promises are made in church. He wants his little sweetheart and doesn't care about a silly promise. He better walk in and break this up.

"Come on Bobby Joe. Let me just play with your dick and you can stick your finger in me and make me feel soooooo goooooddd." Sharon said which stopped Hiram dead in his tracks.

*What was that you just heard?* He asked himself.

"I took a condom from daddy's sock drawer. He won't miss it. They don't fuck much anymore." Sharon reached between Bobby Joe's legs, feeling a rock hard cock, begging in its own way for freedom.

"Please Sharon, let's wait till we get married." The weakening voice of Bobby Joe was heard along with his zipper Sharon pulled down.

Using both hands, Sharon freed the cock she sought for weeks. Grasping his throbbing erection with both hands on the shaft, she moving those hands in an up and down motion, watching Bobby Joe's face. He looked to be in pure ecstasy, and pain at the same time.

*This feels a lot better than when I do it to himself,* he thought.

"Let me just kiss it for a minute honey," Sharon lowered her mouth over his swollen member. Her hot wet tongue swirled around the head of his cock while he moaned in delight.  Her eyes looked into his eyes which looked like they might pop out of his head.

When he got to where he couldn't stand it, she thought she would have him do things to her. Who knew where this might end. She was happy Bobby Joe was a whole lot bigger than her old boyfriend, Ted.

"Oh Lord mama. I tink I'm gonna break dat promise to ya. I gest caint help it," said the shaky voice of Bobby Joe, in total ecstasy just now. He did not care about anything but what Sharon was doing and how great it felt.

Hiram was shocked. He could hear the sucking sound where he stood in the kitchen.  It was his slutty little daughter who was the instigator in this tryst. Bobby Joe was begging to wait while she was begging for it. She must take after his sister Louise. She was a slut in high school he remembered.

Hiram walked to the back screen door, opened it and banged it shut with a fast motion, almost taking the hinges off the door as it slammed hard.

"Hi, Sharon. Are you home? The plant had a problem and we had to shut down. I'm gonna make a pot of coffee. You want a cup?"

## Shooting Mario

Four days after the fire, Mario was suffering through another bandage change. A male nurse administered his treatment. His burns were healing nicely. He was also told that tomorrow he would be transferred to the prison infirmary. Mario hid his emotion well, as his face was re-bandaged. With two eye holes and a slit for his mouth, he looked like a modern version of the old movie, "The Mummy."

He didn't make a move or sound as the nurse changed the dressings. It hurt a lot, but he set his mind he was immune to the pain. He could do that. He tried hard to hatch a plan. Mario knew he had to do something, anything to keep him out of jail. Right now, death was a far better alternative than being bent over a bunk with some animal humping him, making him his sex toy.

As a kid, he and his older brother Miguel, two years his senior, would play many games. The one game Mario always won was who could be the stillest for the longest time. After a while, Miguel got tired of the game he never won and refused to play. Mario continued to play in a new way.

Using a few crumbs of bread, he would sit in the middle of the dirt they called their back yard and scatter the crumbs around him. A bird would land close. It would eat the distant crumb. The statue sitting there posed no threat, so it got closer. Mario would then snatch the bird, often in flight. It was a challenge to play the game with something fast as he sharpened his skills.

Mario learned to pick pockets from a pro who made his living doing just that. It wasn't the money he made as a pickpocket Mario enjoyed but the thrill of the action. Many times, after picking the pocket of a person, he told the guy he just dropped his wallet, much to the dismay of the mark. Many would open their wallet instantly and discover nothing was missing and give Mario a ten or twenty dollar bill as a reward.

At the hospital now, Mario didn't make a move when anybody else was around. He sat or laid perfectly still all the time. It was another "catch the bird" game for him. One game he was very good at.

During his treatments, he was shackle free, making it much easier to clean and dress his wound. A police officer stood against the wall and just watched or read a magazine. When the treatment was over, the officer would clamp the handcuffs on one wrist, then the bed frame. Today would be a little different.

Officer Paul Evers, a relatively new member of the county police department, had the duty again this afternoon. Evers stood five foot eight inches tall. His belt size 48. Officer Evers was rotund. Two years after completing his time in college, his major "Criminal Justice," it took Evers many applications to find this job. His college grades were not spectacular and his weight hurt his interviews. When he got on with the county, Evers worked very hard to keep his job.

Since Paul started with the county force, he put on more weight. His mom and dad were big people. He thought it had to be hereditary. The last three weeks, Evers started working out more and eating less. Later, he would look back and see if this had anything to do with what happened. He guessed not. He just got too complacent. He got lazy.

"He's all yours Evers," said the orderly, picking up the wrappings from the gauze bandages he used on Mario.

Officer Evers walked up to the rolling bed Mario was on, casually reached over Mario to grab the handcuff on the far side of the bed.

He was in the process of grasping the cuff with one hand and Mario's hand with the other when Mario let out a shriek. Officer Evers thought he somehow hurt Mario and jumped back a few inches.

As he did, the holster containing his handgun was practically resting on Mario's belly. Mario unsnapped the holster and removed the gun. Evers never felt the gun leave his holster.

As Evers reached over Mario again to secure the handcuff, this time not touching Mario's body, Mario gave Evers a hard shove, pushing Evers into a tray stand, knocking it over. The shove had the benefit of pushing the rolling bed away from Evers. Mario raised the handgun. He pointed the barrel four feet from Officer Evers face.

For the first time since getting burned, Mario, in a croaking voice said, "This is how it's gonna be. I want you to arrange an ambulance and get me out of here. When we get in the ambulance, I'll tell you where we will go." He had no idea where that might be.

Officer Evers backed up a couple of steps with the red bead sight on his handgun following his nose. Just then, a nurse walked in with a tray of instruments, saw the gun and dropped the tray. The clatter when it hit the floor was loud. The nurse ran out the door.

The surprise was over. There would be no sneaking out now. Thinking fast, Mario decided the best thing would be to put the gun under his chin or in his mouth and pull the trigger.

It takes a tremendous amount of courage to kill yourself. People say it's the easy way out. The cowards way. Those people never tried it or they would not say something that stupid. To take your life takes either a deranged mind or determination far exceeding what could be expected. Unfortunately for Mario, he had neither.

Ten minutes later, the hallway, the adjoining rooms and the outside of the hospital were swarming with the state, county, and local police. That is what Wade encountered as he pulled into the parking lot at the hospital.

A warm shower, typical for this time of the year, just ended. The wiper blades on Wade's Audi flicked for the last time and shut down. Wade pushed a button on the door, lowering his window and smelled fresh rain on the newly mown lawn. A state patrolman stood in the center of the driveway. In his dripping rain poncho, his right hand extended, palm out, the officer demonstrated a signal to STOP.

I showed the officer my badge and asked, "What's up Sergeant" to the state cop.

"All I know is there's a guy with a gun and he has hostages Mr. Nash."

I walked in the hospital, holding my badged credentials in front of me. I made it to the hall where the action was and ran smack into Floyd Johnson.

"What's going on Floyd? What the hell are you doing here?" I asked.

"I was coming to see you when the alert hit the air. I was on the road almost in front of here. What luck huh? I came to see about the kid you saved and what progress you've made with getting him to talk," Johnson said.

"The kid is glued to Diane. He won't leave her for a second. So far, all we have is his name. They've been testing him here every day and they tell us he has some serious problems. He has autism or something like that and they don't think he'll be able to help us much. I was on my way here to see if I could get Mario to talk. Now I hear at the desk he has a gun and hostages. Damn…"

"Yeah, all we can figure is he got it from the cop guarding him. Nobody's been to see him unless it's a hospital staff that got him the gun. I doubt that."

"Well Floyd, we can stand out here until the cows come home or I can go in there and see if I can talk some sense into him. I'm the one who arrested him but I'm also the one who saved his sorry ass on that burning boat. There's only one way to find out what's on his mind." I walked past Floyd, who was objecting quite loud. He grabbed my left arm. I shook it off and walked into the room. The front sight on the gun moved from Evers to me and did not quiver a bit.

I looked at a mummy sitting on a bed, wrapped up from his chest to the top of his head. I could not tell if the person was showing fear, hatred, scared to death or whatever. I had to play this as it went. I had to go with the flow.

"Yeah, I got a gun on me, Mario. It's in a holster on my right side, under my belt where I wear it almost every day. I got a callous on my side from wearing the damned thing more than half my life. It's a 40 caliber Glock, not too different than the nine you have pointed at my nose."

"I'm fast Mario but no way as fast as you, already sighted on my face. I don't want to die today. I won't make a move for my gun. I hope you don't need to pull that trigger on anybody but if you do, it better be me because if you shoot somebody else, I'm fast enough to put one in you before the gun recycles a new round into yours."

"I remember you," said Mario. "You're the guy on the boat by the ladder. You stuck your head down inside when I struck the lighter and blew the thing up. How the hell did you get out?"

"Huh. Not only did I get out but I also got four boys out of the V berth in front, and came back and got your ass out of the damned burning boat too. Look, I got burned too." I showed him my bandaged right hand.

"Why? You think you did me a favor? No way. I ain't going to jail."

"Yes, you are Mario. I came here to talk to you, so before one of us does something stupid, let's talk. I need to know what you know. Talking to the four boys, they said you treated them real good. The guy before you and the boat captain, Fletcher, they weren't very nice to those boys. They liked you. You've got that going for you and if you cooperate, I see you in a far better jail than the hard ones. Do you like basketball?"

"Basketball? Do I like Basketball? Yeah, what's that got to do with this?

"The ball's in your court now Mario. Whatcha gonna do bro?"

"You're lying. All you cops lie. No, I think I have to shoot somebody and you can kill me. It's my only way. I'm sorry man. I can't go to jail."

"So, who you gonna shoot man. The nurse or the cop? Or me? You aren't a killer. A killer would have done his thing already. Do you really want to die now? Do you?" I said, watching his eyes through the cutout holes, as they flickered from one of us to the other. He was scared.

"I got no choice man. I don't want to kill anybody so I'll try and hit somebody in the arm or something. I'm a pretty good shot. Then you shoot me as you said. OK?"

"OK, OK, here's the deal," I said. "I'll kill you but I don't want anybody else shot. You shoot one in the ceiling and I'll draw and take you out. You won't feel a thing, I promise you. What do you say? Nobody gets shot except you. Shoot one in the ceiling and if you see I don't shoot, you can kill all of us for all I care, but me first. Now I have a good reason to shoot you. How about it Mario?"

Mario's eyes are moving from one of us to another. First, a male nurse who I later learned spent time overseas, a Corpsman for a Marine Recon unit, and showed no fear, just a cool look back at him. Then the police officer who looked like his pants might be wet, or worse. Now, the gun moved to my chest. Mario made up his mind.

"OK, let's do it. It won't hurt me you said?"

"No Mario, you won't feel a thing. I won't miss, I promise. I sure wish we could talk first and you could help me out. Can we do that?"

"No. I'll give you the address of the safe house in Miami. That's where I got on the boat. I don't want to say any more. My boss was real good to me."

Mario recited the address from his memory and again stated this is the house where it started for him on this trip.

"Just a minute," I said. "I want to let the boys know what's going to happen, so they don't all rush in and kill all of us. Let me go out in the hall and tell them." I turned and walked out before Mario realized his main hostage walked out on him.

"Are you crazy? I heard you," said Floyd. "You can't make a deal to kill a guy like that. How the hell can I protect you from that? We have witnesses all over.  Your ass will be in jail Wade."

"Just tell the boys they will hear two shots. If they hear more, well, it didn't go as I planned. Two shots and they stay where they are. Two shots."

"Anybody comes through that door with just two shots I'll shoot them myself. Make sure they all know this. Five minutes." I looked at my watch then said, "Go."

I walked back into the room, returning in less than a minute. "Listen, Mario, shoot straight up. It's a concrete ceiling and thick enough to stop a nine millimeter round. If you shoot at an angle, the bullet will ricochet and maybe kill one or two of us anyhow. I gave them five minutes to get the word out." I knew Mario heard every word I said, in spite of bandages over his ears.

The hands on the twelve-inch white face Seth Thomas clock on the wall crawled the second hand around the face at half the speed it normally moved. Well, not really but it seemed like it until five minutes finally passed. I shouted out to Floyd who said the word was passed on and understood. Floyd then begged me to change my mind.

"OK, Mario. Are you sure I can't talk this out of doing this? I came here today to talk to you. Once I pull the trigger, our talking is never gonna happen."

"No man. I forgive you for killing me." Mario raised the gun pointing it directly above him. He took his left hand and made the sign of the cross, his fingers touching his forehead then his chest, his left shoulder then his right shoulder. He then closed his eyes.

When he closed his eyes, I reached with my bandaged hand and slid my Glock 40 out of its holster. I had my gun half way up when….

Mario pulled the trigger. The explosion sent chips of concrete and dust flying from the ceiling down on him.

The noise was intense and briefly deafening. Mario felt the debris fall on him and for a split second, wondered if one could feel things after one died. No, the guy didn't shoot. He turned toward the guy, gun still raised, next to his head.  The scream that followed could be heard well into the hospital hallway, echoing off the walls.

Mario shot the ceiling using his right hand. As soon as he pulled the trigger, the recoil forced the gun down to his head, ear level. He was a profile to me. I had to wait. When he turned, facing me, I shot.

 The blood-curdling scream that followed was one the nurse or Officer Evers would ever forget.

The scream was from Mario, holding his right hand with his index finger broken and bent back, the slide on the Glock gun smashed, taking part of his right hand with it.

"You lied man. You fuckin lied to me. Why did you lie to me?"

"Well Mario, once more the ball is in your court. You can cooperate and talk to me and I will see about a better jail.  Or keep quiet and spend the next twenty years bent over for Bubba. Think about it. I'll see you tomorrow.

I walked out the door, brushing the concrete dust from my shirt. Three steps into the hall, I saw Floyd walking toward me. He was followed by two officers holding sniper rifles. *Meant for whom? I wondered.*

"He's all your boys," I said.

"I saw that and heard what you did Wade. It looks like another medal for you. That was brilliant. Absolutely Brilliant." said Floyd.

"I'll tell you what. I'm going home now and lift a beer or two. If you want, stop by, in say an hour or so, I'll order one of the crappy pizzas they have here and we can have a drink and talk. What do you say, Floyd?"

"I'll be there in an hour. Don't start without me."

I added, "Oh, and bring my retirement papers with you. We can start filling them out. I'm too old for this stuff."

*Yeah, sure you are thought Floyd Johnson.*

# *Abbas's Diagnosis*

"He's Autistic Ms. Mason," said Doctor Molly Epstein sitting in her office, bent over, a pencil in her hand, doodling on a sheet of blank paper. She now had to try and explain what Autism was to Diane, sitting in the chair across the desk from the doctor.

"What do you know about Autism Spectrum Disorders, ADS as they now call this?"

"Not a lot doctor. I keep hearing the incidence of autism is rapidly on the rise and nobody seems to know why."

"That's true," said the doctor as she continued to doodle on the pad of paper, no longer blank. "Autism can be hereditary, and in many cases, it appears so. It also doesn't have to be connected with hereditary issues in many cases. The degree of social interactions and communicative skills can be all over the board."

"Autism is a very complex neurobehavioral condition. It includes impairment in social interaction and communicational skills as well as language skills. There are rigid, repetitive behaviors in almost all cases."

"This gets trickier to diagnose and speak about all the time. Abbas, as you call him fits into a slot called Pervasive Developmental Disorder, or PDD. That's the category we put people when they don't fit the true nature of another category. In other words, we just don't know."

"This boy is smart. Far smarter than his age which we are estimating to be ten years old, although we could be off by a year either way. In our study, we found quite by accident he has a rare skill. He can work Rubik's cube with lightning speed, no matter how much we twist those colors on that block. We believe he has had little or no formal education which means nothing to you in an attempt to locate where he came from. We've had people of varying ages like this. Some come from remote places while others come from big cities. I have no idea how you will find out where he lives."

"Thank you doctor. How about his general health? He's so very frail. I believe he's had little food for several weeks. How is his general health? Would you know that?" asked Diane, an anxious look on her face, no longer sporting that sunburned look from the fire.

"Oh, he's in pretty good health. We don't think he's ever had a vaccination which is another indicator he came from a remote part of the world. I'm sorry Ms. Mason, we just don't know."

"My partner is going to question one of the guys who was on the boat with the boys. The one that was burned pretty bad and held a few hostages the other day. I'm sure you heard about that. The boat captain was carted off the same day and we hear he isn't saying a word. I wish they left him here for a few days. These alphabet agencies are all trying to make a name for themselves. We know who he is and where he's from but nothing about him for the last several years."

"Good luck Ms. Mason. Abbas has taken to you so intensely you may be the only one who can get anything from him. I wish you luck." The doodling stopped. The page full as the doctor stood up.

# Mario's Answers

"So here's the deal, Mario. I don't lie, so I'll give…"

"Bullshit you don't lie. You said you'd kill me. You shot me in the hand and broke it up pretty good. Why should I believe you now?" said Mario looking hard at me, holding his bandaged right hand up to show his wounds. The bandages on his face were small, letting the air get to the new skin growing under the burns. A few places would need plastic surgery but that was down the line a way.

"Aw, for chrissake Mario. You gotta know I ain't going to go to jail for you or anybody else. I couldn't kill you and besides that, you don't need killing. You aren't a bad guy. You were put in a bad spot is all. The kids all liked you compared to the guy you replaced. So, tell me about him."

"Tell me again. If I cooperate, you will put in a good word and I won't be in a bad jail? You promise?"

"I'll do what I can for you. I promise that. That's all I can promise." As I crossed the room and looked out the secure window in Mario's room used for police and security cases. The bars on the window made sure escape that way near impossible. The palm trees in the distance swayed indifferent to what happened in that hospital as they waved their fronds to the world in the bright sunlight.

"I'm gonna set up this recorder on the table in front of you. Now, tell me your name clearly and today's date. And where you are as far as you know."

After the preliminaries, I went on and asked Mario:

"So, who was the guy you replaced and where did he go?"

"His name was Polo. That's all I know. I got a call from my boss who told me Polo had to go someplace else and I had to take his place and it would take two or three weeks. There would be a big bonus for me when it was over. I had to help that guy on the boat and when I got to where we were going, I would be given money to get back to Miami by bus. Not even fly.  By Greyhound. I found out we would end up in New York but not exactly where in New York. I guess the city of New York but Fletch wouldn't tell me anything else. I think Polo was killed."

"Why do you think that?" I asked

"Polo left a little tape recorder and I found it. I told Fletch about it and he told me to destroy it. Where Polo was he wouldn't need it. I took it out behind the building and was going to smash it with a brick then for some reason, I slipped it into my boot. When I got on the boat, I stuck it in the first aid kit sitting on a shelf. I stuck it behind some bandages. I guess it burned up in the boat."

"Did you listen to it?" I asked

"Just for a minute. It was in a foreign language so I didn't listen very long. I don't know what he was saying."

"In a first aid box huh? Where was it hanging, exactly?"

"It was above the refrigerator, on a small shelf next to the ceiling. It was easy to get to and yet it wasn't in the way," said Mario, who had a little hope in his eyes now. Maybe he could survive.

"So, who's your boss Mario. What does he look like and where does he live? In Miami?"

"My boss's name is Arthur Dalton but everybody calls him "The Money Man. I don't know where he lives but I think he has a lot of houses and one in the suburbs of Miami I think."

"Why do you think that?"

"My job was to get girls for his business. Every once in a while, Mr. Dalton would call and have me get him something special. I don't think they were for him but a friend or a client. He'd ask for a tall black girl with long legs one time. When I asked how tall he said his friend was almost six foot seven so the taller, the better. Another time he wanted a redhead that was younger than twenty years old and looked good. Once he asked me for a real young girl. Under sixteen he said. I had the feeling they were never for him. I don't know though."

"So, you'd get the girls and take them to his house?"

"No. We met at a fancy bar on the beach. I don't think he lived far away though as they always walked to where they were going. Heading north. That's all I know. I don't know where he lives or even if he lived there."

The questioning went on for another half hour but nothing much more was revealed. I would try again in another day or two. As soon as I was clear of the hospital, I speed dialed Floyd who picked up on the second ring.

## *Abbas's Home*

I was on I-95 heading south in my black Audi A6, pushing ten over the speed limit, getting passed in spite of my speed. I had the AC on max cold, a hundred thoughts running through my head. Could the recorder still be there? If they found it, would it be in one piece? As thoughts raced through my head, Diane pulled in the drive of my house with Abbas next to her.

Wade didn't have much of a library in his house. Mostly cookbooks that must have belonged to Catherine, his wife. A few magazines, most were trade magazines along with a Motor Trend and a few Car and Driver magazines nestled in the stack. Diane was hoping to find a travel book on South America amongst them but no luck.

Armed with two peanut butter and jelly sandwiches and a glass of milk for Abbas, Diane turned on the twenty-four-inch monitor for the computer on Wade's desk and found travel sites for South America. Abbas devoured one of the sandwiches as he looked hard at the screen, acting like he too was looking for something. With pictures of Brazil, Argentina, Chile,and Paraguay popping up with the keystrokes from Diane, a lot of pretty scenic pictures were met with a somber face from Abbas until one in Peru opened on the screen. It had a waterfall.

Uhhh Uhhh Uhhh grunted Abbas, pointing at the waterfall. Pieces of his sandwich falling from his mouth as he grunted.

"Is this where you're from Abbas?" said Diane, now on full alert and very anxious.

With hand gestures, Abbas held his right hand up, curved his palm and plunged his little fist, going over something, down to the floor. A waterfall. But was this the one?

Diane typed in "Waterfalls in South America" and came up with a list. The largest first to the smallest last. It was on the first listing, the largest waterfall, that Abbas jumped up and down and pointed at the fall then thumped his chest and said over and over Abbas. Abbas.

Using her Apple smartphone, she found Kaieteur Falls was located on the Potaro River in the Kaieteur National Park, in Essequibo, Guyana. It was in the Amazon Forest.

Abbas could not stop his animated antics of thumping his chest and pointing to the falls. Diane was certain this was where Abbas was from. Her speed dial #1 was for Wade which Diane pressed. He connected on the second ring.

"Hey, Diane. I didn't get a chance to tell you. I was just about to call you myself. I may have a good lead on a recorder hidden on the boat and a chance it survived the fire. If it's true and I can find it, we may be able to find out where that boy came from."

"I know where he came from Wade." Diane went on to tell him how she came to this conclusion and was sure without a doubt this was the home of Abbas.

"That's fantastic Diane. What brilliant work. Floyd and the rest of the management team will be thrilled to hear this. They are really glad you came on board. They pushed hard to get you here."

"Sure. OK. What I want to hear is you are happy I'm here. I know. I just like to hear it again."

"Huh? Like you don't know? Yes, I'm so very happy you are here. I can't imagine life without you now."

Diane smiled on the other end of the line. Wade had no idea why but he knew she was smiling.

# *Recorder*

The Coast Guard station in New Smyrna Beach was quiet this afternoon. I hit the gate and was ushered into an office with windows overlooking the intra-coastal waterway. "Mr. Nash. I'm Commander Mark, Fred Mark. I'm the CO of this base."

"I got the call from the top gun so to speak. Rest assured you will have our total cooperation. Whatever you need, just ask." The Commander extended his hand. I gripped the calloused hand of a man who knew what hard work was all about.

I said, "I got the word from the guy on the sailboat that got burned pretty bad that he hid a small recorder on the boat. The recorder belonged to another guy that was on the boat from wherever they departed. The guy left the boat in Miami. Then he just disappeared. If indeed it exists and we can find it, we may have a big lead in helping us get to the people who are the cause of human trafficking in our area. If we can save lives, well, you know the rest."

"What I'd like Commander is a video documentation of me entering the boat and searching the area I was told it was hidden. I don't know if this would ever go to court, but if it does, well this is more of a CYA move. There is nothing as good as covering one's ass at times."

Looking out the window, resting on the back of the command center, a football field away, I saw the "Grasshopper," totally out of the water. She rested on a cradle designed to support her when on land. The 44 foot Catalina sailboat rested at ease. A rolling platform, about 15 feet tall with stairs leading to the top was placed on the left side of the sailboat, near the stern, the top platform even with the boat's deck.

Fred Mark lifted a phone and seconds later said, "Mr. Nash if you'll wait just a minute, I have the video camera coming with some disposable Nomex suits. It's pretty dirty in the cabin now. No sense getting all messed up if we don't have to."

"It's Wade, Commander. Just Wade, please. Mr. Nash was my dad."

"Gotcha. I'm Fred. Here she comes now." The two men watched a petite female carrying a bundle under one arm, the white Nomex apparel.

"Ah, Petty Officer Dawes I believe," I said, smiling at the second class petty officer who was the translator on the sailboat of a group of girls who got this whole thing started, not long ago.

Smiling back, Dawes extended her right hand after setting the bundle on the desk. "Mr. Nash. It's nice to see you again."

"I see you two know each other," said Commander Mark. I went on to explain how we met.

"Let's suit up then. I'll go topside with you but I'll stay on deck until or unless you find something. Then I'll go below to verify the find. Ellen, you go first. No, belay that. I'll be first on deck. It should be perfectly safe, but well, I'll go first."

The three of us dressed like snowmen, white coveralls with elastic snugly on our wrists and ankles. We headed out of the building toward the boat. The white booties we slipped over our shoes were tougher than I thought as we walked through crushed shells making up the compound. The booties held up. Our dress for this visit finished with white gloves, a white cap, and a white disposable face mask.

"We just got permission last night to dig into the boat and see what we could find," Commander Mark said as we walked to the sailboat. "I had a section of the keel cut open to check inside. I think I know what the packages are though."

"There are packages in the keel huh?" I asked. "I'm not surprised. In for a penny, in for a pound."

We made our way up the ladder, Petty Officer Dawes recorded us, using a Sony Minicam. I noticed I began to perspire almost at once. Those Nomex suits let no air transfer in or out.

Ellen Dawes went down the ladder into the cabin first with the camera running then stepped back a few feet and recorded me entering the cabin from above. I moved a few feet to my right, around the sink, past the stove, and to the refrigerator.

Most of the interior was charred a charcoal black from the fire. The area around the stove was spared much of the damage as this boat had a modern fire control system over the stove. A white foam covered much of the immediate area by the stove.

 I looked above the stove where Mario claimed to have hidden the tape recorder.  A white box, the paint smudged in black, a red cross painted on the face, sat on a small shelf above the stove. Exactly where Mario said it was.

"Commander, I think you better come down. I have the location and the item I was told I would find. "

When Commander Mark stood next to me, he said to Dawes, "Ellen, you're getting this aren't you?"

"Yes, sir. Five by five."

I pulled the first aid box from the shelf and set it on the cook stove top.  The box was white, approximately twelve inches wide, ten inches deep and four inches thick with a simple wire loop handle, two clasps holding the hinged top in place. The face of the box was scorched a little, spared by the fire suppression system on this boat.

I snapped open both clasps, lifted the lid and moved it to the side. My face mask was wet from my breath as I asked Dawes to get a close up of the inside of the box. The right side held a packet of what appeared to be four by four gauze bandages, individually wrapped in paper. Lifting the bandages out of the box, below them sat a small black box, slightly smaller than the size of a pack of cigarettes. It was indeed a recorder.

Fifteen minutes later, in the Commander's office, feeling much more comfortable without the hot Nomex clothing, I asked Petty Officer Dawes the question I had to ask, hoping for a positive answer.

"Ellen, do you know exactly how to work this recorder? I mean for sure how to work it?"

"Yessir. It's a simple basic recorder. It has five buttons on it. Record, stop, rewind, play, and erase. Most small recorders like this are all the same."

"OK, let's hear what is on it," I said, holding my breath.

Dawes hit the rewind button for a minute, then hit play. The voice that we heard sounded Portuguese, but I was not sure. One minute of listening and I asked Dawes to stop the recorder. We did not know the language.

"Great. Now, all we need is a translator," I said, looking at Commander Mark and Seaman Dawes.

"I'll do one better for you, Mr. Nash. I'll run this through my computer which has a program on it with over a hundred languages it can translate. You'll hear what is said in English. On top of that, it will save and print the words for you." Ellen Dawes smiled, knowing this was making my day.

Darkness was coming to this part of his world as I pulled out of the Coast Guard complex. On the seat next to me sat an eleven by fourteen manila envelope with the entire content of what that recorder held.

The recorder and a CD of the conversation were safely locked in my gun safe in the trunk of my car. Just in case. A copy of the video recording was forwarded to my computer on my desk.

A CD made of this, now sat in Commander Mark's safe in his office. This was overkill but what I had was a gold mine of information.

Pushing the talk button on the steering wheel of my black Audi A6 turbo diesel, I spoke to the mechanical voice and said, "Call Diane."

The phone on the other end was picked up on the second ring.

"Diane, honey, we have a long night ahead of us. Order some food. Pizza. Chinese. I don't care. I got it and I've got a gold mine baby. Wait until you hear this."

# *A Break!*

Pushing "End" on the screen on his car dash ended my call to Diane. I followed with another request to his system. "Call Floyd Johnson." A phone rang in the background, picked up on the third ring. Floyd was very excited to hear the news garnered from the recorder and the information from the translation.

"Nice going, Wade. That was a great move on your part to get that Mario guy talking in the hospital. This could be the break we were looking for. Maybe get some scumbags off the street. Maybe we can take his whole organization down. This could be a big hit. How about this Mario guy? Do you think he has more he can tell us?"

I was on I-95 passing the U.S. 1 exit, holding my speed to just five over the limit. I had the feeling my cargo today would change history just a bit. A quarter mile behind me, two dots suddenly materialized in my vision, in my outside lane. I moved to the center lane when the two dots became Crotch Rockets.

I think they were men but couldn't be sure as they flew past me, lying prone on the bike tanks, traveling well into triple digit speeds. The engines screamed a high pitch whine as they passed me. Insane speeds. My exit was next. I hoped I wouldn't see them again because if I did, they would not be in one piece.

"His name is Mario Escalante. He's an American, born in Miami. Yes, he is part of the group but he's not a hard criminal. He was burned pretty badly on the boat and I did save his ass. Before the fire, he was a real good looking dude but not so much now. He will be scarred for life."

"The kids on the boat said he was good to them. He didn't rape them like the captain and that Polo guy did. He cooperated because I told him I'd try and get him a softer prison. Can you help me out there Floyd?"

"You must be getting old." Floyd said. "I never knew you to want something easy for a bad dude Wade."

"Listen, Floyd, how about you think about it overnight. I made a promise to try and help for his cooperation.  I'll see you tomorrow and we can talk about it, OK? He helped us a lot already. Yeah, normally, I'd say fuck it, but this guy really helped us and I promised. You know a promise from me is like a written contract."

Floyd called a special meeting for seven the next morning in the county courthouse in Bunnell.  Our phone conversation was over as I slid off the freeway and on to Old Dixie Highway and the beautiful tree lined John Boardman road toward home.  The coffee pot full, a steaming cup in front of us, Diane and I started going over the information I got from the recorder. We began from the time the tape started running in South America. The midnight oil would be burnt tonight.

# *Lester and Jill*

That same evening, thirty miles away, lay a sleeping Lester, covered with a well-worn cotton bed sheet of a low thread count, dotted with a plethora of stain spots. Some spots, daddy's blood stains that wouldn't wash out. Moonbeams found their way between the branches of the live oak tree next to his house. The light from them on his face woke Lester for no apparent reason. Tree frogs croaked and an owl hooted outside his window. Just normal night sounds.

The air in the room hung heavy. The humidity was high but normal for this time of the year. Lester woke up with the strangest feeling he was not alone. The clock on the old dresser showed 12:23 AM. The old lace curtain hanging on the window was silent.

A Cardinal came again just before dark and like the past, he banged on Lester's window repeatedly until Lester thought it would kill itself. Lester didn't see Cardinals here all that often and wondered why the crazy bird did what it did, bang on the window over and over again. Lester grabbed his pillow and put it over his head, searching for asleep again. The ancient sagging mattress had no problem holding him securely in the middle of the bed.

He was certainly tired. He spent the better part of the day working the land and trying to determine where the boundary lines were on the land he was to sell to that nice lady. That finger of land the river surrounded on three sides.

Miss Olson, just who is she? What does she look like? Jill told him she looked a little like his mama. Lester felt something deep inside him that made him feel warm and good and could not understand why. Jill made him feel that way and doing what she and mama asked was the reason. He sure missed his mama, more each passing day.

Daddy never did much with the land although he talked about moving the trailer to that spot a few times. For some reason, the finger was about two feet higher than the surrounding land and never flooded in all the years Lester could remember.

Cabbages grew well on that land but it was an awkward parcel to work as it was narrow. The north side of the land was the best place to fish because the river flowed north here. On the protected north side of the finger of land, delicious catfish could be caught here almost any time if you wanted to wade out past the cattails, in knee-deep muck. Lester thought of putting a dock out past the cattails but never had the money to do it. Nor the ambition, truth told.

Stink bait, made from rotting entrails from most any animal or fish mixed with a bit of bread to hold it all together made excellent bait. Despite eating the rotten smelling bait, catfish meat was sweet to the taste. Lester could skin a catfish faster than cutting filets off a bass he sometimes caught. There wasn't much better eating than a pan fried catfish with hush puppies for a great meal.

Lester had the feeling something was not right as he turned over on his left side, now facing the open window, peeking at the nearly full moon. He felt he was being watched. The feeling wasn't new to him. He just had that feeling as he peeked out from under the pillow over his head, then nearly jumped out of bed in shock. He sat up fast, let out a startled yelp. Jill Douglas was smiling at him, as she sat in mama's rocking chair.

Jill wore a beautiful pink dress. The moonlight through the window shone on her which lent her a glowing effect. The dress was almost translucent as was Jill herself. Her smile was radiant, her eyes soft, as she gently rocked in mama's rocker.

"Hi, Lester. I'm sorry to wake you like this but I had no choice. Your Mama sends her love to you and asked me to tell you she's very proud of you. Remember, I told you we would not let you down if you did your part and you have done what she asked."

Lester had the old sheet covering his body from the waist down, sitting on the edge of his bed. He had on boxer shorts but felt it was inappropriate to sit in front of Jill without being covered.

"Uh, don't you think you should have knocked on the door, Jill? I mean, I could have thought you were somebody here to do me harm and maybe shot you."

"Oh, I wasn't worried about that Lester. I came here with good news and more for you to do."

"When can I see my mama? You promised I could see her one day."

"Not yet Lester. Not yet, but one day you will see her. And a lot of other people who want to be with you too. Right now, we have to move ahead. On your nightstand is a pad of paper and a pencil. You need to write this down."

Lester didn't keep pencil and paper on the stand next to the bed. But when he looked, there they were. "Can't you just give me the list you have in your hand?

Save me the trouble of writing it down seems to me." Lester said, taken aback finding the writing pad he didn't put there.

"No Lester. I need to keep this list. This is a list for you, but it's too soon for you to see more now. One step at a time. Now write this down."

"Next month, you will close on the property. You will have a nice amount of money. Mama said for you to go to town and see John Dempsey where they sell the manufactured homes just west of town. John will do you right. He will help you pick out a new home that might seem a little too big for you, but it won't be. Soon, it will seem just right."

"Make sure the deal includes that they haul this old one away and burn it. Burn everything but your personal belongings. Even your clothing needs to go. Your life is going to change a lot in the next few weeks. You will be much happier soon. Much happier Lester. I promise."

"Jill, are you real? My neighbor Alex Swanson says you ain't real but you are an angel. He sees you too."

"Oh, I'm real Lester. But I live in a slightly different way I guess you could say. Let's say I'm your guardian angel right now. Some day you will understand all of this." Alex is special too. He's a good man. He will see his Prudence one day soon. You remember Prudence, his wife don't you?"

"You promise I will see my mommy and daddy again?"
"You will be with your mother one day but not your father I'm afraid. He is in another place for now."

"Uh, Jill. Why is there a cardinal bird banging on my window sometimes? Do you have something to do with that? It's gonna kill himself he keeps banging like that." The bird just came to his thought.

"Cardinal birds are special Lester. They don't do that for everybody. When they show up, I won't be far behind them. One day, they won't be a mystery to you."

"Go back to sleep now Lester. When you wake up, this will seem like a dream to you. You will remember all of it though and if you do as I told you, we will move on. You will be much closer to being happy and closer to seeing your mother. Did you get all of this down on the pad?"

Lester looked. Of course, he did. Buy a new house and get new clothes. He looked up from the pad to tell her so. But she was gone without a sound.

## *Max Saves the Day*

Max, the Yorkshire terrier, slept at the foot of Danny's bed most nights. If for some reason Danny wasn't home his sister Debby would be honored with a sleeping partner. Danny was OK with letting Max sleep at the foot of the bed while Debbie wanted to hold and cuddle with Max who preferred the foot of the bed. Cuddling was OK for a short time, but…

Max couldn't tell time but knew it was the middle of the night. Something woke him and he didn't know what it was. They say all dogs are descendants of wolves, so maybe that's what woke Max up. If one Looked at him, there was hardly a soul who would think Max had ancestors back that far.

Max heard a crinkle sound. Just barely a sound but he heard a noise that didn't belong in the house. He jumped off the bed to the floor covered with thick tan carpeting. Max was silent himself. Danny's door was open about two inches, enough for Max to squeak through, his body opening the door an inch more.

 As soon as he was in the hallway, Max's nose went into overdrive, detecting an odor he knew well.  A campfire.

While living with his first family, the Masters and his brother Rambo, the red Doberman Pincer, Mr. Masters had a fire pit on the back patio and sometimes lit a fire when guests were over. They would cook marshmallows and hot dogs using long sticks to hold the morsels over the fire.

The smell of cooking meat mixed with the odor of burnt marshmallows was etched in his memory. So too were the sounds a friend made with his guitar.  He played songs while they all sang. It was that smoke smell he remembered just now. This family had a fire pit too. Much like the Masters, they would cook outside and sing songs with the neighbors. Max was very familiar with the smell of burning wood.

Max scampered to the stairwell then headed down to the main floor. The room just to the right of the entrance was Brian's office. The door was open and this room was the source of the smoke. Flickers of orange and red flames danced on the wall.

Max ran up the staircase to the first door on the left. This door leads to the bedroom of Bonnie and Brian. As usual, the door was closed. Standing on his hind legs, Max used his two front paws to scratch on the door.  His little paws are working overtime, scratching, marring the gloss white paint, Max started to howl for all he was worth.

Bonnie heard him and yelled at him, "Max, go lay down. I'm not letting you out."  She looked at the bedside clock showing 2:07 in bright blue digital letters.

The smoke sneaking to in the upper hall was getting thick. Max ran back to Danny's room, jumped on the bed and charged to Danny's head where he started licking Danny's face. Danny, a sound sleeper started to wake up in a sleeper's stupor then woke up with a cry as Max started clawing on his arm hard enough to leave welts he would carry for a week.

"What's the matter with you boy?" asked Danny, now sitting up, holding his scratched arm while Max ran circles on the back of the bed, crying and whining.

"Oh, all right. I'll let you out, you bad boy. Look at what you did to my arm."

As soon as Danny got into the hall, the smoke odor was strong.  He started to scream for his mom and dad and sister.

"FIRE. FIRE. MOM, DAD, DEBBIE, GET UP."

The smoke was building fast. Getting down the stairwell was not possible. Brian had purchased a set of stairs for just such an emergency. They were stored in Danny's closet with strict instructions to keep the stairs free and easy to get at.

Rushing into Danny's room, Brian got the box holding the emergency stairs, a series of steps on a chain. He opened the window, and threw the stairs down the side of the house, hooking the top of the stairs over the window ledge.

While Brian was setting up the stairs, Bonnie used her cell phone to call 911 telling the operator the emergency and how they hoped to get out. Just then, a smoke detector in the hallway downstairs let out its shriek.

"OK Danny. We practiced this before. You know you can do it. You go first then mom will go. I'll carry Debbie." Brian took Danny's left shoulder and guided him to the open window. Danny slid one leg over the window sill, his left foot finding the first step and in just seconds, Danny was on the ground. With the sounds of sirens getting ever closer, Bonnie climbed over the sill and soon was on the ground too.

Now it was just him and Debbie.

"Honey, you get on my back once I get on the window sill. You wrap your arms around my neck and your legs around my body and hold on tight. I won't let you fall."

The sirens turned the corner of their street as Brian slipped over the top of the window sill. Debbie's arms found purchase around Brian's neck in a choke hold. She wasn't going to let go. In less than a minute, the two of them were on the ground just as two firemen carried a ladder rounded the corner of the house.
"Is there anybody else in the house?" asked one of the firemen.

"No, sir. We're all safe. I have no idea how a fire started" said Brian. "We have a smoke detector in the hall upstairs and It never went off."

"Dad," said Danny. "Max is still in there. Dad, he saved our lives. We gotta save him, dad." Tears are streaming down Danny's cheeks.

"Oh, our little dog is in there yet. He's a Yorkie and he did wake us and saved our lives. I just forgot about him. I'm sorry kids.

"Sir, we will do what we can and try and find him for you.  Please go to the front of the house where the chief is and talk to him."

Lights from nearby homes started to come on. As they rounded the corner of the house, the man from across the street walked out and over to them. Harold Washington was a black man. About 60 years old, he looked like a stevedore working the docks. With a heavy muscled upper body, it was easy to see him that way, not the Chiropractor he was.  When the Washington's moved in, Brian was a little apprehensive. "Well, there goes the neighborhood." one neighbor said.

The Washington's, Harold and Alicia, were about as nice a couple and great neighbors as anybody could hope to have. In fact, Harold was the one who played his guitar for the barbecues they had. Harold was once a member of a decent band rock in the 80's. He could rock the yard like he once rocked crowds of people with the band, The Ace of Hearts.

"Folks, come to my house. Alicia is putting the coffee on as I speak. I'll tell the chief where you are. You all aren't even dressed proper and there's a chill in the air tonight."

"Mr. Washington," said Danny, "Our dog Max is still in the house and he saved our lives. Please ask the firemen if they can save him," said Danny, choking back sobs of dread Max would die.

The fire was struck out in short order. Except for the smoke, the damage was contained to the office. It was apparent the cause was not negligence but a cell phone hooked to a charging cord. The phone had been on a stack of papers on the desk.

The papers, notes from the last homeowners meeting of which Brian was the Secretary/Treasurer this year caught fire when the cell phone overheated. The phone, a new one, would eventually be recalled, but today, that fact was not known.

Over the headset came the sound of, "I got him chief. He's lying by the window those folks escaped from. I'm sorry to say but looks like he's dead. I'll bring him out."

Fireman Collins picked up little Max, not more than fifteen pounds of love. He felt sorry for those kids as he too had kids and a dog they all adored.

Fire chief Upton was standing with Harold Washington when Jim Collins brought little Max over to him. Danny, standing at the window of the Washington home saw Max in the hands of a fireman and charged out the door toward the trio. He got to the group just as fireman Collins repeated the little guy was dead. Sobbing now joined the tears from Danny.

Harold Washington took the body of Max in his arms, not sure if he should give him to Danny or not. Calloused as his fingers were from years of playing guitars, Harold thought he felt something move in Max. He picked him up and held Max to his ear. He was sure he heard a heartbeat.

"He's alive chief. I hear a heartbeat." Just then, the rookie volunteer firefighter, Tom Perkins, walked up to the group. Tom was a volunteer for a little over seven months and turned out to be a good hand. A handsome man, just over six feet tall, his athletic swimmers build suited him fine as did his short cropped hair and 'Pepsodent smile.'

A single man, Tom had girls chasing him all the time. While he dated, he didn't seriously connect with a special woman just yet. He was playing the field and enjoying himself.

"Let me have him for a minute," said Tom, taking Max into his arms. Tom opened his mouth and put it over the little mouth of Max, then blew into Max, giving him artificial respiration. On the third breath, little Max sneezed three times, shook his head and wagged his tail a hundred miles an hour, looking at his best friend, Danny.

"Don't any of you guys let out I gave a dog artificial respiration. You'll ruin my reputation," said Tom, smiling at the group of guys.

"Like hell, we won't," said Chief Upton. "I can see it now, Fireman saves dog's life with mouth to mouth. You'll have every woman from sixteen to ninety-six chasing after your ass Tommy. I'm gonna invest in Chap Stick. You're going to need a semi-trailer of the stuff. Hot damn boys. We got us a hero here," beamed the Chief as little Max started licking the face of a very happy boy holding him.

# The Wheels of Justice

"So let me get this straight," Diane said, her voice under control but her face showing control was itself a strain. She stood behind a huge desk in room 103 in the Bunnell courthouse where their meetings were held. Her hands splayed open on the desk, she leaned forward, getting as close as possible to the recipient of her words across the desk. "You're telling me that Justice Stapleton said we can't use Abbas to track down the leader of this group of assholes?"

"It's what they told me," said Floyd Johnson. "I know your point, and I agree with you. We have a huge asset and there is very little danger to him. They tell me he has to be twenty-one and of sound mind to do this. We all know he fails on both counts."

"Yet," Diane replied, "the country will take eighteen-year-old kids and teach them how to kill and be killed and that's OK. It's so routine we don't even show the coffins coming home anymore. Unless it's for some political reason."

I stood up now, feeling angry. "We risked our lives getting this far and we have a chance to cut off a tentacle from the octopus's arm and do some good and we get stopped. How in the hell can we do any good if our government stops us?"

A slight smile crossed the lips of Floyd Johnson who said, "OK, I get what you are saying. In seven minutes we will be connected with a conference with Justice John Stapleton. He will hear your arguments and give you his reasons why this can't be done. Let's keep it civil huh."

The La Crosse atomic clock on the north wall of the room kept perfect time, ticking away the seconds and minutes until the video conference started. Diane and I started thinking of a rational argument to persuade the powers that be why they should follow up with this case. While Diane paced the floor, I just stood and looked at a blank wall.

Soon, the sixty-inch television on the wall under the clock came to life and the face of John Stapleton, sitting behind a large mahogany desk, lit up the room. A family portrait on the left side showed the director and his family with the family pet, a golden retriever. Everyone in the picture smiled. Even the dog seemed happy. The portrait of the President of the United States hung on the wall behind him.

As Wade and Diane returned to their seats, Floyd spoke first.

"John, this is Wade Nash. He heads our team down here and to his left is Diane Mason, his partner. We borrowed from her assignment in Europe. The big guy next to me is Marco Rodriguez. You're going to be hearing more of him in time."

"John, I told the team here of the decision and they have an argument against that decision. I'm grateful you will hear their side of the story and tell them why you made the decision you have. "

"Listen, guys. Oops, sorry. And Ms. too," said John, "I can sympathize with your situation, but it's a legal situation Congress passed many years ago. Believe me, I've heard the arguments before. I have just ten minutes to give you so who wants to go first?"

Diane was seething and it showed as she jumped up out of her chair, looking directly at the television capturing her image, relaying it back to the director.

With a Dixon #2 yellow pencil in her right hand, she manipulated the writing device between each finger First left then right The maneuver calmed her down a bit and yet she let go with both barrels. She kept the tirade civil without the swearing that sometimes escaped her in her anger.

Diane gave the director a complete synopsis of the entire event and how Abbas was responding to her and how he could lead them to the main man, the Money Man. How they had two other witnesses, the boat captain who gave them one address in Miami but had amnesia on locations in Guyana. The other, Mario Escalante gave a different location in Miami but knew nothing else. Abbas, challenged as he was, knew where the safe house was located. Also, he knew where he lived in Guyana.

"So Mr. Stapleton," said Diane, "this is the perfect opportunity to cut off an arm of the octopus and slow down the trafficking in this area. At least for a while.  On top of that, doesn't the State Department want the boy to be back with his parents? He was kidnapped as far as we know. Wouldn't that make a nice story on how the United States reunited a boy with his parents?"

Looking at his watch, John Stapleton saw their time was up. Wade never got a chance to speak but probably could not add anything Diane hadn't already covered.

The director responded, "I'm sorry folks, but the law is the law. For somebody to be used like this is against our laws and to get Congress to change the law is virtually impossible, so I have to say no."

Diane was seething. The number two pencil between her second and third fingers snapped with a loud audible crack. All this work. Getting burned and risking their lives for what? A bunch of political hacks. In an instant, Diane knew exactly what she was going to do. She was going to quit. Right now and directly to the director. They could take their bullshit and shove it where the sun don't shine. Just as she was about to scream out, "I fucking quit," the director held up his hand to stop her.

"Before you say anything, Ms. Mason, let me say this. I've looked over the law and could find no statement or law that says the boy cannot be brought back to his legal parents. As you are a clandestine group and not officially on the books, at least where the press can determine, I see no reason you cannot bring him to his home. If on the way there, something comes up and you have to take care of a problem, well, I'm directing you to bring the lad home and keep him safe. Do I make myself clear?"

"Yes Sir," I said, before Diane could say a word.

"Good," Said the director. "I think two weeks should give you enough time to get the lad home. What do you think?"

"Oh yes sir," said Diane. "Damn, I broke my pencil."

"You sure did," said John Stapleton, again looking at his watch, a smile on his lips now. "Just don't break the law to where it comes back and bites us in the ass. Good luck."

The screen was suddenly blank again.

# Ready, Set, Go!

The teleconference with Justice Stapleton behind them, Wade, Diane and Marco sat with Floyd to put together the start of a plan. They only had two weeks to do the near impossible. So much of what they would do would be on the fly. All three of them were good at doing that, proving it many times over the years.

"I think the best thing to do is fly the four of you to Miami," said Floyd. "I will have another man with you to help. He's a very good guy and knows a good deal about the northern part of South America including Guyana where Abbas seems to have come from and where a lot of human trafficking is passing through. His name is Adam Poe."

"I know Adam," said Diane. "I worked with him a few years ago on a drug problem in London. He's a good guy, and as I recall, he speaks a lot of languages and also knows several dialects too."

"Yes, he does Diane. He'll meet you in Miami tomorrow at the hotel. I will book the Marriott on the river. It's centralized and will be a good place to stay. What I'm hoping for is to see if the kid can locate the safe house they use in Miami. We've already staked out both possibilities. Both places look normal. We need to find the right one," said Lloyd.

"If and when you do, there will be a private plane to take you to Guyana where I will have a special boat for you. It will be plenty fast yet be able to navigate those waterways. We'd like to get the top dog in this organization and shut him down. I don't need to tell you that once in Guyana, you're on your own. Need I say if any of you get hurt or killed, well, you are on your own. We will help where we can, but it won't be a lot. You all know the drill."

Floyd continued, "I'll see all of you at six this evening, at the Daytona Beach airport. Diane, I guess we'll see how much the lad knows. If he doesn't, well, it was worth a try so don't worry about it."

"He knows boss. I'm not worried about that at all. It's just the thousands of miles of waterways in Guyana that have me concerned. It will be like looking for the proverbial needle in the haystack. I know the general area he lived in, so that's a big positive."

As soon as they got home, the two of them started the ritual of packing. Both packed travel bags so many times, it was second nature to them, yet, both consulted each other on what they needed.
.

Abbas was staying with Vickie this morning. Abbas was afraid to be alone but got along well with another woman figure. Marco would be along in an hour with Abbas. Wade asked Vickie as he dropped Abbas off this morning to take Abbas shopping and pick up a few things for him. A new outfit with extra underwear and socks would be good. Uncle Sam was paying for it.

Done packing, Diane and I toted the suitcases to the garage, then went into the kitchen where I made a huge corned beef sandwich topped with spicy mustard and cut the sandwich in half. A wedge of a dill pickle sat on each plate with a cut up tomato for each. With tall glasses of iced water to drink, they sat at the kitchen table, both thinking of something, yet not sharing their thoughts.

It continued to be warm in this part of Florida as I was suddenly aware the air conditioner kicked on another cycle. A cool breeze from the ceiling register blew on my neck as I sat at the table, looking at Diane who looked back at me. Just as natural as taking a sip of water, I bent over and kissed Diane tenderly on her lips while putting both my arms around her in a somewhat awkward position with the corner of the table between us.

That's all it took to start the flame. Deep in the recesses of our brains, we both knew this could be the last time we might kiss like this. The assignment meant guns and the possibility of never returning. We both are committed to each other and we both never want our time together to end.

A simple kiss became not so simple. Diane felt Wade's lips touch hers, her tongue darted out and between the lips of her lover and best friend and soul mate. Just a flick of her tongue started it. Half of a half sandwich eaten on their plates looked on as both stood up and moved to where the table was no longer a hindrance separating them. They molded into each other as one.

Wade's hands roamed her body then took purchase on Diane's lower back as he held her tight. Both tongues waged war with each other, passions rising to blow torch temperatures in just seconds. As was often the case with the two of them, both thinking this could be the last time. Together, they walked to the bedroom. They had an hour perhaps. An hour when they wanted a lifetime together. They better make the best of this. And they did.

# *Getting Some Answers*

A half-moon overhead on this clear night turned the ripples on the water sparkling like diamonds, casting in a repetitive pattern at the top of each wave crest. Several hundred feet to the north, the diamonds became a sea of emeralds interspersed with rubies and other colors, reflected from the Italian restaurant's neon sign. The restaurant is a famous haunt of many locals. Located on the east shore, it has boat access. What a treat to drive up in your million dollar cigarette style offshore racing boat. Until two A.M. when the ordinance says they must stop serving.

It was 10:44 P.M. when a Coast Guard boat, a 32-foot Osprey powered by twin 250 horsepower Honda outboard motors slid across the channel, just three hundred feet wide at this point. The sounds from the restaurant covered up the whisper quiet outboards running at near idle.

The Coast Guard boat held four figures dressed in all black apparel. Wade Nash, Diane Mason, Marco Rodriguez and the new man, Adam Poe. They rode in silence now. With this quartet were three Coast Guard men who regularly patrolled this area.

Wade, Diane, and Adam were here earlier in the day. Along with Abbas, they cruised the river, first a mile south where Gustav Fletcher swore was the location of the safe house. Then north past this location. With Wade and Adam in Coast Guard clothes on deck, Diane wore an auburn color wig and stayed in the cabin with Abbas. Abbas seemed to know what he was supposed to do.

As they got to this location, Abbas started mumbling. Talking in a speech of some sort Diane could not understand. He then started pointing at the building slipping past on the shoreline to the east. He got excited to where Diane had to hold him inside the cabin.  This was the place that Mario Escalante said was the safe house. They asked the Coast Guard to motor up the river a couple of miles then return at a leisurely pace. This time Diane asked Adam Poe to sit with Abbas and see if he could understand him.

Like before, Abbas started mumbling and pointing and getting excited as they returned and he viewed the building again. Adam said Abbas was saying "this bad." Over and over. They had the right building.

The past three days, the building was watched carefully. While people came, entered, and left, they were residents of the building. All the people were checked and rechecked. Most had shady backgrounds but not connected with human trafficking in any way.

It was 10:20 P.M. when Wade's cell phone rang. The lookout sitting in a clump of mangroves in a camouflaged Jon boat spotted a powerboat stop in front of the building and tie up to the seawall. Two adult males got off the boat ushering five children into the building. They appeared to be young girls.

Five minutes later, as Wade and the group were already on their way, one of the adults came out and started the sleek boat, supporting four white Evinrude outboards on the stern. He idled to the restaurant and turned it over to one of the guys who parked boats like one would park a car in a fancy restaurant. The man walked back to the building and let himself in.

While talking on his cell phone to Wade, the lookout never took his eyes off the building. He reported the three floors above all had identical picture windows facing the water.  The ground floor window was the same but was darkened and blacked out with heavy drapes. The second and third-floor units had the blinds open. One occupied by one adult male and one female. The other units seemed empty. Those that just entered were not on the upper floors in his opinion and observation. That left the ground floor as the one they wanted.

Sometimes luck has a way of finding the righteous. The Coast Guard boat barely touched the seawall in front of the building while Wade and the others prepared to step on shore and dash to the building door. Marco was carrying a heavy battering ram made for breaking down doors, ready to do his thing.

As they stepped off the craft, a young man on a bicycle with a carrier box on the back glided to a stop in front of the door. The box had printed *Pizza King* on the side. The kickstand was one people rarely see any more. It's a stand where you kick it down then pull the bike back several inches and the stand keeps the bike totally level. An "H" type stand no longer in fashion.

The young man looked at a slip of paper then looked at the number above the door. Satisfied he had the right address, he opened the carrier box fastened over his rear fender and removed two large pizza's just as Wade and the group walked up, almost totally invisible in the dark clothes they wore.

Startled, the delivery guy gasped and stepped back. In his surprise he uttered: "Man, take the pizzas. I only have change for a twenty on me. You can have that too."

"Easy son," I said. "What apartment are you taking this? I flipped out my ID with my name and picture on one flap.

"Apartment 1-A on the first floor the ticket says."

"Are you in high school son?"

"Yessir. I go to Archbishop Curley, Notre Dame. I'm a senior sir." He looked at the waiting Coast Guard vessel and the armed men aboard, black rifles in their hands as apprehension shown in his eyes, then looked back at Wade.

"How much is the bill?" I asked.

"It's $32.88, sir. If I don't come back with the pizzas or the money, I have to pay for them, and it's more then I'll make all night."

Looking over to the Coast Guard boat I said, "Captain, my wallet is in the console under the helm. Please take out fifty bucks and give it to this young man." In a minute, the money was in the pocket of the delivery boy, grateful he didn't get robbed and thankful for the generous tip.

"Son," I looked sternly at the delivery boy, "this is a federal operation. You go on back and keep your mouth shut. If you don't, well, just be quiet. It's best for everybody you were never here." He patted the delivery boy on the shoulder who pushed his bike forward, freeing the H style kickstand, turned the bike south and rode away at a rapid pace.

"Talk about luck," said Wade. "Get on both sides of the door and I'll make the delivery. He held the pizza boxes up to the spy hole and rang the bell. A shadow crossed the peep site, the sound of a safety chain on the door heard just before the door swung open. Wade kept the boxes head high as he walked in and said,

"That'll be $32.88, sir." Then stepped further into the room, the space behind him suddenly filled with bodies in black clothes.

With his hand in his pocket, reaching for his wallet, the man would soon be known as Wallace (Wally) Pounder. He had a startled look on his face but said nothing as the gun barrel of Marco's Sig Sauer 40 caliber struck him just behind his left ear, dropping him to the gray carpeting. The blow was just hard enough to knock him out for a minute or two.

Setting the two pizza boxes on the cocktail table, Wade and the others looked around knowing another adult should be in the room. What they saw were four small, very young girls sitting on top of each other in the corner of the kitchen next to the refrigerator. All of them very dirty with a terrified look on their faces. Their Fingers in their mouths. The shook in fear. A quick guess made them twelve years old or younger. None made a sound as they clung to each other. They shivered, although it was not cold in the room.

A partially open door on the other side of the room had sounds coming from inside. In just a few quick strides, Wade and Marco were at the door and opened it wide with one quick motion, guns out, pointing straight ahead. Instead of shooting, both suddenly felt sick to their stomachs.

In the room, on a double bed lay another girl. So very petite and frail looking from what they could see. Later, they found her age to be ten years old She looked younger. Her face was partially hidden and darkened with dirt. Her eyes shut tight as tears formed streaks down her cheek.

She whimpered in pain as the man above her moved, his cock thrusting in and out of the tiny girl as he approached his orgasm, grunting with each accelerating thrust of his body. He held the tiny girl's hands above her head. His pants down to his ankles, his ass moved up and down at a quickening pace.

Stunned, the two men were incapable of moving for a couple of seconds when reality hit both men at the same time. Marco was a step closer and crossed the space to the bed in two strides. He holstered his gun as he moved.

He reached between the man's legs from behind and grabbed his testicles with the stronger of his two hands, his right. He squeezed with all his might. The pain was so intense, the scream from the guy died in his throat, only to be compounded when Marco lifted him off the bed and the girl by his balls.

Marco's left hand took purchase in his grease laden hair. He lifted the guy shoulder high, then with a grunt, he threw him across the room, watching him land on the top of the dresser, shattering the mirror and slipping semi-conscious to the floor. The scream still deep in his throat. Panic in his eyes and seven years of bad luck. Seven years. He should be so lucky.

The next thirty minutes were hectic but well planned. The girls huddled and clung to Diane like she was the salvation all prayed for and perhaps she was to them. The five girls were abducted from Guyana a week before. Three spoke good English and told a horrifying tale of a man they called the Money Man who tricked them into coming to the water for food then kidnapped them. All but the little one had been raped on the crossing to America. The bad man Wally was saving her for a party tonight. The girls were to be passed off to others tomorrow.

Wally's partner, this guy named Chick, raped all of them more than once and he was the meaner of the two. A couple of girls had cigarette burns on them to prove how mean he was if they didn't do what he wanted.

A phone call had forensics arrive with many pictures taken of everything and everybody, including the bed which was bloody from the abuse the little girl suffered. The two scumbags were handcuffed, blindfolded and their mouths duct-taped shut.

One was in the bedroom on the floor while the other dumped in the bathtub with the door closed. After forensics left for the night, Wade and his crew were alone in the room with the two kidnappers. The Coast Guard boat waited to take the perps to the naval brig.

The girls were already taken to the Naval infirmary to guard against the word the young girls were rescued. Somebody was coming for them tomorrow and they wanted that somebody pretty bad.

"Listen, guys," I said, "We only have a very short time here to work. These two assholes will be in the Naval brig before long and they won't talk. We need information.  I want all of you to get aboard the Coast Guard boat and give me a half hour. That's all I'll need to talk to one of them."

"Uh uh no," said Diane. "We're a team, Wade."

"Fuck you Wade," said Marco, not smiling.

"I'll turn the faucet on," said Adam. "I know what the fuck you're gonna do."

The bathroom was crowded with Wade and Adam in the room and Wally in the tub, giving an evil eye to the two that approached. He knew he was one tough son of a bitch.

Pulling Wally's body into a sitting position, I closed the drain on the tub and turned on the cold water full, then lay Wally back into the tub. I reached over with my Benchmade knife and easily sliced the duct tape from his mouth, careful to slice his lower lip just a little. Wally leered at me. Blood dribbling down his chin.

"Here's how it's going to go. I despise anybody who hurts kids. You and your partner are the worst mankind has. Each breath you take sours the breath other good people take. The best a man can do with you is put you under the dirt. But I don't have the time for that. You're going to tell me what I want and if you don't, your death will be horrible and very slow. First, we'll play in the water. Next, it will be fire. Then a drill through each joint until you pass out when I'll wake you and do it again. Let's start the fun." He might have thought I was not serious. Oh, but I was.

The tub was half fullWithout a word, Adam grabbed Wally's legs and pulled him back, banging his head on the bottom of the tub. I took his face and submerged it under the cold water pushing his head down deep enough to cover his eyes but not his nose. I watched as the eyes of Wally grew larger in size but held contempt. I reached over and turned the hot water faucet to the full on, increasing the flow of water. Thirty seconds later, the water was deep enough to cover Wally's nose who started to choke, struggling to sit up in vain.

Half a minute passed and I let him raise his head. When it looked like Wally was going to say something, I slapped his face viciously and said, "Shut up asshole. You're just going to lie. I'll tell you when to talk. I'm enjoying this," then pushed Wally's face now well under the water getting deeper every moment.

Wally's cruel eyes became eyes filled with terror as bubbles escaped his lips, just a few small ones at first.  Soon, the bubbles became much bigger as his body searched for oxygen just inches in front of him. Once more, I let him up, gasping for life-giving air.

Three gulps of choked air mixed with water entered his lungs, burning like a fire inside his body. Lungs were not supposed to have water inside them. His headache from Marco's blow forgotten, he went under again. This time Wally gave in much sooner than the last time, the bubbles came sooner, and his eyes held a total panic mode as I let him up again.

"You've got one chance asshole. Tell me everything I want to know and you'll be sitting on that Coast Guard boat. But if you lie, I'll have you back here in a jiffy and watch the life go out of your eyes and thank God a scumbag is off the face of his green earth."

"Your partner is next, and if your stories don't match perfectly, you'll both be in hell before the bar down the street closes tonight." I looked at my watch. The bar was already closed. They didn't know it.

Diane came in with a mini tape recorder and in ten minutes, Wallace Pounder found himself chained to a cleat in the helm of the boat resting outside with the letters U.S. Coast Guard stenciled on the side in bright orange.

Chick Robbins was evil. And why not. His father named him "Lucifer" when he was born. His last name held no relationship to Marty Robbins, the country and western singer. Nor was he related to Harold Robbins, the writer of many fine books. He sure wasn't related to the award-winning motivational speaker and author Tony Robbins.

Doomed from the cradle on, saddled with parents that lived on crime themselves, they raised the devil themselves and were proud of it.

The fires of hell burn hot they say, so perhaps it was the luke warm water of the tub and the continuing baptism I performed on Lucifer that had him change his tune after a while. He was tough and held out longer than his partner, but he did cave in.

The stories were the same.  My crew and I had something to go on. A good starting point and with the help of Abbas, we had a chance to make a little difference and hopefully help a few kids along the way.

"Captain," I said to the Coast Guard vessel as Lucifer "Chick" Robbins was chained at the bow, away from his partner. "They're all yours, but I'd ask a favor if I might."

"Sure, Mr. Nash. I will if I can."

"When you get these two pieces of shit to the Naval base and the brig run by those hard-assed Marines, tell them these two are child molesters and worse.  And tell them a Marine put them in the brig."

And he replied, "Semper Fi."

# *Ambush*

The Cessna Citation M2 Company jet with no markings other than the mandatory tail numbers touched down in Georgetown, Guyana in a light drizzle the following afternoon. Georgetown, the capital of Guyana, is located with the Caribbean Sea to the north and east, Suriname to the south and Venezuela to the north. Georgetown was soon to be infused with wealth. Exxon's director Rex Tillerson announced that their research oil well called "Liza-2" off the shore of Guyana was the world's biggest discovery of the year.

The porous sandstone reservoirs could hold more that 1.4 billion gallons of high-quality oil reserves. Guyana, once controlled by Britain, was a sovereign country and the only English speaking country in South America.  While English is spoken with much of the population, the inner parts of the country spoke many other languages for thousands of years in the Amazon jungle the country inhabits.

Known as the land of many waters, Georgetown is nestled at the mouth of the Essequibo River which emptied its contents into the Atlantic Ocean, starting from the Acarai Mountains, 630 miles through the Amazon jungle.

Stepping off the air-conditioned jet, the trio of Wade, Diane, and Mario, felt like they were slapped in the face with a warm wet towel because of the proximity to the equator. Only Adam Poe, who lived in this climate and Abbas, smiled with the familiar and welcome feeling they embraced. Central Florida could be hot and sultry in mid-summer but nothing like this.

Floyd got the group out of the country as soon as possible. Wade wanted to stay and catch the group coming for the girls in the safe house. Floyd did not want them involved with the capture as that could tie them up for a long time.

They did hear from Floyd the operation was successful as it caught two men who came for the girls. Two more low lifes caught. Two more bad guys off the street.

A vehicle waiting for the group was reminiscent of the vehicles Wade saw in the Philippines years ago. Jitneys are jeeps converted into small buses. In the Philippines, the vehicles are painted outrageous colors. This one was drab green. Wade climbed in the front passenger seat while the others found room behind him. The luggage found a place in the very rear.

Passing the clock tower above the Stabroek market, the vehicle turned a sharp left down a street taking the group through shoppers laden with goods along with a few obvious tourists, cameras in hand or hanging from straps around their necks. Many in very colorful attire. Tents with vendors lined the street on both sides. The odor of a variety of items cooking found them as they passed. The misty rain did not affect anybody. It just was. The Essequibo river bank was just a short distance ahead and where the vehicle reached the end of this journey.

Tied to the seawall, they gazed at their transportation and home for possibly the next week. It looked to be an oversized Zodiac boat with large pontoons wrapped around the hull, obviously made for shallow water. This extra wide boat looked all business to the trained eye of the group. Sitting on the stern, just under the canopy of the upper deck sat two men dressed in what could only be described as casual junk attire. Each wore cargo shorts of a dubious age. One a faded olive drab green, the other was probably tan at one time.

One had a colorful Bob Marley tee shirt that had seen far better days while the other had a likeness of Che Guevara, well faded and worn, now a dingy white. Both men looked to be in their mid to late thirties and neither had seen a shower or had a razor touch their faces for quite some time.

Both men stepped off the craft just as Wade walked up to the boat, his eyes covered the entire vessel and the two men he was about to meet.

Reaching out a hand, the closest man said, "Staff Sergeant Pete Ortiz. I take it you're Wade Nash sir."

Wade nodded acknowledgment as the second man reached out.

"Gunnery Sergeant Angus Norlin sir. Pleased to meet you." Shaking Wade's hand.

"Angus Norlin? How the hell did you come up with a Norwegian name and look like a native here?" I asked. A quizzical look came on his face, a smile from ear to ear, anxious to tell his story.

"Remember Grenada sir? My daddy was part of the invading force and met my mother there and well, after the war, short as it was, he returned on leave. And here I am sir.  They're still happily married by the way."

"Listen, fellows, let's drop the Sir stuff huh. I'm Wade. I've been called a helluva lot worse and you may call me worse before this is over, but no "sir" please, gentlemen."

The smell of rotting fish and decaying wood surrounded the group as all introduced themselves to each other. For this trip, Staff Sergeant Ortiz would go by Pedro while the Gunny would answer to Angel. The names they used with the locals who thought they worked for the Guyana government. In truth, they worked for Uncle Sam.

Marco and Adam made fast work of transferring all their personal effects while Diane stood next to Abbas in the misty rain. Abbas stood like a statue and looked south, southwest toward the distant mountains. He was remembering. And smiling.

*What is he thinking* wondered Diane who glanced sideways at Abbas. *Probably about his home near the base of Kaieteur Falls where he appeared to live before he was captured.*

As is the way of the Amazon region, the mist passed and the intense sun turned the wetness into a steam bath, steam vapors rising from the ground all around them. "Like spirits rising from the dead" Angel said as he made ready to travel. Wade walked toward the stern of the boat as the others attempted to settle in and find a place they would claim for themselves on the crowded vessel.

With his foot on the huge cleat anchored to the dock, Wade sent an encrypted message to his Floyd. *"Here safe. On our way."* Then walked back and stepped aboard and said, "Let's go. We're burning daylight."

Pedro piloted the boat back into the Amazon, going against a three miles-per-hour current. Angel gathered the group at the rear and gave a summary of what they might run into as far as animals and reptiles they might encounter.

"The Tapir, although rare here, is the largest mammal in South America. Its diet is vegetarian and it's afraid of man for a good reason. Natives kill them for the food they provide. They resemble a hog and can reach a weight of near five hundred pounds. You may not see one but if you do, don't worry. He's more afraid of you than you of him."

Angel went on to brief the group of the Ocelot and Jaguar and the variety of monkeys they might see as well as a sloth. "None of these animals will harm you unless they are cornered which is pretty hard to do in the jungle."

Soon, he talked about a subject he loved. Snakes. Of course, there was the Boa which comes in several different forms. The Tiger snake looks like a cobra. The Black Mamba is very poisonous and a few others.
"By far our biggest threat is the species Homo sapiens," said, Angel.

"While the Amazon is far less dangerous to man when it comes to the animals, it has never been this dangerous than now as we confront humanity himself. The jungle is the route or home to many men and some women too, that run drugs or many illegal products under the triple canopy above."

He went on, "In this mission, we are tasked to break up a human trafficking ring. To catch the very elusive leader. Ha. We plan to succeed but I tell you with a heavy heart, should we succeed, you won't even be back to the United States, and another will take its place. It's very sad but this is the way our world is today."

I spoke up. "Thank you, sergeant. I think we know what you are saying but we have to somehow slow them down here, at least for a while."

"And you will sir. But the intermission will be very short indeed. Unless you can catch the boss. He's very elusive. Catch him or stop him and the intermission can be a few months. But it will start again, I promise."

"With the thousands of miles of channels running through the jungle, finding him will be, well, let's say it will be tough and let it go at that."

As darkness settled in, so too did the predators, including the human kind. With Angel spelling Pedro at the helm, he maneuvered the boat near the shore, just far enough out of the main channel to not interfere with another boat traveling by night. The boat sat a few feet under the dark canopy of trees, making stargazing a chore.

The gently waving branches above and the busy day soon lulled most of them to sleep in short order. Diane watched a distant brilliant star that could have been the planet Mars. She thought back a long time ago, lying in the grass next to the house and Grandpa Cletus telling her stories about the heavens. Back then she believed them and never forgot the Walt Disney song, *When you wish upon a Star*. Oh so very long ago.

Living on the ocean in Florida, sunlight starts with a pre-dawn. The eastern sky brightens up a bit then wham! The sun peeks over the horizon and it's light out. Under the canopy of the jungle, the light just creeps up on you a little at a time.

Curled in a light sleeping bag on a roll up foam pad, Diane opened her eyes to the sound of footsteps she not only heard but felt through the pad. Then a voice spoke softly, "Diane, don't be afraid. Please wake up. Just don't move." It sounded like Angel's voice.

Lying on her left side, Diane opened her right eye and searched for the voice. She saw Angel on the other side of the boat, close to her feet tucked in the sleeping bag. He held a rod about eight feet long with a loop of rope on the end.

Between that rod and her foot was a snake. A big one at that. It was over ten feet long and several inches thick. Its red tongue flickered out every few seconds as it looked at Diane with its piercing black eyes. It started to slither toward her, never taking its eyes off of her.

Angel extended the rod out toward the head of the snake. The loop of sturdy nylon line on the end gently slipped over the head of the snake, which was now near her knees and moving toward her head. Angel let the viper slide over the loop until six or so inches of the loop was behind its head.

With an easy movement, Angel took most of the slack out of the line. Then with a firm and fast tug, he secured the hook over the snake which coiled over and over around the pole Angel held.

Lifting the pole, he pivoted and put the snake in the water. He then let slack in the loop and watched the snake slither to the bank of the river.

"It was just a small Boa," Angel said. "I heard him drop from the tree into the boat about an hour ago but it was too dark to see him until now."

Having been holding her breath, now Diane could breathe again. While not afraid of snakes, she avoided them whenever possible. The toilet was close and a good time to make use of it. Now everybody was up anyhow. Welcome to the Amazon, she thought.

Breakfast was a fast affair made by Diane and Adam Poe. Boiled instant oatmeal with a can of mixed fruit was distributed for everybody as Pedro pushed the boat up the river at a good pace. The brown mud river was a series of turns, with much of the river under the canopy of the jungle.

Walking up to the helm with the breakfast for Pedro Wade asked, "I never got a chance to ask about the boat here. What'll she do?"

"This baby has a 440 horsepower Cat diesel with twin jet drives and will do 44 knots with four aboard. With all of us, I'd say she's good for 40 knots anyhow. She'll run in ten inches of water and her range is near 400 miles. A lot of fours huh."

"Yes, there are. What do we do for fuel back here?"

"No problem. There are some good size settlements we will visit. There's plenty of fuel. The prices are high. Price gouging is rampant back in the jungle.  With our GPS, finding fuel is no problem."

Three hours of running had them to the first junction point and a decision must be made. The Essequibo continues but two other rivers branched out both left and right in a double-Y pattern. Which one was the one they wanted? It all looked the same to them. Abbas looked left with a hard stare then grunted to Diane pointing they should go left.

"Left it is Wade," Pedro said. "The GPS shows this to run for twenty miles or so then peter out but there are a few branches that run off it on the way."

A half hour later, they came to a very sharp right swing in the river, almost doubling back on itself. The river was shallow here. Rocks were not far under the surface. Some protruded out of the water creating a series of white foam around them.  Once past the sharp bend, the GPS showed the river opened up again.

Diane and Abbas stood on the bow platform, Abbas transfixed on the river, while Diane sipped on a half-full bottle of water. As the boat was almost through the sharp loop in the river, the right jet drive hit a submerged rock sending the craft a foot left just as the bottle in Diane's hand exploded, water spraying both she and Abbas.  The sharp crack of a rifle sound cut the air.

Grabbing Abbas, Diane hit the deck as another shot rang out followed by the sound of Adam Poe cry out, "I'm hit."

Diane looked back and saw Adam holding his right thigh just below his shorts, blood pulsing out of the wound. An artery must have been hit looking at the amount of blood escaping and the way it was shooting out.

I crawled to Adam and was opening a package, a tourniquet, when Pedro shouted, "Hold on folks."

He pushed the throttle to the stops full forward as the boat lunged through the remainder of the sharp curve. The back slid sideways on the surface. Geysers of water flew fifty feet in the air, helping to conceal the boat.

*Had the boat not hit the submerged rock, that round would be lodged in the center of my chest* thought Diane.

Angel climbed on the roof and with an AR-15, a hundred round drum magazine attached. He tore up a section of the jungle with rapid multi-round bursts and was rewarded with a scream from the bush.

By now, the boat was past the curve with a straight stretch of the river in front, moving at top speed.  Soon, the boat was well out of range of the ambush.

With Poe's leg wrapped with gauze from a first aid kit, the bleeding much slower now, Wade grabbed his satellite phone and called in the ambush to the base in Georgetown, which relayed it to the states.

After the message was sent, word came back to Wade. "Seventeen and a half miles ahead of you is a village on the left bank. Get there. We will have a bird pick up the wounded man. If you run into any more problems, call it in. We have other aircraft that may be able to help if necessary. We have two Blackhawks heading your way as we speak."

Standing next to Pedro, Wade said, "You heard the man. I don't feel comfortable doing this but we have no choice. Let's get moving my friend."

"We'll be OK Wade," said Pedro. "Angel, it's rock and roll time. Bring out the toys."

Wade turned and saw Marco open a storage box on deck and hand a fifty caliber machine gun to Angel on the roof along with three boxes of ammo. In less than a minute, the gun was live and ready to go while Marco handed Diane an AR-15 and Wade a Heckler and Koch 9 mm machine gun.

Angel called down to Marco, "Buddy, the box on the other side has a nice toy you may or may not be familiar with. It's experimental, but it works great. It's a modern bazooka with fragment and napalm rockets. We'll keep these fuckers away. Oops, sorry Maam."

"Fuckin A, Angel," We'll keep the fuckers away. No problem," said Diane.

Wade gave Adam Poe a shot of morphine to ease the pain now settling in on him and checked the tourniquet once more.

Angel said, "These are drug runners. They think we are Narcos. That's why they hit us. The jungle is full of them."

"You know guys, we're in way over our heads in this. Let's get Abbas back home and get our asses out of here and regroup."

Through gritted teeth, Adam answered, "Fuckin A Wade."

Across the deck, Marco said, "Fuckin A boss."

In the front, Diane answered, "Fuckin A big guy," as she smiled. Snakes. Shot at, and all in a couple of hours. She could leave without regret after getting Abbas home.

Everybody looked at each other and suddenly all were laughing so hard the boat started rocking from side to side. Pedro laughed hard with them. Fuckin A.

## *Hot on the Trail*

An hour on the switch back river, negotiating boulder strewn waters was the reason for the time it took to reach the village we learned was called Burro Bono, so marked on their GPS screen. It was a swatch of land, perhaps two hundred acres, once a jungle, now rich fertile farm land.

The freshly plowed earth gave off the pungent odor of decaying moss. Thatched roof huts sat in a semi-circle facing the river, a hundred yards back from the bank. Clothing hung from bushes. A woman bent over a cauldron stopped her task as we arrived. We saw women and children leave the river bank with clothes they were washing as we pulled up to their dock.

The dock on the river was about a hundred feet long and made of a mix of logs taken from the forest, including a quantity of mahogany. The top of the logs grew green moss interspersed with streaks of black. The setting could have come from hundreds of years ago.

Angel pulled the boat against the dock, with the nose pointed into the current. Marco jumped off the boat, slipping on the slimy moss, almost falling. Wade tossed him a line to secure the bow. That secured, the stern slid against the dock by itself.

Angel killed the Cat diesel engine. The ensuing silence was eerily quiet. Everybody just froze in motion, including the pair of oxen plowing a section of the field near the jungle. Everybody just looked at the boat with a heavy machine gun on its roof, manned by a person they knew worked for their government. They saw the boat before but never with a machine gun on the roof.

Many of the residents worked the drug trade in one way or another. With the government boat showing up and the men armed, it could mean there would be arrests coming.  Wade watched men slide off into the jungle leaving their women and children to stand and stare.

Getting off the boat and on the dock made of round logs, I carefully made it to land and walked up to two men that had not moved since the boat docked.

Their age was hard to determine as anybody growing up in the jungle environment aged fast and lived short lives for a variety of reasons. Still, I guessed the men to be younger than me by ten or more years.

"Do either of you men speak English?" I asked both men and got a blank stare from them.

"English. English." I repeated, with the same blank stare returned from two men who could have come from another planet as far as I could tell.  Playing a hunch, just a thought, I went on and said, "We have a wounded man on board. There's a helicopter coming any minute to pick him up and they need to land in your field.  It will do a little damage and I want to pay for the damage." I took out a wad of American cash folded over, a hundred dollar bill on the top.

"Yes, we speak some English. You are not here to arrest us?" asked the man on the left.

"Nobody is going to get arrested. We are taking a young boy back to his village by Kaieteur Falls. He was abducted and smuggled into the United States and we are bringing him home is all. We have no interest in what you do here or any other place in the country."

"If he was stolen, it was the Money Man who took him. Or maybe he bought him. People sell their children to live a better life in another country. We do not trust him and he is a bad man. He stops

here for food and fuel for his boat. He never stays here though."
Spoken by the same illiterate man now speaking very good English.

I peeled off two one hundred dollar bills. I handed the money to the
man I was talking to as I heard the whap whap of the chopper blades
cutting through the air. The helicopter cleared the treeline, coming
into view from the east. Two hundred American dollars was a
fortune to the village and worth probably more than all the produce
they grew for the season.

With Adam Poe between them, looking pale but smiling, Marco and
Pedro made quick work getting him to the helicopter, it's blades
winding down.  From out of nowhere appeared two Blackhawk
choppers, manned to the teeth. Each side door had a fifty caliber
machine gun facing down.  The pods under each bird carried a
variety of armament.

I walked to the helicopter with them and wished Adam well and
promised to get together soon. *If I can get out of this mess,* I thought.
With that, the helicopter with its two support birds was soon out of
sight.

I stepped over the furrows of the fresh oxen plowed field.  The
helicopter did no damage at all I could see. Just two furrows a few
inches deep, about twenty feet long. I walked back to the two men I
had spoken with. Neither moved an inch from what I could see.

The other man who never spoke to me then turned toward the jungle
and gave out a very loud screech which I thought could be the sound
a Jaguar. He then came out with another of a slightly different tone
as men materialized from the jungle and went back to whatever they
were doing.

The first man then said, "The Money Man was here three days ago
and said he was heading to Kaieteur Falls. You may see him on the
way."

"Hmmm. I have no idea what he looks like or what his boat looks
like," I said. "Can you describe him and his boat to me?"

"For ten American dollars, I will show you a picture," the man said as he reached in this homemade purse-like sack on his side. He opened the bag made of woven grass, reached in and removed a modern cell phone.

I guess I had a shocked look on my face as the man said, "We are not savages sir. Oh, our children don't stay here. They go to the big cities like Georgetown and even out of the country, but us old ones choose to stay here and live a simple life. That life is not so simple anymore because generators power our water pumps and provide lights for our homes.  We voted to turn off the generators at dark.  It helps us live the lifestyle our ancestors lived. The phone was a gift and while we don't have phone service, it takes fine pictures. I took one a few months ago of the Money Man and his boat. You can see it for ten American dollars."

As the man scrolled through the pictures, I dug out a five and five singles and exchanged the money for the phone. There on the little screen was a picture of a small boat with a cabin, very similar to several boats we saw, except for the exhaust pipe running up the side of the cabin. Another picture was one of a man in boots that laced up to his knees. In a leather vest and a wide brim hat, he looked like he stepped out of the century before.

I asked the man to hold his camera still.  I took out my cell phone and took three pictures of each of the two pictures on the other phone. Checking to make sure they came out. I would transfer these to the satellite phone once under way. Peeling off another twenty dollar bill, I thanked the two men and went back to our boat, walking carefully over slippery moss covered logs.

As I walked to the boat, the man called out, "The Money Man is a bad man. He has two with him that are evil. Watch them. They are truly evil."

Marco untied the bow line, gave the boat his hardest shove, pointed the bow into the current and stepped aboard as the gap widened to four feet between the dock and the boat. We were underway again.

# Death on the River

Travel that day was brimming with anxiety, knowing the little huts they occasionally passed could harbor people who did not want them here. Because of the way their world was now, most were armed.  Every hut we passed had us look where we could seek shelter if bullets began to fly. Nothing happened but the tension was high.

We finally decided to take the machine gun off the roof but keep the other weapons close, hidden from view. We were preparing to stop for the night and were looking for a suitable location, far enough from the shore, yet not in the channel.  And not under a tree like last night. We saw a suitable location and motored to it when around the bend in the river came the needle that was lost in the haystack.

A river boat with the engine exhaust stack running up the side of the cabin, little black puffs of smoke popping out every second or two, chugged into our space. A giant black man at the helm guided the boat away from our craft.

At the stern stood a man with one foot on the gunnels of the craft, leather boots laced up to just below his knee. The man waved and smiled at us as we passed not ten feet apart. The boat and the man in the back were on the pictures I had on my phone in my pocket.

Diane and Abbas stood at the bow. Abbas stared intently as the boat approached.  Diane had all she could do to hold Abbas still. He was pointing and speaking a language none on board knew, but in his way, he made it clear that the boat passing was the bad man. The Money Man. He was found but so were they.

Arthur Dalton didn't get to where he was by being a fool. He had spotted the boy before the boy saw him, but it was too late to get under cover, so he just waved a friendly gesture. He knew it was the quiet one who knew how to work a Rubrics' cube easily. How the hell did he get back here he wondered, now knowing they had a problem.

The big African at the helm spotted Abbas too and as soon as he could, he slipped the machine pistol to his side from its spot under the steering wheel.

He spotted the woman and the kid and one man on deck amidships and somebody at the helm. That was all he saw. It would be child's play to clean up this group.

"We go back and get dem," said the giant at the helm. "We keel dem all."

"No," said Arthur. "They will turn around and come after us. I'll take the helm. Go below and get Basil. He can break the girls in later. Get out the bazooka. I'm going to find a spot to back the boat in, under cover. We will ambush them around the next curve or two."

I watched them pass then said, "Ok, The guy at the helm spotted us and pulled a machine pistol out.  The Money Man was far too casual for meeting strangers in the jungle. He knows too. He probably spotted Abbas right away and the way Abbas was acting, he knows we know."

"We have to turn around and go after him as sure as hell, this will be our one and only shot to get him. Now, does he have more kids in the boat? It's a good chance he does. So we can't just blow them up. Any ideas?"

Marco and Angel were below fixing dinner but heard the conversation when Angel walked on deck and said, "Wade if I were them, I'd sneak in a little hidey hole and wait for us to come looking for them. What do you think?"

"Yes, that's exactly my thoughts. They can't outrun us. But where will they hide is the thing?"

"Hey Pedro, I'm putting Tinker Bell in the air." Angel spoke to his partner at the helm.

"Tinker Bell is our little drone with cameras only. She's very quiet and can stay up for hours if need be. What do you think Wade?"

Pedro turned the boat around, well out of range of the other boat's sight or hearing.  Angel sat at the kitchen table and looked at the screen in front of him, two hands on the control board as he set Tinker Bell in the air and down the river. The drone scanned both sides, looking for the telltale mud trail the boat would leave as it left the main channel.

Two curves down, to the right about a half mile, a mud water trail pulled out of the main channel.  The boat was backed into a clump of mangroves, the bow barely visible.  The camera on the drone showed a man is standing waist deep in the water. A huge black man, hiding behind a fallen tree with a tube in his hand. It was clear it was a modern bazooka looking weapon. One shot and they would be toast. Literally and figuratively toast.

Angel took the drone up several hundred feet to get a good bird's eye view of the area. It was all swamp with no dry land between their boat and the quarry.

 Angel pointed this out to Wade who understood what they were up against then said to Wade, "You guys relax. Pedro and I will handle this. Just sit tight."

"Belay that Sergeant. Marco and I will handle this. You stay with your boat and the lady and the kid. If things go bad, get them back to

Georgetown asap" I said. Both Angel and Pedro looked put out. They were primed to go.

Digging into one of the bags we brought along, I removed three ear mic's giving one to Angel and the other to Marco. "Keep the drone up and keep looking for anybody else, not on the boat. We don't know who or how many are on the thing.  Our lives are at stake here."

We motored back to just a couple hundred feet from the Money Man. I wanted them to know we were coming. I also didn't want to slog a mile on foot in the muddy river.

Testing the microphones, making sure all was working well, Marco and I slipped silently into the water from the stern of our boat. We fanned out and made a loop behind the boat We stayed in contact with Angel who kept an eye on each of us, although difficult to see in our camouflage setup with the fast approaching darkness.

Marco said, "I've got the guy with the tube Wade. I hope you don't want to talk to him because I doubt you can when I put one in the back of his head."

"Do it Marco," I said, watching Marco slither through the putrid water.  He never gave a thought to a Cayman or any other animal that could do him harm. Not even a snake which he hated. Just the animal with the tube in his arm.

Marco slid through the water without a sound and soon lost sight of Wade to his left. Angel spoke in a whisper to Marco saying, "he's twenty feet in front of you, and three feet right of you."

Two minutes later, the giant was just an arm's length away in front of Marco. Reaching for the gun in his holster on his right hip, Marco slowly drew the Sig Sauer 40 caliber from its home, then he slowly raised the weapon. Tilting the barrel down to drain the water, the gun barely cleared the surface when the giant heard a drip from the water running out of the gun just behind him.

The drip was alien and with a quick motion, the tube forgotten, the huge man turned to attack and almost turned in the right direction when the side of his head was punctured. A metal object traveling at over two thousand feet per second pierced his head just behind his right ear.  The bullet expanded as it traveled through gray matter and grew to the size of a half dollar. It exited the left side of his head, his ear totally disintegrated along with a large portion of his skull. His lips formed an "O," but the word never came out. Just blood and brains. His body settled to the mud bottom.

A thought came to Marco. Words he heard just hours ago. "They are evil men."

Sometimes evil men die so suddenly they feel no pain and no remorse. For a fleeting second, Marco wondered how God dealt with evil men. A second later, his mind was back on the job.

Even with the silencer in place, the sonic crack of the shot sent dozens of birds into the air that were resting for the night in the branches above them. A movement at water level to his left had Marco look to the source which materialized from the middle of a swamp bush.

The black giant's partner. Another giant of a man who had a gun pointed directly at Marco. He folded his legs, attempting to sink below the surface, but in the fraction of the time he had, the big giant had the laser sight on Marco's left eye. The red beam blinded him.

Marco knew he was too late. He was done. In that partial second, he thought of Vickie and how he loved her and how many plans they had. And they were all gone. He saw the flash and an instant of pain as he sunk below water.

The bullet snapped Marco's head back as he felt his body slide under the surface of the water.  Warm, soothing water all around him. He was under for several seconds thinking dying wasn't so bad after all. Then he exhaled and could feel air bubbles escape from his mouth. His breath was gone. He was dead.

Tinker Bell noticed a slight movement in a bush just right of Wade's position.  Angel told Wade about it.

"Could be a bird or an animal. I don't know, but it's something that moved. About 7 or 8 feet to your right."

I moved with all the caution I ever knew and I was good at that. Then I could smell him. It was the smell of diesel fuel. No animal other than man could smell like that. And then I saw him. A huge black man with an AR-15 with a laser sight attached, held just above the water, sticking out of the bush he hid in.

Three feet. Now two feet and just a bit less, my trusty Benchmade custom knife in my hand, my arm free of any obstructions.

I heard the soft crack of Marco's gun and saw the giant in front of me look over to Marco, seeing him for the first time. Birds squawked and flew above as he raised his rifle and put his index finger of his right hand in the trigger guard. He steadied the laser beam on Marco's head. His finger closed on the trigger taking up the slack. Only six pounds of pull needed.

He pulled, just as a spray of his blood shot several feet into the air. His right carotid artery was severed by my knife. The gun went off a fraction of a second after the slice and Marco was missing. I was too late. A second sooner and….

That's it I thought. If I ever get out of here, I'm done. Now I lost my best friend. I was too late. You're too old for this game old man.

Birds were flying through the trees making a racket above him. The giant in front of him was jerking in spasms in his death knoll. The blood escaping from his severed carotid now slowed to a trickle as Wade watched the life fade from his body.

It was too dark to see the pool of blood around me which I knew was there.  I made my way across the gap to find Marco. Find him and carry him home with sadness and grief all the way. To Vickie. To tell her I let them down. I was too slow. Too old. I would live with the memory of this moment forever. If I was just a fraction faster.

Marco's world was black.  No bright light appeared as is often reported by those who died and came back. No relative was waiting for him at the pearly gates. *I guess this is where hell starts he thought.*  Then he remembered to open his eyes. He wasn't dead. What happened? Suddenly, the top of his head caught on fire with pain.

Like Phoenix rising from the ashes, a head emerged from the water, gasping for air. It was Marco and he was alive.

## *Surprise Turn*

In the seconds it took Wade to cross the gap to get to Marco, excited his friend and partner was alive, it was enough time for the Money Man to bring out a powerful hand held searchlight and a shotgun to his shoulder. He snapped the light on, illuminating the two men in the water with a million candlepower beam.

The bright light illuminated both of us as I saw blood streaming down Marco's face. Rivulets of red dripped off his chin from the wound on his head. The blood flowed freely and had me thinking his wound was very serious. Later, we discovered the bullet that hit him just grazed the top of his scalp, tearing a three-inch long portion, a quarter inch wide off his skull, taking just a small part of the skull bones as it traveled past his head. Scalp wounds bleed excessively but rarely are the cause of death. Had the bullet traveled a quarter inch lower, death would have been a certainty and our Phoenix would not have risen as he did.

The brilliant searchlight shining from the bow of the boat fifty feet away startled both men in the water. With just enough backlight, they could see the Money Man holding a rifle or shotgun on them. Both of them were dead ducks. It looked like they would die together. The emotions in Wade were screaming for just a few minutes of quiet time. Any second now and he'd be quiet forever. In his haste to see to his friend, he forgot all his basic survival rules. Rules he taught and now somehow neglected.

With an English accent, the Money Man said, "This could be your lucky day boys. You have a choice. Think about this. Do I want or die in this swamp?  By tomorrow, even your clothes will be in the belly of something that lives here. What'll it be?"

"Well," I said, "I think you hold all the cards. You know if you let us live, we'll be back for you. But we'll be much better prepared. And we'll get you."

"Oh, I know that. I have a huge "get out of jail" card and I want to use it."

"You do?" I asked. "And what's that?"

"I know all about this operation. Every single detail of it and well I should as I designed much of it. My get out of jail card is I turn it all over to you. Your government can shut down a huge operation. Multi millions of dollars come out of this every year. I have every name and every payout to every player and there are many."

"And what do you get in return?"

"Your government has the best witness protection program in the world. I want in on that. Me and my family."

"You would shut down your own operation?"

"My operation? Are you kidding me? I just work for the man. Do you really think I'd be in this backwater if I were the boss?

"The word is the Money Man is the man behind all of this. Is this not true?"

"My name is Arthur Dalton. I am just a piece of the business. OK, a good chunk but I'm not the boss for sure."

"So, who is the boss?" I asked, knowing what he would say before he spoke.

"Not so fast my friend. I'll give it all to you. It's all documented and you won't believe all the people and names that are involved. This will be the story of the month, maybe the year, and it will make your career for you."

"Come here to the boat," Arthur said. "I'll drop a ladder, and you can come aboard and I'll give you my gun. There are two girls below deck. Young girls, I stole for the trade. They are scared but they are OK. When you are aboard, call your boat here and the whole thing here is yours.

I know I can't beat the United States government so maybe I can help on my way out. I want political asylum or whatever. But I want my freedom and I want in your witness protection program. Big heads will roll and they'll be after me."

Marco needed attention. He may not die but he would be very sick if not treated soon. The man had a gun on us and with a simple pull of the trigger, we'd be toast. Or Caiman bait. I could say no and get shot for certain. Or I could say yes and play it out.

It was as dark as black ink in a black jar when the two boats touched bows and were tied together securely. Tree frogs and night predators echoed in the night. Sounds that would make your skin crawl and have you seek shelter.  A gangplank stretched from one boat to the other on a slight incline, the Money Man's boat a foot taller.

True to his word, Arthur Dalton surrendered his weapon and told where others were stored on the boat. Diane took custody of the two frightened girls with the help of Abbas who seemed to know just what to do, calming the two little children.  He spoke to them in a language only they understood.

As agreed, Dalton was handcuffed and loosely chained to a cleat on the boat but showed no interest in escaping. Quite the contrary. He would give up no more information on the operation. He was no fool.

The secure satellite phone to my ear, I spoke to Floyd and discussed the situation and went over options.

Floyd said, "Get to that village you were at this morning, Burro Bono I believe, and we will fly all of you out. I'll bring in some Rangers to get both of the boats out safe. You should be there by noon."

"No, that won't work. We are just a few hours away from the falls and Diane won't hear about not getting Abbas home. She's determined and I am too, that we get him home. And now we have the two new girls to get home. Dalton is cooperating and will guide us to where he picked the two of them up today. They are OK and just scared. Why bring them to the states then bring them back?"

"I see your point, Wade. As for political asylum, I'm sure we can work this all out. I'll start on that now. Good luck. Keep me posted. Great work Wade. I'll see you soon."

The Amazon River black caiman can grow to a length of sixteen feet. They may not have been quite that large but with blood in the water, alligators of the Amazon came to the area at the same time both boats touched bows. Just to the stern of Wade's boat, several caimans dined on two very large meals.

I turned on the spotlight as water thrashed and splashed. Two caimans fought each other over the meals and while the two fought, a third came in and bit off a chunk for himself.

Soon, several caimans were involved in the feast which brought other carnivores to the scene. The water boiled with activity for several minutes. Finally, everything calmed down, each victor swimming off to feast on fresh meat. Even the bones disappeared.

Dalton was secured and the girls attended to by Diane. Angel worked on the head wound on Marco and whistled, "Man, you can't get much closer to death my friend. A quarter of an inch and your skull would have been blown apart from that bullet. You can learn to part your hair down the middle now because you will have a permanent crease. Damn, that was close."

He doused the wound liberally with hydrogen peroxide, bubbling out the river dirt before adding an antibiotic cream and a surgical dressing that covered the top of his head. He secured it with a gauze strap that went under his neck. The bandage looked like a homemade bonnet. A crude rendition of what a Quaker girl might wear.

We couldn't do anything more until daylight, several hours away, so I dug into my bag and extracted a brand of medicine I thought perfect for the occasion. A fresh bottle of Templeton Rye whiskey. Nicknamed "The Good Stuff" during prohibition, it was the smoothest rye whiskey I ever tasted.

With a couple of ounces poured into Solo plastic cups, we all enjoyed the celebration and the treat. We were setting up a rotating watch and watched Marco crash right where he sat. Diane placed a light blanket over his head and around him to keep him comfortable and keep the bugs off. He looked like an Indian teepee.

I took out my phone and took a picture of him. All that was visible was his nose and closed eyes but it was enough. I sent it to Vickie, calling the shot "Sitting Bullshit." We needed to laugh.

# Reunion

By 5:45 A.M., it was light enough to see. I had the last watch, so I was up already, looking at the swamp around us. I saw no sign of anything out of the ordinary, like clothing or body parts. Nature takes care of itself.

Marco was on the deck, on a foam pad with the same blanket over him. He opened his eyes which showed a lot of pain in his squint. The pain was like looking into the sun, but the sun was not visible yet.

"I guess you saved my life, Wade. Thanks. Huh, like that's enough," said Marco, slowly sitting up.

"Marco, I damned near cost you your life. I'm too damned slow now. We were both lucky. Maybe when we both get back, we should take to driving a cab for a living."

"Hell no. That job's too dangerous. I'll take my chances out here, thanks."

Our talking had the gang up. Diane headed to the potty. The guys just hung it over the side. The whiskey must have helped everybody sleep. None had a headache, except Marco, of course. His was a dandy.

The food was passed around from government rations and Arthur Dalton's boat was secured. They hoped to be back later to pick it up, but accurate GPS coordinates were taken just the same. With everybody aboard the government craft, the group, guided by Dalton, motored up the river about ten miles to a small clearing. A woman was standing ankle deep in water, washing clothes in the brown water, beating the clothing with a stick. She stopped her labor. The woman watched as the boat pulled up to shore and the two little girls were handed down to Angel who jumped out as the boat touched shore.

With screeches and yelling, the three embraced, all crying and laughing at the same time. As the boat backed into the channel, those on the boat looked on with happiness.  None on the beach would ever know how close they came to a life they would never want to be a part of.

"Forget the GPS. I know a way to get us to the falls a lot faster," said Arthur Dalton, very relaxed. He was so very close to freedom himself.

The way Dalton suggested they go and the GPS was, in fact, the same. Because Dalton suggested the route made the crew a bit uneasy. Did he have a trick up his sleeve?

They could hear the waterfall quite a while before they saw it. Kaieteur Falls is the largest single drop waterfall in the world by volume of water flowing over it. The water is donated by the Potaro river and as it goes over the edge of the fall, it crashed down 741 feet before it flows over a series of smaller falls for a total of 822 feet. Even with the jungle damping the sound, the fall can be heard for miles away.

As the boat docked near the base, several tourists were standing, snapping pictures of the magnificent falls. Tourists with money flew into the airstrip just to see the attraction. Having never been here, Wade had no idea the falls were a tourist attraction.

As he looked up information on the area, he discovered they came by air. Why couldn't Floyd send a plane for them and extract them from here? He didn't relish the idea of fighting the jungle and its villains another day. And a day sooner back to civilization was a huge plus for Marco.

His satellite phone went into action again and soon had Floyd on the other end.

"I was just looking at that and about to call you. Now that you have the boy home, how about I fly you out from there?"

"That's a deal. When can you get here?"

"I make it four this afternoon. I will have six boys coming which will take care of the other boat and spell your crew."

"That's perfect Floyd. That will give us enough time to get Abbas home and get squared away here. Oh, listen. When these two guys get back to Georgetown, arrange for them to get the finest meal in the best restaurant in town. And from me, a bottle of the best Scotch whiskey they have here and a case of beer. These guys deserve it."

"OK, Wade. I think Uncle Sam can afford it, no reason for you to pay."

"No Floyd. That's on me." Angel and Pedro listened on, smiling.

***

With a terrible headache that even three Advil could not control, Marco elected to stay aboard the boat and relax. Arthur Dalton was already planning on what his demands would be to the U.S. government. He once read that Idaho was pretty. The city of Coeur d' Alene stuck in his mind. That would be a good place to spend the rest of his life with his family. He had multi-millions of dollars stashed in several locations so financially he was in great shape. Nobody knew what he had and they never would. Other than his wife who had the bank account numbers well hidden.

Abbas clutched Diane's right hand in a grip far stronger than she thought possible from the boy as he dragged her through a trail that went past the waterfall, practically under it. Wade kept up, increasing the length of his stride. Fifteen minutes of brisk walking got the trio to a clearing with several grass thatched huts, not at all dissimilar to the homes seen at Burro Bono.

Abbas stopped suddenly causing Diane to bump into him. She watched his face light up, a smile on his lips and a sparkle come into his deep brown eyes. Two little children were playing with a stick in the dirt in front of a hut. Their mother came out with a pan of water then looked up and froze herself. Seconds later, she called out to a neighbor hut, not turning her face from them.

The woman that came out must have asked what the other wanted, not looking across the clearing until the caller pointed to them. The woman that came out was the mother of Abbas.

You could hear the sob all the way to them as the woman started to shake, then found enough energy to practically fly toward her son who dropped Diane's hand and flew himself to his mother. They met closer to the side of the homes as Abbas never ran faster in his life. Clinging to each other, both sobbing and rocking from side to side, his mother started wiping the tears from her son's face, continuing to cry herself.

In a couple of minutes, Diane and I walked to them and was thankful his mother could speak a little English. Others came out of their huts and gathered. Mostly women and children and a few old men. It was learned the younger men and older boys were out hunting for food.

The gathering was a festival as bits of food was brought out. None looked appealing to the two Americans. They tried little bites. The story was told of how the parents of Abbas sold him to the Money Man and the promises made. Diane tried hard to make it clear what would happen to Abbas had they not rescued him. She wanted the word passed around to the other villages. Later, she would find, her words were all for naught. The Amazon was a different world.

A scurry erupted from behind them, as voices rang out. The men were returning from a successful hunt as a very large Boa snake rested on the shoulders of five men carrying it. It was food for several meals for the village.

The women started making preparations to clean the snake and prepare it. Each house meal would be a slightly different taste. There would be a feast this afternoon.

Seeing the look on Diane's face, knowing the last thing she wanted to eat was a snake, I looked at my watch and said to Diane we had to leave. Saying their goodbye's to Abbas and his mother and father, they started back across the clearing. As they walked away, Abbas ran into his hut for a moment, then ran up to Diane and give her another big hug. From his pants pocket, he took out a Rubik's cube and put it in her hand, then smiled the biggest smile he ever had.

"Thank you, Abbas. I will cherish this forever," she said with a tear in her eye. In a minute, they were on the path to the boat and swallowed up by the Amazon. Soon, they would be back into another century of time.

# *No Safety Here*

Air transportation for the group was right on time. Pedro and Angel took care of their gear, toting the bags to the runway. Marco still suffered with his concussion from his near escape from death. He sat in the cabin, out of the sun. His head throbbed and his eyes felt like they were replaced with burning coals.

Handshakes and goodbye's said with promises to get together when the boat got back, the four were soon airborne, heading for Georgetown. The Piper Cherokee 6 held only five on the trip back. Diane and Marco sat in the back. I sat next to Arthur Dalton for several reasons. I never really relaxed on the flight yet did my best to try and get more information out of Dalton who would talk but said nothing helpful.

The Piper was not a fast aircraft but the jungle streaked by below us significantly faster than the boat could have taken us. It wasn't long and the pilot set the aircraft on cruise control as he followed the Essequibo river to home.

It was near 5:30 in the afternoon when we touched down and taxied to the private terminal on the south end of the field. The sun was on its journey heading west, the temperature in the low 90's and the humidity near 100 percent. Wade thought a nice shower with plenty of soap and shampoo would be in order before dinner. After a few days in the jungle and the putrid water he splashed in with Marco, he didn't care how hot or cold the water would be. Just clean and fresh.

The pilot removed the last bag from the aircraft luggage hold. He passed my duffel to me. Behind me, I heard a loud "splat" sound and felt, more than saw, Arthur Dalton fall.

From years of experience, I knew what it was before the sound of a rifle shot got to us. I turned fast and saw Arthur Dalton face down on the tarmac.  The shooter must have been a half of a mile away judging time between the hit and the sound of the round going off.

Arthur's right shoulder and collar bone were missing. Some of his body parts were on me and the tarmac between us.  His eyes were open wide with a shocked and a frightened look. His mouth moved. He spoke, but no words came out. Grabbing the nearest duffel, I pulled the zipper open and grabbed a shirt from the bag. I crawled on my belly the ten feet to Arthur and pressed the shirt on the open wound, just as another round came in, inches above my head.

They hit the plane's left tire, exploding it, and taking out the landing strut, shattering the frame.  With the landing gear broken and the tire shattered, the plane tilted radically to the left side, the wing tip just inches above my head. It has to be a 50 caliber I thought, to shoot that far and hit that hard.

"Marco, can you get that forklift over there and get it between us and the shooter?"

"I got it," said Diane, sprinting the fifty feet to the parked vehicle. She hit the starter and spun the wheels, circling, putting it twenty feet between Dalton and myself and the shooter. Diane jumped off the forklift and started to sprint towards me when another round found the LP gas tank on the forklift, striking it, causing it to explode. The force knocked Diane flat on her face, her hands and her chin scuffed on the rough tarmac as the force of the exploding LP tank pushed her toward me. A ball of LP flame passed over her head.

"Are you OK?" I asked, now really shook up. This shooter was good.

"Well, now I'm pissed," said Diane. "How bad is he?"

"His shoulder is gone. He's losing a lot of blood. We'll lose him if we don't get him some good medical help real soon." I kept strong pressure on his wound, yet blood escaped between my fingers. Arthur was ashen. His bottom lip trembled. His eyes held a blank stare.

Sirens sounded in the distance but not that far. Somebody called for help, perhaps when the forklift gas tank blew. Apparently, the airport had its medical crew.

 A fire truck and an ambulance came from the other side of the airport, stopping in front of us. The LP tank and fire on the forklift was extinguished with a hand extinguisher as a medic came over to Arthur, taking the bloody shirt out of the wound and looking at it.

"I want to clamp this artery and start an IV and get him to the hospital. If you put the shirt on the wound and applied pressure, sir, you probably saved his life." Arthur just looked at me.

It was just after nine that evening when the doctors did all they could for Arthur Dalton tonight. He would need constructive surgery but not at this hospital.  A nurse cleaned and dressed the contusions on Diane's hands and chin and re-dressed the head wound on Marco. Another doctor seeing Marco ran a CT scan and pronounced he had a pretty severe concussion. That was no surprise.

Adam Poe resided on the second floor of the hospital, recovering but heard the news we were here.  Adam borrowed a wheelchair and talked his way into the emergency room. It was good to see he would recover fine.  Marco was shot.  Was it luck? Divine intervention? Whatever. A quarter of an inch from certain death. Diane was banged up and almost killed. Two or three steps closer when the LP tank exploded, and well.  What a sorry bunch we were.

At 10:20 that night, a nurse found me sleeping in a chair in the waiting room. Following my orders to be woken as soon as Dalton was awake and could talk, she shook me enough to startle me from a deep ten-minute nap. I walked into Arthur's room, rubbing my eyes with my knuckles and looked at a sorry mess of a man. Two intravenous tubes dripped fluids into him. One was red and blood. The other fluids contained strong antibiotics. Dalton was still in shock.

"That was a close one Arthur. Whoever the shooter was knows his stuff. He almost got all of us. What will keep me awake is how the hell did anybody know we would be there?" I said.

"The only one I talked to was my boss on a secure satellite phone. I know Floyd is as straight as they come."

Arthur just looked at me. He didn't even blink an eye,

"You know I saved your life out there Arthur. Whoever is the boss has to be in a helluva high position with a lot of people on his payroll."

Arthur gave a slight nod. He was heavily sedated and could do no more.

"Come on Arthur. I saved your life. These bastards may just take my crew and me out. You'll be back in the states in a few days with the best surgeons in the country working on you. You'll probably never use your left arm again, but you can still have a good life, secure in some nice place. I got this thing going with Diane now that my wife is dead from a car accident and I like it. I want it to continue. I'm getting out of this crap and so is she. Give us a chance."

Arthur's lips moved, but no sound came out. I walked closer and asked again. "How about it Arthur. I got you another chance. How about helping me?"

In barely a whisper Arthur Dalton said, "Randolph Frederick Edward Spencer Churchill. That's the code. The Georgetown Bank downtown. A safe deposit box. The key is on the keys with the boat. The code is those first letters backward. The son of England's greatest man ever. CSEFR. Box 642. It's got it all." A wan smile faded as Arthur drifted off to sleep.

Who could I tell I wondered? The secure sat phone must be compromised, or somebody in our system is on the payroll. Then I thought of a way to communicate that might work.

I called Floyd on the satellite phone. "How's he doing Wade?" asked Floyd

"It looks like he won't make it through the night Floyd. I think we will pull security off before too long. He's sliding fast. We never got a thing from him. We wasted a trip, but hey, we had to try. How about Neptune. Any word on that?"

Neptune was the key word. Everything Wade said was false. Neptune meant he needed to talk to Floyd but not on the secure phone. It was urgent.

"I'm in Miami," said Floyd. "I can check later and get back to you." "How about that spot under the cars?" I asked.

"Sure. Give me an hour."

Under the cars was a pay phone under a bridge in Miami in a seedy part of town. For some reason, nobody vandalized it. Maybe because nobody seemed to know it was there. An hour meant a half hour. Floyd would be there. Something was radically wrong.

# Shooter

Floyd lifted the phone off its cradle on the first ring. The phone was in a booth under a freeway bridge in a part of Miami where security bars on windows and doors were the rule.  It was amazing the phone was there in the first place, and that it wasn't vandalized was impossible to believe. Yet, here it was. Both Floyd and Wade had the phone number memorized, both grateful the phone was still in place and it worked.

The next five minutes were spent telling Floyd what happened and how we were compromised. Neither of us had an answer.  Floyd had an idea how he could find out if the leaks were internal. I didn't ask and didn't want to know. I doubted Floyd would tell me his plan. I said I thought we would have access to what they needed in three days. That meant probably tomorrow in our code. After what just happened to us, I didn't feel comfortable with the secure phone anymore. Or the staff monitoring it.

We ended our conversation and promised to talk tomorrow on the satellite phone. If we didn't use it, the leaker would be suspicious.  I went to bed after that hot shower I desperately craved. Even with the long shower, Diane never woke but smelled of fresh soap as I slid into the right side of the bed next to her, then passed out for seven hours. Floyd worked through the night.

Our boat and crew arrived at the dock with Arthur Dalton's boat just after noon the next day. The crews pushed through all night and made good time. There were no incidents out of the ordinary including the area of ambush we had on our way up the river.

As soon as I got word the boats were close, I walked down to the dock with that bottle of scotch and case of beer in tow. Greeting the guys, I soon found myself checking the boat thoroughly with one thought in mind - get the key off the ring. I dismissed the crew to get a meal and said I would stay with the boats and watch them. I gave them fifty bucks for the first round and told them to have fun, but the duty group should be back in two hours.

The Jeep spun its tires heading for the town. Finding the right key wasn't a problem. There were only two keys on the ring.

Slipping the key off the ring, I dug into my pocket and found a somewhat similar key among the dozen I brought along, picking them up in the market up the street. I slipped the new key on the ring. The exchange was made. I sat back and relaxed.

So far, so good. Boat traffic passing by had water lapping at the side of our boats. The sound was so comfortable with the accompanying gentle rocking, inviting one to close one's eyes, which is what I did. I didn't sleep but spent the next hour and a half wondering and trying to figure out how somebody would know where we would be yesterday afternoon when I didn't exactly know myself. Once more, I could feel that 50 caliber bullet pass just inches over my head. The bullet that thankfully didn't have my name on it.

Yesterday's late night call under the bridge had Floyd and I agree I would get into the vault in the bank and remove the contents. Floyd said we could remove the contents legally, but it would take several days or longer. With Arthur Dalton now out of the picture, his bosses would know what happened and probably close ranks. It was those bosses we wanted most.

As soon as I took possession of the vault contents, I would call Diane and Marco, head to the airport where the Cessna jet would be waiting and get us out of the country. We could examine those documents in the air.

Angel loved driving fast and skidded to a stop, sliding sideways, near the dock. Pedro and two other guys got out of the Jeep, all relaxed, no doubt with a couple of shots of whiskey or some other alcohol they had with lunch. These boys earned it. We talked and joked for a few minutes then I said my goodbyes and walked casually into town, past the vendors in tents, hawking their wares. I think I looked like a tourist as I reached the bank.

The bank security chief walked with me. I was admitted to the secure vault room and walked up to the box marked 642. I pushed the keypad letters in the order.

The first letter of every name of Winston Churchill's son, in reverse order. Inserting the key, I twisted a quarter turn to the left, heard an audible snap and the door popped open.

I pivoted on my right foot, turning one hundred and eighty degrees and faced the security chief standing directly behind me.

"Please leave. I need my privacy," I said to him.

You would have thought I committed some crime on his person the way he acted. Like I spit in his face or something.

"Well, I never…" he harrumphed as he turned and walked out of the room in a huff.

I opened the door and slid out a black metal box that was heavy enough to require two hands to hold it. Opening the box on top I removed two black books, each eight by eleven and a good inch thick. A quick check showed both filled with names, dates and dollar amounts. In the back of the box packed neatly sat stacks of money. All-American. All-banded. All one hundred dollar bills. A quick estimated guess put the amount north of two hundred thousand dollars.

In the room, on another table sat a stack of heavy duty burgundy color plastic bags the bank provided for customers. They looked like a shopping bag from a high-end retail store. I put the two ledgers and a handful of loose papers from the vault, into a bank carry bag. I sealed the box and was about to call the guard, then had an idea.

Opening the box once more, I took two bundles of one hundred dollar bills. One from the top and one from the middle of the pile. Perhaps the money was traceable? Then I called the guard, looking put out and grumpy.  I snapped the door shut and watched as he checked the vault was sealed properly. He turned without a word and walked out with me two steps behind him.

I walked out the bank door, turned left and spotted him right away. About thirty-five years old, six foot tall, about one eighty and left handed. He held his cigarette in his left hand. Twice, I caught him looking. If he was the shooter, he was good. As a spy and a tail, not good at all. No, he was a shooter.

I've been around shooters most of my life. They have a way of carrying themselves that sets them apart. While not exactly arrogance, it was something that told others he was special. And he was. All shooters were special, or they would be grunts.

I got on the phone with Diane on the other end. I told her I was being followed. Somebody knew all about our secret mission. To kill time I confirmed how and when we would meet at the airport, which was within the hour.  I asked she pass the word on to Marco. All the while laughing loud and cracking a joke in between serious lines of conversation as I walked past the shooter.

"Bye love. See you in a couple of hours. I need a drink. Dinner at eight? OK, See ya." I hung up then walked into a smoky bar around the corner.  My first thought was I didn't want to cause a scene and hurt the guy. With what I carried, I just wanted to get out of the country. Then I thought if this is the shooter, why let him walk away?  I took a stool at the bar and ordered a local beer. I didn't like the beer, but it was cheap and I didn't plan on drinking much of it. An American dollar covered the cost.

I pretended to look at my cell phone, watching the smoke stained mirror. Sure enough, the guy followed me in.  He sat alone at a two person table across the room behind me. Another sip of beer and I asked the guy next to me where the bathrooms were. He pointed to the back. I switched to my best English accent when I asked for the bathroom, then said, "Please watch me beer mate. I got up and walked back to the bathroom door. I opened it then shut it and walked farther into the dark back room.

I found the back door and found it had a security alarm. It was locked with a heavy steel bar across the door, a huge padlock secured the bar. Getting out this way was not an option. I stepped behind a tall stack of beer cases and waited. As I expected, the guy came back, saw the bathroom empty and hurried to the back door and saw it shut. As he turned toward me, I noted a knife in his left hand. A four-inch blade that glistened in the dim light. Before he could slash out with it, I hit him behind his left ear with a full bottle of beer, dropping him to the floor.

There wasn't much light in the room but enough that I could see him reach down to his boot. His knife was somewhere across the room.

"What do you want asshole? Why are you following me?"

"I was looking for the bathroom. What'd you hit me for?" His hand slowly reached that boot.

"You're the shooter aren't you. I can see it in your eyes. And in your hands. The short fingernails and you keep those fingers soft." I was playing a strong hunch.

"Shooter, watcha mean? I ain't no shooter." His left hand near his boot now.
The pressure point on the shoulder where it connects to the neck, if done properly, will tear the heart out of a man. He will experience incredible pain. The pain is so intense he couldn't even scream. Both his hands went around my hand, but I just squeezed harder.  I eased off the pressure and asked again. "Are you the shooter?

"I won't miss next time Nash. A puff of wind was all it took to miss you at near a mile." He looked at me with tears in his eyes, inflamed with hatred. I could sense he was ready to get up and get it on with an old man.

"You're right. You might not miss the shot. But there won't be a next time for you."

"Ha, watcha gonna do, call the cops?"

We will never know if he felt the snap of his neck being twisted as I placed one hand on the side of his head and the other hand on the other side. A practiced move I knew well, I gave a violent twist, the sound of a snap was audible. The shooter convulsed for a few seconds then his bowels and bladder released, the odors mixing with stale beer.

I took his legs and dragged him behind cases of beer, leaving a wet trail on the floor. His eyes open, a foggy stare looking into hell maybe, I took out my phone and took a picture of him to share with Floyd.

I picked up the burgundy bag and walked past my waiting beer. The old timer watching it hollered out, "Hey, your beer is still here."

"You can have it mate" I said, walking out the front door. I headed toward the airport. I had a mile to go in twenty minutes. A song popped up in my head as I walked at a brisk pace. My favorite singer, Elvis Presley, back in 1970 sang, "Walk a Mile In My Shoes."

Walk a mile in my shoes
Walk a mile in my shoes
Yeah, before you abuse, criticize, and accuse,
Walk a mile in my shoes.

I knew the lyrics and sang the song to myself. By the time the song was over, I saw the shiny silver Cessna in the distance, with just tail numbers, engines running, waiting to take us home.

# *The Spy*

It was one day short of a full week after leaving Guyana when I found myself back in my office at home, on the satellite phone with my Floyd.  It wasn't the phone that betrayed us, but a member of Floyd's staff.

Floyd had eleven people on his office staff that could have leaked information about the program. He divided the team into two groups. Each group received a different memo about a possible path to hitting the operation hard. One group was silent. The other had a traitor working against them. All of his employees were thoroughly vetted.  Floyd couldn't believe it, but it was true. He had a traitor in his group.

The message contained a thought about Arthur Dalton's boat possibly having a ledger stowed in a secret location under the deck. It should be located below the seat the captain sat on as he piloted the boat. He made plans that the boat would be searched the following day.

That same evening, a demonstration against the Guyana government started on the dock.  A Molotov cocktail found the cockpit of the boat. The thirty or so students suddenly broke off the conflict, much to the relief of the nine police in riot gear on the scene. The gang of protesters headed for town. The leader's pocket had folding money to buy all a couple of drinks with plenty of money left for him.

Of the five in this intel group, only one stood out. The person was Cynthia Cade. Age forty-two and holding.  Cynthia had been with the group for just over five years, coming from one of the alphabet divisions in the government. Cynthia stood five feet ten inches tall, six foot with the high heels she often wore. At 135 pounds, she was model thin with very long legs. She sported shoulder length blond hair with a complexion that could support a model's roll for a facial cream that worked wonders.

A graduate of Wesleyan College in Macon, Georgia, Cynthia had it all. Beauty, brains and a sweet southern accent she could turn on or off at her whim.

Cynthia Addleson became Cynthia Cade when she married Terrance Cade of the Cade and Cade law firm in Atlanta, Georgia. The law firm specialized in serving high-end clients. The four and a half years they were married, Cynthia suffered the high life of Atlanta. She didn't want children while Terry did. He never knew about the "pill" she took daily to ensure pregnancy would not interfere with her lifestyle.

The high life suited Cynthia just fine until the day Terrance came home unexpectedly and caught his truly beloved in bed, with another couple. The other woman was her girlfriend, Jennifer. The guy was unknown and would remain so. A true ménage trios. He would never look at the wine with the same name without remembering that scene.

Cell phones take good pictures too, and after several are taken, Terry made his presence known He then walked out of the bedroom. The divorce was fast and final with the agreement the reason for the divorce not be divulged but sealed. Cynthia got a paltry quarter of a million dollars and got to keep her vast wardrobe and the Mercedes sports car. The money would not last long.

A friend of a friend got her the first job she had. She got this one on her own. Cynthia was a good worker. Smart, efficient and kept her personal life to herself She was a model employee all the while she was with Floyd and his group.

One day, she looked into her mirror and saw reality creeping up on her. Crow's feet began to show at the corner of her eyes. Her skin wasn't quite as tight and her ass not quite as firm. She liked sex and knew every trick in the book, but it wasn't quite as exciting as it once was. Perhaps it was time to find a steady mate. One that had money and promise and perhaps find the high life scene once more.

The cocktail party was just like the dozens of other cocktail parties she attended. Cynthia usually found somebody interesting to take her home for the night. Tonight was different. He was older. Quite a bit older in fact. She preferred younger men. More stamina. More ambition and often she could teach them a trick or two in bed. This older man couldn't have the stamina she needed. Nor the looks as he had a paunch which she hated. Love handles were not sexy to her. But he obviously had money. And her mirror didn't lie.

He took her home and at her front door, she kissed him briefly and said good night using her best southern accent. He wanted more. She said no. He promised to call. And he did.

"Her name is Cynthia Cade," said Floyd Johnson. "I was able to get a peek at her closed divorce papers. It's likely she was a bad girl at one time. Well, bad to some anyhow. She has a good education and has had a perfect work record with the company we hired her from and with us too. She lived in a nice apartment. She is a semi-socialite. She's a real looker but she always behaved at work."

"About six months ago, she suddenly got an infusion of money. She moved into a very nice place on the ocean. Her Camaro was replaced with a Porsche 911, the high-end one at that."

"I checked and her bank account remains steady. Her lifestyle habits haven't changed from what I can tell. I did hear that one-day last week she came in with a bracelet that was a showpiece. Somebody commented on it. She said she got it from a special friend."

"Is there some way you can send her up here on assignment?" I asked. "Maybe work with Diane on something for a few days."

"Let me think on that. I think we can do something."

"Is this Cynthia hooked up with anybody special you can see?" asked Wade.

"Well, that's a problem. She seems to be with Bradford Carlton a lot. She's been seen going to his mansion several times. That's a problem for me."

"**The** Bradford Carlton? The philanthropist? The multi-billionaire who gives so much to charity? That one?" I asked.

"Yes, the one and the same. The one who has a party and half of DC shows up.  The one who inherited his fortune from his daddy who was an early partner with Rockefeller and Henry Flagler before they started Standard Oil. Bradford's been a widower for eleven years, but Cynthia has been to every one of his parties the last several months. She seems to dote on him too."

"Send her up here Floyd. We can make up a good story and get her involved. We will find out once and for all if the leak is truly her and who she is leaking too. I can't believe it's Carlton."

***

Two days later, Cynthia's fire red Porsche 911 carefully rode over the speed bump into the parking lot of the Hilton Hotel in Daytona Beach. Floyd's staff arranged for a nice ocean view room which would take in the morning sun. She would meet this old bitch Diane Mason here for dinner at six. It was just 4:30 so she had time to freshen up after she checked in.

Sitting at a table for two by the window, at six P.M., if one looked inside from the beach, they would see Cynthia looking like a southern belle from Gone with the Wind. Her pale yellow and white dress was a perfect match to the southern wide brim bonnet she wore. As Cynthia removed her white gloves and placed them on her handbag, the bitch showed up.

A radiant smile on Diane's face greeted Cynthia, as Diane reached across the table to shake Cynthia's hand. The smile stayed as Diane said, "Honey, I don't know what you think you are into here but it doesn't require a dress like you are wearing. This is Daytona Beach. A few miles west of here is the first and greatest race car track in the world. The smell you'll find, once you get out of here, is the smell of high test gasoline and oil. And burning rubber. This isn't Miami. These boys are good old boys so cut the shit girl. My name's Diane Mason and we are going to work together for a few days."

Cynthia's mouth dropped open. She wished she could say something clever. words escaped her now. Cynthia looked at Diane, dressed in casual attire. She wore black dress slacks and a black and white blouse, with shoulders and upper arms exposed. Her short salt and pepper hair showed she was not a kid but she sure wasn't what Cynthia expected either. Diane looked like she could handle herself.

"I just thought, uh, well, I just. OK, I won't do this again. Tomorrow, when we start work, I'll dress differently."

"Tomorrow hell. When we finish dinner, you can follow me to the office. We have a lot to do tonight sweetie. Let's order. The chitins and rocky mountain oysters are good here." Diane watched Cynthia suck in her breath, screw up her lips, and look not well.

***

Diane had a reason for pushing Cynthia like this. She just drove over five hours to get to Daytona Beach. She drove a fantastic sports car but it's a sports car, not a luxury barge like a Mercedes S-class or an Audi 8 series. Sports cars will wear you down on drives such as the one she just took. Diane could see Cynthia was tired. Tired people are prone to making mistakes. Wade and Diane set up a plausible scenario that while untrue, it could happen.

In Wade's office, crowded with Diane and Cynthia huddled around the laptop on the desk, Wade standing behind them, Diane laid out the story.

"The story is out that Arthur Dalton is dead when in fact, he is still in Guyana, in a small hospital just on the outskirts of Georgetown. It's called St. Anne's hospital. Dalton is in pretty bad shape. He was hit by a fifty caliber round that took off his left shoulder. He is stabilized and will recover if he gets the proper medical attention. He also knows his boss put the hit out on him. Or that's what he thinks. Who else could it be anyhow?"

Diane continued, "He has agreed to tell us everything. He had a ledger with everything in it, secured on his boat which burned and sunk. Most of the ledger was destroyed but a few local names in Guyana survived. Just low-end people he agreed that helped in the operation. Mostly food and fuel sources."

"He has agreed that if we get him the best medical care and security, he'll give us everything he knows. He knows it all, or so he says."

Wade piped in, "We're going to move him to Panama where we will fly a team of doctors down to get him in shape to travel to Rochester, Minnesota, to the Mayo Clinic where they specialize in problems like he has."

"You come in this scene because you were picked to travel with him from Guyana to Mayo in the states. You're a new face. He's seen all of us. More than he ever wants to see us again. You're new, pretty and very smart so get close to him, and sympathize with him just a little. Maybe get some information from him. You'll have a recorder, so you won't have to memorize anything."

"You will leave in two days," said Diane. "Tomorrow, we have some free time and I want to show you around. I see you like hot cars. I do too. I grew up around race cars and love them. I've set it up for a little test drive at the Speedway in a NASCAR stock car. You'll love it."

In bed, several hundred miles away lay Arthur Dalton, heavily sedated. If he could look out the window, he might recognize the coastline was in Costa Rica.

Diane kept Cynthia busy for another hour then finally said, "Go
back to the hotel. I'll pick you up at nine. We can have breakfast at a
neat place I know then I'll show you around a bit. Dress casual
huh."

## *Fun at the Track*

Diane was a customer at the Daytona Speedway several times after her first visit. She knew Jerry Dooley quite well by now.  She rode with him around the track, paying for lessons. Discounted, because of who she was.  He learned from her too.  He was a top notch instructor, yet never too old to learn. She became very proficient in piloting a 700 plus horsepower beast around the 33-degree steep bank track. She didn't want to be a driver, she just loved the speed. Speed kills. Yes, but speed thrills too.

A phone call from Washington DC to the track manager had Jerry Dooley in the manager's office along with Wade Nash. The plan was in the incubator, ready to hatch. Diane would take Cynthia on a nice ride around the track. All responsibility would be transferred to Uncle Sam with the caller from DC saying a silent prayer Wade Nash and Diane Mason knew what they were doing.

The only reason the ride would not happen was if Cynthia would be silent. But Cynthia didn't disappoint them as she pulled into the parking lot on Rt. A-1-A and Granada Boulevard, on her way back to her hotel that first night. Parking in front of T.G.I. Friday's, she dialed a number not in her phone directory. The call was answered on the first ring with a "Yes?"

It would be safe to say there were more tracking and listening devices on and around Cynthia Cade's car and person than in the entire city of Ormond Beach Florida at that moment. Her car had been visited by an expert team in Wade's driveway that night Now the effort was paying off. While the person answering said nothing, Cynthia said everything. They had their mole.

Wearing NASCAR regulated fireproof clothing, Diane helped Cynthia through the passenger side door before climbing in the driver's side window of a Chevrolet Super Sport painted to look like the wheels Dale Earnhardt Jr. drove, including the number 88 painted on the sides.

It was ten minutes to twelve on a bright, beautiful day. A breeze blew out of the west at seven miles per hour. The breeze wouldn't be a factor in today's drive. The track was officially shut down from noon to one today. A special driver would be on track so everybody else was ordered to stay off.

Making sure both Diane and Cynthia's shoulder harnesses were secured properly, Jerry Dooley said to both ladies via their headphones, "Diane, you have the track for an hour. Try and bring her back in one piece this time. You're only cleared to 180 so keep your speed below that huh?"

Take gasoline, oil, burnt rubber and plenty of body sweat and you have the smell of the Daytona International Speedway. Cynthia, remembered what Diane said the night before about the smell. The aroma found its way under her helmet. She much preferred Chanel.


The big electric clock on the pit wall showed it was two minutes to twelve when Diane hit the toggle switch that fired the monster engine to life. Even with her helmet on secure, Cynthia could hear the rumble and bark of the engine and felt the entire car shake. It felt like being on the back of a wild beast about to be unleashed. One hundred and eighty? She had her Porsche up to one ten a few weeks ago and that scared her. Diane said this would be a slow ride. Just for fun.

Snicking the shifter into first gear, easing off the clutch, the NASCAR engine had so much torque, it required but a touch on the accelerator to move #88 out of the pit and on the track. Diane kept her speed down and stayed low the first lap, all two and a half miles. The slow speed was to warm up the engine and other working parts.

Cynthia could feel the enormous power this car had. By the time Diane hit the start finish line after the warm up lap, she had the speedometer showing 120. Wow, this was fast she thought, but it felt like it had no springs. It rode very hard, shaking her body and teeth. This was probably as fast as they would go she hoped.

The second time around, five miles were covered, it was show time. Mashing the go pedal to the floor, Diane chose the middle lane and swept through turn one at 150 and turn two at 165. Cynthia felt ill. Her stomach was turning inside out and she felt like her breakfast was about to revisit her. In her helmet no less.

The long straight stretch had #88 moving at 190 and gaining speed as it swept high into the turn. Cynthia had trouble breathing but managed to yell, "Diane, you promised just a slow ride and that guy said you couldn't go over one hundred and eighty. What are you doing?" Everything to Cynthia was a blur now. This was certain death she thought.

"I'm having fun sweetie. We've got a ways to go. Hang on."

The tri-oval was coming up, as Diane backed off to one eighty then mashed the pedal down again. The back stretch saw two O five on the speedometer when Jerry Dooley's voice came over the headsets.

"Back it down Diane. That's way too fast. You're gonna wreck again."

Wreck again? Cynthia was crying and shaking uncontrollably and pleading, "Please Diane, I don't want to die. Why are you doing this?" said through sobs and tears.

"You should have thought of that before you turned traitor to your country sweetie. We got you dead to rights. You stopped last night on your way home. We have you recorded. Every single word."

Barreling out of turn four now, the tri-oval again, Diane deliberately oversteered for a moment causing a slight drift out of the rear, Cynthia screamed thinking they were going to roll over or something worse.

"So tell me Cynthia, who did you call?"

"I called my boyfriend."

"And who was that?"

"I called Chambers. Brad Chambers. Please slow down. I'm sorry. Please slow down."

"Chambers is behind all of this? Are you sure?"

"Behind what? He has tons of money and I can live as I want with him. All he wants is to know what's going on with my group. It's nothing serious. He's a business man and not into our stuff. He likes to pretend he's a spy or something. It's just pretend with him. It's all an act. I tell him what's going on and he pretends he is 007 or something.  With him, I can have a good life. He loves me and will take care of me."

"Oh, I'll bet sweetie. Just like he took care of Arthur Dalton."

"Carlton wouldn't do anything like that," Cynthia said over the microphone in her helmet, recorded in the control room.

The fun ride was over, but it paid off. Diane eased off the throttle and took #88 in the pit, the speedometer showing sixty-five miles per hour, the car moving much slower. The speedometer was geared to show thirty-five miles per hour faster than the true speed. The whole thing was a setup, and it worked.

Diane pulled in behind the wall, stopping next to two federal agents, waiting with a special bracelet for Cynthia. This one was shiny but had no diamonds mounted in it.

"Thanks, Jerry," said Diane. "If only I were younger, I'd give Danica Patrick a run for her money. If only, huh?"

*Bradford Carlton, a billionaire. He gives away a fortune and does this. Why* she thought.

# *Dressed Up*

"Wade, it makes absolutely no sense Bradford Chambers is involved in this. He's a billionaire for chrissakes." Floyd said. "He gives away more money to charity than almost everybody in Miami combined. Why would he do something like this, human trafficking and drug running?"

"Damned if I know Floyd. Everything we have points to him. The phone calls. Cynthia's visits to his home all the time lately and she said it was him. Hell, she ought to know. Why would she lie? She's looking at some serious jail time the way it is. Is it possible she is just that dumb to believe Bradford is playing spy?"

"I know, I know. I just don't see any reason for doing something like this. His record is perfect. We checked, and his businesses are all doing well. His son was killed in Nam but that has nothing to do with something like this. We have no choice but to come down on him. He's what, near eighty years old and will end like this?"

"How do you want to handle this Floyd? This can be very sticky. What if we're wrong? Can you imagine how that will look?"

"Chambers is holding another special party tonight to announce more money to two special charities given under his wife's name again. It will be held in his banquet room. They say there will be one hundred significant guests who will all donate along with him as they always do. We don't want to make fools of our selves or him, so after the ordeal, when the guests leave, we can talk to him and see what he has to say. I have a plane on the way to Daytona Beach and want you and Diane to get down here. You will be here by five. The event isn't until eight tonight. Got a tux?"

The plane was early and the flight fast, arriving at a small airport near Miami just after four P.M.  A car awaited taking Wade and Diane to a custom shop where Wade got fitted with a tuxedo and Diane, a beautiful lavender gown befitting tonight's occasion. Her clutch bag was exchanged for a larger purse to hold her Glock nine-millimeter handgun.

"You look very handsome my man," said Diane, walking out of the building with me at her left side. Today, I saw another side of this beautiful lady I hadn't seen before.

"And you look stunning my beautiful lady," I replied. "Now that we're all dressed up, how about we get married?"

"Say what?"

"Married. You know, like standing in front of a preacher or judge or priest or a boat captain or something. I make you legally mine and me yours. Forever."

"Oh cut the crap, Wade. You know I like you a lot but we're too old to get married. And this job sucks. There's too much danger. We are both too old to change.  You're joking, right?" Later, Diane told me she was sure I was just joking because we were dressed so nice.

"If you say so, sweetheart. No, I'm not joking.  I love you and you know you love me. This job sucks for sure.  I've told Floyd enough times that I'm quitting. You're tired of this stuff too. So, how about it? Want me to get down on my knees here? Will you marry me?" I felt like I just embarrassed myself. She liked me, but….

We stopped half way to the Suburban that would take us to Chambers house. Diane had a look on her that was a part shock, part disbelief, and mostly happiness.

"Well, maybe it's too soon, huh? Maybe you can't wait to get out of here and go back to England, or Spain, or wherever. Maybe I push too hard. Maybe, aw hell Diane, maybe you like me but don't love me as I love you. I'm sorry I brought it up," I said, looking down at my patent leather shoes, shining like mirrors.

"Oh Wade, shut up, please. Yes, I will marry you. Right after this is over. Today if we can. I love you so much."

"Well, that's good news sweetheart. I planned this since this morning and made a couple of phone calls. We have a marriage license waiting for us. Floyd has it and doesn't know it yet. I used his name and pulled some strings."

"I've arranged we two can see someone tonight after this is over. We both quit this racket and retire. We get married and bon voyage. You love traveling, so I've rented a motor home. We've got three months to see our beautiful country. Just take our time and do what we want. Yes, you can drive too. What do you say beautiful?

"Yes. Yes yes yes."

***

Dinner for the two was a quick trip through a drive in and a delicious quarter pounder with cheese for both famished people. They finish their meal as the driver of the black Suburban pulled up to the front of the mansion of Bradford Chambers.

Floyd was waiting there, with six other agents, his driver making it seven men plus the three of them in their car. Ten able bodies against one old man. Their federal credentials got them in with surprised looks on the faces of the doormen.

As planned, they all fanned out and mixed with the crowd, not expecting anything out of the ordinary to happen. Just a room full of millionaires wanting to be part of a big scene of giving back to society, making them feel a little better about themselves. As none of the agents were rich, far from it, they had no idea how good it felt to help others in the best way the rich knew how. Donate money and time and not necessarily in that order.

331

## The Main Event

Bradford Chambers looked at his watch. It was time again. He had done this countless times over the years, yet it gave him a slight chill to walk out in front of his friends and do what he would do. Give money away to a much-needed charity. Giving made him feel good every time. He and his friends were helping. Making a difference in this world.

Once considered an icon in the business world, Bradford didn't need to read the occasional column stating his status and judgment was questioned. He turned down political positions on two occasions. Once during the term of George Bush senior, his friend. The other time, Bill Clinton asked. He was truly apolitical, although he didn't think much of the politics of either party now.

He walked out from the side room after checking himself in the full-length mirror one last time. Just like every time past, an old song came to him. It was their song. *Daisy Daisy, give me your answer true. I'm half crazy over the love for you. It won't be a stylish marriage, I can't afford a carriage.* He was at the podium, the tune in his head. He almost sang the words as he looked around.

Applause greeted him as it always did. *Oh Daisy, if you could only see this,* he thought. Bradford Chambers raised his hands for silence. A pin drop could be heard.

"Friends. Neighbors. Ladies and gentlemen all. Thank you for coming tonight. As some of you know, we do this two or three times a year with me giving a bit of money to a worthy charity and hitting on you to do the same. This time will be a little special. After the presentation and donations are pledged, I have something special to say to all of you. Let's begin, shall we?"

Five charities were chosen by the committee with Bradford choosing two winners. The remaining three would be automatically on the next list. The top two chosen would be the recipients of a million dollars each from Bradford Chambers in memory of his wife Daisy.

Any monies from the gathering would be equally divided between the winning two charities. It would be a sizable donation with each donor listed in tomorrow's newspapers. Not the amount the donor gave but the larger the donation, the higher on the list one's name appeared.

The awards presented and check already written were passed forward then totaled and tallied. The award was substantial indeed.

Bradford Chambers took the podium once more, amidst heavy applause. He held his hands high, quieting the gathering.

"Now for the surprise I have for all of you. As you can see, I'm old and getting older. I miss my Daisy and in truth if God took me tomorrow that would be OK too. But I'd like to think the charitable work would continue. We've done a lot of good for a lot of people. I know or would like to think one of you fine people would continue this great tradition we have here, but just in case, I have this announcement to make."

Diane and I were now just a few feet apart, at the front of the gathering, waiting for the special announcement. What could it possibly be? Bradford Chambers seemed elated, so it had to be something positive."

"Unbeknownst to all of you," Chambers went on, "I have been reacquainted with my brother's son Bradford. It's a long story and won't be told here, but my brother Otis died some time ago as did his wife, Amy. They had one son they named after me."

"Young Bradford had a somewhat turbulent life growing up, what with my brother General Chambers moving so much and all. Well, I lost touch with my namesake for many years. The last several months, he's been living in the guest quarters here and well hidden. I want this tradition to continue. He is my only living relative, so I've been bringing him into the business quietly. He will take the place of my son, Otis, who died in Viet Nam as some of you know. With that, please let me introduce my nephew, and one day successor, Bradford Chambers."

From the side of the room, into the limelight came his nephew, Bradford Chambers. The one hidden in plain sight in the community. Dressed in a tuxedo matching his uncle, young Bradford looked a little uneasy. His cummerbund concealed his stomach bulge enough to make him look trimmer than he was.

Bradford's long hair was salt and pepper, slicked back with some hair gel. His gate waddled from side to side like an ape. With deep-set dark eyes that kept moving from one side of the audience to the other, he missed little. He had a visible scar from the corner of his left eye to the corner of his lip. His face was cruel although he tried to smile. Something about his look gave the appearance of a dangerous man.

Diane and I looked at each other. *So, this has to be it* I thought, as I walked to the back of the room. Taking my cell phone from my pocket, I dialed Floyd somewhere in the room.

"This has to be it, Floyd. The nephew has to be the one, not the senior man. Can you get some background on him ASAP?"

"I'm already on it Wade. I'll let you know as soon as I have something."

I walked back to the front of the room, next to Diane as the presentation was ending. The applause tempered, an undertone of words spoken. Perhaps it was the sneered expression on young Bradford's face, or the less than refined words the younger spoke which caused an uneasy feeling in the room. Young Chambers was play-acting in front of this group. It was easy to see. He was not at all comfortable in the presence of people accustomed to the better life.

Bradford senior spoke after his nephew chopped off his prepared speech. "Enjoy yourselves folks. Food is served and I've been assured the shrimp is the freshest available. Have a good time. You've all earned it. Thank you again."

Bradford senior walked amongst his guests while the younger left the stage and back into the side room, shaking away from his uncle who wanted him to join in the gathering together.

"Did you see his nephew looking at us?" asked Diane. "Like he knew we were here for a reason. He was sneering at us. I bet the prick knows we're on to him somehow."

I picked up my phone and called Floyd, asking him to get a few men outside and behind the building. I told Floyd I was going to follow young Bradford into the room and confront him, detain him in some way. Was this the head of the gang? Could Bradford senior be so deceived? Perhaps, I thought. He was his only living relative after all.

I turned and discovered I was standing alone. Diane was half way across the room heading for the side room Bradford entered. Calling out to her, it was doubtful she heard me over the noise. If she did, she didn't respond but just kept on ahead.

As she walked into the darkened room, a figure stood outlined across the room, about twenty feet away. The room behind the open door was well lit. She recognized Bradford at once. Diane raised her handbag, reaching for her handgun, and suddenly saw a flash, and felt a thunderous jolt to her chest. She felt instant pain, a swoosh of her breath leave her and felt herself falling backward until everything turned black and the pain stopped.

Hearing the shot as I rushed to the entrance I drew my handgun. I was ready to fire, only to see the door opposite the room swing shut and Diane on the floor.  In the dim light, I was able to see the expanding pool of blood on her chest, turning the lavender gown an ugly red where it escaped. Diane was motionless. *That son of a bitch is mine,* I thought. I wanted him more than I ever wanted anybody else.

"Officer down. Officer down" I shouted over my phone. "It's Diane. She's in the side room. It looks bad. Get an ambulance right away. The shooter is his nephew. He headed out the door to the beach I think.  I'm going after him."

I looked at Diane for a moment. Hopefully, there would be a doctor in the group. Almost certainly there had to be. I desperately wanted to stay with Diane, but even more, I wanted young Bradford. I wanted the man who just ruined my life again.

The French doors leading to the beach were open. In the distance, I could see a figure running north along the beach. He had a good hundred foot lead on me as I slipped my gun back into its holster and cleared my mind of everything but making tracks fast. I would catch him. I had to catch him or go insane with the thought that he got away from me.

While the younger Bradford Chambers ran in soft sand, I took the hard packed stuff near the water. Soon I was close to Chambers who finally figured out soft sand was harder to run on and angled down to the hard-packed sand along the shoreline. Adrenalin or something kicked in. I felt a burst of speed somewhere from deep inside of me as I closed the gap fast.

Chambers must have heard my fast approaching footsteps. He turned and stopped.  He brought his gun up to fire at me. The speed I found closed the gap fast enough Bradford could not raise the gun and fire as my body made violent contact with young Chambers, both of us flying to the wet sand. The gun went flying off into the water and was washed over by an incoming wave as Bradford staggered up and ran to try and retrieve it.

My gun was secure and safe in its holster. I could have easily shot him. *No, not this time,* I thought. This time I would teach this guy a lesson and make him suffer. I felt I owed it to the thousands of people this guy desecrated. But most of all, I wanted his life for what he just did to Diane and me.

Bradford was on his hands and knees, searching for where he thought the gun landed in the surf. As the tide washed back to the sea, his gun was now visible as he crawled toward it. As he reached for it, I plowed into him again, dragging his stunned body deeper into the surf.

Now waist deep in the water, I clipped Bradford behind the right ear with my fist, disorienting him. I plunged his face well under the water for several seconds. His body fought me, trying to get to the surface for life giving breath. He was stronger than I thought, as he used every ounce of energy he had in him, trying to survive.

Although he was several years younger, he was no match for me. Not an enraged Wade Ivan Nash. I let him up briefly, just to tell him he was going to die tonight, then pushed him under again.

Several seconds later, I let him up again, Bradford coughing and spitting out salty sea water.

"You're gonna die asshole," I said.

Suddenly, torturing him seemed alien to me. This was torture for sure. Just kill him I thought. Hold the bastard under until his life is gone so that he can kill no more.

"I want a lawyer," He choked out. "You can't do this to me. I have my rights. I want a lawyer," He gasped, sucking in his last breath of air.

"Your lawyer will be with you very soon. His name is God. I wouldn't want to be in your shoes," I plunged him under one last time.

"Wade, don't." It was Floyd yelling from the shore.

"Are you shitting me? The thousands of lives this miserable son of a bitch ruined and you want mercy? He deserves worse."

"Yes, he does. Don't you see? You're giving him the easy way out. He will never see daylight and we may get his whole organization if he lives. You kill him and it's just one asshole scumbag."

He was right. Of course, he was. I knew it and pulled the now unconscious Bradford Chambers to the shore where he involuntarily spat out water and started breathing again. There was no way in hell I would give him one breath at all. Never.

The tide rolled out, exposing the handgun. An agent walked in ankle deep and retrieved it. Wade was too much in shock to get it himself.

"Diane. How's Diane Floyd?"

"I don't know. She took a hit in the chest and I see this guy was using a 45." Floyd looked at the gun taken from the water. "You know what those bullets can do. It doesn't look good. I haven't heard and that isn't good either. I'm so sorry, Wade."

I started to cry. I never felt so sad.

# *Hospital*

The drizzling rain started an hour ago, causing the black tarmac to shine like a mirror, reflecting the neon sign above saying Mount Sinai Medical Center. The man in black stepped between and over puddles trying to keep his feet dry.

Mount Sinai Medical Center had an ambulance roll in at ten P.M. With the sirens and lights flashing and wailing, came carloads of federal law enforcement and state agents. The man in the black suit tried to enter the emergency room but was stopped by two very large agents. The man in black showed his identification as he spoke to the men. A phone call was made and after a cursory body search, the man in black was admitted. The white collar was a giveaway. He carried nothing but a bible.

"The last door on the left, Father," said the larger of the two agents. They assumed he was there to administer Last Rites.

*I'm not a priest*, the man thought but did not say anything to either agent again. He just walked toward the last door on the left, his Bible unchecked, clutched firmly in his right hand.

***

"Do you Wade Ivan Nash take Diane Mason to be your lawfully wedded wife? To have and to hold. In sickness and in health. To death do you part?"

"I do."

Do you Diane Mason take ….

"I do."

"I now pronounce you man and wife. You may kiss the bride but be careful buddy, she was almost killed you know."

"Thanks, padre. I appreciate you coming over so late and all. It means a lot to us," I said.

"No problem, Mr. Nash. Our parish owes Floyd Johnson a great deal. And I don't mind coming for a wedding, even though it's almost midnight.

Diane was lucky. She raised her handbag to retrieve her gun as Bradford fired. The bullet struck the gun inside the purse she carried. Some of the bullet splinters passed through the handbag causing several small wounds that did little more than pass through her skin. The bullet shock from the impact knocked her unconscious. The bleeding looked far worse than it was. Had the bullet hit an inch either way… Well, it didn't.

A day in the hospital would be all that was needed to keep the wound clean to prevent an infection. Their honeymoon would start soon.

"We quit Floyd," I said with a smile on my face a mile wide. I couldn't help but remember starting my life in the military. I was eighteen, in a small smoke-filled recruiting station in downtown Chicago. Everybody smoked back then. I raised my right hand and took the oath with fifty-four other men.

It was a long and turbulent ride to where I was now. I guess, in a way, it was like most people that buy a boat. Glad the day they get it and glad the day it's gone. It was a huge burden suddenly lifted off my shoulders. I felt free. And happy. I would not change any of it for all the tea in China. I loved the military, all the branches, especially my Marine Corps. Semper Fi.

Wade Ivan Nash. W.I.N. My initials. I was a winner in life. I looked at Diane and knew I just won life's lottery. I won the jackpot.

# *Wrap Up*

Young Bradford Carlton wasn't talking but Arthur Dalton at the Mayo Clinic in Minnesota was. A great deal would reach the press about the massive human trafficking bust that took place. The bust was so successful that it was highly unlikely that any of its "players" would resurface anytime soon.

After the stories had been told and most of the agents gone, the clock on the wall approached two A.M. Wade and Diane told Floyd they were retiring effective immediately. It was the third time they told that story too.

"Yeah, I know. Tell me, Wade, Is Marco ready to take over for you?"

"Yes, he is. One hundred percent. I'll be around for advice only."

"Good. I wish you kids well. Did I just say, kids?"

***

Not too far away a phone rang. Someone answered.

"Carlton is out. He's done. I'm taking over. Chill for a few weeks. Nothing changes, got it?"

# *Epilogue*

Looking up at the sun just over the tree line, Lester gauged it to be about 8:30. He just finished sweeping and mopping the kitchen floor after heating a bowl of leftover grits, last night's dinner. He had the mobile home about as clean as it could be and yet it was a sad sight to see. It sagged in a few places and leaned slightly toward the back.

It was old and worn out. This old place was home.  It had so many memories attached. Especially the memories of his mama when he was so young. Now, that angel said he should get rid of it. He would start a new life.

Ever since he started seeing his one-time schoolmate, Jill Douglas, his life changed radically. He changed from being a petty thief and con man to somebody even he didn't know. He went from being slovenly to taking much better care of how he looked. Before the transformation, town people shunned him. Now they said hello and smiled.

Nothing could be so powerful as the dream of Jill in his bedroom last night. She rocked in mama's chair, talking to him about good things to come. He didn't know what to think or believe at times. Since meeting Jill, his life changed for the better in every way. He believed. But he wasn't sure why.

Lester took the half bucket of dirty soapy water and slushed off the side of the seashell walkway, careful to not get any of the dirty water on the few flower plants he planted on each side of the steps to his house. Wonders, he thought. He, Lester Frabill, digging up wildflowers from the roadside and planting them at his house. When he walked up now, he smiled. Those silly flowers made him feel good. Especially the purple ones.

The chug chug chug sound of an old John Deere tractor could be heard coming up his driveway. He was well familiar with the sound. The tractor belonged to Alex Swanson, his next door neighbor. A man daddy hated while Lester never knew why. Since daddy died, he and old Alex spent time together, more all the time. Old Alex rode his old tractor up here, or he would walk down in the evening. They would share an iced tea or lemonade. And talk.

Chug, chug, chug, came the tractor until it was almost next to Lester.  In the worn steel seat sat old man Swanson, dressed in old bib overalls and a Florida Gators ball cap, sweat stained and looking like it seen better days years ago. Swanson twisted the key on the panel in front of him shutting down his old workhorse.

Reaching down, Swanson offered a gnarled, liver age-spotted hand to Lester who took it and shook the strong hand while thinking, *before daddy died, he never shook this man's hand. Daddy never let him on the property saying Swanson wanted to steal his land. Now he was a welcome guest.* And that was good to Lester's way of thinking.

Lester found out Alex was eighty-three years old, yet worked like he was sixty and thought like he was forty years old. Alex was religious, or so it seemed to Lester as Alex praised God for most things. He didn't go overboard or preach to Lester.

"Mind if I get down and we talk a spell, Lester? I got sumtin to say to you. Needs saying and I don't know how you will take it."

"No, I don't mind. I gest washed the floor and its wet. How about we sit on the swing over there? I'd offer you some water but the floor's wet and all. What you got to say that will upset me? I own this property outright and I paid my taxes."

The old man took his time getting down off the tractor with the metal seat, perforated with holes to let water pass through. Old Alex Swanson shuffled behind Lester to the old swing hanging from the live oak tree. That swing is hanging for as long as either could remember.

"Well son, I could beat around the bush and blow smoke at you and lie to you cept I don't lie. Never did and I ain't about to start now. You see, the past few weeks, I've been having the darndest dreams. So real I swear they are true. This young girl comes to my bedroom and talks to me. I never believed in that spooky stuff, but this is just too real."

"Mr. Swanson, did she have on a yellow flower dress?"

"Why yes, the last time she did. Do you know her? What's going on? I mean, just plain scared the bejesus out of me. It's like for real."

"So, what did she say to you, Mr. Swanson? You tell me what you know and I'll tell you my story. I best get us a pitcher of water because this is going to be a long story. I can wash the floor again.

Five minutes later, a pitcher of cold water, as cold as the tap would allow, sat in front of them in the crushed shells. Swanson held a plastic mug with palm trees printed on it while Lester's mug was his favorite. A Florida Gators glass. There was just enough of a breeze to set the Spanish Moss moving in the tree above them. A faint whiff of gasoline and hot metal passed over them coming from the old tractor.

"Well, son, this girl and I talked a long time the first time. She told me to make friends with you. You needed friends, and well, we both do.

Then she told me you were going to sell a little land by the river, the piece that runs out into the Saint John's. A lady was gonna buy it and build a home on it and that same lady would one day save my life. And we all needed to be friends and good things were gonna come out of all of this."

"Go on," said Lester, anxious to hear what the old man had to say.

"Well sir, she told me to help by letting you use old Sally here. I call that old tractor Sally cause she's so pretty and all. Don't know why I call her that. Well, yes I do. Once had a girl I was sweet on in school and her name was Sally. Then I met Martha. We had a lot of good years together. No kids. Martha couldn't, but we had a good life,"

"So tell me, Lester, what do you know about this?"

It was near noon when Lester finished his story which started from his grammar school days through high school. His thievery and going to jail and stealing dogs and the same girl sent by his mama to talk to him.
Lester talked and refilled their water glasses, finishing his story about the same time the pitcher of water was empty.

"Oh, I know the girl Mr. Swanson. She's Jill Douglas. Jill was in my class at school during grade school and high school. Well, until I dropped out when I turned sixteen to work the land here. Next time she shows up, I'm gonna ask her to stay for dinner and I'll invite you over, and we can all talk. My mama sends her. You'll see."

"You know son, that ain't ever gonna happen. I'd like that but I don't think she is for real."

"Sure she is. You'll see. Mama sends her so she must have some connection with God and heaven. She sure changed my life for a fact."

"That's just it son. I think she comes from heaven. Just a feeling I got from her. And she tells us both the same thing. Helping each other and you selling a slip of river land to some stranger. How can that not be something not from this earth? I hope she comes back 'cause I want to ask her if she knows my Martha."

Alex went on. "She come to see me three times and each time she looks, well, kind of like an angel or a spirit. So, I asked my friend, Reverend Rollins about such a thing and he believes she is most likely an angel sent to help us. He said God works in mysterious ways.  I dunno?"

The old man and the young man sat on the swing, moving to and fro ever so gently as both men appeared to be looking in space for something neither could see.  The sound of footsteps crunching on the shell driveway came to both at the same time. Somebody was walking up toward them.

The sight of the woman took Lester's breath away for a moment. He was sure she was his mama. About fifty-five years old he guessed standing about five feet four inches tall. A nice adult figure dressed in denim pedal pusher style pants with a tan blouse open at the neck, showing an abundance of freckles. Her brown leather walking boots, now coated with mud, made the crunching sound of crushed sea shells as she walked.

Both men could see she wore minimum makeup and looked very well without it. Her eyes were bright and her smile infectious.

No Lester, he thought.  Mama's been dead for a long time.  No, this was the lady Jill spoke of and it was confirmed when she said, "Hello, gentlemen. My name is Lynn Olson and I'm stuck."

"Oh?" said Alex Swanson, looking at Lester and giving him a sly wink.

"I'm from Bluffton, South Carolina and I'm visiting a friend in Palatka and it's such a beautiful day. Carolyn, my friend, has chemotherapy this afternoon, so I thought I'd take a ride just to see the sights. I guess I got distracted by the land and the river and took my eye off the road and ran off a little. My right wheel is buried and I need help. Can you gentlemen help me or get me some help?"

"Got distracted by the land on the river huh. Yes, I'll sell it to you. No worry about that Mrs. Olson." Lester said.

"Oh, the land here is beautiful and it would be perfect for what I want to do, but I'm not here to buy land. I raise dogs you see. I have what I think is the world champion dog I'll show next year when he is trained. He is a Chesapeake Bay Retriever."

Alex leaned forward and said, "Don't you need room to train? And when you win the championship, don't you need room to breed more champions?"

"Why, yes. I live in a beautiful gated community and I have so much to do, but my true love is my dogs. I don't know what made me turn down this road. It's like my car just turned. It's so peaceful and beautiful here but I can't afford to buy land here."

Lester Frabill and old Alex Swanson just looked at each other, winked and smiled.

# About the Author

T. Vincent Beck recently lost his wife of fifty-four years. In his grief, he was inspired to write a book, which kept him sane during the most difficult time in his life. He lives in Flagler Beach, Florida. With his new-found passion for writing, this is his second book in this series.